A LILY *in* DISGUISE

WYCLIFFE
FAMILY
BOOK 1

D1738906

JESSICA SCARLETT

REDWING PUBLISHING

ALSO BY JESSICA SCARLETT

Managing Mary

A Lord of Many Masks

A Lady on the Chase

A Maid for Melbourne

To Allie, Elaine, and Kjerstin.
What a lovely bunch of idiots.

CHAPTER 1

LONDON, ENGLAND
1811

I HAD ALWAYS BEEN GOOD AT LYING, BUT THAT DIDN'T MAKE IT EASY.

Light bathed the blue parlor in yellow tones, blinding me whenever I looked directly out the large, east-facing window. Beneath the folds of my dress, in a little pocket I had sewn myself, I could feel the outline of my father's pocket watch, twitching for every two of my heartbeats. My gloved hand fingered it for luck as I tried to withstand the smiling scrutiny of the young woman sitting on the chaise lounge.

"Gad, but you're not at all what I expected," Miss Mary Raynsford said at last.

"I rarely am, miss." I bit my tongue, hoping the comment didn't sound as impudent as I felt. I couldn't afford to give the wrong impression. Lowering my chin, I added, "My previous employer told me the same on many occasions." True. "She would say, 'Stop being so surprising, Julia, or I shall turn you out.'" Half true.

"And this previous employer of yours, did she give you any references?"

I swallowed. "Impeccable. But unfortunately I had a dreadful bit of luck on the road to London involving a clumsy coachman and a bit of wind." An outright lie.

Miss Raynsford's gaze went to my hand still rubbing my dress in search of the pocket watch. "What is it you have there?" she said.

Drat. I let my hand fall away. "Forgive my twitching. This is my best dress, but I hardly ever wear it because of its prickliness."

She tittered. "I know just what you mean—style over function and all that befogging nonsense. Though I can't say I've worn anything as horrendous as that outfit." She covered her laugh with a petite hand. "What did you say your name was?"

"Smith. Miss Julia Smith." Another lie, though it hardly registered as one. The name had rolled off my tongue so many times in the past eight years that I'd started to believe it was my real identity. I bobbed a curtsy then studied her face for any suspicion.

With a round chin and a small face, she seemed young for an unmarried woman running a household. Perhaps only eighteen. Straw-blonde curls adorned her head, and her neck and wrists flashed with jewelry as she stood and sashayed closer.

"I admit, when I posted the advertisement I had not expected someone so . . ." Miss Raynsford circled me, a twinkle entering her eye. She never finished.

The expectant silence prompted me to say, "As requested in the advertisement, I have some experience as a ladies maid, and am an expert in the modern styles—"

"I do not need a ladies maid." She turned in dismissal.

My shoulders sagged. Personal attendants received better pay, and I already had two years' experience in the coveted position even though I couldn't be much older than Miss Raynsford herself. *Blast it, Lily.* Perhaps it was the eye contact. I always made too much eye contact for a servant.

". . . Nor am I looking for a maid of any kind." She spun back, a secret dancing upon her lips.

My brow wrinkled. The notice had said Hampstead House needed both a ladies maid and a housemaid. "But ma'am—" I stopped, rethinking how I wanted to proceed over this patch of dangerous ground. High society didn't particularly like being told they were mistaken. "I believe the advertisement specifically asked for—"

"Please, would you turn for me?" She made a squiggly motion with her fingers, her smile growing.

I paused. If not for a maid, what did she want me for? I shuffled in a circle, fighting the impulse to squirm under her eager gaze. She didn't recognize me . . . did she?

As soon as my feet came to a stop, a torrent of giggles burst out of her. "You're perfect! Excellent posture, soft hands, regal bearing. Your hair is a little dark—more of a light brown than a blonde—but no one should know the difference. Not too short, not too plump. Yes, you shall do quite nicely."

"Not too plump for what, ma'am?" Surely size wasn't a factor in hiring maids?

Her hand caressed the polished wood of the chaise on her way over to the stately desk in the corner of the room, where she began to rummage through one of the drawers. "Miss Smith, the duties I should ask you to perform upon employing you are not the most . . . socially acceptable. Indeed, because of this, I have had a difficult time locating someone who not only will agree to it, but can look and play the part. I confess I am already keen upon hiring you, for you seem to possess a —" she turned back, waving a folded paper in the air, "—a natural grace and elegant manner. You do not cower. Curious traits for a servant, I should think—but that is exactly the sort of thing I need."

"Need for *what*, ma'am?"

"Why, to be me, of course." Miss Raynsford returned and held out the paper for me to take. After a few moments, I did, although I didn't open it. "You see, Miss Smith," she continued, "I have an aunt. She is a good, dear aunt, but often absurd in her requests. I shall inherit her fortune when she dies, so it is wise for me to comply with even her most whimsical desires. A fortnight ago, I received this letter from her . . ." She indicated for me to open it.

I unfolded the letter, noting tear-stains that blurred the sophisticated cursive in places. I quietly began to read, wary of Miss Raynsford watching me.

My dear Mary,

I am writing to you on a matter of much importance to me—for it has come to my attention that you have no intent to marry, and expect to squander my money once you inherit it. You will exhaust my funds within a month of my passing, girl, if you are not properly supervised.

With this in mind, I have secured an invitation for you to spend the summer at Ambleside, the estate where my valued friend, The Dowager Viscountess Wycliffe resides. I'm sure you recall me mentioning her previously.

She has a very amiable son, Lord Peter Wycliffe. Such a match would be most advantageous if you were able to secure him. It is my wish that over the summer you might form an attachment to him, or any other eligible gentleman, for that matter. A husband will assist you in breaking your ungodly spending habits—if he is anyone but Mr. Harrington, that is.

It would please me for you to accept this invitation, as your inheritance depends upon it.

Regards,
Aunt Phoebe

PETER WYCLIFFE. THE NAME WAS FAMILIAR. AFTER A FEW MOMENTS of contemplation, I had placed it. His name was whispered about London—in tones of both reverence and rapture. Even the lower class seemed to know of the stunning Lord Wycliffe who had inherited his title a few years ago. Excepting that, I didn't know much about him, other than that he was said to be incredibly wealthy. But one thing was for certain: he was an influential figure in the *ton*.

I squinted up at Miss Raynsford as soon as I made the connection. She wrung her hands and bit her lower lip.

"Oh," she said, throwing her hands up, "how I hate the country! Nature and I have not been the best of friends. It is so awfully far away from civilization, and I should *die* if I cannot go to Paris this summer. But I must conform to Aunt Phoebe's wishes, you see—for if I don't, I shall not inherit her fortune. And you really are perfect; just my size in nearly every way. The only thing that is dissimilar is our eyes. You have blue, and mine are green—but I don't think it shall make much difference—"

"So," I said, eyes wide and struggling for words, "you want me to go in your place? For the summer? To pretend to be you?"

She nodded and I nearly guffawed.

What an idea!

"You shall be reimbursed for your trouble," she said hastily, a plea in her eyes. However, despite my desperate need for employment, I wasn't about to expose myself to even greater scandal—or risk hanging or imprisonment for impersonating someone in a higher class. I couldn't earn my ticket out of the country if I were dead.

"I am sorry, Miss Raynsford, but I cannot." I turned to leave.

"Nine pounds for two months. That is my offer."

I halted in my tracks.

My vision lost focus as I rotated back to face her. *Nine pounds?* That was half a year's wages for a ladies maid. For two month's work? Quickly doing the math, I realized the money would put me just above my goal—that if I agreed to this foolish plan, I could at last make my way to America. And, more importantly, to my sister.

My jaw started working. It was tempting—too tempting. But I was not yet convinced. "Have you not already met the Wycliffe's?" I thought it unlikely she hadn't been introduced to such a prominent family when she most definitely had the connections.

"Aunt Phoebe didn't think it wise before now—some nonsense about being a fractious girl with obscene puerilities, whatever that means. And though I confess I should like to meet Lord Wycliffe, I would much rather go to France. Aunt Phoebe wants me to find a husband, but I've already found one, you see, and cannot tell that to my aunt. So you see my predicament?"

I didn't see. I wanted to ask her where her guardians were and who this "husband" of hers was, but decided I didn't need to know. I wasn't going to go through with this foolish plan anyway. Still, for the sake of argument, I said, "Surely someone in your acquaintance will be attending? And then they will see I am not you . . ."

"I had thought of that," she rushed on, "so I wrote to Aunt Phoebe asking after the guests who will be there—she thinks I did so to look into eligible gentlemen, you see. Silly old bat. The list she sent me contains every individual who received an invitation, none of whom I am acquainted with. All introductions will be made through Lady Wycliffe, who has, luckily, never met me in person. The only thing the Wycliffe's know of me is a vague description. Tall, blonde hair, green eyes." Miss Raynsford seemed pleased with her foresight to my question.

I drew my bottom lip between my teeth, trying to ignore the grim truth: if the past few days were any indication, this was my last chance to earn the money—at least in a respectable way. Not that impersonating someone was particularly respectable, either.

I shook my head with a sliver of shame. Was I really considering this eccentric notion?

I was. My heart beat wildly in my chest, believing for the first time since being let go a month ago that I might see my sister again. Might hold her close once more.

She would be twenty-four next month. It had been eight years since we were separated, but it felt longer than a lifetime. There were nights I cried myself to sleep, dreaming that all of the horrible things people said about me were washed away by the sound of Jennie's lullabies. Now, here was an opportunity that could make those dreams a reality.

Even as my hope ran rampant, common sense trailed not far behind. Something about the name "Ambleside" tugged at my memory, and it made me nervous. "Where is this estate?"

"In the northern part of Hampshire, I believe."

My blood chilled. It was too close—*much* too close—to Newington. Thomas would find me. An image of Jennie darted into my head; of her languishing for months on end, waiting on the docks for a boat and a sister that would never come.

I chewed my bottom lip. "May I see this guest list?"

Miss Raynsford retrieved another piece of paper from the drawer. She hastened across the cobalt blue Persian rug before handing it to me and stepping back, trepidation written on her face.

I studied each name on the list scrupulously. My half-brother was not there. None of the names sparked my memory, and I started to believe I could actually go through with this. There was no evident reason why I could not. If by chance I found myself in a predicament, my quick mind would always be there to get me out of it. And I did need the money terribly. If I was successful, I could leave—break free of the limits of social class. Only freedom would await me.

Freedom, and my sister.

"When do I leave?" I said in a definitive tone.

Miss Raynsford brightened and clapped in victory. "They are expecting the guests by the beginning of next month, so you shall depart in three weeks." She half-danced to the door, where she tugged a tasseled rope twice.

"We have so much to do!" she continued, spinning back around. "First, we shall get you fitted and order all the clothing you shall need. You are about my size, so we shall make minor adjustments to some of my less favorite dresses." A maid entered. "Oh, girl! Send for the dressmaker immediately, and tell her I shall make it worth her while." Miss Raynsford turned back, not even pausing for breath. "And then there's the matter of teaching you the rules of etiquette. There is much to learn! I have already broken it down into segments. Today, you shall learn posture, curtsying, how to behave when—"

"Miss Raynsford." She halted, surprised at the interruption. I didn't give it a second thought, feeling her equal under the circumstances. "I trust you have a promissory note for me?"

Her face pinched. "Why would you require that?"

"I do intend to do my best, but I want a guarantee that I shall be compensated for my efforts."

She cocked her head, as if the thought was only now occurring to her. My, what an impulsive thing she seemed. "Now that I think on it," she said, "you could cause much scandal in two months, using my name. How Aunt Phoebe would scold me! That wouldn't do at all. I shall write you the note, but you shan't get the nine pounds until after the deed is done; and only if your real identity remains a secret."

A smug smile tugged at my lips. I had kept my real identity a secret for the past eight years.

Two more months wouldn't be too difficult.

CHAPTER 2

WE HAD BEEN TRAVELLING FOR THREE DAYS, AND I FELT EVERY
bruise. The carriage rolled forward, occasionally jerking when it hit a
rock or a dip in the road.

The previous weeks had been filled with shopping trips and fitting
sessions, readying my wardrobe with chemises, stockings, petticoats,
nightgowns, pelisses, bonnets, handkerchiefs, and slippers. Miss
Raynsford had taken it upon herself to teach me the refinements of
the upper class and had covered everything from social calls to escorts.

Unbeknownst to her, I didn't have much use for her tutelage
because I still remembered what I'd been taught in my youth. And, my
last employer, Mrs. Wilshire, had treated me more like a daughter than
a servant, enabling me to practice the other delicate arts on my own.
In fact, the only skill to be found in a young lady that I seemed to be
lacking was dancing.

Impressed with the supposed progress she'd made with me, Miss
Raynsford was, more than ever, certain her plan would work. I,
however, fed my doubts with incessant worry that someone would
recognize me.

When I'd first been admitted into Miss Raynsford's presence, I'd planned on one lie—one little lie—to land me a job. But that little lie had blossomed and stretched until it was an elaborate plot. This was pure, unabated deception, and I'd have to perpetuate it for weeks.

The only thought that kept me from changing my mind was Jennie. I would go through with it—*must* go through with it, or I might never see her again.

So, with a full trunk, an upset stomach, wringing hands, and a fluttering heart, I rode in the carriage, anxious for when I would arrive at Ambleside. I glanced at my reticule lying on the empty leather seat across from me. It held my father's pocket watch, the letters from my sister, and the document Miss Raynsford signed, folded up neatly so they would fit. The reticule was a safe place for them, at least for now. I swallowed and glanced out the window.

This whole plot posed an unfortunate dilemma: Mary's Aunt Phoebe wanted her to catch a husband. As I was pretending to be Mary, that task fell to me—but of course a husband was out of the question, along with falling in love. Love would only complicate matters when my two months were up and I left for America.

Mary had made it clear in her promissory note that flirting needed to be in the cards. She had to be able to report to Aunt Phoebe that she'd at least tried. Being acquainted with the Wycliffe's, her aunt could easily solicit a report on "Mary's" activities during her stay, and if they didn't match what the real Mary said . . .

Flirting simply needed to be in the cards.

It mattered little to me either way. It was all pretend anyway, and lying was what I did best. The hearts I might break would be Mary's problem. Still, it didn't hurt to be cautious, and as I bumped along through miles of countryside, I resolved to not grow attached to the place—or to anyone residing there.

The carriage crested a hill. My jaw went slack as I blinked in surprise.

In the valley below, people bustled around fences, carrying feed and leather saddles. Horses with shiny coats and muscly flanks clopped in and out of the stables. On the other side, vibrant gardens with stone paths and dark green hedges wove through the grounds. Bridges spanned a stream that moseyed through the park, and beyond it grew an aspen grove, quaking and yawning as it stretched for the sun.

In the middle of all of the grandeur stood Ambleside, a sprawling estate, even more noble than its gardens. Twin protective wings guarded the entrance, and I glimpsed the mushroom color of its hewn stone before we delved into a copse of nearby trees.

Though it was only a preview of where I would be staying for the next two months, it was enough to reignite the flame of apprehension in my stomach. I didn't know what I'd expected, but it certainly wasn't something so royal and . . . important. The people who lived in that— that *palace*—were the ones I had to fool. People of noble blood.

You are of noble blood too, Lily, I told myself. *You are a baronet's daughter. You are just as significant as they.* But eight years as a servant had shattered that confidence. Gentleman's daughters did not fetch water, or tighten stays, or arrange hair. My hands, clutching my seat, started to slip inside their gloves as the carriage rolled up Ambleside's lengthy driveway and came to a crunching halt.

I retrieved my reticule and filled my lungs. The driver swung my door open, revealing two ladies and an adolescent boy. The boy, no more than thirteen, had dark brown hair cropped shorter than the present style. His features were pleasant, and I could tell he would be very handsome in his own way when he grew up.

"Welcome!" greeted the older of the two women with a warm smile as my driver helped me down. "I am Lady Wycliffe. You must be the young woman Phoebe has told us so much about. You are Miss Raynsford?" Curly wisps of gray hair peeked out from beneath her matronly cap, framing bright blue eyes and a face that must've been strikingly beautiful twenty years ago.

I dipped into an effortless curtsy, but inside I felt wicked for the lies I was about to—and would for two months more—tell them. "Indeed I am, and I am much honored to make your acquaintance, Lady Wycliffe. My dear aunt has done nothing but praise you." The words felt natural on my tongue, like I'd been born say these sorts of things.

And indeed I had been.

Lady Wycliffe beamed before she turned to the young woman beside her. "This is my daughter Eliza, and my younger son, Matthew."

I curtsied to the blossoming young woman, thinking she must be sixteen at the most. Then Lady Wycliffe hooked my arm, suggesting I retire to my quarters and freshen up. Before we had taken two steps, Matthew piped up.

"I thought you were supposed to have *green* eyes."

I turned back to find Matthew's glare fixed upon me. Miss Wycliffe shushed him, muttering something about being impolite, but I smiled. "It is quite all right." I walked up to Matthew. "You received my description from my darling aunt, I trust?" He eyed me, but after a while gave a curt nod. "That explains it. You see, her eyesight is not as serviceable as it used to be—nor is her memory. It is quite understandable she would mistake my eye color. You will forgive her, will you not?"

Despite my confidence, Matthew's eyes were disturbingly penetrating, and I wavered. He squinted, trying to decide whether or not he should believe me. He would eventually, I was sure. I had given him no reason to suspect me.

Had I?

"Of course he will," Lady Wycliffe answered for him. "We all know poor Phoebe has been out of sorts lately. A mistake is quite understandable. Come, it is certain to rain soon, and you must be exhausted." My hostess steered me toward the grand house. When I glanced over my shoulder, Matthew was standing in the exact same spot, scrutinizing me as if he were an artist and I his masterpiece.

Even as the worry crept in, I stifled it. He couldn't possibly know who I was, he was only a young boy. Besides, people didn't go about suspecting others to be imposters.

We hiked up the steps, and as the great doors to the entrance opened, I had to stop myself from gaping.

A lustrous crystal chandelier hung from the ceiling of the spacious entryway and an elaborate motif curled the center of the tiled floor. Double doors on either side of the entryway led to sitting rooms and parlors, and at the end of the hall, arched marble staircases ascended and conjoined.

The *click-clump* of retreating footsteps echoed off the tile, but I didn't look away. I couldn't.

A balustrade that wrapped the perimeter of the second floor, and the same marble railing wound around the room higher up. I stared up in wonder, feeling insignificant in the rich, hollow house.

Newington, my childhood home, was distinguished; but it paled in comparison to this wealthy estate. The room reflected the luxuriant status and elegant taste of its master. I knew I should be afraid—afraid of what such wealthy people could do, if I were caught—but instead, my pulse buzzed with excitement.

A simple painting, hung on the wall in the little alcove underneath the staircases caught my eye. Brows furrowing, I moved closer to study it. Someone followed behind me, and after a while, Miss Eliza Wycliffe spoke.

"He is handsome, is he not?"

Without taking my eyes off the painting, I replied softly, "Indeed."

And he was.

He was young—only a few years or so older than I—his face possessing a boyish quality. His jawline was firm, dark lashes hooding deep blue eyes that seemed to pop out of the painting. Dusky brown hair swept his forehead, and all his features combined gave his face a look of gentleness. He resembled an older version of Matthew.

"Many ladies visit Ambleside, hoping to catch a glimpse of my brother," Eliza said. "He is the most sought-after bachelor in all of England—perhaps even further—and some women will do outrageous things to ensnare a husband. I daresay he's had to endure some awful scrapes, though he always takes them in stride. Peter does not come home often, but mother made him promise to stay for the whole summer. You're guaranteed an introduction."

She cast me a sideways, knowing smile, like *I* was one of those devious young women. But of course I wasn't. At least not in that way. I was here to tell lies, not get a husband.

I inclined my head. "When is he to arrive?"

"Mother said it will not be for another few days, so you shall have time to freshen up." Her eyebrows lifted suggestively.

Knowing we were going to be fast friends, I decided to play along with her little joke. If she insisted my reason for coming was to ensnare her brother—as Aunt Phoebe wished me to, as well—perhaps I could pretend it was so. It might help allay the suspicion caused by Matthew's outburst.

"What a relief," I said with a devious quirk to my lips, "for that is the sole purpose of my visit, and I would hate to make a negative first impression on my future husband."

Eliza giggled before turning to a maid that was standing nearby. "Katherine, do show Miss Raynsford to her room and get her settled." Then, turning to me, she added, "Dinner will be served at seven. If there is anything you need, you might ask myself, or Mama, or when he arrives . . . my *brother*." Shooting me one more meaningful smile, she turned and disappeared through one of the side doors.

Glancing around, I realized that Lady Wycliffe must have known Eliza would see to me, for she was nowhere in sight. And, thankfully, neither were the apprehensive eyes of little Matthew.

Katherine curtsied and said, "If you will just follow me, miss," before leading me upstairs to one of the guest rooms.

The furniture consisted of a nightstand with a porcelain basin, a vanity with half a dozen vases of flowers, a dressing screen, a stuffed chair, and of course, the bed. Simple, compared to the rest of the estate, but still extravagant in its taste. Lavender wallpaper lined the walls, except where silky white drapes overhung the window. A knock sounded at the door, followed by two manservants carting in my trunks then leaving.

Still taking in my chambers, I asked, "Am I the first to arrive?"

Katherine set about unpacking my bags. "No, miss, nor I daresay the last. Sir George Stanton—oh, and Miss Clarissa Caldwell arrived just a few minutes ago. Then the day before there was Lady Agatha and her twin daughters. If I am correct, nearly a dozen guests have been invited! A rather large party, don't you think?"

"I suppose it must be exhausting for the staff."

"I think it is quite exciting, and truth be told, the viscount could probably afford to invite another dozen more. But inviting too many guests and not being able to spend time with each of them would be rude, don't you agree? Plus, there's always the possibility someone uninvited will show up."

I spun toward her, blanching. "Do you often receive uninvited guests?"

"All the time." She sighed dreamily. "Perhaps someone will come who is so important, no one dares to ask him to leave. Oh, and he's the handsome sort, of course. No other kind of strangers will do."

Glimpsing my letters from Jennie spilling out of my open reticule on the bed, I stuffed them back in and placed the reticule in a small desk drawer next to the bed. The whole plan would be forfeit if anyone were to discover those letters. I smoothed my dress and chewed on my cheek, hoping Katherine hadn't seen—but she was still airing out my dresses.

Grateful when she finally excused herself, I sat on the bed, the silence enveloping me like the ghost of my father's embrace.

Here I was, thrust into wealth, parading around as an heiress. This life, which had once been so comfortable, felt foreign now. The supple, embroidered dresses in place of drab, brown ones felt as if they didn't fit, and the kind suggestions in place of commands left me unsure of my place. Not that it was unwelcome, only . . . strange. I felt detached from my body, watching these events playing out like a whisper of someone else's dream.

There was still a little time before dinner. Inhaling the scent of freshly pressed sheets, I pondered all the possibilities my newfound freedom afforded. When I peered out the window and saw gentle rain-drops falling, I knew just the thing I wanted to do first.

By THE TIME I GOT OUTSIDE, THE SHOWER WAS ALREADY THINNING into a sheet of mist, sprinkling onto the grassy fields of Ambleside. The earthy scent of rain hung in the air, fresh and musky. I tracked up a swollen hillock sporting bluebells and foxglove, taking deep breaths and enjoying the feeling of cold air in my lungs.

Rain reminded me of Newington. When I was little, after Jennie had told me the story of Noah and the ark, I'd insisted I wouldn't have drowned like everyone else; I would've found the tallest tree in the world and climbed it. The next time it rained I did just that, and Jennie joined me, reenacting the bible story. We hugged the glassy trunk and pretended the world was flooding, trying to scramble higher than each other.

I smiled at the memory and continued up the hill. The hem of my dress collected bits of mud as I walked, but I didn't mind. Would Mary mind? Probably not, as it was the least fashionable dress she'd given me to wear.

At the top of the hill, I stopped to crane my neck up. Rising before me stood a tall ash tree, almost identical to the one Jennie and I had scrambled up, at Newington.

An ache trickled into my chest, along with bittersweet memories.

Jennie admitting defeat during our verbal matches, and the blur of her waggling finger after I'd been uncharitable toward someone. Her form curled up on the window seat, head against the glass as she read Shakespeare—or her warm back pressed against mine after I snuck into her room on particularly cold nights. Her stories, filled with cinnamon and magic. Her bright eyes and ready smile.

In the distance a dog barked, dashing out of a cluster of trees, chasing a fox across the meadow. When the fox dove into a hole, the dog snuffled at the ground and howled.

Snarling, the dog turned, sniffed the air, then sprinted toward me, bringing my musings to a grinding halt. Foam dripped from its mouth. I took a step back, chest clenching. The dog wasn't slowing down. In fact, he was speeding up.

I panicked, looking around. There was nowhere to go, nowhere to take shelter from the mad creature. Nowhere except—

The dog neared, barking and scowling and baring its teeth. I whirled around and clambered up the ash tree as fast as one could in a dress. I barely made it up the first branch before he reached me, leaping up the trunk, jaws snapping. Shaking, I climbed the next branch up, trying to widen the distance between my feet and the beast's teeth.

His barking turned shriller. I unlaced one mudded boot and dropped it to the ground. He clomped onto it, thrashing it around, emitting a low guttural noise. I watched in fascinated horror as he shredded the leather to pieces.

Then, somewhere in the expanse of countryside came a piercing whistle, a man's voice calling the creature back. His ears perked up, he glared at me one last time, and then scampered away, my boot still in its jaws, disappearing into the tree line.

I let out a slow, wobbly breath, muscles relaxing against the trunk. A life-threatening altercation with a mad dog wasn't exactly what I'd hoped for, my first day here. But it could be a lot worse. I might've had to drop *both* my shoes to appease him.

Danger abated, I blinked at the ground far below. When I extended a leg toward the branch below me, it met nothing but air. Pulling it back in, I tested the other side, gripping the trunk to add length, but came back with similar results.

I surveyed again the distance between the branches, the distance to the ground. There was no way I could climb down by myself. I frowned at the tree. If I couldn't climb down, then how on earth had I gotten up in the first place? Should I call to the man who had whistled? Was he already too far away to hear?

"Help?" I called, voice wobbly. "Help!" The shout sounded muted, like someone yelling through a thick fog. There was no response, and not a soul as far as the eye could see. I heaved a sigh, resting my head against the trunk.

"Why do these things happen to you, Lily?" I whispered. "First Mrs. Wilshire, then Mary Raynsford, and now this."

A twig snapped.

I jerked up, nearly tumbling out of the tree. Hugging the branch to regain balance, I searched for the source of the noise. A man atop his horse clopped his way beneath me. His steed stopped, and he dismounted. I opened my mouth to call to him, but something about him seemed familiar, and I faltered.

"There she is," the man said, gazing at Ambleside while patting his horse on the neck. "Home again."

I swallowed, debating what to do. I could cry to him and ask him to help me down, or I could continue to try and find a way down myself after he left, ultimately falling in a heap in the mud. The latter seemed less humiliating.

"It's been a long time, hasn't it, Royal?" he continued. "Mother will be surprised we're a few days early. She'll be overjoyed that she has more time to try and get me married. Thinks I'm waiting for a wife to fall from heaven." The man chuckled, patting his horse. His voice was quieter when he said, "Perhaps I am."

Slowly, it hit me who he was. This was my host. The viscount. Lord Wycliffe. The man from the painting.

And now, because I had neglected to make my presence known in the first place, I would appear to be some ridiculous girl that had no sense of propriety, willing to go to the extreme of climbing a tree to snare him as a husband.

I cringed. Of all the people to be a fool in front of, my host was definitely not on the list. I would be ridiculed, gossiped about. Not to mention how being found up a tree would tarnish Mary's reputation. This was not the right way to start my two months.

I'd simply have to stay put until he left, and then either wait for someone else to come along, or somehow find a way down myself. Pressing my lips in a firm line, I tightened my grip on the branch, determined to go unseen.

Fate had other ideas.

My grip slipped on some wet moss, my balance wavered, and I tumbled out of the tree, emitting a little yelp. The man looked up in astonishment, just before I toppled him to the ground beside his horse. The horse reared back, whinnying and stomping his legs near our heads.

Body and pride both bruised, I groaned. Rotten luck! Not only had someone witnessed my inelegant fall, someone *participated* in it. And my host at that! I planted my hands to either side of his head and reared back, then gawked. My mind screamed at me to do something —to salvage what little dignity I might still possess. But I couldn't.

I sat there, frozen, staring at Lord Wycliffe as if he were the devil himself. He was certainly handsome enough to be. Obviously he couldn't bring himself to do anything either, because he looked at me like I looked at him. Horrified.

And there we were, both of us gawping at each other while lying on the muddy ground under a wet tree.

One corner of his mouth curved upward. His eyes lit up and he said, "So *you're* my wife."

My cheeks burned. Why couldn't I move? What must he think of me? Could it possibly get any worse?

Yes, it could.

I had a history of sneezing whenever I felt humiliated. It didn't surface often, but when it did, it was at the most inconvenient times. Like now. Before I'd formed a coherent response, I let out an "achoo" right into Lord Wycliffe's spectacular face.

He blinked.

My insides exploded as he gingerly wiped my spit off. I stumbled to my feet, embarrassment scrabbling in my stomach. My first instinct was to run, but I thought better of it. An explanation might lessen the severity of what would certainly come. Perhaps Mary's reputation could still be rescued.

"I'm dreadfully sorry, Lord Wycliffe," I began, breathing hard, "but you see, my allergies have been horrid this season, and I'm afraid I couldn't hold it in. Please accept my deep regret for . . . for sneezing at you."

He got to his feet, brushing himself off. Chuckling, he said, "And though you may not have been able to prevent it, could you not have aimed it in another direction?"

He was laughing, but I felt horrible. He seemed delighted to be knocked to the ground by a—for all he knew—conniving young woman, willing to go to extremes to catch him as a husband. Didn't Eliza say that he was used to these sorts of things?

He was much, much handsomer than the painting. With rich, brown hair that fell softly across his forehead and dark lashes hooding vivid blue eyes that matched his stormy tailcoat, he was breathlessly picturesque. His face was ruddy from his ride, countenance glowing with health and magnificence. All in all, he looked practically perfect. I wouldn't have felt so ashamed of my muddy dress and disheveled appearance if he didn't.

"It came on so suddenly, you see," I said, hiding my shoeless foot by putting it behind the other, "I did not have time to think on which direction to point it. Please accept my apology."

"Oh, I accept. But you must first tell me what you were doing in that blasted tree."

He seemed amused, but I did not like being the object of his amusement. I would've rather he yelled at me, or merely stormed away. But to *laugh* at me, deserved or not—that was something that even as a little girl, I'd never been able to stomach.

And most certainly would not. To be sure, I could tell him about the rabid dog, but that wasn't going to wipe that charmed smile off his face.

"I was spying on you."

His head knocked back, face forming into a question.

Forwardness was not attractive in young ladies. That fact alone should have prevented me from continuing, since the *real* Miss Raynsford would probably act with more decorum. But I was strangely pleased by his reaction, and before I could realize fully what I was doing, my need to best the man convinced me to go on.

"I saw you coming, my lord, and quickly climbed this tree to get a better view—for I knew that the woman who catches you is a lucky one indeed. I had not planned on finding you directly beneath me, but then suddenly, you were. I saw an opportunity to pounce, so I did. Literally." I did my best to keep my face straight, but knew by the pull of my lips, I wasn't fully succeeding.

His eyes lit with interest, then started to dance. He could tell this was a game, and he wanted to play. "I see you are missing your shoe," he said, pointing to my hiding foot. "It must make pouncing a difficult business. As for myself, I prefer barefoot women, but surely you could not have known that. What is the reason for its disappearance?"

"Ah, that." I returned my socked foot to its rightful place, wiggling my toes and mentally swatting down the heat rising to my face. "I only ridded myself of it so you'd be forced to sweep me into your arms and carry me back to the house. Men do love a good damsel in distress. A rather romantic notion, is it not?"

"Indeed. So you abandoned your shoe, climbed the tree, and then toppled me to the ground—intentionally. To catch a husband."

I smiled, pleased. "Yes."

"Quite a believable tale. But if so, why did you not kiss me? Any woman with your intent would have seized that opportunity as well." He said it so simply, one would think we were discussing the weather, or how the sun comes up every morning.

A few moments passed before I realized I had no retort.

"Or perhaps a kiss was your initial intent, but in the heat of the moment you decided a sneeze was more fitting." His lips twitched. "I cannot fault you in your execution, madam. Though I do wish you had asked my opinion first, as I would've rather preferred the kiss."

I gulped, face flaming. My mind raced, but nothing came—and when I still did not answer, he smirked as if he'd already won the unofficial verbal sparring match.

Oh, bother. I'd have to tell him the truth—about the dog and about being helpless to get down. Not to mention that he would've bested me. The shame I'd surely suffer! *What to do? Think, Lily, think!*

And then it came to me. A feeble argument, but I didn't care.

"Your breath stunk."

He laughed out loud—an infectious laugh. "But how can that be? You couldn't have smelled it through the rain. And our faces weren't *that* close."

I put my hands to my hips. "Yes they were. I leaned in to give it to you, but the smell overpowered me. Truly, I could not bring myself to do it."

He laughed harder, and I decided I liked the sound. My own giggle bubbled up, and soon we were both laughing. It was a long moment before we finished.

He took up the reins of his horse. "You clearly know who I am. May I have the honor of knowing your name?"

The effects of my amusement still wearing off, I opened my mouth and said, "Miss Julia Smith."

It was two heartbeats before I realized my mistake.

I gasped, hand flying to my mouth. I had pretended to be Julia Smith for so long, it seemed like a natural thing to say—but a slip up so soon after the start of my charade? Only a few hours into my stay, and already I had compromised my plan twice.

"Are you going to sneeze again?" Lord Wycliffe asked, eyeing my hand over my mouth.

"No, I simply . . . that is I—Oh, dash it all!" I stomped my foot, my hopes for my sister and I shattering into a thousand pieces under my heel. A sick feeling settled in my stomach as I realized that I had failed. The lessons, the dresses, the lies; it was all for naught.

"Are you ill?"

"I am quite all right." I swallowed my emotions. "Please forgive me, I—I fear I have been away too long and must return to the house."

Before I could turn, he gently grabbed my arm. "Why not take my horse? It's faster, and I was planning on walking the rest of the way anyway." He held out the reins to me, eyes expressing the kindness from his painting.

But accepting his offer would only heighten my disgrace. "Thank you," I shook my head, "but I believe the exercise will do me good."

"Then let us walk together." Before I could think of an excuse, he led his horse away. Knowing he expected me to accompany him, I caught up, and we walked in silence toward Ambleside. I did my best to disguise my bobbing, one-shoed gait, grateful that Lord Wycliffe seemed to sense I was upset and didn't inquire after it.

When we reached the entrance, I was half certain he would make his way toward the stables without another word, or command me to pack my bags and leave the estate immediately, but he surprised me.

"I don't believe I saw a Miss Julia Smith on the guest list."

My pulse quickened, and I swallowed in despair, knowing the climax of my shame was about to commence.

His head tilted in thoughtful recollection. "But I did see a Miss Mary Raynsford. You are she, are you not? For that is the only person you could be. Your name was the only one I had not recognized, and believe me," he grinned, "I would have remembered if I had met you before."

"Yes, I am Miss Raynsford." I tried to look dignified, straightening my spine and lifting my chin. He could make me leave, but he couldn't take away my pride. *So what if my plan fell apart after a few hours? Better sooner than later.*

"Please, Miss Raynsford, you must tell me. Why did you pretend to be someone else?" His eyes gleamed, just as they had under the tree.

And then it hit me: He thought all of this was part of our little game.

I blew a breath of air. What relief! All would be well after all. He hadn't a suspicion. I permitted a small smile to emerge as I thought up my explanation.

"Because I was *not* myself, my lord. Miss Mary Raynsford does not climb trees, or fall on top of men to try and catch a husband—but Julia Smith, does."

His smile was almost ripe enough to bloom into a laugh. "And will I ever get to see her again?"

There was no doubting that Lord Wycliffe would be a valuable ally, should the need ever arise. "Perhaps." With a smirk, I turned on my heel and headed into the house, but not before hearing Lord Wycliffe's laughter in the air.

Damp and coated in mud, I returned to my room. Exhausted, I asked Katherine to make my excuses for dinner, relishing the rare feeling of power and control. Nearly half my life had been spent on the other side of the coin, serving my betters and making sure they were comfortable.

Before, I had been allowed two meals a day, to be taken downstairs in the dirt of the kitchen and which often consisted of gruel and humble vegetables. There was no plate for me being kept warm in the oven, if I were tardy; I simply had to go without. But here, I could take my dinner in my quarters if I felt so inclined. A dinner consisting of steamy scalloped veal, curried eggs, potatoes, cutlets, and jam tart.

I sighed in bliss despite my shivering skin, shucking off my water-logged dress.

Here I was, surrounded by luxury at every turn, able to go where and when I pleased.

And it felt magnificent.

CHAPTER 3

I STAYED SEQUESTERED IN MY ROOM FOR MOST OF THE FOLLOWING
day. I told Katherine I was unwell and still recuperating from the journey, but the truth of it was, I was yellow to the core.

Matthew had suspected me. What did he know about Mary? Was I
not as competent as I thought I was? And most importantly, if my
story was already compromised on the first day, how on earth was I
going to last two months?

I used the day to re-read Jennie's old letters and boost my wavering
confidence. At six o' clock sharp, Katherine appeared to help me dress
for dinner. I selected a forest green tiffany trimmed with gold lace, and
though it was one of Mary's old pieces, it had been altered to remain
stylish.

While Katherine arranged my hair, I pondered Lord Wycliffe. I
didn't know what I expected in a wealthy viscount, but it certainly
wasn't him. In my experience, lords were rude and brash, using their
affluence to gain what they wanted. Perhaps he *was* conceited and
yesterday I had simply caught him in a good mood, but part of me
doubted it. He had been affable, and unassuming, and . . . *genuine*.

Katherine soon finished. After studying myself one last time in the mirror, I rolled my shoulders back and walked out of my room, bracing myself to face the throng of guests that had arrived. I followed the hum of chatter to a drawing room just off of the entryway. Ten or so guests mingled, shifting weight, inclining heads. Eliza spotted me and made her way through the crowd.

"Miss Raynsford! I was beginning to worry you were still out of sorts."

I smiled. "I am feeling much better, thank you."

Though Eliza's eyes were more of a frost blue, they were uncannily like Lord Wycliffe's in the way they sparkled. "I saw that you had not left your room today," she said. "I was afraid we'd be deprived of your company for another evening."

"Oh, I was recuperating. The carriage ride was very taxing, and already I have met so many new people."

"You have met Peter?"

My stomach turned to lead. Did she know? Had he told everyone of our embarrassing encounter? "Why do you ask? Did he say that we have?"

She laughed. "No, nothing like that. I only wondered because he keeps looking this way." Eliza motioned, and I turned. Lord Wycliffe stood in the furthest corner, leaning against a wall, deep in conversation with a striking woman. He nodded at something she said.

His eyes lifted to meet mine, as if they had known exactly where I would be. One corner of his mouth rose. Then, slyly, one of his eyelids closed in a wink.

I repressed a smile. The nerve.

"He asked after you, you know," Eliza continued. "Wanted to make sure you were comfortable."

I saw his lips move, and realized that he was still conversing with the woman, but that his stare was permanently fixed on me. His pushed off the wall, his conversation finished.

Mind sprinting, I broke eye contact and spun to Eliza.

"It appears he is on his way over to speak to us. Oh! My allergies are acting up again. They must be brought on by wealthy men. Please excuse me."

Eliza laughed again. "Is that what I shall tell him when he asks after you?"

"Please do." I made my escape to the other side of the room just before Eliza stopped Lord Wycliffe. As they discussed, his face poked around her figure, mouth working in an attempt to morph his grin into a glare.

I smiled playfully. I'd won the first round of tonight's games.

Lady Wycliffe appeared at my side and led me on a stroll about the room, introducing me to all of the guests. There were so many names and faces, I doubted I would remember half of them.

Lady Agatha carried a perpetual scowl, and her twin daughters, Margaret and Molly, twittered at everything said with a false enthusiasm, giggling at things that weren't remotely humorous. There was Mr. Charles Quincy, a bachelor who laughed a little too loudly at my jokes and made ridiculous statements as if they were common expressions of speech. Miss Helen Batten held her chin down as if she had something to hide. Mr. Oliver Wentworth seemed at ease, though I doubt he could seem like much else with his nose barely leaving his newspaper as we were introduced. At last we came to a stop in front of a gentleman introducing himself as Sir George Stanton.

We made light conversation until a servant entered, announcing that dinner was served. Couples lined up, and Sir George offered his arm before I had time to worry about not having an escort. He led me to my seat at the enormous, rosewood table.

Lord Wycliffe sat at the head, and I, two places down on his left. Closer to him sat the woman he had been talking with earlier—Miss Clarissa Caldwell. I studied her, wondering what had earned her that position at the table. She acted familiar with the family. Was she related?

Servants entered carrying platters filled with our first course. Diverse conversations started up at both ends of the table, ranging from the dreadful weather to who would be coming out next Season. My fidgeting hands under the table relaxed with each uneventful minute that ticked by. This was simple enough. *Act pleasant, but aloof.* I could do this all night.

Several times, I resisted the urge to look in Lord Wycliffe's direction when I heard his laugh, persuading myself it was because I didn't want to be winked at again. Oh, but what a pleasant laugh it was. And perhaps one more wink wouldn't hurt.

Miss Caldwell lightly tapped the table in quick succession. "Oh, but Peter, you promised! Eliza heard you too, didn't you dear? You will hold one, won't you Peter?"

How casually she used his first name. She must know Lord Wycliffe intimately. *Perhaps they shared a childhood?*

"I beg your pardon, 'hold one' what?" inquired Mr. Quincy, seated across from me.

"A ball, silly! In London, Peter promised me he would host one this summer, and now he tries to go back on his word!" She pouted.

Lord Wycliffe chuckled, saying, "On the contrary, I merely doubt our guests would enjoy such an affair." Several of the visitors piped in, giving their approval and commenting on their personal tastes.

"You see?" declared Miss Caldwell. "The idea is well received. You will give one, will you not?"

I could feel everyone lean forward, waiting for his response, the apprehension in the air as thick as the pea soup in my bowl.

Lord Wycliffe let the anticipation ripen, before saying, "And how would you feel toward a ball, Mary?"

It took me a moment to realize he was talking to *me*. My eyes shot up, face burning up under so much attention. How informally he spoke! Only a day had gone by since we were introduced—and not even properly, at that. Addressing me so familiarly in such a public setting was surely meant to further my humiliation from earlier, under the tree.

Others would now assume Lord Wycliffe and I were more intimate than we really were. But perhaps that was his plan. Cheeky man.

I hardly had time to consider his question. Dancing was definitely not my forte. I was terrible, truly terrible, and would likely be found out if forced to attend. Even Mary, after a few hours of attempting to teach me, had determined I was a hopeless case, advising against any functions which included dancing.

"I must confess, Lord Wycliffe," I emphasized his name, attempting to put us back on formal terms, "my dancing skills are quite unpolished. If you were to host one, I should probably not attend."

"Surely, you would go. You cannot be so dreadful to refuse." He stared intently at me, as did all of the other guests.

I blinked. "I'm afraid I am, my lord. I have not danced since my Season." I returned my attention to my soup, but not before catching a minor glare from Miss Caldwell.

"Certainly that would not deter you from hosting one," she said. "The majority of your guests think it is a marvelous idea."

Again, everyone waited for Lord Wycliffe's answer. This time he did not disappoint. "I will host a ball—"

Miss Caldwell tittered and clapped in excitement.

Lord Wycliffe held up his hand. "But only on one condition."

"What is it?"

"I will host a ball . . . on the condition that Miss Julia Smith attends."

Soup sputtered in my throat and I dropped my spoon. It *kerplunked* into my bowl with a fantastic splash, and once again all the focus turned to me. Lord Wycliffe smirked at me.

So this is round two.

Through a silent meeting of our eyes I sought to convey a message of revenge, but Lady Wycliffe spoke before I could.

"Miss Julia Smith?" Lady Wycliffe set her napkin down, eyebrows slanting up. "Peter, I don't believe I have met the girl—or even heard of her, for that matter."

"No Mother, you remember Julia," he said. "Tall, clever . . ." His gaze settled on me. "Exceptionally pretty." Heat rose to my face, my stomach twisting into unsolvable knots. "Why, I ran into her just yesterday." My heart hammered, and I was able to take two deep breaths before Lord Wycliffe spoke again. "I believe you are acquainted with Miss Smith, are you not, Mary?" His grin was so wide it barely fit on his face.

Mary this, Mary that. He was growing bolder by the minute.

I couldn't very well tell the table that Miss Smith didn't actually exist, so my only option was to play along. I gathered my wits and cleared my throat, forcing myself to sound much more collected than I felt. "Yes, I know her quite well. Practically *inseparable*, she and I."

I had not thought it possible, but Lord Wycliffe's grin broadened. "My thoughts exactly. Perhaps you could pass the invitation along?"

"I will tell her," I said offhandedly, "but I believe she will be due for a headache at that hour."

He leaned forward in his seat and we locked eyes. "That would be unfortunate, for we will not be holding a ball without her."

Eager to direct the focus away, I conceded with a false smile. "I'm sure she will be delighted."

Mollified, everyone returned to their original conversations and then moved on to talk of the upcoming ball. But Lord Wycliffe continued to stare at me, his gaze gloating of his success all through dinner.

AFTER DINNER, SOME OF THE YOUNGER GUESTS STARTED A GAME OF whist, Lord Wycliffe and Miss Wycliffe among them. Cards slapped against tables and laughter rang out every so often.

I busied myself with a piece of embroidery I'd had since before being hired by Miss Raynsford. Though not much time had passed, that life felt more distant than the stars.

After being thrown out at sixteen, Jennie was hired by Mr. Melbourne. We'd worked alongside each other, chapping our delicate hands as we scrubbed dishes and floors. A few months later, the Melbourne's could no longer afford to keep me—and that's when we had been truly separated.

Mrs. Wilshire had taken me in as a ten year old girl. She sheltered me, provided me with every comfort of life, and loved me as a daughter. Despite my bumbling first attempts to please her, she continued to be patient with me. Under her steady guidance, I blossomed into a young woman, educated in the art of being a lady's maid.

I was Mrs. Wilshire's constant companion and most secret confidante—until the day she learned my real name. Early one morning she tossed me onto the street without a goodbye, much less a reference.

No one wanted to be connected with Lillian Markley.

With only a suitcase full of my few personal belongings, I walked all the way to the busy streets of London. In my small purse I kept all of my salary since being hired by Mrs. Wilshire—a large sum, but not quite enough to join my sister in New York.

Deep down, I had thought it was useless. No lady of respectable means would hire a maid with no reference. Not to mention that the rumors spread by Thomas practically guaranteed unemployment. Over the years, my reputation had become so scandalous that I was forced to create Julia Smith.

I never supposed I'd end up playing someone else entirely.

"Miss Raynsford!"

I glanced up to see the players at the card table watching me, Eliza motioning me over. Standing and nearing, I inwardly hoped they weren't going to ask me to join. I didn't know any card games. Miss Raynsford's "lessons" were beginning to seem more and more worthless, as the only things I hadn't already known she had failed to teach me.

"You look so secluded over there by yourself," Eliza said. "Why don't you join us?" Mr. Quincy nodded his head enthusiastically.

"I do appreciate the offer," I said. "But I was not lonely, merely occupied with my embroidery."

"But you will join us, will you not? After all it was Peter who suggested it to me."

"Oh?"

Lord Wycliffe smiled at his cards, seeming almost unwilling to look at me. Somehow, he had orchestrated this. Another round, another challenge—this one over whether or not I would enter their game. To join them would be to admit defeat, if only because that's what Lord Wycliffe *wanted* me to do.

And I would never admit defeat.

"I'm afraid my card playing is just as rusty as my dancing. Please forgive me, but you all seem to be having such a wonderful time. I would hate to spoil your evening by forcing you to play with an amateur like me."

"You could ask *Julia* if she would like to play," Lord Wycliffe suggested innocently. "I believe I saw her in the library. Perhaps you ought to go and fetch her?"

The little lout. He was outdoing me at every turn.

Eliza and Quincy's brows wrinkled. Before they could ask any questions, I plopped in an empty chair and swept up my stack of cards.

The score was now two to one, and Lord Wycliffe beamed with the knowledge.

They were playing whist, and I, not knowing the rules of the game, decided that the best course of action would be to put down something similar to whatever Quincy played. It proved to be a good strategy, as I took many tricks that way. Overall, I thought I did a decent job of concealing my ignorance.

Then they changed the form of the game to something called the 'elimination version.' From what I could gather, failing to produce a trump card would eliminate you from the game. Eliza left the table first, followed by Quincy a few short rounds later, until, as misfortune would have it, only Lord Wycliffe and I remained.

Had this somehow been his doing? My survival was certainly no thanks to my skill with cards. Lord Wycliffe shuffled and cut the deck.

"Did you do this on purpose?" I asked.

He chuckled, dealing out the cards. "Whatever would give you that idea? Do you have so little confidence in your card playing abilities?" After he set the pile in the middle of the table, we both picked up our cards and rearranged them in our hands.

"No," I lied. "But like I said before, I was a little rusty and couldn't have won without a little help."

"You haven't won yet." He was not just talking about a card game. Without removing his gaze, he said, "Trump is spades."

I analyzed my hand, trying to decide if spades was good news. "And by the way," I added, wanting to best him in some form, "it is cheating to use the same strategy twice. You cannot bring up Julia Smith every time you are about to lose."

"How else am I to meet her again?"

"That is the thing with Miss Smith. She is a woman of her own rights, and she will make her appearances as she pleases, not at the behest of any one person."

Lord Wycliffe's lips puckered in thought. "I admit, that seems a fair rule. Duly noted. From this moment forward, no idea can be used as a weapon more than once in the battle of wits." He laid down a two of clubs.

Despite myself, I smiled. We hadn't said a word about it until this moment, but we both understood we were competing. Just like under the tree. I selected a card at random and set it down.

He laughed. "You really have no idea what you're doing, do you? What a mysterious conundrum you are, Miss Raynsford."

At the sound of Mary's name, I remembered something else. "Why did you address me so informally at dinner?"

After placing down a different card, he said, "What makes you think I can't?"

"We are not well enough acquainted. It's not as if I will call you,

'Peter.'" I selected another card and set it on the pile. He studied me, and I ducked my head.

A boyish grin split his face. "Oh yes, you will."

"You cannot force me to. And it would be most improper." I willed my blush to stop, attempting to bury all evidence that he had an effect on me. It was uncharacteristic of me to blush. Perhaps I was simply unaccustomed to having attractive, wealthy lords paying me their attentions.

"If you do, I will let you even the score."

Fanning my cards out, I said, "Just like that? That is all it would take to gain one whole victory point?"

"It's not a one-time circumstance. This victory point will be given to you on the condition that you will call me 'Peter' for the rest of your stay. And if you violate these terms, the point is automatically withdrawn." Sweeping aside the finished round, he spun a new card onto the table.

A conditional point. I laid down a seven of diamonds.

I shouldn't accept. It was indiscreet, and Mary would probably be scandalized at the suggestion of calling someone their Christian name. It simply wasn't done. Not to mention that it was probably just a ploy to outsmart or embarrass me.

But a warm glow spread through me—a feeling caused by this man who laughed with looks and won with wit. Before I could stop myself, I said, "Very well, *Peter*. So long as we are in private, I shall do as you ask. And now, we are even."

"So we are. But someone must win tonight, otherwise our efforts will feel wasted. What shall be our last contest?"

I observed him closely. "Judging by your expression, I'd say you already know."

"Indeed I do." His voice took on a playful tone, and he leaned in confidentially. "The outcome of this card game will determine our winner."

My mouth dropped open, ready to tell him how unfair it was, when I glimpsed that irritating gleam again.

Touché.

"There is only one more trick to play," he said, holding up the single card in his hand and placing it down on the table. A king of hearts. "Your card will decide tonight's champion." He watched me evenly, waiting for me to reveal the last card. But something about the way he was looking at me made it seem like he already knew what it was.

Hesitantly, I put it face up on the table and sat back, reading his face. It gave nothing away, and for a while, he was silent. Then, all he said was, "Interesting."

Peter gathered the cards and shuffled them, preventing me from counting the number of tricks we each had taken. He stood, stepped aside, and tucked in his chair.

I desperately wanted to ask him who had won, but my pride was a large thing to swallow. After a good hour of pretending to know how to play whist, admitting the truth now would be more humiliating than losing. I knew I couldn't. But more importantly, *Peter* knew I couldn't.

He bowed, watching me the whole time with a smile. "Goodnight, Miss Raynsford, and thank you for your company." Turning on his heel, he ambled away.

I stared at his retreating form, eyebrows dipping into a scowl.

Who on earth had won?

CHAPTER 4

FOUR DAYS LATER, I WOKE TO THE SOUND OF TWITTERING BIRDS AND a conversation outside.

I was still unaccustomed to such lavish treatment. Rose-scented baths, pressed day-dresses, refreshments at all hours of the day. My bed swallowed me whole when I lay upon it, the mattress stuffed with a fortune of the finest feathers. I had little trouble falling asleep amid such luxury.

Though . . .

That could not be said of my second night at Ambleside. Thoughts of Peter and our card game had rolled around in my head, making me toss and turn. Over and over I replayed the scene in my mind, trying to decipher his face and catch something I hadn't noticed before. It was hopeless. He had packed up and left in a hurry—and did that mean he was elated that he had won, or that he was being a decent sport because he had lost?

I couldn't decide.

I'd spent the past several mornings munching on breakfast while everyone in turn explained their plans for the day. My afternoons consisted of tea and cookies while visiting neighbors. And my evenings found me lounging in the drawing room, furthering my embroidery, or dodging requests that I sing or play the pianoforte.

But the thing I avoided most was Lord Wycliffe.

It had been relatively easy. After all, he had an estate to run, as well as seeing to all of the other visitors. Yet, though there was never a time when we found ourselves alone, there *were* times when we made eye contact. Many, many times. Whether he was already looking at me, or we happened to glance at each other at the same moment, I didn't know; but always he was ready with a secretive smile, reminding me of those cards and taunting me with the truth of them.

Shrugging off my drowsiness and my reminiscence of the past few days, I slid out of bed, reaching for a shawl draped over the chair. Wrapping it around my shoulders, I unlocked the latch on the window and pushed it open, letting the morning swathe me in its dewy smells.

A blur of movement caught my eye. Eliza strolled down one of Ambleside's many pathways with Miss Clarissa Caldwell clinging to her arm like ivy crawling up a trellis. In fact, she always seemed to be clinging to Eliza, or Peter, or anyone within her reach . . . mostly Peter. They halted beneath my window, their discussion drifting up to the birds and my eager ears.

"But the fair will be here sometime next week," Miss Caldwell said. "I find it unreasonable that he would not even consider it!"

"Peter is merely being mindful of all of the guests. He cannot afford to attend only to one person." Eliza sounded like she was trying to be kind, but was somewhat disappointed herself.

"I see no reason why not. Where is he, anyway? I told him that I should like him by my side most of the summer, and yet here it is the fifth day, and he has gone off somewhere."

'Clingy' headed down the path in a huff, leaving Eliza planted in her spot, shaking her head.

"Miss Eliza!" I whispered fiercely out the window, cupping one hand to my mouth. She turned about. After a moment, when she still couldn't spot me, I added, "Up here."

She threw her head back. "Why, Miss Raynsford! What on earth are you doing at the window? Have you been listening all this time? And is that—why you are not properly dressed!"

Realizing how indecent my situation actually was, I began to regret drawing her attention. But I had to satisfy my curiosity. "There is to be a fair?"

"Indeed there is. It is to come sometime next week." Her eyes lit up, and suddenly her voice was laced with excitement. "There are to be exotic dancers, strange foods, goods for sale from all around the world, and games and performances of every kind. Oh, the experiences to be had!"

I smiled down at her, mind already working. "And your brother says he will not go?" I tried my hardest to ask the question casually, but inside I was grinning like a fool. Eliza's answer only broadened my secret smile.

"Indeed. Miss Caldwell was distressed by it, I daresay."

"If Lord Wycliffe does not go, is it likely that you—or any of us —shall?"

Eliza shook her head, before her expression brightened, bit by bit. "Could you convince him to go, Miss Raynsford? I've never known anyone that could change his mind after it was established on something, but he seems to like you."

I chuckled. "I shall certainly try. And please, you must call me Mary. Now, if you'll excuse me, I must dress for breakfast."

Eliza, still smiling, nodded and retreated.

Now I had my goal. All I had to do was find something to use against Peter to force him to go, and I would win. Maybe then I wouldn't be ashamed to show my face around him. And, though I had not said so to Eliza, I was also looking for any reason to go into town. I needed to send a forwarding address to Mrs. Wilshire in case any new letters from Jennie arrived during my stay. Whatever the cost, I had to persuade Peter to go.

After clothing myself quickly, I made for the door. My hand paused on the handle. Katherine would find it suspicious if I didn't ring for her to dress me. And servants were the worst gossipers.

I sighed, disrobed, and pulled the rope that rang for Katherine. By the time she arrived, dressed me, and put my hair up, twenty or so minutes had passed. I was sure to arrive late to the breakfast table, drawing everyone's attention. Inwardly, I groaned. Undue attention was the last thing I needed. And I had missed my chance to trap Peter before breakfast.

Perhaps after dinner would do. I wasn't likely to see him before then.

The long dining room was empty. After piling my plate at the sideboard, I occupied one of the chairs. Delicately slicing my toast into bite-sized pieces, I wondered where everyone could have gone.

Mr. Quincy entered, flushed and disoriented, sporting long leather boots and a riding crop. Seeing me, he smiled and tipped his hat politely. "Good morning, Miss Raynsford." He took a seat next to me. "That was quite a game the other night. You really oughtn't to lead all of us on like that. Rusty indeed! Why, I've never seen better card playing in all my life."

I chuckled. "Oh, do go on, sir! I believe it was quite the contrary, and I forced a dull evening upon you."

If only Mr. Quincy could shed some light on the results of the card game. But Peter had been the only one there, and was thereby the only one who could know the outcome . . .

Or was he?

A plan began to formulate.

"Nonsense!" he laughed. "You soundly thrashed us! You must tell me your strategy Miss Raynsford, for one day I hope to become as great a player as you." He paused. "And as for the evening, it was anything but dull." A candid smile graced his face.

I folded my hands in my lap, uncomfortable. Flirting was acceptable, but not forming attachments. And an attachment was surely what Mr. Quincy must be hoping for, if the way he inched closer was any indication. The balance between a harmless flirtation and insinuating something more was difficult to get just right—and apparently I hadn't mastered it yet. I needed to discourage him, but how?

Put him in the race with someone else.

"Dull is relative, I suppose," I said. "True, it might not have been a boring game while you were there, but the most thrilling part was near the end, in my match with Lord Wycliffe. How clever he is! And so very handsome, is he not?"

Mr. Quincy's expression plummeted. He had come to the assumption that I had hoped he would—that I had formed an attachment to Peter.

Swallowing my guilt, I continued. "In fact, I found the last trick to be the most fascinating. Trump was spades, and Lord Wycliffe laid down the king of hearts. When I revealed my card, it turned out to be its queen." He raised his brows, making my pulse race with hope. "Now what do you make of *that*, sir?"

"I—"

"Why Quincy! I had hoped that you would've joined us this morning."

We both spun in surprise.

There, in the doorway and in all his glory, stood Peter, a pleasant smile plastered on his face. He had obviously been riding, for he looked much like he had when I had toppled him—windblown and wonderful. I frowned, despite his appearance. Of course it would be him that spoiled my plans.

"You'll be sorry to know that the game was remarkably good today," Peter said, stopping before us on the opposite side of the table. "Gave us very good sport."

"Is that right, Wycliffe? I confess, I had planned on joining the party this morning, but sleep rather got the better of me. Perhaps tomorrow, eh? Should be agreeable weather."

"Indeed. Moresby got quite a few of the rascals, if you should fancy a look at them. Last I knew he was behind the stables, displaying his trophies to the young ladies. Some of them need rescuing."

So that's where everyone was.

"Well, I believe I'd be keen on taking a look at the devils, at that." After standing, Mr. Quincy bowed in my direction.

Peter waited until the sound of his footsteps faded to silence before turning to me. How long had he been listening to our conversation, and how much had he heard? Had he heard me tell Quincy . . .?

Oh, no.

Fearing the possibility, I bridged the river of silence, before he could. "One might wonder why *you* don't feel inclined to rescue those unfortunate young women. Instead, you're sending poor Quincy to do the job. One might think your masculinity is at stake."

Peter sighed dramatically. "To be sure, I feel sorry for the distraught maidens, but you see, the sight of dead creatures upsets my delicate disposition." His stare remained open, but he was lying, I could tell. Somewhere under the surface, there was a smile ready to break through; and I, quite unavoidably, wanted to see it.

"So your honor *is* in question, for it is cowardice that brings you here, sir."

"Nay, not cowardice, but an empty stomach." He reached over, plucked a piece of toast off of my plate, and stuffed it in his mouth. The crunch of his chewing punctured the silence as he pulled out the chair opposite mine and sat, reclining in it comfortably.

I cleared my throat.

"One might further assume, Lord Wy—*Peter*, that *when* you appeared was anything but coincidence. Quincy was just about to tell me his opinion on our card game the other night."

And there it was: his full smile in all its brilliance. "Indeed? The thought never occurred to me."

Yes, it had. He obviously didn't want me to know who had won, forever delighting in my doubt. "Of course the thought never occurred to you," I retorted, sipping some tea. "I find it hard to believe that any thought occurs to you at all."

He chuckled, plucking a flower from a vase on the table and twirling it between his fingers. "On the contrary, thoughts occur to me at least twice a day—three times if you count the inclination a person has to eat when they are hungry. Which as you know, brought me here in the first place."

Returning my cup to its place by my plate, I bit my lip to hold the laughter in. My wit hadn't had this much exercise in almost eight years. Perhaps never.

"I pity the man," I said, face assuming concern, "—or *woman* as the case may be—who is so unfortunate as to witness any of your three displays of wit. For, though it is quite an improvement from your regular self, it is rather out of character, and must cause no small amount of alarm."

Peter's laugh sounded as if he hadn't expected to be so amused. His eyes twinkled, and I waited for him to retort with his own clever remark, but he didn't. After a few moments of lingering laughter, he finally said, "I concede. You win this one."

Victory marched through my blood. "What?" I teased. "Couldn't you think of anything?" I knew I shouldn't vaunt my triumph, but winning made my head swirl with giddiness, making it hard to think straight.

"I would not gloat so if I were in your shoes. After all," he stood, "remember the card game?"

The words were tantalizing, and I latched onto them like I would a floating log in the middle of the ocean. "Are you implying you won?"

"Are you implying you don't *know* who won?" he countered roguishly. I clamped my mouth shut, wishing I had not spoken so hastily.

I decided to change the subject. "Eliza says there is to be a fair."

"Indeed."

"She also said you will not be going."

"Indeed I will not."

I clucked my tongue. "And why ever not? It promises to be exciting."

"Mm, not to me."

I stood, leaning forward onto the table on the tips of my fingers. "And what if I give you the victory of the card game? Would you go then?"

Eyes narrowing, he stepped forward and leaned over the table himself. "And what if it is not your victory to give?"

"It is." But really, I wasn't so sure. Peter was smiling at me in a private way, both charmed and amused. Had he won, or had I? He wouldn't be smiling like that if *I'd* won. But if *he'd* won, surely he would've told me about it so he could wallow in it. Wouldn't he?

A small, elderly fellow I didn't recognize entered the room. "Lord Wycliffe?" He was graying, his lips thinning, his long nose crooking ever more, but he wore a soft expression that was etched into his face, making him seem kind.

Peter's head turned. "Yes, Mr. Minton?"

"You do remember our appointment this morning?" His words were quiet, but not timid. "I've been mailing you for weeks to get these documents signed, but you haven't responded."

Peter rocked back. "Ah, yes, I nearly forgot. If you'll be kind enough to wait in the study."

"Of course, sir." Mr. Minton bowed then left.

As the echoes of his steps faded, Peter turned back to me. "I've been meaning to ask you, do you have plans today?"

I scoffed, ignoring the skip my heart did at the thought of what he might be suggesting. "I didn't, but now I find my schedule to be full. I must track down some more breakfast, as my toast seems to have been devoured by someone else."

Peter went on, not the least bit fazed. "But after that, you are free?"

I leaned in closer, giving in to intrigue. "Free for what?"

He leaned in too. "Well, I thought it would be nice if . . ." He trailed off and the butterflies in my stomach burst from their cocoons. I couldn't tell if he was in earnest, or if we were playing one of our games. And all the uncertainty was driving me mad.

". . . if you spent some time with Quincy," he finished, his look souring to sympathetic. I couldn't decide if I was relieved, or disappointed. It didn't matter much, because his next words froze me in place.

"He is such a tender-hearted fellow you know, and I daresay he won't take your refusal lightly. It's a hard blow to any man when they discover they are competing with the likes of the Lord Wycliffe; for I am *so very* handsome, am I not?"

I stiffened. The all-too-familiar feeling of mortification ate away the butterflies in my stomach and snaked its way up my spine, a blush spreading to the tips of my ears in the face of Peter's meaningful smile. My throat constricted, my nose tingled, and I knew I wouldn't be able to stop it no matter how I tried.

I ducked my head into my elbow as the sneeze erupted.

Peter looked off in the distance, biting his lip to contain his laughter. Again, I was the object of his amusement!

After somewhat transforming his face into a sincere one, giggle barely restrained, he turned to me and said, "My, my, Mary. You really ought to get a physician to look at those *allergies*."

And then, he couldn't hold back any longer. He doubled over with laughter. I watched him for a few moments as he clutched his middle, reveling in my folly. At least he had the decency to turn from me as he did so.

He *had* been listening to our conversation. Which means he had heard Quincy express his interest in me. Which means he had heard me turn Quincy down by claiming an attachment to him. Which means he had every right to never let me hear the end of it. I had just surrendered a heap amount of ground in our battle of wits.

Levelling my features, I suppressed the urge to slap him. Let Peter tease me all he wanted. His turn would come soon enough.

"True, that. And you know, I *do* feel rather sorry for Quincy. I shall attempt to console him once I am finished with my breakfast." Sitting, I turned my attention to my plate but found I was no longer hungry.

Peter's fits of laughter subsided, face sobering into a perplexed but fascinated expression. "What are you up to?"

"'Up to?' Why, whatever could you mean?"

"You're giving up rather too easily, I think. You wouldn't do that unless you wanted to fool me into a false sense of security, patiently waiting until the perfect moment to exact your revenge. Which means that you must have another card up your sleeve. So, Miss Raynsford." He leaned over the table, capturing my eyes and holding them prisoner. "What *are* you up to?"

I couldn't help the demure smile that crept across my face. Peter was clever enough to guess that I had a plan, but was he clever enough to guess what it was?

"If you must know, then yes, I *am* up to something." Pushing my plate aside, I rose from my seat. "And indeed I would tell it to you, but you see, I must rush to Mr. Quincy's side. A dear friend of mine told me that his heart is in desperate need of repair, and I'm afraid I cannot delay any longer."

Flouncing my skirts, I departed from the dining room, leaving a very captivated Peter behind.

THERE WAS SOMETHING AGITATING ABOUT BEING IN A THRONG OF gossipers.

I sipped the last of my tea while Betty Hartford updated us all on London's scandals. Apparently, she had a friend whose sister's maid found Lord Ashby in a shocking embrace with Miss Van Couth in an alleyway after Lady Callahan's ball. And Betty's cousin had fallen ill after he had received a mysterious note from his wife's uncle while promenading through Hyde Park last Wednesday morning.

We were taking tea outside, and I was situated between Eliza and Miss Caldwell. A gentle breeze played at my hair, and I shifted in my seat, angling my parasol so it would stop. I set my cup back on the table. Perhaps I despised gossip so thoroughly because of the awful times I had been on the other end of its sword.

"I've been meaning to ask you," Eliza said to me quietly, "about how you plan on convincing Peter to go to the fair. He can be rather stubborn, you know."

The others kept conversing unhindered, and I grinned. I thought about our conversation at breakfast this morning. "Yes, I know. I'm still deliberating it."

"Well, whatever you do, you had better do it quick. The men are keen on taking a hunting trip, and who knows how long they shall be gone."

"But is the fair not for another week?"

"You are talking of the fair?" Miss Caldwell leaned over and asked. Her eager eyes oscillated between me and Eliza.

Eliza nodded. "Mary has promised to change Peter's mind."

"Has she?" Miss Caldwell sized me up. No doubt she was wondering what influence I had on him. It was very little indeed, unless I found something to use against him.

Lady Wycliffe called to Eliza, pulling her attention away.

"I have promised to try," I said to Miss Caldwell, twirling my parasol. "Though, I find Lord Wycliffe to be stubborn. And arrogant. And if he cannot find a way to have a little fun, I doubt he shall ever find a wife."

Miss Caldwell inclined her head. "Oh, he shouldn't have difficulty there."

I chuckled. "Indeed, what with all the female attention he receives."

Miss Caldwell set her teacup down, a confused smile touching her mouth. "Why no, Miss Raynsford, that is not at all what I meant."

My twirling stopped. When she didn't elaborate, I said, "To be sure, I don't know what else you could mean."

Her mouth curved further, and the hair on my arms stood on end. The happy jabber of the rest of the company was drowned out by Miss Caldwell's next words, low and boastful.

"But didn't you know? Peter and I are engaged."

CHAPTER 5

MY PARASOL TUMBLED TO THE GRASS.

With a monumental effort, I tried to keep my face neutral, but my eyes widened a fraction. I glanced at Eliza for confirmation, but she wasn't paying attention. A swarm of questions buzzed within me, flies bumping against windows.

Annoyance started to simmer—and then boil at the realization it was there in the first place. What should I care if they were engaged? I mustered a polite smile, thoughts darting over everything that had happened in the past few days.

Miss Caldwell's cheeks dimpled. "I daresay he is quite a catch. Rich, titled, and handsome to boot! Indeed, I count myself to be the luckiest woman in England!"

Finishing my evaluation, I was sure of it. No one had cared to mention an engagement between Lord Wycliffe and Miss Caldwell— much less Peter who, under these enlightened circumstances, had behaved inappropriately.

I had behaved *atrociously*. How rude of him to withhold the truth. And I'd agreed to call him by his Christian name in private!

"Indeed," I said at last, licking my lips and retrieving my parasol from the grass. "My condolences."

"I beg—" Her voice lowered, stare hardening. "I beg your pardon?"

Clicking my parasol closed, I said, "From what I've gathered regarding Lord Wycliffe's pursuit of a wife, he is rather enamored with my dear acquaintance, Julia Smith."

"Enamored?"

"Yes. Did he not refuse to hold a ball unless she attended? Is that the sort of thing an engaged man would say?"

Miss Caldwell faltered, mouth dropping open.

"And," I went on, "if that is truly the type of man he is—rich, handsome, titled, but unfaithful—then what more is there for me to say but that you have my pity, and I hope you will find consolation in spending his money." I batted my lashes. "Or, if that is not the case, one must conclude that he is not engaged and you are lying, which I can hardly bring myself to say as we are seated here together."

Miss Caldwell stammered something incoherent before managing, "Well, yes, he has been acting rather outlandishly. That is because our engagement is a secret and he is trying to keep up the pretense."

A secret?

My mind started racing, digesting the news.

Miss Caldwell prattled on, and at the appropriate time I gave her an empathetic response, but my attention was far, far away.

Peter. Miss Caldwell. Engaged.

The muscles in my face relaxed. It was a secret. Something Peter clearly didn't want others to know about.

And it was certainly worth one victory point.

The cogs in my brain began working a mile a minute. As far as Peter was concerned, he still believed me ignorant of this attachment. As my mind began to formulate a plan, overcoming obstacles and taking on shape, I couldn't help the slow smirk that stole across my lips.

Peter was not as invincible as he liked to think.

WHEN RICHARD CUNNINGHAM III—AN ELDERLY MAN IN HIS LATE
fifties—began a winded and detailed description of all of England's
kings during dinner, he monopolized the conversation. He was a little
eccentric, and no one had the heart to stop him from getting the
attention he so rarely received. But when I created silly poems for each
monarch, everyone roared with laughter, eager for Mr. Cunningham to
continue so I could craft the next humorous poem. More than once I
heard Peter's laugh during dinner. And more than once had I caught
him staring.

Now, with all of the guests gathered around in the drawing room, it
was my chance to trap him into going to the fair. The opportunity was
soon lost, however, as the young men began to devise plans for a
hunting trip. Before I knew it, they had determined to start their
journey tomorrow, not to return for a week or so, at least.

I wanted to stomp my foot. A week! I couldn't wait that long. The
fair would be gone by then, letting Peter out of the noose he didn't
know I'd placed around his neck. And maybe I was as equally disappointed about his engagement as I was about this hunting trip.

I suppressed a scoff at the thought. Through mere looks over the
past few days, he had wormed his way into my mind. My mind drifted
to my conversation with Quincy, and how I'd insinuated that I was
attached to Peter. Perhaps 'attachment' was too strong a word, but
there was no denying that I liked—even preferred—his company.

*Why shouldn't I miss him? I shall be bored with him gone, for there shall be
no one to banter with.* The thought persuaded me, charming away any
deep meaning from my muddled feelings. And it was that moment
Peter chose to saunter over and continue our game.

"I've been meaning to tell you, Miss Raynsford, what a delightful
meal that was. I have yet to live a dull moment in your presence."
He stood languidly in front of my sofa, perusing a book. "Tell me,
have you ever taken lessons in entertaining?" His gaze remained

glued to his book, but it was apparent that he enjoyed the game as much as I did. That he would seek me out was both flustering and flattering.

"Naturally." I folded my arms, reclining back on the sofa. "I used to be in the theater, you know."

"Oh?" He angled his head to the side. Closing his hardcover, he swung it behind his back an clasped it there.

I kept my tone light, teasing. "Indeed. Performing was my livelihood for a few years before I became the elegant Miss Raynsford."

It was partially true. Mrs. Wilshire had called upon my talents many times when she was entertaining guests, since an accomplished servant was a rare thing. In fact, that was how it had been made known that I was Lillian Markley.

Mrs. Wilshire had insisted I sing, only when I entered to perform, I came face to face with my half-brother. Shaken, I fled the room and holed up in my quarters. Thomas soon left, along with Mrs. Wilshire's other guests. He did not reveal me—not right away—but I knew it was only a matter of time.

But then the letter from Jennie had come, beckoning to me from America. So I stayed with my employer for as long as I could, needing the money to join my sister. When the rumor finally reached Mrs. Wilshire's ears, she confronted me about it, and, learning the truth of who I was, had bidden me and my belongings to be tossed into the gutter.

Though I hadn't known it, the whole ordeal turned out to be a blessing. It wouldn't be long now before I had the funds to travel to America—Ambleside being the steppingstone.

I knew exactly how Peter would view the information that I was an entertainer, and I was glad I could offer him a scrap of truth, however small—even if he thought it was a silly joke.

"Performing," he said thoughtfully. "That is so very broad a subject. You must tell me the sorts of things you were called upon to do."

"I am sure you know the wild world of show business. I did

anything the theater required. Acting, playing the pianoforte—" I stopped short as I noticed Peter's eyes beginning to sparkle.

Oh no. Where had I misstepped? What had I overlooked?

"Is that all?" His stance was much too blasé, his smile much too concealed. Yes, he was toying with me. My mind scoured for what I could be missing.

I gulped. "Singing . . ."

". . . Dancing?" he finished.

There it was. I winced.

Peter's act disappeared, his stunning features twisting into a cheeky grin. "You know, theaters all about London are known for their dancing, and you said you did *everything* the theater required." His smile expanded with my humiliation. "Ah yes, Mary, I have caught you. For I thought you said you didn't dance."

Replies bashed on the prison walls of my mind, but none became fugitives. Instead, my mouth hung open, unintelligible sounds slipping out, until I finally managed, "I don't!"

"No, perhaps you don't." He strolled to the edge of the sofa and braced his arm on its back, trapping me. "But Julia Smith *does*."

The cheek of the man!

"And that is why she *will* be attending our ball, yes?" He stayed close, adding low enough so no one else could hear, "I believe I have won this one." Peter pushed off and straightened, face glowing with his success. My pride reared at the knowledge that he had bested me—and in such a flippant manner. I needed to say something, and fast.

He turned away, no doubt intending to make a famous exit, when my mind seized from my spinning thoughts the one thing I held over Peter. The one thing that could give me the win.

"Have you, sir? Have you *really*?"

Peter halted. Little by little, he turned back. For a glimmer of a moment, his confidence slackened, but he covered it. "I see no reason to assume I have lost."

"Do you not? I should think it was quite obvious. However, if you are having trouble reasoning it out, perhaps you could think on our conversation this morning concerning 'one more card I have to play.' You may even want to solicit the opinion of . . . your *fiancée,* Miss Caldwell."

Peter's expression froze so completely, I wondered if he had even heard me. Then, slowly, he frowned, even as something like admiration shone in his eyes. I smiled smugly, quite pleased with his reaction.

"So. This is your card. Your plan." His words were soft and deliberate, but held an undertone of enchantment. If not for that enchantment, I might have been afraid that I had crossed a line that shouldn't have been crossed.

"My plan? Why, I am merely curious about your engagement."

"I am not engaged."

"Are you not?" I stood and sashayed closer.

"Indeed I am not," he said so convincingly that I almost believed him.

"Miss Caldwell would claim otherwise."

Peter laughed suddenly, the reason for his frown forgotten. "That is because she fantasizes about having a husband who is *so very* handsome." He walked away.

How dare he mock me again? I sucked in my cheeks, following him to a table where he poured himself a glass of wine. Why was he skirting my question? Why wasn't he simply admitting the truth?

"Or perhaps one who is so very arrogant," I countered.

"When I marry, it will be to a woman who can tell much more interesting lies. While I am a perfect fit for Miss Caldwell, she is not a perfect fit for me. No, the one I marry must be tall . . . clever . . ." Peter glanced at my face, then my toes, and then back up again. ". . . and exceptionally pretty."

He obviously loved to play on my heartstrings, his words exciting, intoxicating. Pleasure washed over me, followed instantly by guilt. Here I was, dallying with a gentleman at a rich estate, while my sister waited for me an ocean away, probably slaving away.

Resolved not to let him distract me from my true purpose here, or to let him win this round, I rolled my shoulders back. "Now I *know* you must be teasing when you say you are not engaged, for that description fits Miss Caldwell to a tee."

Peter laughed, and what a nice sound it was. It contained all the radiance of birdsong and all the warmth of a sunny day. He stared thoughtfully into the bottom of his glass as he swirled it. "And of course, whoever I marry must also be a brilliant conversational partner." Peter watched me above the rim as he took another swallow.

"Well then," I said, hoping he hadn't noticed the blush rising to my cheeks, "I shall be sure to let Mr. Cunningham know of your interest."

He swallowed his drink quickly, snorting on a chuckle. "Well played," he said, setting his glass down. "I think you have rightfully earned tonight's trophy."

"It is not the trophy I desire, but something else entirely."

I paused. I promised Eliza I'd change his mind about the fair, but now that I was faced with it, I wasn't so sure I could. Peter watched me, waiting.

"What is it you want?" he asked, and I got the sense that whatever I told him, he desired to give it to me.

Before I lost the nerve, I took a deep breath. "The fair. I wish to go to the fair."

"Goodness, do you think we tie up our guests and chain them in the basement to prevent them from leaving? You needn't ask my permission. You can go to the fair if you please." He picked up his glass again and leaned against the wall, continuing to churn it and raise it to his lips.

Peter looked so at home, so graceful yet comfortable. He clearly belonged among the privileged class, taking hunting trips, playing cards, and dancing with a beautiful woman on his arm. Yet there was something familiar about him too. Endearing, even. Almost as if he were a little boy.

And that little boy knew very well that none of us would go to the fair if he did not.

"Peter . . . I want you to go to the fair *with* me."

He raised his eyebrows dramatically. "Madam, do you not think you are too forward? Besides, I already told Miss Caldwell it wouldn't be prudent."

"What is imprudent about taking an outing with your fiancée?"

He shook his head. "I told you, I am not engaged."

He seemed in earnest. Was he really not betrothed? But then why had Miss Caldwell said that they were? Obviously one of them was lying.

But which one?

"Eliza has been craving to go, and I promised her I would change your mind."

"How certain you are that you can convince me to go. This, I must see."

This was proving to be disastrous. Not only had my plan failed, but he was making fun of me again, and I did my best to turn my eyes into daggers. How I hated being made fun of.

Peter bit his lip and looked away—something, I noticed, he only ever did when he was trying not to laugh. I pursed my lips.

"Lord Wy—*Peter*, you really oughtn't laugh at a lady. It is most indecent."

"Careful there, Mary," he said. "That's twice now that you've almost slipped up."

"At any rate, I don't appreciate it when you laugh at me."

"Ah, but you're so lovely when you're angry."

Of course he would say that. I fought off the flush before it could surface. "You must go to the fair. Eliza is counting on it." I didn't want to mention that I was counting on it too—especially considering how he might use the information against me.

Peter studied me a moment. "And if I refuse?"

"Then I shall tell everyone you are engaged." My hand clenched in a nervous fist. *Don't call my bluff. Don't call my bluff.*

He squinted at me, and I could see he saw the truth. Drat.

"No, Miss Raynsford, I do not believe it. To do so would force me into a marriage practically without my consent. That would be much too cruel, and you are too sweet. So in all actuality, you hold nothing over me."

Drat it all. Why was it so easy to lie to everyone else?

"However, I am a good sport—one that is so very handsome, I might add—and can see when someone's efforts should be applauded."

I bit my tongue from telling Peter just what I thought of His So Very Handsomeness as he finished off the last of his drink.

"I shall go to the fair," he said, "but you must give me something in return, since we shall have to cut our hunting trip short to accommodate you."

I glanced around. Most of the guests had retired for the night, but a number of the young men still huddled in a corner, discussing plans and swapping ideas. Turning back to Peter, I said, "I don't have anything of value to give you, except perhaps tonight's victory."

His mouth twisted. "I am not so sure that you have it, now."

It was true—and how on earth he had managed to win again?

I had played my card, gambling high, and he had called my bluff. The tables had turned so quickly—just like with the card game, and at breakfast this morning. At all costs, I was going to make sure that he went to the fair. I still wouldn't have won, but it would be a balm for my wounded pride.

"No, perhaps I don't have the victory. But I have nothing else to offer you, and I must ensure that you go."

"Then I am afraid that we are at an impasse, for I must have *something*."

I huffed. He was being so difficult. And he knew it. In the way his eyes lit up and how his chin was held high and how his smile was a riddle, he knew it. He really was like a little boy.

He sucked in a breath. "Perhaps, we don't have to decide right now. We can simply say that you are in my debt."

I scoffed. "I would rather not be indebted to you, sir. You'll just use it to win the verbal sparring."

He held up a hand in promise. "On my word, I will not."

"Fine," I said at last, giving in.

"Do you promise you will agree to it, no matter what it is?"

I sighed. "I suppose. If it is not improper."

"Perfect."

I was quite uncomfortable with how pleased he seemed, and, as if Peter knew I might change my mind, he bid me goodnight and joined the remaining men in the corner, telling them the change in plans.

As I ascended to my quarters, I shook my head. What an odd conversation that went nowhere near according to plan. Not a week had passed since our meeting, and already Peter and I conversed like longtime friends. And though it felt relieving to have a friend after all these years on my own, it made me nervous. The closer I grew to the people here, the harder it would be to leave them.

I needed to remind myself why I was really here.

After climbing into my nightgown, I sat at the writing desk, a lone flickering candle casting shadows across the walls from its resting place next to the parchment. I dipped my quill in the ink and began a letter to Jennie, thinking long and hard about every word.

Dearest sister,

I shall forego asking after you, as this letter's purpose is more for me to organize my thoughts (though I suppose I shall write you again asking after your health and whatnot if you desperately desire it). I am selfish, I know.

So much has happened. At this moment, I am encircled about by an opulence not even Father could have provided; but the best part is that I am earning the money to come to you. I won't tell you the details, as I'm sure it will spark an uncharacteristic scolding in your next letter. (Also because there is a risk that someone might intercept this letter, and this matter must remain confidential if I am to be successful.) It is not dangerous, if perhaps reckless.

I am happier than I can remember being since Father died; and that, I never expected. Though you might think it is because of the lavishness of my surroundings, it is not the reason. I feel important; needed, even. Things I have not felt in a long time.

Forgive me, Jennie. I know I should not feel so content in this corner of paradise—but then he comes with that quick mind and that childlike smile and that bottomless stare, and I forget all over again.

Do you remember when I broke my arm from leaping out of that tree behind the stables? I was convinced that I could fly. You said some things should only ever be regarded as fantasies, or dreams, not as things that could become reality.

You might not remember, but I do.

Well, perhaps this place is my opportunity to fly—a chance to see what it's like to soar limitlessly. And even though this fantasy ascends into the velvety clouds of heaven, it will come to an end. When this lovely dream closes, I shall tuck these memories into my box of wishes, grateful that I ever had the chance to belong to the sky. I will come to you with happiness.

I do not know how you will take this letter, Jennie. Truly, I do not know what to make of it myself, but I want you to know that nothing shall stop me from coming home. And home has always been, and ever will be you.

It is possible that when this letter reaches you, I am already on my way.

Yours,

Lily

CHAPTER 6

SNUGGLED IN A CORNER ON THE THIRD STORY, THE LIBRARY SMELLED like stories and adventures.

Though it was vast, there was a coziness to it that the rest of the house envied. Having Peter gone provided me with a delicious opportunity to peruse the shelves at my leisure, and perhaps gain some skill with cards before he returned.

Ornately carved cedar trimmed the doorway and the columns lining the edges of the room. Every inch was filled with shelves bearing books that begged to have their contents discovered—philosophy, history, poetry. It wasn't long before I discovered the section devoted wholly to proper etiquette.

I scanned the row, excitement dampening. There were several on the history of dancing or conventional gentlemanly pursuits—and even one surprisingly thick volume on when it was acceptable to serve quail —but no books on card games. Disappointed, I instead selected one on horse riding, determined to better myself in some form. I stood there, reading for some minutes.

"Are you going to leave anytime soon?" a voice behind me called.

I whirled around, losing my hold on the book. It plummeted to the floor with a loud *thwap*. A figure lounged in an over-stuffed chair near the window, not looking up from his book.

Matthew.

No rustle came from his clothing, no fidgeting or shifting in his chair. He sat as still as a statue—stoic, but at home among his tomes. Stacks of books several feet high surrounded his chair and boxed him in, giving the impression that it had been a few weeks since he'd moved.

Clearing my throat, I rescued my book from the floor, stroking it as if it were a child in need of comfort. "Have you been here the whole time?"

He turned a page in his book, apparently refusing to acknowledge my presence a second time. His feet were propped up on an end table before him, eyes travelling the pages of his hardcover and never once lifting.

I approached him. "What are you reading?"

He held his book higher. The move was either to let me more clearly read the cover, or to try and block my face from his peripheral. I couldn't decide which.

The Wealth of Nations. I had heard of it before—it was a detailed discussion concerning economics, and hardly a suitable book for a boy of thirteen. Tilting my head sideways, I read each title making up the stack of books next to Matthew's chair. They were all similarly difficult.

"Do you often read such challenging books?"

Still, he didn't look up. In fact, nothing in his expression suggested he knew I'd spoken, and when the heavy silence was broken by another one of his page turns, I huffed.

"You know, conversations work so much better when both parties participate."

"I know," he said. "I didn't respond because I hoped if I ignored you, you would go away."

I rocked back. What an insolent boy. "You don't like my company?"

"No."

I laughed emptily, hoping that perchance he was playing some cruel joke; but when I was met again with silence, my brow furrowed. Should I be friendly? Worried? Angry? What would Mary do? Matthew was being unquestionably rude, and I wanted to scold him—but to do so might cause a rift between the Wycliffe's and me. After all, he was their family.

"I cannot know what I've done to offend you," I said, probing.

"Nothing. I just don't trust you." Finally, he set his book down, and the eyes that met me were Peter's. But the effect was remarkably different.

Instead of a soft, lively gaze, Matthew's eyes had a hardness about them—though perhaps determination would be a better word. They spoke of great intelligence, while Peter's spoke mostly of mischief. The brothers looked so similar, but they couldn't be more divergent in personality.

As if Matthew could read my thoughts, he added, "And it is one of the many things my brother and I differ on. I've told him countless times over the past few days that you can't be trusted, but he never listens to me. Peter means well, but he can be rather stupid sometimes."

"He wouldn't believe you?" I don't know why my mind focused more on that scrap of Matthew's speech than on the fact that someone was catching onto my charade.

Matthew scoffed, closed his book, and tossed it onto the floor. "Of course not. I'm only the little brother, after all. Who would listen to me?"

It would surprise me if no one paid attention to Matthew, like he claimed. He was too unorthodox to ignore completely. "What is it about me that you don't trust?"

He snorted. "Like I know. There are just too many things that don't add up." He squinted, expression turning harder than thoughtful. "Like, your hair isn't blonde. And, your eyes aren't green. And mother was told you were silly and would probably be angry that you were here."

He had obviously spent a lot of time considering me since my arrival. I smiled my most teasing smile. "Am I not silly?"

I expected him to grin—like how Peter would—but instead he looked me up and down, weighing my question seriously. "No. Peculiar perhaps, but not silly."

I nearly guffawed at who was calling who peculiar. Instead, I decided to take a different approach. Even though he was catching on to my disguise, I doubted I had anything to fear from him. For the oddest reason, I didn't feel threatened.

"All right, Matthew. You've said what you think is suspicious about me. Have you determined what it all means?"

He sat up, his hands coming together—thumbs under his chin and forefingers to his lips—as he studied me from head to toe.

"Well, there are a few different explanations," he began, as if he were assessing a medical condition. "One could be that your aunt really doesn't know you very well—or perhaps hasn't seen you for some years and still believes you to be obnoxious. However, I don't think that's the case, because she wouldn't be so ignorant about her heiress. Another one is perhaps we were misinformed, and some of the communication between my mother and your aunt had been tampered with—a highly unlikely scenario, but a possibility all the same.

"Or your aunt may have deluded us accidentally because of her poor eyesight, like you claim. You could have had an epiphany since your aunt last saw you, changing your entire personality—or a frightening experience, changing your hair color. Perhaps you haven't had much sun, recently. Perhaps your eyes are green under London light. Perhaps you are only *acting* like you love it here. *Or . . .*"

He paused, folding his arms across his chest, brows dipping into a scowl. "Or perhaps you are not who you say you are."

My, he was brilliant. I couldn't help but be impressed. I found myself wanting to challenge him, like how I would Peter—but in a different way, for Matthew's mind worked differently. Once again, the familiar urge to be cleverer overruled the need to be wise.

"Then let us say I am not. Let us say that I've been fooling everyone for some bizarre reason, pretending to be a silly girl with blonde hair and green eyes . . . What then?"

Matthew faltered, doubt creeping onto his face. He'd obviously not quite thought that far. And just as I couldn't help sneezing on Peter, I couldn't help my next words.

"For it will surprise you to know, Matthew, that you are right. I am not, nor ever will be, Mary Raynsford."

For a few, immeasurable moments, complete silence reigned.

"I . . . I am right?" He looked so uncertain, it was difficult to believe only moments ago he'd been exuding confidence. Jerking to his feet, he said, "Then . . . I—why are you here, then? To trap Peter and marry him for his title?"

"Don't be absurd. What would I do with a title?" I stooped my head to his level. "No. No, I am here to make sure that snobbish boys behave themselves."

His mouth parted and he stared at me in humble fascination, quite unaccustomed to being put in his place. It gave me a twisted satisfaction. Clasping my book on horseback riding tightly, I turned and paraded out of the library, feeling pleased with myself.

After an hour or two of reading in my quarters, I set the book down, no longer possessing the patience. My mind returned to the scene in the library. Perhaps I had made a wrong decision. What was to stop Matthew from telling everyone the truth?

The more I thought on it, the more my nervousness festered.

The next day, as soon as breakfast finished, I trudged up to the library. Sighing, I knew I couldn't avoid it any longer and opened the door, peeking into the stuffy room. I hoped to find it empty. But there was a familiar form in the chair near the window, book propped up in its place.

My lips meandered to one side, disliking the idea of groveling. But what else could I do? I plodded toward the window.

Matthew appeared to be completely engrossed in some philosophy, so I was surprised when he spoke, words dripping with derision. "Come here to read again, 'Not Mary'?"

My pride reared its hideous head, and I knew I would not be groveling today. "Actually, yes." I plopped into the chair opposite his and reached for a nearby stack of books. I seized the one on the top and pretended to read.

After a few minutes of silence, I peeped over the top of my page, analyzing Matthew. Did he possess any sympathy for me? Would he keep my confidence anyway? He must've felt my scrutiny because he glanced up, forcing me to look down again.

A few minutes passed before I noticed Matthew studying me like I had been him. He pulled his book up to cover his eyes, but not before I saw that the antagonism in his eyes from yesterday was replaced with curiosity.

On and on it went the whole afternoon in total silence: Matthew catching me staring, and I catching Matthew staring—both trying to make out the other, trying to decide whether the person across from us were friend or foe. We read . . . and stared . . . and read some more . . . and stared.

When I grew hungry I consulted a clock on the mantelpiece. Dinner would be served soon, which meant I needed to change for the evening and have Katherine fix my hair. Finishing the book would have to wait for another day. Rising from my chair, I turned to leave.

"See you tomorrow," Matthew called to me when I reached the doorway. And as I exited the room, despite myself, I smiled.

On the third day since the men had left, Matthew was in his usual spot. I took my place in my chair and continued plowing through my book, prepared to pass the afternoon in the same companionable silence as yesterday. Matthew had other ideas.

"What is your real name?"

My eyes shot up. Matthew was watching me with interest. "Why do you want to know?" I finally asked.

He shrugged. "It feels wrong to call you 'Miss Raynsford' now that I know you are not her."

"Even if you knew my name, you still could not call me it. Everyone else knows me to be Mary."

"Not Peter. He refers to you as 'Julia,' sometimes."

My hold on my book slackened. This was new information. "Peter . . . talks to you about me?"

He nodded disinterestedly, returning to his book. "These days he talks to me of little else."

I bit my lip to suppress my growing smile. Matthew looked up again, but if he saw my blush he didn't acknowledge it. Instead, he said, "Is that your real name? Julia?"

I chuckled, though it wasn't exactly funny. "It is much more my name than Mary Raynsford, to be sure." Matthew studied me for a long moment, until I was squirming under his scrutiny. Hoping to draw his attention away, I said, "So, Peter confides in you?"

Matthew stood, walked to the window, leaned against its frame, then shrugged again. "When he's here. Most of the year he's in London on business, but you could still say that we're close." He stared out the window, the sun streaking his dark brown hair with patches of gold. Yes, he would be very handsome indeed.

Suddenly, I realized what he had said. *Peter confides in him.*

Which meant that he must know about our card game, and . . . who had won.

I licked my lips and tried to make my voice sound offhand. "Matthew, do you know how to play whist?"

He blew a puff of air. "Peter was right. You *are* sneaky. I'm sorry, but I cannot tell you who won." Turning back, Matthew put his hands in his pockets.

"Why ever not?"

"Because he made me promise not to."

I sighed, collapsing against the chair. Perhaps I should despair of ever discovering the truth of the matter. Whenever I came close, something, or some*one* ousted me. I scowled at nothing, exceedingly tired of being bested.

"I may not be able to teach you the rules of whist," Matthew said slowly, "but, I *could* teach you loo, or bridge, if you'd like. If we started now, you could be quite proficient before he got back."

"Why would you help me?"

"Peter's my brother, and loyalty forbids me to teach you whist so he can win the round. But truthfully," the barest whisper of a smile touched his lips, "I want you to win the game."

"Why?"

Matthew gave a halfhearted shrug. "Because against my better judgement, I find you satisfactory."

In Matthew Wycliffe's book, that was probably as close to a compliment as he came. I laughed through my nose and gave a small nod. Matthew pushed himself away from the window, fetched a deck of cards, and sat.

We passed another summer afternoon together—but instead of silence surrounding us, there was discussion as he taught me the rules of all the card games he knew. Game after game we played, making sure I memorized the differences between each version, and all of the many rules correctly. As the hours flew by, the cards felt more natural in my hand, and before I knew it, it was time for dinner.

We finished our game of bridge. Crossing the library, I thanked Matthew over my shoulder, and he grunted a response. But something made me hesitate in the doorway. Slowly, I twisted back.

"You know . . . it's not that I don't *want* to tell you my name."

Matthew looked up from collecting the cards. "Then why don't you?"

I hesitated, pinching my hands together. "It's a rather long story, and one I can't really tell you, either. If everyone knew the truth, I would lose something very precious to me. And you would loathe me forever. And Eliza would never trust me again. And Peter—"

I stopped myself from finishing the thought. After a moment, I sighed and said more softly, "Peter."

"Yes, Peter." Matthew's face was full of understanding. We shared a moment then, Matthew and I, where he seemed to grasp how much Peter's friendship meant to me—and I was glad I didn't have to say the words.

I sighed again. "He couldn't bear to look at me, if he knew."

After a moment of contemplation, Matthew nodded and said, "Well, then. I suppose it's better for all of us if we don't."

Matthew returned to his book, but I remained glued to my spot— incapable of believing that this boy could so readily forgive what he didn't know.

And in that moment, I decided that, though he was condescending, and hostile, and quite peculiar at times, Matthew was also genuine, and open, and had a heart that was good. That perhaps he was not so unlike his brother, after all.

I waited for him to take it back—to reject me the same way Thomas Markley and Mrs. Wilshire had—but all he said was, "See you tomorrow."

CHAPTER 7

THE MAID BOBBED A CURTSY, ANNOUNCING, "THE MEN HAVE returned from their hunting trip."

Miss Caldwell and the twins dropped their embroidery and rushed from the room. Eliza cried with delight, not far behind. The maid slipped back out, and I found myself alone in the morning room.

I had missed Peter, and I'd been anticipating his return more than anyone—but to reveal that to him would surely give him the upper hand. If I didn't die of his teasing first.

So instead of going to greet them, I slipped away to return my embroidery to my quarters and continue my reading. After fifteen minutes, I became acutely aware of how uncomfortable the chair in my room was compared to the stuffed library ones, and, after attempting to ignore it unsuccessfully, decided to relocate to a better reading place.

To my surprise, Matthew's regular spot sat empty. But all thoughts of him vanished as I positioned myself in the window seat of the library and delved into *Robinson Crusoe*. When I finished a chapter, my thoughts drifted to the people downstairs. It hadn't occurred to me that it might be rude not to make an appearance. Was it expected of someone of Mary's station? Perhaps I should've gone to greet them.

The honeyed voice of Miss Caldwell filtered through the door. "No, no," she said, "I think the library will be a perfect place to—"

I slammed my book shut, jumped off the window seat, and ran to the closest corner, hiding myself in the shadows shrouding one of the wide bookcases. As a guest, I had the right to the library just as Miss Caldwell did, but I hadn't conversed with her since I'd insulted her engagement, and I'd rather avoid a conversation about it. Not to mention she was undoubtedly with Peter, and I was not in the mood to watch her fawn over him.

The creak of a door and the padding of feet were followed by, "My! Look at all the books!"

Someone else entered behind her, and he spoke, his voice dripping with sarcasm. "Yes. That is, after all, what libraries are for. To keep books in." It was Matthew. Though it was difficult to tell because Matthew always spoke condescendingly, he sounded even more annoyed than usual.

Miss Caldwell laughed. "Are there any books on poetry? I should like to write a poem for Peter now that he's returned, and I need inspiration."

"They're to the right of the window over there." I imagined Matthew motioning over to where I was hiding, and panicked—for I was standing directly in front of the poetry!

Rotten luck!

Lamenting not making my presence known before, I looked around. Miss Caldwell would find me, interrogate me, and perhaps scold me for eavesdropping. Her footfalls grew louder.

Clenching my book harder, I moved away from the sound. My back bumped into the wall. I had nowhere to run. My fingers brushed something cold, and round.

A doorknob.

I spun around. Hidden in the shadows between the bookcases was a door, completely camouflaged by the shades and darks of the room. Without thinking, I turned the knob and stepped through, shutting the door quietly behind me.

I slumped against it.

The sounds of Miss Caldwell removing a book from the shelf, and then her voice as she went on to read to Matthew aloud trickled through the cracks. I visualized him plugging his ears, striving to finish *Gulliver's Travels* amid her horrid inflections.

Despite my recent panic, I smiled at the picture. Perhaps Matthew had realized there were worse companions than me to have in the library.

Miss Caldwell went on and on, apparently not planning on leaving anytime soon. My pulse slowed and when my eyes adjusted to the limited light, I studied my surroundings in detail. Though, there really wasn't much to study.

It was a simple room; small, and square. Only perhaps three paces in each direction. And it was completely empty besides a single, black winding staircase that disappeared into the gloom above.

Curiosity piqued, I clutched my book and ascended. The only light beamed from under the door, and as I got higher up, the darkness increased, until suddenly, the metallic click of a latch rattled when I bumped my head against something. The stairs must lead to the roof.

I pushed the hatch open and traveled the few remaining stairs before emerging onto the roof. The sudden light was bright, and I shielded my eyes with *Robinson Crusoe*.

The rooftop terrace was large and clean. Instead of several different quarters linking together, it was like one vast, topless room—a bond between the earth and the heavens. The view was bright and airy, stirring within me a deeper appreciation for the lush gardens and lofty trees below.

In my moment of enthrallment, I failed to notice that the roof was already being occupied, until I heard, "Well, if it isn't Miss Smith, come to dance."

I whirled about. He was leaning on the ledge about ten paces behind the hatch—which was why I hadn't immediately spied him.

"I'm glad you've returned. Er, that is, that you have *all* returned." I bit my tongue, inwardly bemoaning that I had just disclosed what I promised myself I would not. "And on my word, I had thought we had already discussed this. I do *not* dance, Peter." I closed the distance between us, resting my hands and my book on the ledge as I looked out at the park. "And certainly not up here. And *most* certainly not with you."

"Is that a challenge?"

"Think it what you will, it matters not to me."

"If not to dance with me, whatever could be your reason for coming up here? Did you miss me all that terribly? You could not keep away any longer?" His expression warped into artificial sympathy, and I scoffed, though really, he wasn't far from the truth.

Peter looked the same, but . . . somehow different, too. He made the same expressions, and still radiated arrogance in an endearing way, but perhaps the *way* that he did them was changed. He seemed even more relaxed, even more warm, and even more like we had a childhood together with incalculable pooled secrets.

"You flatter yourself, sir," I said. "I simply came up here to escape Clingy's pestering. She seems to have found all my other hiding places, and when I noticed the secret door in the library, it couldn't be a moment too soon because—" I stopped short when I noticed Peter's surprised but blooming smile, realizing what I just revealed.

"'Clingy'?" He folded his arms across his chest and looked at me as if I had been very naughty. "Who on earth could *that* be?" When I didn't respond straightaway, he prodded, "Mary?" sounding a bit too like a father scolding his child.

Blast my running tongue! He undid me in ways that took the

longest time to do-up again. "Yes," I sighed. "I have an awful habit of nicknaming people. My er, *aunt* has reprimanded me for it on several occasions."

What he must think of me now!

I would have wallowed in my shame, if not for the tone of amusement that entered his voice. "Yes, your aunt must think it a rotten little habit." His eyes darted to me. "But I confess, I find it rather attractive . . ."

What a ridiculous thing to say. He probably did this with everyone. And if he did indeed find me attractive, it was because of Mary and her money.

He took a step toward me, a playful smile on his lips. His hand moved along the ledge until it came to rest upon mine in the simplest touch, sending my heart bounding out of my chest and jumping off the roof. I cleared my throat and looked away, trying to tear down whatever it was that was building.

"Attractive?" My laugh sounded a tad too like a whimper for my liking. "Why, that is not something a gentleman should say, Peter Wycliffe."

"Why ever not?" He was much too close.

"There are *two* reasons, actually." I casually moved my hand out from under his, grasping my other arm with it so he wouldn't be able to touch it again. The wind teased at my hair. "For one, it isn't chivalrous. You should defend their honor, or at the very least, be so dumbfounded at my cynicism that you withdraw yourself from my company."

Peter laughed, not seeming to notice the way I'd extricated my hand. "Believe me, Miss Raynsford, this is not the most shocking thing I've seen you do. On the contrary, I find this instance to be the most ordinary."

"That does not make it commendable." I refused to look at him, and it was a long moment that I felt Peter's gaze, studying me.

"And what is the second reason?" he asked.

I concentrated hard on the top of a nearby sycamore, pushing any sentiment to the farthest reaches of my mind. "The second reason, sir, is that it undoes me when you call me attractive. A true gentleman would never, both for my comfort and the propriety of the situation." My eyes flitted to their corners, trying to see without moving my head how Peter would react.

He shrugged. "It is not proper for young ladies to fall on gentlemen from trees. *Or* to take on a second identity. One should not call another by their Christian name after only one day of being acquainted, or call a man 'handsome' in his company. It is also highly inappropriate to be alone on this rooftop with me, right now. But Mary, nearly everything you've done since I met you has been improper. So, I say, hang propriety."

Everything? The thought wasn't heartening. He leaned in further, his whispers nearly drowning in the wind. "As for your comfort. Though I hate seeing you uncomfortable in any way, I must speak my mind. And if your comfort prevents that . . . well, then I say hang that too."

"Truly, you are teasing."

He backed away. "On my word, I am not. Now tell me," Peter reached across me, took hold of my book, and started perusing it, "do you conjure nicknames for every person you meet, or only the disagreeable ones?"

"Only the disagreeable ones."

Peter turned thoughtful. In fact, he looked much like Matthew with a furrowed brow and a book in hand. "Hm . . . then you *must* have a name for me." Peter's eyes remained on *Robinson Crusoe*, but when he knew I was looking, he started to smile.

"To be sure," I said loudly. "I have a rather horrid one for you."

Oh, why had I said that? Now I'd have to think of a name for Peter, who laughed for a moment, then waited. I cleared my throat and folded my hands, trying to stall the inevitable. "Well, it's . . . horrid . . ."

"Yes?"

What were Peter's faults? Did he *have* any? *Oh think, Lily, think!*

I must've remained quiet for too long because Peter said, "I do believe you're making that up. Rather than trouble yourself, why do you not admit you have no name for me because I remain—as I have always remained—a perfect saint?"

Now I had to think of something, if only to wipe that self-satisfied smile off his face. I snatched the first thing that came to mind. "I call you 'His So Very Handsomeness.'"

Peter's chuckles quieted. I savored the image of his mouth prying open, his eyebrows rising on his forehead. "Rather clever of you."

His praise lifted my spirits to towering heights. "Isn't it just?"

And then we both turned and looked out on the hills, waltzing to the music of the sky, a comfortable silence settling over us as our smiles faded in time. It really was beautiful. The stream was a gold chain through the scenery, with Ambleside as its jewel; the gardens, the shimmery, landscaped gown. And all of it—the manicured gardens, the tough wildernesses, the little patches of daylight and happiness— all of it, danced.

"I've told you why I came up," I said, breaking the silence, "but you've yet to reveal your reasons for being here."

Peter shrugged. "I simply like it up here. I can think. Clear my head. There's something about being above all the world that helps you view it in a new light."

"And how did the hunting go?"

His lips screwed. "Disappointing."

"Why is that?"

"Because for the first time in a *long* time . . . I found myself wishing I was here, instead of away." He glanced over, something substantial in his face, but I couldn't put my finger on it. His voice turned quiet and his face grew distant, as if he were drawing from pure memory and had forgotten that I was still there with him.

"My father used to take me up here, you know. It was our secret place. He would set me on the ledge over there, gesturing to all the grandeur as he told me stories of the histories of my ancestors, of the legacy that was Ambleside. As a little boy, I gobbled up the descriptions, passing many an afternoon here with my father, dreaming of sword fights and conquests and creating a legacy of my own. But the thing my father told me most was that one day, it would all be mine."

Peter's eyes were fathomlessly sad, storm clouds dampening his usually sunny face. For some reason, these memories were painful. I tried to understand why—and then remembered how Eliza and Matthew had both mentioned that he was hardly ever home.

"But you did not want it?" I ventured.

Gaze still fixed on the estate, he smiled wanly. He seemed so different wearing a serious expression. More . . . human.

"No, I wanted it. I've loved this place for as long as I can remember. I grew up here, on this land. I collected its rocks, swam in its rivers, climbed its trees."

A tingling feeling crept over my arms.

"It's not that I didn't want it, but that I knew I'd never deserve it." Peter stared at his hands resting on the ledge, struggling for the right words. "My father . . . he was a good man. And well, I was a foolish and rebellious boy. I wanted the estate, but didn't want to learn the ropes of managing it. Again and again my father tried to make me take an interest, saying that he would not be around forever. At that age, I didn't believe him. I had no doubt that if father dueled with Death, his sheer stubbornness would guarantee him the victory. One time he stormed off in the middle of our discussion, saying Matthew could inherit for all he cared."

Peter paused, and laughed, emptily. "What a fool I was. I was away in London when the news came. He'd grown suddenly ill and died. I could not believe it. I was a viscount.

"I came back for the funeral and services but immediately returned to London. Mother thinks it was because of my overwhelming grief—and no doubt that played a part—but mostly I could not stand to look at this place that my father had loved so dearly, because I knew I had let him down. I could never step into my father's shoes, because I'd never be able to fill them.

"Over the years, my visits became more infrequent and less lengthy. I've come to learn all the things that are necessary to run the estate, but I still find myself wondering how much more I would know if my father were still here. What else he might have taught me."

Peter turned from the ledge, his confident bearing replaced with one that was fidgety and unsure. "I don't know if this is making any sort of sense to you, Mary, but I guess what I was trying to say is, I come up here because I miss him, and wish I'd learned how to *be here* before he died." After a moment, he laughed at himself. "I suppose that sounds rather weak and pathetic of me."

I studied Peter for a long while, the firm line of his lips, the regret in his brow, realizing for the first time that Peter was not all teasing and conceit. He had a soul that was deeply wounded—a soul, I thought, not unlike mine. And he was baring it to me like I was a trusted and treasured friend.

"No," I said slowly, "it does not sound weak to me. I think everyone has their moments when they are not the person they wish to be. To be sure, it sounds cowardly."

Pete's eyebrows came together. He didn't seem angry, though, only curious. I took a deep breath before plunging back in.

"I understand your grief, Peter, truly I do. I too, have lost my fa—" Was Mary's father alive? ". . . Well, have lost someone dear to me, and I know it's a hard thing. But can't you see that by never coming home, you are disappointing your father much more than you would if you were undertaking the task? That being here doing your best—even if you never fill your father's shoes—is doing a much better job than not even trying?"

Peter's lips parted, but I went on, suddenly and inexplicably heated.

"And another thing, leaving home sounds rather selfish. Matthew nearly worships the ground you walk on, you know. Did it ever occur to you that he might need an example to follow—especially with your father gone? That he *needs* an older brother? And Eliza misses you dearly. I know for certain she wishes she had another opinion on even silly things like what ribbon best complements her complexion, for her mother is bound to love anything she does. And as for your mother, she lights up every time you enter the room, so happy is she to have both her sons with her."

I swallowed, my resolve starting to waver. "Peter, I understand that you want to please everyone. But what about you? What do *you* want? I can see in your eyes that staying away from the family and hating this place for its memories does not make you feel content. I didn't know your father, but I am sure he would not have wanted to see you miserable. If you look deep enough, I think you will find that what makes you happy will make everyone else happy, too."

Peter stared at me for perhaps a whole, silent minute. But instead of a smile or admiration on his face, there was something I had never seen before . . . something I could not name. Perhaps 'significant' describes it best, though it was also detached and confused. His eyes went all over my face, as if trying to decide what exactly I was.

"You frighten me, Mary." His voice was deeper, and hushed.

My insides gave a little squeeze at the sound of a different woman's name on his lips, reminding me that I was not myself. "And why is that?"

"Because you see through me when no one else can. Because you have just stated so simply what I have been running from for years. Because I tell you things I can't even tell myself. And that is terrifying." His face was the solemnest I had ever seen it. "I'm sure my mother—and likely Eliza—has wanted to scream at me those exact same words, but no one does. No one ever talks to me that way."

My blinking stuttered. While I felt he needed to hear those words, they probably should have come from a close friend—someone he'd known more than a week. "I'm sorry. I was too forward." The words were stiff and clumsy, just like the mood.

Peter held up his hand. "No, do not apologize. You were perhaps the only person it could've come from. And, to be honest, when you talk to me that way," a glimmer of a smile started to tiptoe onto his face, "I find it rather attractive . . ."

"That is not something a gentleman should say, Peter Wycliffe," I said, relishing the buoyancy that had returned. It was then that I decided that, without a doubt, I rather liked nearly everything about Peter. The way his eyes lit up, the way his hair curled at his temples, the way he always smiled at me for no reason at all.

After the lovely moment passed, he asked, "So you've spent time with Matthew? Last I knew he loathed the very sight of you. However did you change his mind?"

"My feminine charm. Young boys find it nearly irresistible. In fact, we spent a whole afternoon together where he taught me the rules of every card game."

"Oh?"

I nodded.

"Including whist?"

My nodding slowed, then stopped. "Well, no. Apparently he had made a promise to you or some other such nonsense. Also the library lacked a book on the subject, so I . . ."

Peter's eyes lit up. He quickly looked away, but it was too late. I had seen his expression, and my gut told me it had been no accident there were no card books.

My eyes narrowed. "Rather odd, don't you think, that a library as vast as Ambleside's could be so empty of books on cards?"

"Ah, Mary." Peter looked back. "You always underestimate me. A clever little thing like you. I had to be sure you would not find out on your own."

"You little sneak!" I stomped my foot. I should've *known* it was no coincidence. He was, it would seem, obstinately determined on winning this one.

"Yes, it was rather sneaky of me. But not against our rules."

"Why can you not just put me out of my misery already? Are you planning on keeping it a secret forever? You already know I don't know who won!" I huffed, my dignity a little damaged. I had eventually admitted what Peter had always wanted to hear me say.

He smirked, obviously pleased with my confession. "My dear, all you had to do was ask."

AFTER MAKING SURE THE COAST WAS CLEAR, WE REENTERED THE library. As I took a seat, Peter disappeared, returning with a few books and a deck of cards. He set them on the small table in front of the window and pulled up a chair. My skin tingled in anticipation, burning with a desire for the truth. He opened the top book and began.

"Whist is a relatively simple game, though perhaps difficult to figure out if the rules are not explained. Now, the last card dealt declares trump, and each player takes a turn. The goal of each round is to take the 'trick,' and thereby win the round. But it is not always wise to play whatever is highest in your hand.

"For example, if someone leads a round with an ace of clubs, the rest of the players will want to play low because they already know they cannot win the trick. However, if perchance trump was diamonds and a player were out of clubs, they could play trump—even a two—and it would win the ace . . ."

Peter went on, clarifying all the basic rules, extracting the cards and explaining the wisest course of action in certain scenarios. And as I watched in fascination, little by little, the mystery pieced itself together.

Trump had been spades. Peter had played the king of hearts. And I had played . . . the queen of hearts.

So, I had lost.

Or maybe we hadn't taken an equal number of tricks? But if I had lost, why hadn't Peter revealed it right then? Did he simply like watching me squirm? Or was it something else?

Peter stopped his narrative. "I see you've figured it out."

"Yes. Though, I don't know why you refused to tell me before now. You could've been gloating all this time."

One corner of his lips quirked. "See, I knew you'd say that. But I want to show you something." Peter removed a book from the bottom of his stack. The pages ruffled and flapped as he searched for the right spot. At last satisfied, he set the open book on the table.

"Whist became popular in the mid 1700's, and several altered variations sprang up as a result. Countless cultures developed their own twist on the game, so that over the next fifty years, more than twenty different versions had arisen. There's bid whist, Russian whist, and elimination whist—all of which we played that night. And then," he pointed to the open book, indicating to the page, "there's German whist."

Peter rotated the book around so I could clearly see the pictures. I studied it with riveted eyes, barely registering that Peter was moving around the table and sitting next to me on the window seat.

The picture depicted a woman at the top of a tower, calling to a man wearing a jeweled crown who was being thrust through with a sword. Swarms of men surrounded him, trying to save him. On the next page, the woman knelt at the dead man's body, weeping over him with her hands on his ears, a pool of blood at his side. It was a gruesome sight, and my stomach turned at the images.

Peter leaned in, pointing to the pictures. "You see, the Germans have a folk tale that goes like this: Once upon a time, the kingdom had been celebrating a peace of ten years under their new king. There was singing and jubilee, and the king and queen joined in the dancing in the town square. But while all the kingdom reveled, a wicked man stole the beautiful queen away, locking her far away in a tower. He was a sorcerer in need of royal blood to heal his only son, blind from birth. The king soon discovered the absence of his beloved wife, and marched about the land, eventually learning of the wizard and of his terrible intent.

"He hurried to the tower, arriving just as the sorcerer raised his knife to the queen's throat. 'Stop!' he cried. 'Do you not need the blood of royalty? Why take the blood of a queen when a king's is ten times more valuable? Now then, I pray thee, harm not my queen, but take my life instead!' The sorcerer let the queen go, rushed out of the tower, and thrust his sword through the king, filling a goblet with his blood. As the sorcerer scampered away to heal his child, the queen cradled her husband as he died in her arms. And so the story goes: that the king loved his queen so much, that he gave his life for her."

Peter's narrative came to a close, and I was suddenly extremely aware of his nearness; of how he smelled of soap, and leather, and wind, and heaven. It was intoxicating—his soft voice mixed with the stories and the closeness. I didn't want it to end.

"And what has all this to do with the card game?" I asked a little breathlessly.

"We were playing the German version. That's the only variation that can finish with only two players, and the Germans incorporated this folk story into their version of the game. The rule is, whenever the king of hearts is played with its queen, the queen will always trump."

There was something in Peter's voice that was changing, morphing into something resembling . . . longing.

His voice faded, and after a tension-filled silence, he lifted a gentle hand to my face, angling it slightly so I would look at him. I didn't want to, for there was something different about this moment that frightened me. But I did, and I found Peter's chin, and then his lips, his nose, and then his eyes. Oh, his eyes.

"Because after all," his voice was so very quiet, "the king loves his queen so much, that he will give his life for her. She will *always* win him . . ."

My thoughts stuttered. He was so close, so intoxicating. The air shriveled up, the corners closed in, and time suspended itself as Peter's eyes began to shift slightly . . . down . . .

I jerked my head away and stood, needing the air to return along with my senses. I rubbed my temples, not sure what had just happened, nor what to make of it.

Don't be a fool, I scolded myself. He hadn't been about to kiss me— why would he? I was no one to him, just another one of his guests. A maid.

Was I a maid, though? I was Mary Raynsford, a wealthy heiress. She wouldn't let herself be kissed by a man who hadn't declared his intentions. And, neither would a girl who was pretending to be her, just to collect her nine pounds.

Resolved that no matter his reaction—hurt, shamed, or confused— I would pretend nothing had happened, I schooled my features and turned back. He stared at me with a curious, warm smile.

"So. I won you after all?" It was more of a statement than a question.

Peter's smile twisted as he stood. "Yes, my darling. You have won me."

I colored up. "Why, that's not at all what I meant—"

"Didn't you?" He walked around the table. "For you would not have phrased it that way if you did not wish to imply it."

"On my word, I did not think on how to phrase it! I was merely glad I had won!"

He nodded sarcastically. "Of course, madam. Of course."

"Honestly, Peter—!"

"Peter, *there* you are!"

We turned at the interruption. Caught up in each other, we'd both failed to notice the doors opening and an upset Miss Caldwell stepping through them.

"I have been looking for you all afternoon, and I vow I had already checked here." Miss Caldwell strode toward us, her frown more fixed upon me than upon her subject of interest. "Wherever have you been hiding? We need to prepare for the fair tomorrow. Come, we still have so much to plan."

Before she reached us, Peter turned back to me and said in a low tone, "A rather *clingy* sort of girl, don't you think?"

Then, just as Miss Caldwell grasped his arm and began pulling him back across the room, he flashed me the most conspiratorial smile the world had ever seen.

CHAPTER 8

TODAY WAS THE DAY OF THE FAIR. I THREW OFF MY COVERS AND
rang for Katherine, before stepping behind the dressing screen. She
entered a minute or two later.

"Oh Miss Raynsford, is it true that you and all the other guests are
going to the fair today? How exciting! I'm sure you'll have a wonderful
time—with the dancers and jugglers and sights and such." Katherine
finished lacing up my stays and pulled a lavender muslin gown over my
head.

The sights were the last thing on my mind today. My real purpose
for going into town was to arrange for my mail to be sent to Ambleside, on the off chance that Jennie had written again. The real Mary
couldn't arrange it because she was touring France, but if I asked, I was
sure Hampstead House would send my forwarding address to Mrs.
Wilshire's.

After Katherine finished, I grabbed a petite parasol, as well as my
reticule containing my letter to Hampstead House, and dashed from
my room. Well-dressed guests mingled in the grand entryway.

Eliza rushed to my side, giving me a quick and excited embrace.

"Oh Mary! I still can't believe you convinced him. What a day we shall have!"

I didn't notice Peter entering and wearing a deep green tailcoat, cream trousers, and a black topper until he announced, "Let us be off!" He offered one arm to his mother and the other to a radiant Miss Caldwell, before leading the party out onto the drive and into the barouches.

Seeing him brought back the memory of yesterday, making me question for the thousandth time what had happened in the library. He had acted so . . . familiar. Something between us had definitely shifted. I was glad he hadn't sought me out again—it would have forced me to make sense of the confusion I was feeling.

After asking a white-wigged footman to have all mail addressed to Julia Smith delivered to me, explaining it as a small mix-up, I joined the others in the carriages.

The ride into town was short but scenic, and we could hear the festivities before we saw them. Tents wandered along the banks of the river, just outside the little hamlet. Already, throngs of people among the rows of pitched canvas awnings lining the streets tried their luck at a game, or sought to have their fortunes told. Men and women promenaded in overdresses, turbans, sashes, and toppers, adorned with canes, buckles, pins, and broaches.

Eliza clapped beside me, eager for our barouche to park. She clutched my arm and dragged me from the contraption, pointing in delight. "Look at that man throwing knives! Oh! And that ribbon-dancer there!"

The air was bloated with the smells of apple, thyme, and roasting meat. Shouts rang out from the booths as men endeavored to draw in customers; a tambourine and flute played above the noise. The crowd swayed and expanded as each spectacle was re-discovered.

"Look there, Eliza," I said, pointing to a purple booth displaying colorful seashells and chests.

Eliza's mouth opened in smiling wonder as she approached the booth, examining a small, rusty-orange starfish. "My," she marveled, "what a strange looking creature." She turned it over in her hands, tracing every edge and crevice.

The old man operating the exhibit grinned, and I thought perhaps his teeth were the other—and far more fascinating—half to the display. They crisscrossed along his gums in unimaginable ways.

"Starfish are as ordinary as can be along the coastal villages. Perhaps you've never been to the sea?"

Eliza shook her head. "No. In fact, I have never been outside Hampshire."

The old man tsked. "Shame, that."

"I should love to go, though," she said. "Someday." She looked around the makeshift shop, taking in the strange shapes of shells, horns, trinkets, and baubles. "In fact, I think I have already gone much further than Hampshire." She glanced up at the man again. "How much for this starfish?"

He told her the amount, and Eliza sorted through her reticule and produced the coins. The man turned to me, gracing me with his crooked smile. "And for you, miss?"

"Oh, no thank you, sir."

"Nothing to your liking? I s'pose you're not much of adventurer, eh? Unlike this little lady here, you'd rather just stay at home? Well, there's nothing wrong with that, miss. Nothing wrong with that."

I frowned. "It isn't exactly that . . . It's true I am content to stay at home. But if I could go anywhere in the world, it would be to a person, not a place."

The man clucked his tongue and tapped his nose. "Not an adventurer at all, but a dreamer. I have just the thing for you."

He vanished through the back wall of the display, rummaging through things that tinkled and clanged. I avoided Eliza's curious gaze, focusing instead on the sound of scuffling feet and clacking canes on the cobblestones behind me. The man emerged again with a necklace dangling from his extended hand.

I gasped, softly.

It was a watercolor of a crepe-colored lily. The porcelain brooch hung on a dark gold chain. Metal had been worked around the frame, weaving intricately in a delicate and elegant design. I took it in my hands, letting my fingers wander its surface.

"The water lily is the flower of the dreamer, you know," the old man said. "They're said to be made of fallen stars and maiden's tears. Of course, it's just a silly old tale that fathers tell their children as they tuck them into bed at night, wishing them sweet dreams of their own. But it's a lovely thought, I think, that something so ordinary could be so priceless."

I stared in wonder. "It is lovely." I held the necklace out to him. "I'm afraid I don't have the coin to buy this, sir. But I thank you for allowing me to look at it. It is beautiful."

"Ah, but it fits you so well, miss."

"I'm sorry, but I simply cannot afford it."

"Cannot afford it?" Eliza cried incredulously. "By all accounts, you are an heiress! Buy the beautiful thing."

I did love it. But to purchase such an extravagance would set me back weeks—months, perhaps. It would render my whole visit to Ambleside purposeless. Mary might have enough money, but I certainly didn't.

"I am not so attached to it," I said. "Besides, my aunt threatened to cut me out of her will if I didn't curb my spending—"

"Nonsense, I can see you love it. I shall buy it for you." Eliza dug back through her reticule while asking the old man how much.

"One pound, miss." It was worth at least three times that.

"No, Eliza," I protested. "I cannot let you—"

"If you don't, I shall simply tell Peter all about it when next we see him, and *he* shall buy it."

He would, too, confound him. And that *definitely* wouldn't suit.

After exchanging coins, Eliza placed the necklace in my hand and bid the crooked-mouthed man farewell, stepping back out into the sunlight. Stashing it in my reticule, I followed.

"You really shouldn't have," I said once we had reached a less noisy section of the street.

Eliza laughed. "Please, Mary. If not to buy pretty things for each other, what are friends for? Think nothing of it."

But I did think something of it. It wasn't so much the necklace, as it was why Eliza had bought it. *Friends.* I had friends now; people who cared for me. People I cared for in return. Something about that thought warmed my core.

"You long to travel?" I asked.

Eliza handled her starfish as we walked, sighing. "Yes. Mama lived in Spain for a time, Peter went on Tour, and even Matthew stayed one summer with a cousin on the coast. I've spent long hours fantasizing about ancient Rome or faraway India. The people I would meet, the sounds, the smells, the sights! Sometimes I am a powerful duchess, other times, a pauper. I suppose that is why I long for adventure. Perhaps after I've had my Season I shall go exploring."

I laughed. "Why after? Why not go now?"

"For one, I'm much too young. Peter would never let me. In fact, I don't think he'll let me at all no matter how old or capable I grow."

"That is because he loves you too dearly." That made Eliza smile.

"For another, I wonder if I would enjoy the thrill of *being* somewhere as much as I do *imagining* being there. Do you see?"

I nodded. "I think so. And I think that old man had it all wrong. You are the dreamer, not I."

Eliza stopped, and I found we were at the end of the street, which had an open view of flourishing hills and pockets of forest. Her voice took on a distant quality. "But I think in the end, I am too in love with my England."

I gazed out at the scene, silently agreeing with her. An ocean of green stretched to the horizon, herds of sheep and dirt roads weaving through its depths. The air, thick with sun-soaked pollen carried the buzzing of bees and children's laughter. Nowhere else on earth could possibly be this beautiful.

Unwilling to dwell on that, I said, "Still, that does not explain why you would wait until after your Season."

"Oh." Eliza looked down, and I saw she was blushing as she clasped her hands behind her back. "It is because I want to fall in love." Her eyes darted to me, then away. "It sounds silly, I know. And I know I am still much too young. Only, I've never even been to London, and I think it's as great a place as any to begin an adventure. You don't have to journey to exotic places to have one, you know. They can be a warm fire on a chilly night, or a race as the sun is rising. It is spontaneously finding the thrill in everyday things. Things like falling in love."

I pondered Eliza as I beheld her, thinking of her zest for life, her vibrant soul, of the way she deserved to be cherished. A sisterly instinct to protect her came over me.

"What a romantic, you are," I teased.

She laughed again. "Indeed."

My eyes strayed to a yellow ribbon woven through Eliza's hair, one I'd noticed several times that day, and I asked after it.

"Oh that!" Her smile broadened. "Wouldn't you know it, but yesterday after dinner, a whole boxful of ribbons sat on my bed! And what luck, for all the ones I own are plain and couldn't be worn with this dress." She smoothed her golden floral-patterned day dress. "There was a note with it too. 'For your complexion,' it said, and that was all. Do I have an admirer, do you think? Oh, I could kiss him for giving me such a lovely gift!"

It was mysterious, to be sure. That is, if one hadn't had a conversation with a certain someone regarding ribbons and Eliza's complexion yesterday. I kicked the pebbles at my feet, beaming inside and out. An admirer Eliza certainly had, but not one she could kiss. Perhaps on the cheek would do.

We dove back into the fray of bustling bodies and fluttering colors, visiting more booths and loitering at each one. When our stomachs started to growl, we made for the river's edge. We crossed a bridge and settled down onto a blanket underneath a canopy, next to the rest in our party.

"I'm starved!" Miss Caldwell said. "Peter, aren't you going to get the baskets?"

"It might rain soon," Lady Agatha added as if it somehow contributed to the conversation. "It is always going to rain." The wispy clouds above had defiantly waited until the hot morning was over to shade us.

"It's no good to have an empty stomach during a rainstorm, I always say," said Quincy as he appeared suddenly with a twin on each arm.

Peter laughed. "A full stomach is always better under any circumstance, I should think. But there are at least four baskets, and I only have two hands. Perhaps you would like to help, Miss Caldwell?"

"Silly Peter!" She hit him lightly on the arm. "I could not lift even one, I am sure."

Peter looked forward at nothing with a wistful expression. "If only Julia were here. I'm sure she could lift the baskets."

I bit the inside of my cheek, striving to maintain a neutral expression. I got the distinct impression that this was Peter's way of breaking whatever ice had formed between us.

"Who is this Julia you are always talking about?" Miss Caldwell propped herself up on her knees. "None of us besides you have met her, Peter. I am beginning to think she doesn't exist!"

A chuckle escaped my lips. The whole company looked to me with crumpled foreheads, trying to understand the joke. Peter saved me from having to explain by insisting that Quincy help him, and within minutes, a feast sprawled before us.

As I ate my cold chicken and apple slices, I considered the town, craning my neck in search of the post office. The moment lunch was finished, I would set out to find it.

"How about a riddle?" Quincy asked suddenly. After a few notes of encouragement, Quincy stroked his chin. "Aha! I have just the one. Surely it will stump you as it stumped me. 'My first has the making of honey to charm; my second brings breakfast to bed on your arm; my third bores a hole in leather so fine; while united, the whole breaks the heart most kind. What am I?'"

As one, the group hunched forward with scrunched faces. Then Miss Margaret exclaimed giddily, "A bee! The first one is a bee."

"And the second," added Miss Molly, "is a tray."

Lady Agatha scowled. "That is no riddle, Mr. Quincy. For the third is an awl, and the word is 'betrayal.' You shall have to do much better than that if you wish to flummox us."

They continued on, bantering and laughing gleefully at their riddles. I tuned out, concentrating instead on finishing my lunch. Standing, I brushed myself off and uttered a small, "Excuse me," to Eliza before heading off to find the post office, their laughter following me into the throngs. Ribbons atop wooden spikes billowed in the wind, pointing down the lanes to stands of coin tossing, bizarre creatures, and deranged mirrors.

"Where are *you* going?"

I spun around, nearly colliding into Peter who followed closely behind. "I—I uh . . . I was—why are you following me?"

"It is improper to wander about a crowd unattended," he said simply. "You needed an escort, so I followed."

"I am surprised Quincy did not fight you for the honor."

"He put up a valiant effort, but where you are concerned, I always succeed."

A begrudging smile came to my lips.

Peter's eyes narrowed in interested suspicion. "At any rate, what was so secretive that made you leave us all behind in the first place?"

Before thinking, I glanced to the letter I clutched with both hands, bringing his attention to it.

Blast.

"What is this?" Peter whisked it away, reading the address. "Ah, Hampstead House? And who lives at this house, hmm? A close friend?" He smiled cheekily. "An *admirer*?"

"*Mary Raynsford* happens to live at Hamp—" I cut short, realizing my blunder. By all England, why did he always make me blunder?

After a lengthy pause, Peter's brows shot up. "Strange, that," was all he said, eyeing me.

"That is, *I* do. I live at Hampstead House. That is where Mary lives after all, and Mary is me. That is, I am Mary—" I shut my mouth before I could blabber out more idiotic sentences.

"Ah," he said, face clearing. "Now that I think on it, I do remember. Hampstead House. London." His face crinkled. "I wonder I have never seen you about London before. True, it is a large city, but we run in the same circles. Rather strange we never met before now . . ."

"My, er, aunt. She is ailing, you know, and has needed my constant attention. I'm afraid I never got out much. It was only because it was her dearest wish that I came to Ambleside at all."

Peter seemed to be weighing my reasoning, and I could see that doubt was winning the battle—probably because I was acting so strangely.

"I worry about her constantly," I lied again. "In fact, that is why I have written this letter to her, to see how she fares and if she wishes me to come home."

"But then why is it not addressed to your aunt?" He was clearly still suspicious.

I rallied a confident façade and forced it into place. "Oh! Did you think that was what I meant? No, no, no! How offended Aunt Phoebe would be if I asked her directly! She doesn't think she is ill at all, you know. Rather stubborn. If I sent *her* the letter, she would lie about her condition. No, it is to my trusted housekeeper. She and I have been in close communication, for she is the only one I trust to tell me the truth of how my aunt fares." How easily the intricate lie came to me, and how easily Peter accepted it. His expression cleared, and we both started in the direction in which I hoped lay the post office.

My stomach folded in on itself. Half of me wished that he simply knew the truth; for with every lie I told Peter, I hated myself a little bit more. How long would it take until I loathed myself entirely? Would it be worth seeing my sister again if I shredded my standards in the process?

No! What has gotten into you, Lily? A few lies aren't worth your sister? You've let him worm his way into your affections. Stop thinking about Peter and concentrate on the goal. Nine pounds. America. Jennie.

"How long has your aunt been ill?" Peter asked, snapping me away from my inner turmoil.

"She became ill right after I had my Season." The lie was bitter to taste.

Peter let out a low whistle, shaking his head minutely. "Then she has been ill for quite some time."

I stopped in my tracks. "What on earth is that supposed to mean?"

He turned, walking backwards as he said, "You don't have to hide it, Mary. It is nothing to be ashamed of. Lots of women don't marry until their forties! I shouldn't worry if I were you."

I scoffed. A spark lit his eyes, and he was obviously teasing, so . . . why could I feel my temper rising? "Are you implying I am an old maid, sir?"

"Oh, you make me sound so cruel! I would never be so blunt as to say 'old.' I believe you are more of a . . . *middle-aged* maid."

The shock gushing through made my limbs quiver. He presented this next battle like an itch on my skin, irritating it and then inviting me to scratch. With a mountain of control, I resisted, biting my tongue and brushing past him. And on my word, it was my every intention to let it go, but when he muttered from behind, "Silence implies consent," I knew I couldn't leave it be.

"Or," I said, twisting back around, "silence implies that it is so childish, it does not merit one's attention."

He grinned. "I do believe I've struck a nerve." Taking off his topper and holding it over his heart, he looked to me in gratitude, as if to say, *Thank you for giving me yet another weapon to use against you.* A few people milling about looked on, curious at the sight Peter and I presented.

Leaning in and lowering my voice, I said, "I can see how confusing it must be that my wit has advanced well beyond my meager eighteen years. I forgive you for believing me to be so far superior." I smiled sweetly at him, gratified when he laughed, though it made more spectators stop to watch us.

"Superior? I am at least four years your elder!"

"Twenty-two? Ha! If I am an old maid at eighteen, what does that make you, sir?"

"Ancient, I suppose. Perhaps I was wrong then, and you really do have cause to worry. In a scant few years, you shall be as old as I, and too old to marry, my merry Mary." He laughed attractively at his little pun, drawing several more feminine eyes our way.

I realized then it was not our conversation that drew them in, but Peter himself. Most of them were sure to recognize Lord Wycliffe. And didn't Eliza say he was the most sought-after bachelor in all of England?

These young ladies probably saw his wealth, his title, his handsome face. But I realized with a start that when I looked at Peter, I saw his ambition for Ambleside, his desire to please his family, his need to be like his father. How many of these women with jealous stares would ever see that in him? Probably none.

And for some strange reason, it saddened me. Peter was going to marry one of them. Some young lady who was genteel, generous, sophisticated. Honest. Someone like Miss Caldwell. He was going to marry someone who was everything I wasn't.

The thought sobered me. "Well. I doubt I shall ever marry anyway, so it needn't matter."

Peter's face blanked. "Why ever not?" He paused. "Surely you know I was only teasing. I can think of scores of fellows who would—"

"Oh no, Peter, it's not that. I just . . ." I looked down, suddenly vulnerable. "I only don't think I'd want to, after . . ."

He hesitated. "After what?"

You.

The word came unbidden to my mind, followed by confusion and dread. I blotted it out. Peter may be fascinated with me, but he was fascinated by an illusion—by a woman who didn't really exist. And how could I ever hope to tell him that?

"After what?" he prompted again.

"After . . . my aunt dies and I inherit her fortune. I shall have so much money, I won't need a man to take care of me." It was the perfect lie. Just enough truth to make it believable, yet not enough deception to discredit it outright.

Glancing sideways, I saw that my answer stumped Peter. His lips parted, and he opened his mouth as if he wanted to say something, but at that moment, I spotted the guild of the post office, hanging from a hook a few buildings down.

"There!" I pointed happily, flinging the serious atmosphere away. "We have found it at last!"

A small bell tinkled when we entered the sunlit space, the smell of dust and wood hitting my senses. The postmaster was friendly, promising me the letter would be delivered by the end of the week. Having completed my task, a weight lifted off my shoulders as I stepped onto the cobbled street.

The masses were even more swarming than they had been this morning, the fair reaching its climax. We wound our way down the street in search of some quiet and shade. Peter said something, but I didn't hear him above the shouting and bustling of the people nearby. There were so many bodies streaming through, so many voices crying in gaiety, so many faces blurring by. And without warning, one of them stuck out in sharp clarity.

It was a man, elaborately dressed, with a woman on his arm. He had light brown hair and eyes of such a pale blue, they were nearly gray. Even from a distance I could make out the scar above his left eyebrow, the sharp angles of his face, the frown upon his lips.

Thomas.

CHAPTER 9

"THOMAS LIKES CHARLOTTE."

The maid pulled on my hair, trying to make sense of the tangled, wind-blown mass of curls. My nose crinkled. "Who is that?"

"Charlotte Nagel, silly," Jennie said, sitting down on the bed. "She's the pretty one that's coming to dinner tonight, and Thomas likes her, so you must promise to be on your best behavior."

I rolled my eyes, lips turning into a trumpet. There was never any fun in behaving.

Jennie fingered her silken gloves. "And Charlotte is not the only one of Thomas's friends who will be here tonight."

"Who else?"

Jennie sighed. "I'm not entirely sure. But you ruin this evening for him and he will have your head. There are to be no repeats of the incident with Mrs. Pruitt."

"Mrs. Pruitt had it coming to her, I daresay," I grumbled, picking at fake threads on my golden evening dress.

"No one deserves to be told that their feet do not match and that their eyes resemble a crow's. Especially from a nine-year-old girl."

I scowled. "I did not put it that way!"

"Even so." Jennie fixed me with a stern glare. "Behave."

I puffed the curls away from my face as she left to go downstairs. Jennie was fifteen, just like Thomas. But unlike him, she worried too much. Tonight would be no different from any other; Thomas always remained unhappy at me, whether I behaved or not.

Soon the maid finished with my hair and I joined everyone downstairs, easily the youngest in the crowd. Children were usually forbidden from mingling and dining with the adults, but Father was unconventional that way, and I adored him for it.

Dinner was served and the conversation dominated by the adults. In a foul mood from being excluded, I stabbed the food on my plate, imagining they were toy soldiers battling it out to see who could claim the victory of being eaten. Or that they were Mrs. Pruitt. Both scenarios were entertaining.

After dessert the adults left, leaving Thomas and his friends, and Jennie, and me. There were seven of them including Charlotte, four boys and three girls, though I didn't know all their names.

"I thought they would never leave," Charlotte giggled.

One of the boys blew a breath of air. "Yes, who wants to spend their evening conversing politics? So dull."

"Politics are actually quite fascinating," I piped up. The cluster turned to me, noticing me for the first time. Jennie gave the barest shake of her head, but I decided to plow on. "And if you had made a study of it, you might find yourself more agreeable than you are now."

There was a pause before the group laughed, all except the young man I had addressed. He frowned. "Are you calling me dull?"

"No," I said, blinking innocently. "You might recall that politics are fascinating. I said it only a moment ago, even a half-wit would remember." The group laughed harder, and I smiled in gratification, stealing a peek at Thomas. He didn't look pleased.

"Are you calling me a half-wit?"

"She is only teasing, Nathan," Jennie said from her seat. "She does this to everyone—please don't mind her." Then she turned to me and cast me that scolding stare of hers that said I was being too unfeeling.

Charlotte stood and sat in the seat next to me, putting one arm around me. "What a bright little girl you are. None of us knew that Nathan was a half-wit, and we are indebted to you for pointing it out to us." Nathan shouted in protest. "What other secrets can you tell us?" She pointed to a girl with auburn hair. "What about Anne?"

I peered at her. "She's nice," I said at last. "But she fancies Thomas, and that indicates very poor judgement on her part."

Again the company laughed, this time dosed with a hearty amount of climactic 'Oh's. Anne blushed, looking away.

"But how can you tell?"

I shrugged. "It is obvious to anyone paying attention."

"Well, since you are so astute," she said, giving me a squeeze, "let me ask you this: Does Thomas fancy her as well?"

"No, he likes you."

The levity in the room left like a snuffed candle. Thomas's eyes hardened, lips pressing into a thin line. Charlotte's smile slipped. The air was suddenly thick and brooding, and I couldn't understand why. Jennie cleared her throat.

"You shouldn't mind her, Charlotte," Jennie said. "She's only nine years old. Half the time she doesn't know what she's saying."

Charlotte swallowed, squinting at Thomas, then down at me. "And the other half she is right?" After a pause, she scooted her chair out and turned to leave.

Thomas's hand rose as he moved toward her. "Charlotte."

"You know, little Miss Markley," Charlotte said, head turning to the side, "even if you are not right about Anne, you were right about one thing. It is poor judgement indeed for any woman to be inclined toward your brother." She pushed out of the room.

A moment of calm ensued before the storm.

Thomas spun around, stepped forward, and clutched my upper arm. "Come with me, Lily," he uttered, his hold cutting off my circulation as he dragged me from my chair, moving out of the room. Jennie followed closely.

"Ow, you're hurting me," I said.

Jennie caught up. "Thomas, you're hurting her. You should let go."

"You!" He whirled around and pointed a threatening finger at Jennie, grip tightening. "You stay out of this." He quickened his pace and lugged me from the room, leaving Jennie behind to stare fearfully after me.

He hauled me down the long hallway until we reached Father's study where he pushed the doors open and practically threw me inside. The room was cold, and dark except for the glow dribbling through the doorway.

"Why did you say that?" he snapped. "Why do you always have to ruin everything?"

"I didn't mean to say it, Thomas."

"Yes, you did. You always do." He raked a hand through his hair, starting to pace. "You never have a thought toward anyone else."

"I didn't know it was a secret. Jennie told me earlier and I merely thought—"

"Blast that sister of yours!" he snarled. "And you too!"

My chest froze in fear, bottom lip quivering. "She is your sister too," I said in a small voice.

He stiffened and stopped. "What did you say?" His voice was deadly, face turning darker than the shadows.

"Why are you being so unfair?" Hot tears rolled down my cheeks. "I didn't mean to. I don't understand—"

"No, you don't understand, do you?" His teeth clenched as he stepped closer, and the sharp sting of water mint assaulted my nose. "You think you're such a clever girl, but the world doesn't work that way, Lillian. There is no cheating life, no outsmarting it when it doles out its unfairness. If life were fair, then my mother wouldn't have died." He grounded the words out, forceful and hoarse. Angry tears welled in his eyes.

My eyes widened with fright. "Thomas."

He closed the gap and grabbed hold of my arms, shaking me violently. "Father wouldn't have abandoned her for your horrible mother. And if life were fair, I wouldn't be treated like this as Father watched from a distance, too preoccupied with his gentle Jennie and his precious little Lily. He was my father long before he was yours. And you! You stole him from me!"

He shoved me hard and I fell, crashing my head on the wooden floor. Pain seared through my skull and down my spine. I cried out, eyes rocking back.

Thomas' face blanched. He looked at his hands, then back at my prostrated form. He took a hesitant step forward and I gasped, raising my arms in protection.

"Thomas."

The doorway darkened, a figure filling its frame. Thomas spun around, gulping.

"What have you done, boy?" My father stepped into the room. When he reached me he bent down, taking me in his arms as I cried into his shoulder.

"Nothing." Thomas' chin jutted out.

Father kissed my forehead, smoothing my damp, wayward locks from my face. His fingers faltered when they came to the goose-egg developing on the back of my head.

"She embarrassed me," Thomas explained. "She embarrassed me in front of all my friends, and now in everyone's eyes I am a fool. Father, she is always causing trouble, always harassing me and turning me into a joke, and tonight she crossed the line."

"No, boy," my father muttered, rubbing my head. "Tonight, you did."

Thomas scoffed, hatred blazing. "You favor them! Mother was barely in her grave when you brought that woman and her rubbish daughter into the house! And now I am forced to watch you dote on those wretches—one not even your own child—while I am to be sent away to boarding school!"

"You sully your character hitting your sister over something so inconsequential."

"It is not inconsequential. Things used to be different—used to be happy. But ever since you got your new family, you didn't want me anymore. You pushed me away—continue to push me away—and I will not stand it any longer!"

"You need not. You will leave for Harrow in the morning."

A sudden stillness overtook in the room, broken by my hiccupping breaths.

"I have three more months yet," Thomas said at last in a low tone.

"I said you will leave tomorrow."

My father continued to brush the hair from my face, not looking at his son. Thomas hardened, jaw working, nostrils flaring.

"Come, Lily," Father said softly as he stood. He grasped my hand and led me from the room, never looking back.

But I did.

It was dark, and I had to squint to see it, but Thomas wasn't watching Father as we retreated.

He was watching me. And there was murder in his eyes.

As they scrubbed the kitchen floor the servants whispered what *a peculiar child I was. "Miss Lillian is so witty and smart—and she is sure to grow into a pretty young lady. But a child her age should not be gifted so. Her older sister is quiet, and though she will not be as handsome, Miss Jennie is sure to draw in more suitors."*

One of the newer servants stopped their scrubbing to ask why, and the older one said, "Because Miss Lily is too clever," and never offered anything more.

I gripped my dress as I huddled and listened, silently resolving to be less brilliant. I fled from my hiding spot near the door and started applying myself to singing, painting, and learning the pianoforte. Anything to change the whispers.

And they did change. As they dusted the paintings, the servants said, "Little Miss Markley is so talented. She shall make quite an accomplished young lady. But I doubt she shall ever marry if she cannot control her cleverness."

Disturbed at the outcome of my efforts, I sought my older sister for consolation. Jennie stroked my hair and reassured me, murmuring the gentle consolation only older sisters are capable of. But the whispers did not change. They worsened.

"Miss Lily oughtn't to have done that to poor Master Thomas."

"What a fiend she is."

"She has the devil's tongue."

When my despair got overpowering, I went to my father. He did nothing but held me, mindful of the unusual burden I felt upon my young shoulders.

Cradling me in his arms, he whispered that his little Lily should not encumber herself so—for her mother would have been proud.

He pulled out his pocket watch, telling me I had exactly thirty more seconds to cry, before I had to be happy again. And with each second that passed, my heart grew lighter, so that when the seconds were up, I was cheerful once more.

It happened so frequently it became routine. When his study doors burst open to reveal my tear-streaked face, my father promptly dropped what he was doing and took me into his arms. Always he pulled out his watch, and always I had thirty seconds.

Then, one day, he was no longer there to hold me, and the weight of the world crashed down. No matter how I tried, I couldn't stop crying for him, even when my thirty seconds were up.

Again, the servants' comments changed. "Poor little Miss Lily—to have lost both her parents at such a young age. Wherever will she and Miss Jennie live?" I didn't understand what they could have meant. We lived here, at Newington.

But we did not inherit, Thomas did. He forced us to leave.

And suddenly, nobody cared about the two little Markley girls.

CHAPTER 10

My limbs tightened. The past flashed before me. A cloying smell, sharp looks, tight grips on my arm, that withering stare when he recognized me at Mrs. Wilshire's. I started to tremble. *Has he seen me? What is he doing here?*

His head swiveled and his dull gaze scanned the crowd.

I turned away with a jolt. Breathing hard, I pressed into Peter, whose arms wrapped around me. I clamped my eyes shut, too scared to be embarrassed.

Does Thomas know about Mary? About Jennie and America? With each second that passed my heartbeat thundered louder, until I was certain Thomas' gaze was fixed upon me, eager to swoop in and take away everything I cared about like he'd done twice before.

Calm down, Lily. Thomas came for the fair, like everyone else. He didn't see you. He didn't see you . . .

Tentatively I glanced up, skimming the mob for his shrewd face, expecting at any moment to meet that lifeless stare. It was a minute or two before I was convinced he must've moved on, and I relaxed.

The feeling was short-lived, as I realized I was still in Peter's arms.

Jumping away with a stifled yelp, I covered my mouth with the back of one hand. "Sorry." I shook my head to clear away incoherent thoughts. Peter looked from me to his now empty arms, inquisitively. He seemed unruffled, though, as if women threw themselves at him every day.

A sick feeling made my limbs feel weak. It came from the shock of seeing Thomas, from reliving those disfigured memories, and from the sudden embarrassment of having Peter see me like this. Having him see me as Lillian.

Unable to meet his eye, fearing he would glimpse the cowardly girl I really was, I said, "Please don't tease me about this, Peter. I couldn't bear it if you did. Not about this."

He stooped a little, forcing me to look at him. Concern etched his brow. "What exactly *is* this?"

I wouldn't tell him—not if a thousand horses tried to drag it from me. Peter's eyes narrowed. He glanced up, searching the crowd.

I shook my head again and waved my hand. "It must've been the heat. I found myself suddenly faint." I put a hand to my forehead. "I think perhaps I should sit down." Not looking back to see if he followed, I moved into the crowd.

I emerged near a grassy area by the river at the outskirts of the fair, and collapsed in the cool shade of a beech tree. The few minutes of walking had given me ample time to finish collecting myself. Peter joined me nearly a minute later, setting his topper on the grass beside him as he sat down.

"You dropped this in the street," he said, holding out my reticule.

" . . . Thank you." I took it from him and opened it, examining its contents. My note from Jennie and my agreement with Mary were still there. I sighed. How close he had come to discovering all! Closing the purse, I resolved to find a safer place for the letters as soon as possible.

The river shimmered before us, babbling as it strolled by. A warm breeze passed through, carrying the reverberations of the fair and rippling the water.

"Something is troubling you," Peter said.

I scowled. How dare he see through me so clearly. "Shouldn't you be getting back to Miss Caldwell?"

"Ah, perhaps." Peter grinned. "But it is good for her to miss me sometimes. Absence makes the heart grow fonder, you know."

"And why should you want her to be fond of you? I recall you saying you weren't engaged."

Peter's smile trickled off his face, his expression sobering. Again, he reacted this way when I mentioned the engagement with Miss Caldwell, and again I wondered why. He sighed. "It is more complicated than that."

"I don't see how. Either you are engaged, or you are not."

"You know, I don't really want to talk about it." He scooted until his back met with the trunk of the tree. I wanted to pursue the matter further, but then thought better of it. Peter had let my episode with Thomas drop, instead of coercing a confession. The least I could do was give him this.

Instead, I said, "Eliza received dozens of ribbons yesterday, all mysteriously complementing her complexion. I wonder who could've given them to her."

I saw the exact moment the twinkle entered Peter's eye. "Hm. That is rather odd. Sounds like we have a scoundrel on our hands. Perhaps we should investigate."

My lips twisted to one side. "Indeed. Or you could confess."

"I?" he laughed disbelievingly. "I, the scoundrel who gave Eliza such a frivolous gift? What nonsense."

"I know it was you."

"You have no proof, madam!"

"One does not need proof to be right."

"No, but you do to pass judgement and give penalty."

"What a shame," I sighed. "For the judgement in this case would be that the man is a caring brother. And the penalty would be that he must receive a kiss on the cheek."

He smirked. "Then I confess."

My face colored. I threw a handful of grass at him, even as he laughed again. "From *Eliza*."

"If you are the one passing sentence, you must deal it out as well." He leaned over, offering his cheek. "Here I am before you, my lady, duly repentant and ready to bear my punishment." He tapped his cheek twice.

I shoved him away.

Once the merriment had subsided, we talked of other things. Simple things. We weighed the merits of strawberries, and argued over whether the river was more blue or green. The hours passed silently by us, too polite to disturb our conversation. I should have been content to stay there for a week, but the other Ambleside guests happened upon us on their way to the barouches.

"Look, they have been here all the time!" exclaimed Miss Margaret. "We had almost lost all hope of finding you." Mr. Quincy, Miss Caldwell, Eliza, and the twins swarmed Peter, while Sir George and Lady Agatha watched on, aloof.

We made our way to the carriages, climbed aboard, and rolled back to Ambleside. Once there, everyone rushed to change for dinner.

Dinner itself consisted of everyone recounting the things they saw, talking in animated tones of their pleasures of the day. I hardly paid attention, content to replay my own experiences, re-analyzing every word and little gesture. Still in a daze, I bid everyone an early goodnight and eventually settled underneath my freshly pressed covers, smiling contentedly to myself.

There was that moment with Thomas, but no matter. Surely he wouldn't recognize me all dressed up—and he certainly wouldn't have been expecting to see me next to Lord Wycliffe.

The day had been nearly perfect, filled with lightheartedness and friendship, soothing my yearning heart just a little. Smiling, I fell asleep visualizing all the beautiful reminiscences that I had added to my collection.

Perhaps I was a dreamer, after all.

CHAPTER 11

TWO WEEKS LATER, ON A DAY WHEN JENNIE'S ABSENCE WAS MORE acute than usual, I pulled out all of her correspondence, stumbling upon the letter that had brought me here. It bolstered my spirits as I read, Jennie's lovely personality seeping through the page.

My dear Lily,

Do you remember how, before I sent you to Mrs. Wilshire's, we would lie awake on Mr. Melbourne's kitchen floor after all the scrubbing had been done? We'd whisper in the dark for hours until the time to begin the work again was near. We made a lot of plans on that kitchen floor, a lot of promises. But there was one that was special—one we've both carried in our hearts.

You might remember the woman I told you about that came to stay last summer? The one that took a special interest in me? Well, she has returned, and . . . I cannot exactly remember the details of how it came about, but she asked after me, and then provided me with what is an inconsequential amount of money to her, but a fortune to me.

By now you must have guessed it—and you are right! I finally have enough to travel to America and make a life for myself. She purchased a ticket in my name, and the boat leaves in a fortnight. I almost fell to my knees and begged her for the same condescension on your behalf, but she doesn't know my true identity, and I fear raising her suspicions.

Oh, Lily. I can hardly bear the thought of leaving you behind. I know we both promised that no matter what, once we had enough money we would leave for America and then wait for the other to come, helping them in any way we could. Yet, somehow I had always imagined us leaving together, waving goodbye to our country on the bow, sailing off to a new adventure, a new life, a fresh start.

But I shall be alone. And I feel terrible that I should be first and not you. Oh Lily, please, please, follow me soon. No matter what, you must manage it. You must not leave me alone. You must come to me.

I will be waiting.

Always yours,
Jennie

THOSE DAYS OF SLEEPING ON A KITCHEN FLOOR WERE NOW A distant memory. Clutching the letter in my hands, I realized that it was becoming harder and harder to remember her—a dream that was passing away like a morning fog when the sun rises.

I no longer needed her as I once did, and I was ashamed because of it. Whether I needed her or not, she needed me. I folded the letter up and returned it to the drawer, resolving to redouble my efforts to keep my heart in check.

I couldn't get too attached, for in the end, I was going to leave. It wouldn't be long now. Shoving my drawer closed, I stood and made for the library, where I was to meet Matthew for another reading day. A few moments after I'd situated into one of the chairs, the library doors crashed open.

I jumped.

"Mary, there you are!" Eliza hurried over, bubbling with excitement. "Everyone has been searching all over for you. I'll wager you cannot imagine who has just arrived!"

I blinked, at a loss for guesses. "The Prince Regent?"

She shook her head. "No, silly. It is Sir William Bentley!" She stared at me with a happy expression, as if waiting for me to reciprocate her enthusiasm—but I'd never heard of the man before. "Isn't that wonderful?"

My book creaked closed. "I suppose. Do you . . . admire him?"

"To be sure! He is a good friend of the family. And there *is* much about him to be admired, with his beautifully dark blond hair, and his bold eyebrows. It is no wonder you should be acquainted. You would make a very fine-looking pair."

I froze, as I grasped what she was telling me. My book tumbled to the floor.

The man, whoever he was, knew Mary.

CHAPTER 12

I SHOT TO MY FEET, HEART ALREADY RACING.

"He is downstairs, expecting to see you." Eliza latched onto my arm. "Come, he is waiting."

Mind in a whirlwind of confusion, I was unable to protest when Eliza led across the room and out of the library. She continued to jabber, but I didn't hear a word of it. My frame shook. *Mary hadn't been acquainted with anyone invited. He must be a surprise guest. But what was I to do?*

We reached the end of the hallway.

I could pretend to faint, or suddenly fall ill. Or perhaps I could run away before he exposed me as a fraud.

We were at the staircases.

My senses returned in time to hear Eliza say something about the well-to-do connections I must have and what a coincidence it was we had one in common. Terror lanced its icy fingers around my throat. I couldn't go down and face the man.

"Stop!" I shook off Eliza's grip.

She fell back and studied me carefully. "Mary? Are you ill?"

I took a moment to reorganize my thoughts, breathing deeply and clenching my trembling hands, forcing them to be calm. "I was not aware that Sir William was invited for the summer. It has merely taken me off guard."

"Oh, he wasn't invited. But he knows Mother and was in town, so he decided to call. Your name got brought up, and he promptly expressed that though he had been unaware you were staying here, he greatly wished to see his dear, old friend again." She scanned my face, and added, "It had not occurred to me that you would not wish to see him."

I studied my options.

I could run. My exposure would be avoided, but I would be kissing my nine pounds goodbye. That wasn't an option.

If I claimed ill, he might return, every day until he could personally see to it that his "dear friend" was healthy once more—drawing equal, if not more attention than meeting with him in the first place.

If I simply refused to see him, he might become suspicious. Who knows what he would do then? He might demand to see me anyway, or talk to Mary's aunt about her irregular behavior.

Though it filled me with unease, my best option was to face him, and hope that his devotion toward his friend and her precarious reputation would overpower any temptation to uncover my mask.

At last, I answered, "I *do* wish to see him—after all, he is a valued friend. I simply wanted to gather my wits and prepare myself for his . . . bold eyebrows."

A look of understanding crossed Eliza's face, and she uttered a slight, "Oh."

"How long will he be staying?" I clutched my middle in an effort to strangle my escalating fear.

"Not long. Likely an hour or two. Mother told him we had room for one more guest, and that he could stay for as long as he liked. But he refused, stating he had business in London."

A bit of luck, that, I thought. *Maybe I could pretend to be sick after all?*

As if Eliza heard my thoughts, she said, "But he was quite insistent upon seeing you, I daresay."

Drat.

There was no use in delaying things. My fate rested in the hands of this Sir William Bentley. I rolled my shoulders back, faced the stairs, and took one more deep breath before descending them, ready to meet my destiny.

Following the low rumble of conversation to the parlor, I saw that all the guests had gathered to be introduced to the visitor. Peter was there too, conversing with the twins near the window. How cruel that my disgrace would be witnessed by so many spectators.

After scanning the sea of faces, I identified my "acquaintance" as the one with his back to me, and approached him with as much self-assurance as I could muster. The various conversations tapered to a standstill.

"There you are, Miss Raynsford," called Lady Wycliffe. "Someone is here to see you."

The man turned his head. His gaze skimmed over me, no doubt looking for Mary and not the imposter in her place.

He was very handsome; though in a different way than Peter. Eliza had been spot on in her description of his eyebrows. They were a coffee brown, starkly contrasted against his dark blond hair, and causing his eyes to appear brooding. He was tall, and young, and from his dress I could tell he was rich. His lips were full, his jawline, pronounced.

Yes, he was very handsome. And the way he held himself suggested that he knew it.

His face screwed in confusion. "I do not see Mary," he said. "I had thought—"

"Why, William!" I said, knowing that I had to stop him from finishing the sentence. "Do you not recognize me? Has it been all that long? It is me. Mary."

He rotated back, seeing me for the first time. Ever so slightly, one of his dark eyebrows rose, and he cocked his head to one side. His expression changed from surprise to casual interest as his mind wrapped around the scandal of my situation.

Here was the moment of truth. Would he pretend I was indeed who I said I was, or would he divulge my secret? I held my breath and returned his stare, much more confidently than I felt. He sauntered forward, stopping just inches from my face.

My heart lurched into my throat. But I held Sir William's gaze, refusing to look away. *Perhaps he will play along after all.*

But then, he smiled.

It was not like Peter's smile, which was one of pure enjoyment; but rather seemed almost wicked—like how a fox would smile at the rabbit caught in his den. My pulse quickened, an urge to run from the room making my fingers twitch. I pushed down the tears prickling behind my eyes.

Still inches away, he said playfully, "Why, Mary! I looked right past you, and didn't even recognize you." Reaching out, he clasped both of my hands in his. "My, you *have* changed. Please forgive me for saying so. You were always lovely, but I had not expected the beauty you have turned into." After a moment of eyeing me adoringly, he raised my hands to his lips, and, still looking at me, kissed them both.

I was almost too stunned to be relieved. Had I misread him?

"Th-thank you," I said, gathering my wits. "You too, have changed."

Without removing his hazel gaze, he announced, "Lady Wycliffe, you have convinced me. I believe I shall take you up on your offer and stay for a few weeks. My business can wait, and I am anxious to catch up with my . . . *dear friend.*" He flashed me his wicked smile again, and a hard knot formed in my stomach, dreading what his words implied.

Sir William waited until everyone's cries of delight quieted before adding, "I must make the proper arrangements." Dropping of my hands, he stepped around me and without a backwards glance, left the room.

Was that it? Why didn't he expose me? And, even more importantly, why would he suddenly change his plans? Out of pure habit, I glanced toward Peter. He watched me evenly, deep in thought.

Eliza jumped up and down, giddy. "What wonderful news! He must regard you very highly to have surrendered his trip to London."

I laughed nervously. "Yes. Very highly indeed. If you will excuse me." I made my way out of the parlor, feeling Peter's gaze on my back.

THOUGH I WAS UNSCATHED AND MY PLAN STILL INTACT, THE TEARS still came once I lay on my bed. Perhaps the tears from the parlor simply needed to be released. But I think that, ultimately, they came because I was tired of having to pretend.

For half of my life, I had been forced to play someone other than myself. As the moisture plopped onto my pillow, I found myself wishing—even if it was only for a moment—that I could simply be Lillian Markley. Not an heiress. Not a servant. Just a girl.

I told everyone such awful lies, stooping to levels I never dreamed of—and with the arrival of William Bentley, it was only about to worsen. Such a game would've amused and thrilled me as a child. Not now. Not with such high stakes and real implications. And yet, to not play meant never seeing my sister again.

It was a vicious cycle, and suddenly I knew that it had to stop.

Rising, I trudged to my vanity and opened a small drawer. From inside, I scooped up my father's pocket-watch, unfastened the little handle, and placed it in my hand where I could clearly see it through my blurred vision.

I stared at it. And breathed.

"There, there, Lily," Father whispered, cradling me in his arms.

"Thomas is so cruel," I said, hiccuping sobs wracking my chest. "I have tried so hard, Papa—t-to please him."

He smoothed away the hair matted to my temple. "Shh . . . I know, my dear. You are too little to worry about such things. You should not encumber yourself so—for your mother would have been proud. Look here." He fished out his watch from his coat, holding it out in his palm. "*You have thirty more seconds to cry, before you have to be happy again. And when thirty seconds have passed, you shall cry no more.*"

I watched the second hand. Tick . . . tick . . . tick. *My breathing relaxed. I sank back into my father's chest.* 27 . . . 28 . . . 29 . . .

The clock hand ticked into place. Slowly, I snapped the face shut, locking the memory away. My tears were gone, replaced only with renewed determination.

The watch had proven useful over the years anytime I felt overly despondent or downhearted. Always I pulled out the watch. Always I had only thirty seconds. And always, it had stopped my tears.

The only time it hadn't was when my father had died.

A soft rapping sounded on the door.

I carefully tucked the watch back in the little drawer next to my letters and mopped my face, trying to cover up the evidence. I pinched my cheeks and cleared my throat before calling out, "Yes?"

"Mary?"

It was Peter's voice.

My mouth ran dry. He couldn't see me like this.

"Mary, are you well?"

Oh, what should I tell him? "No, I think I am not," I called out. "Please, forgive me—I shall not be coming down for dinner." Even the thought of having to confront William Bentley again made me sick to my stomach.

"I know it is more than that. Please, just let me in."

Let him in? How could he even entertain the idea of entering a woman's chambers?

"I shall pretend you said nothing of the kind, Peter Wycliffe, as it is a shockingly improper thing to request."

His voice took on a tone I had never heard before, insistent and determined. "I shall not come in if you will come out. But either way, I will see you."

So suddenly it surprised even me, anger start to churn through my blood. *Why must he always have his way? Why must he always win?* I marched to the door and swung it open.

He reared back as I moved past him, closing the door behind me. "There. You've seen me. You've seen that all is well. Now may I please have your permission to have a moment to myself?"

To an extent, his face darkened. "I was only ensuring you were well."

"I am fine."

"You did not look so downstairs, and neither do you look it now." His response would have fanned my anger, but he doused it by sighing, and stuttering softly as he said his next words.

"Mary . . . please tell me what is upsetting you. I had thought us close friends. True, we keep score and mercilessly compete for an imaginary trophy. But I had hoped that secretly, you feel the same connection that I do—that we are the same, you and I." His voice held such pleading, the sincerity in it nearly overwhelming. "Would you not tell me if something was troubling you?"

He didn't know what he asked of me. But my heart leapt at the thought of trusting him. If there were anyone in the world whom I could confide in, it would be Peter. Surely he, of all people, would be able to understand why I was really here, why I had to deceive everyone. I *did* feel the connection that he spoke of.

But he and I were far from the same. He didn't know how different I actually was. He was a lord, and I a disgraced servant. How could he associate with me once he knew my true reputation? More importantly, how could he ever forgive me for lying to him for so long? Was I really so secure in his faith in me, that I was willing to risk our blossoming friendship? The answer was blatantly clear.

No. I wasn't.

And even if that weren't enough reason, my stay here was going to come to an end, and all my friendships with it.

He studied me quietly. Concern etched his brow as he lifted one hand to cradle my cheek. "You've been crying," he whispered softly.

I turned my face away and his hand dropped. "I only don't feel well," I said, nearly choking on my words. "I simply needed a moment to myself to think. But truly, I don't know why you would concern yourself with me."

For a few, endless moments, he stared at me, blankly, as if we were playing cards again and he didn't want me to know what was in his hand—though why, I didn't know. I had known so little about card games. And I suspected I knew even littler about the game we were playing now.

A foreign feeling crept up my spine.

Then, as if he accidentally let one card slip and tumble to the table, his eyes softened, becoming endearingly familiar. They travelled my face, seeking something, something that he longed for desperately. And he was going to find it.

That *something* warmed my core and bloomed, reaching its branches up to cradle my heart.

His lips parted. "Do you not?"

I held my breath, fearing that if I moved he would discover the turmoil I was experiencing inside—discover the way my heart pounded whenever he was near. Casting my eyes down, it took every ounce of willpower to shake my head no.

I had to push away this feeling and ignore it—ignore Peter and that bottomless look in his eyes—because in a matter of weeks, I would vanish out of his life forever. A moment later, he exhaled, breaking the tension encircling us.

He seemed disappointed, and no amount of talking from me could make it better. I could not say the things he wanted to hear. So when I finally looked up and found that his serious stare was morphing into a willing smile, I was more relieved than I could say.

"I concern myself with it because," he said, "if you are ill, I shouldn't want you jeopardizing the other guests. Indeed, I did not come up to see if you were well, but to ask that you refrain from mingling tonight." Though he was putting on a mask to cover his dejected face, I was grateful.

Familiar ground at last. This, I can do. Letting a small grin develop on my face, I said, "What? And abstain from hearing Miss Caldwell's lively banter? No, sir, you ask too much!"

"I know it shall be difficult for you, but my dear Mary, it is the well-being of the majority you must think of."

"The mingling, you say? What about dinner?"

"I'm afraid that too is a function which you will not be attending." His eyebrows sloped together. "There's nothing else for it. I suppose you shall have to starve. "

Peter continued, doing what he did best—lifting my spirits. Slowly, all my concerns melted away. In that moment, Jennie, Julia Smith, Mary Raynsford, and William Bentley were swept from my mind, replaced only with Peter and his beautiful smile.

Stepping into the drawing room, I closed and bolted the door, still smiling at the conversation Peter and I had had. We had bantered on like the serious moment had never happened. We were still friends. And what's more, I had won the round. I laughed a little to myself.

"What are you laughing at?"

I spun around. Behind one of the sofas, cutting me a calculating gaze, stood William Bentley. I put my hands behind my back as my cheeks grew red. "We were just playing a little game."

"Ah. You and Wycliffe?"

After a moment I nodded, thinking he was going to ask if there was some sort of understanding between us, and then relieved when he didn't.

"You like games, then?"

"I live for them."

"So that explains why you're playing Miss Raynsford." His tone lost all its humor.

My blood ran cold and I swallowed hard as he made his way around the sofa and stopped at the end of it, only five or six paces away. I was acutely aware that the door was not only closed, but locked. It was all *very* improper.

"There is no need to deny it," he went on. "You need not play games with me, Miss . . .?"

"Smith."

He paused, eyes narrowing. "Miss *Smith*. Tell me, what are your reasons for becoming Mary's imposter?" Though his face was serious, he seemed delighted to have the upper hand. Just as he had seemed earlier in the parlor. As if he had decided to stay for the sole purpose of dangling me over a cliff, and laughing when he saw me wriggle.

Well, dangle me, he might. But wriggle, I certainly would not do.

"I woke up one morning and decided I'd like to be someone else for a change. Your precious Mary was the lucky candidate."

William burst out laughing, and folded his arms across his chest. "Oh, I do not think so. I know Mary too well. It is just like her to refuse to come to the country. She is a pretty thing, but there's not much that goes on in her head, you know. I'm curious as to how she thought up something this clever." His voice was smooth, deep. Somehow coaxing.

"But more than that," he went on, tone lowering, "I want to know how she managed to rope in someone as quick—and as lovely—as you. Mary might not have seen the folly in such a scheme, but I'm sure you did. What is she paying you? What could possibly make this all worth it, hm? Whatever your reasons, you must be truly desperate."

I thought back to my agreement. Mary had said that I mustn't be discovered—but did it count when an unexpected visitor knew her, and thereby identified me as a fraud? What if he vowed to keep it a secret? Would it still matter then?

His smile turned light, playful. "All it would take is a few words from me, and your little escapade would be over. A few words, and you will have lost this *game*."

"I am not the only one embroiled in this, sir. Have you no care for your friend? Mary, after all, would take the harder blow."

He chuckled. "Nothing a few well-placed bribes couldn't take care of. And it would be well worth the money just to see your reaction." My face must've registered distress, because his face morphed into satisfaction. His eyes bored into mine, as if they were a mystery only he could solve. "Here I hold your fate completely in my hands. Yet you stand here, and claim that you could win?"

I held his gaze without flinching, calling on every memory of my sister to strengthen me, and said, "I can."

He tilted his head to the side, his dark smile widening. "I should like to see that." Sir William leaned in closer, face uncomfortably near mine. But the move didn't feel threatening, merely interested. "Your name is not Smith, is it?"

The man before me seemed cunning. Unpredictable. Dangerous. Secrets were only ever weapons in the hands of someone like that. I raised my chin. "To be sure, it is Smith."

". . . I don't know that I believe you."

"You cannot change my name by wishing it so. It is Smith."

"You might as well tell me the truth. I will find out eventually, whether or not you confide in me."

"How? By asking Mary? She would only confirm it." I was met with another one of his joyous laughs.

"Yes, of course she would. You probably didn't tell her your real name, either. No, let's just say I have my connections." He leaned in ever closer, wandering my face. ". . . And that I'm very, *very* curious."

I clenched my fists together behind my back, trying to stay calm. "I thought you said you didn't enjoy games."

"To the contrary, I love them. I simply said there is no need to play them with me." He reached behind me, grabbing the handle to the door. The move made his arm wrap about my waist. I looked away in embarrassment.

"But if you *insist*," he whispered, breath touching my neck, "then I'm willing to play." He shot me one last roguish grin, before turning the door handle, stepping around me, and leaving the room.

Whether or not he was planning on exposing me, I still didn't know. But either way, things were about to get much more complicated.

CHAPTER 13

"It is sure to be a crush," Betty Hartford said, talking of the ball. "Just think of that magnificent ballroom filled to the brim with eligible gentlemen!"

The ball was fast approaching, with less than three weeks to get ready. Unfortunately for me, my two months weren't up until a week after that, so I still had to attend.

I sat near the parlor window with a novel, drinking in the sun while Lady Wycliffe, Eliza, Miss Caldwell, Betty Hartford, and the twins took tea at the table. An early afternoon glow lit up the room, turning the light green wallpaper a buttery color. The air smelled of cinnamon from the cookies, and of roses from the fresh bouquets around the room.

"Oh, I wish I could go!" said Eliza, resting her chin on one hand. "Mother, please will you let me?"

Lady Wycliffe sighed. "We have been over this Eliza. Not until your Season."

"Don't be disheartened, dear Eliza," Miss Caldwell said. "Balls are never as entertaining as you think they will be, especially if you have nothing new to wear." She snapped her fingers and sat up straighter. "I know! Let us go on an outing to town and shop for new ball dresses—or at the very least, find a new ribbon or pair of gloves?"

"Splendid idea!" exclaimed Betty.

"Yes, and we can bring Mr. Quincy, and he can decide what looks the prettiest on me!" tittered Miss Molly.

Miss Caldwell clapped to herself. "Then let us bring the men, and they shall ridicule us for being unable to decide what we want."

The table burst into a commotion of bright faces and spontaneous additions to the plan. Lady Wycliffe looked about, bewildered but also amused. Eliza hopped up and rushed over.

"What an adventure! Though I cannot attend the actual ball, I have every intention of pretending as if I will." She pulled me up and twirled me around, sending my book careening toward the floor. I laughed as we wound about the room. Out of breath and bright-eyed myself when we stopped, I sunk back onto the window seat. All the other young ladies had disappeared to make arrangements.

"You must come, Mary!" Eliza begged. "I know the perfect shade of blue to match your eyes."

I exhaled wistfully. "Oh, but I cannot. I promised my aunt I would break my spending habits." I took her hand, swinging it. "Though you must still go and enjoy yourself."

"No, you must come."

"I cannot!"

"Please? Oh Mother, tell her she must come!"

Lady Wycliffe was the only one left in the room, finishing her tea. "Eliza, you cannot force the girl." After she took another sip, she added to me, "Though I would be grateful, Miss Raynsford, if you took her off my hands for the day. She's been rather rambunctious of late."

"Aha!" Eliza cried triumphantly. "Come, let us fetch our bonnets."

She hurried me out of the room to retrieve our things, then back downstairs and out onto in the drive. Servants trotted up barouches and parked them on the gravel as we joined the throng of town-goers. Peter found me through the crowd, managing to flash me a comically pleading look before he was whisked away. I squeezed my lips, tightening my smile.

If I had to suffer through this afternoon, then so did he.

Eliza steered me toward a barouche with Miss Margaret and Sir William, and we clambered aboard. We jerked forward.

"Oh, I cannot wait," Miss Margaret said, one hand holding her bonnet while the other braced against the carriage. "I do wish the ball were sooner." A dusting of freckles bridged her nose, not quite identical to her sister's. I often wondered if the twins' smile—or Eliza's for that matter—ever got tired. It was used so often. The carriage lumbered along, rocking with each dip in the pebbly road.

"As do I," said Sir William from the seat beside her. "It has been a long time since I've been in the presence of three fetching females all at once."

"Oh, Sir William!" Miss Margaret hit him on the arm. "Do go on!"

"I look forward to dancing with each of you lovely ladies." He graced Margaret and Eliza with a beam before resting his gaze on me. "Some more than others."

"Oh sir, cease this flummery! I cannot bear it!" Miss Margaret hit him again, stealing his attention away.

"Miss Margaret," he declared, "you must give me the honor of the very first dance."

"What a bold man you are, sir. But alas! I have already promised the first dance to Mr. Quincy. I hope I have not wounded you."

William's face spoiled. "You have, madam, you have." Then it instantly brightened again as he looked across the carriage. "Dear Eliza, you must dance with me then."

Eliza flushed and fidgeted with the reticule in her lap. I had never seen her so demure and embarrassed. After studying her harder, a suspicion began to form.

"I would love to, but Mama says I cannot attend."

He clucked his tongue. "What a shame." The carriage fell silent for a stretched moment, before finally, William's eyes sidled to me. "I don't suppose you would dance with me, Miss Raynsford?" Each word was punctuated slowly.

Lifting my chin, I transformed my expression into childlike innocence. "Unfortunately, I don't really dance. But I might, if one were to ask like a gentleman."

His lips twitched as he sat back. "What a shame." Then he turned to Miss Margaret and remarked what a pretty nose she had, eliciting more giggles and flirtatious hits from her.

To the left stood a great, green army of forest, stern and disapproving at the merry company that bounded past them. On the other side, a stream wound its way in between copses and brambles. It all muddled together as the chitter-chatter of the carriage propelled us into town.

Once at a halt, William hopped down first. One by one, he assisted us. His eyes pranced as he helped me down—hand tightening just a fraction—before he let go and proffered his arm to Eliza. She took it with a smile. A very sunny smile.

I followed behind them, watching Eliza's secretive glances, her pink cheeks. He laughed and gestured to the guilds for the various shops, leading her toward one after another. At every brush of his shoulder, every sweep of his gaze, every accidental touch of his hand, the admiration in Eliza's eyes deepened, yet he seemed not to notice.

An unexpected protectiveness welled up in my chest. I shot forward. "Eliza, let us visit that shop over there. It seems similar to the starfish booth we saw at the fair." Linking her other arm, I steered her away from William, but he followed.

We entered the little cobbler's store, neat rows of shoes and the smell of leather assaulting us. The shopkeeper eyed us while he dusted his shelves. Eliza surveyed the nearest shelf, selecting a pair and exclaiming, "Oh, what delicate slippers these are! I think I shall die if I cannot have them!" She held one up to her foot for comparison. "And they are just my size. I must see if Peter will buy them for me." She turned to dash out of the shop, but William caught her by the elbow.

"What's this? Have you no money of your own?"

She placed the slippers back on the shelf. "Oh, I do, but I did not bring enough for these. Do not worry, Peter shall buy them for me. I'll return shortly." She hurried out the door. Besides the shopkeeper, William and I were once again alone.

What poor luck I had!

"And you?" he asked me, gesturing to the room. "Are there no shoes here that please you?"

I fingered the laces of some boots, stuffing down a wave of nervousness. "These appear to be of good quality. But Miss Smith's tastes lean toward something simpler."

"Because she can't afford something better?"

I stopped short. He was fishing for information. *Your name is not Smith is it?* His stare now was cunning, conniving.

"No," I said slowly. "I am merely a simple girl. You will find I am an open book, Sir William."

"Ah." He neared and bent down. "A book I am very much looking forward to reading."

Eliza burst back in the room, face distraught. "Peter says he will not buy them for me. What am I to do?" She came over and clasped my hands. "Do you think the proprietor would save them for me, so I could return and claim them another day?"

"I'm sure he would."

"There is no need for that." William swept the shoes off the shelf. "I will buy you the slippers."

Eliza's mouth dropped open. "Oh. But I could never let you—"

"Yes, you can, and you shall." William snapped his fingers, and within seconds, the proprietor materialized. William plunked a handful of coins in the man's hand. "A pretty girl deserves to be spoiled with pretty things, and you, Eliza," he bent and kissed her cheek in a familiar, brotherly way, then gave her a winsome smile, "are the prettiest of all."

He was teasing her. He was being generous in his teasing, but it was teasing all the same. And though I saw through it plain as day, Eliza was even more enamored. She smiled and bit her lip. Annoyance bubbled up in my throat. Once the shoes were wrapped, we returned outside. After ensuring Eliza wouldn't be left alone with William Bentley, I departed, too unnerved to spend another moment in his presence.

The gall of the man! Toying with a girl—a girl barely fifteen!—just to . . . to what? Annoy me?

"Ha!" I said aloud as I marched to the other side of the street. If that was his sole purpose in paying attentions to Eliza, then not only was he a scoundrel, he was a fool as well. I glanced up at my destination, the sign above it reading, "Weston's Threads & Lace."

The shop, sunny but dusty, smelled like flowers and decaying wood. Shafts of sunlight illuminated floating specks. I took in its messy state, not knowing where to begin.

Unlike the last store, there was no order to these items. Grimy bolts of fabric cluttered the floor, and lengths of ribbon hung down from the ceiling like ominous fingers. The small space had so many pins and bobbins and spools crammed into it, it would take far longer than one afternoon to sort through them all.

I shifted down the row of items, sifting through them one by one. Gloves, opera glasses, fans. When I had come full circle around the shop, I twisted my lips to the side and peered out the window. The barouches were still empty. Perhaps I could be a little more thorough. I started on the shelf closest to me, shuffling back through the goods.

A bell tinkled. ". . . can't be worse than that hat she was wea—good grief! What a dirty, drafty place this is!" It was Miss Caldwell, accompanied by Miss Betty Hartford. Spotting me, she made her way over. "Ah, Miss Raynsford! We have all been wondering where you ran off to. It would seem you are always disappearing. A shop of this caliber has nothing suitable for your elegant tastes, I'm sure. Quite a lower standard than London."

"Actually, I find it rather quaint." I pulled out my most guileless smile. "Must be the charm of the country."

"Indeed," agreed Betty, and Miss Caldwell shot her a look of annoy-ance before smoothing it over.

"I suppose we shall have to make do with 'quaint,' as 'elegant' cannot be found—no matter how charming it may be." Miss Caldwell scrutinized her surroundings with a trained eye. "Scruffy, subpar, shrewish. Ah, now this." She clasped one of the ribbons hanging from the ceiling. "This is not half-bad. Shame there's not enough of it though."

It was a fine silk ribbon of the softest pink, and all that was left of it was just enough to go around my waist—too short to really be used for anything beyond decorating a bonnet. Miss Caldwell gestured to the burnt orange ribbon next to it, and called for the proprietor. "Ah well. I suppose I shall get this one. Though it's not as attractive, it still keeps catching my eye."

The proprietor appeared—a middle-aged, unkempt sort of fellow—and cut the ribbon to the proper length. Miss Caldwell and Miss Hart-ford followed him to counter to complete the transaction, but I stayed behind, studying the pink ribbon.

It was the perfect color; and it would match my dress, I was sure of it. I rubbed it between my fingers. The price was a bargain, and it was good quality too.

"Good sir," I said, dropping the ribbon. "Have you any more of that ribbon there?"

His face screwed before clearing again. "The pink? Yes, miss, that's a bestseller here. I reordered it again a few weeks back. Should be here today." He pulled out a pocket watch from a hidden vest pocket. "Within the hour, in fact."

The bell chimed again, and we were joined at the counter by Peter. "I trust you ladies are almost finished? Everyone else is near ready to leave."

I glanced back through the grubby window. Blurry shapes were loading into the carriages.

"What a shame!" cried Miss Caldwell. "Miss Raynsford was hoping to wait for a new shipment of ribbon. Oh, truly it is a shame."

Peter turned. "Ribbon?"

"I wasn't planning on—"

"Yes! Such a shame! The man said it would be here within the hour. Isn't that right, good sir?"

The proprietor nodded. "They've never come later than six o' clock."

"There you have it," said Miss Caldwell. "Miss Raynsford, you must stay and wait for it. We women must have our ribbon after all. I daresay we shall miss your company."

Flabbergasted, weak protests died in my throat.

Betty tapped her lips. "Though I shouldn't think she could stay by herself. It wouldn't do at all for her to make the journey back alone."

Peter looked between us three. ". . . I could stay with Miss Raynsford and see that she is properly escorted back."

Miss Caldwell grasped Peter's arm. "But Peter, you promised to help me with my archery this afternoon and there are only a few hours of daylight left. Let one of the others do the job—Sir William Bentley, perhaps."

"No!" I said, a little too forcefully. Their heads whipped to me, and I cleared my throat and amended in a small voice, "That is, I shouldn't like to trouble him."

"Then why not send a servant to pick it up tomorrow?" Miss Caldwell suggested.

"Truly there is no need. I do not wish to be a bother. I can do without the ribbon."

"It's no bother at all," Peter insisted. "It is settled. I shall stay behind."

Miss Caldwell looked between us, dissatisfied. "But—"

"I shall stay." Peter's expression was kind but brooked no further argument. "We can do the archery tomorrow."

The proprietor, who had just finished packaging the ribbon,

handed it to Miss Caldwell. With what appeared to be a monumental effort, she mustered a nod and frail smile before turning and exiting the shop, Miss Hartford on her heels. They joined the other hazy people through the window.

"Let me make the arrangements," said Peter. He disappeared outside, probably ordering the others to squeeze into two carriages so we could have our own.

I busied myself with rummaging through the items in the shop, and when he returned, said, "You shouldn't have offered. I didn't especially want to stay in the first place, and now Miss Caldwell shall look at me with utter loathing for the next week."

Peter chuckled as he joined me. "What makes you think she would not do that already?"

WE WERE SO BUSY TALKING AND LAUGHING, IT SEEMED NO TIME AT all passed before the clerk came from the back, carrying the packaged ribbon. "Sorry it took so long, miss. My delivery man only just arrived."

I took the parcel with thanks. "We have not been waiting so long," I said. But as Peter and I exited the shop, we stepped into a world where the sun was sinking below the horizon.

"The others will start to worry if we don't return soon." Peter offered his arm and led me to our barouche, which already had a number of packages sitting inside it. "Since everyone crushed into two carriages, there wasn't room for everyone's purchases," he explained, helping me up. "I hope you don't mind."

Peter clambered aboard, picked up the reins, and gave them a flick. The road, an attractive, shimmery brown in the pale sunlight, wound through the forest and over hills, into a twilight that tasted of lavender.

We had been travelling for quite some time when the wheel hit a deep rut in the road. The barouche shot up in the air, sending us careening, the *crack* of splitting wood rebounding off the trees. The horse bolted, breaking its tethers and galloping away as the carriage skidded to a halt. I coughed, waving away the dust clouds.

"Are you all right?"

Looking around, I said, "I think so."

Peter hopped out of the tilting carriage, walking around and inspecting it. He sighed. "One of the wheels is broken, another fractured. As it currently stands, this carriage is useless." He looked to where the steed ran off. "Especially without a horse." His brow scrunched as he bent down again, touching something on the broken wheel that I couldn't see. "Huh."

"What?"

"Nothing. It's just . . . if I did not know better . . ." He trailed off, straightening slowly, rubbing the back of his head. "If I did not know better, I'd say the wheel had been tampered with. Right there—" he pointed again to something I couldn't see, "—it has the look of being sawed halfway through." He shook his head. "I shall have to speak to our stable boy about it."

I tentatively stood on the sloping structure, noting the scattered packages. "In the meantime, what are we to do?"

Peter shrugged helplessly. "I suppose all we can do is walk."

I blinked. ". . . All the way to Ambleside?" We were still a good five miles away.

"Either that or we can return to town, find an inn, and call for a new carriage in the morning."

I gulped. "Spend the night? Both of us at an inn?"

Peter's lips twitched. "In different rooms of course. I know it's a difficult choice, but inconvenient times call for inconvenient measures."

I halted, an outlandish suspicion gathering. "Did you plan this?"

He took a step back, eyebrows shooting up. "I? Plan this? How on earth could I have planned this?"

"I haven't the foggiest, but it is something you would do."

He laughed. "I can't know what I've done to warrant the accusation, or the compliment."

"You can't know?"

"Indeed not!"

"You arranged the card game so I was the last one left. And you eavesdropped on mine and Quincy's conversation. Not to mention the time you took books out of the library when you thought I might read them."

Peter chuckled, hard. "They hardly compare! I would not strand you in the middle of the country—risk your life and reputation—just to steal a few moments alone!"

"Oh?" I put my hands on my hips. "And you didn't saw the wheel in half?"

"No! How could I have when I was with you the entire time? Besides, there were other factors. Staying behind was your idea—and you insisted Sir William not be the one to escort you. Indeed, now that I think on it, perhaps this entire incident is a result of *your* scheming."

I scoffed. "Me?"

"Yes." He came up to the side of the carriage, resting his arms on the wood, and his chin on his arms. "I know how you crave my company."

"Oh, rubbish," I growled and held out my hand. Peter took it and helped me down onto solid ground, gathering the parcels strewn about the carriage as I smoothed my hair. We set off down the road, Peter still noiselessly laughing.

We strolled in silence for some time. The sun drifted below the horizon, and the forest's shades darkened.

"How dreary your spirits are this evening," Peter drawled.

"Upending carriages isn't exactly my idea of a good time."

"It could be." He nudged me with his shoulder. "It all depends on your outlook. For example," he stopped and angled toward me, "you *could* be tremendously happy that you now have my company even longer than you had anticipated."

A begrudging smile met my lips. "I suppose, but I could never tell you so, or it might get to your head."

"Indeed." Then he snapped his fingers. "Now I have it! With all this extra time, we shall play a game."

"No!" I protested. "I shall lose!"

"Yes, you shall. Now let's see, the rules shall be these: You must either confess something you love, or confess something you hate. The first person to run out of confessions loses."

I balked. This didn't sound like a good game for someone with no truth to confess. "Surely it would take all night!"

"Then we had better get started. Now, I shall go first." Peter took on a thoughtful expression. We continued walking, an owl hooting in the distance. "Do you like Beethoven?"

I inclined my head. "I admit I have not tasted it."

He laughed. "It isn't a dish—it is a man. A German composer in fact, and in my opinion, a genius of the modern age. That is my first confession. I love Beethoven. Even though Eliza thinks he is senseless and brash."

"I did not know you were musical." I stopped and turned to look at him. "You know, I do believe I'd like to hear you sing."

He only smirked. "Another time, perhaps."

"So I am expected to dance at the ball—in front of a host of spectators—but you cannot sing one tune while we are alone? Seems rather unfair."

"Yes, well, you should've thought about that before you conjured Julia Smith. Now, stop changing the subject. It is your turn."

Mentally, I stomped my foot. "I . . . I live in London."

Peter squeezed the packages under his arm. "That is not a confession, that is a fact. You must tell me something you love, or something you hate . . . It doesn't have to be profound. Mine was about Beethoven, after all."

I chewed my upper lip. *Anything at all?* Well as long as it was all silly opinions, there could be no harm. Perhaps I could put Mary aside for a few minutes. I thought for another moment before saying, "I hate the color orange."

"Mm. I love strawberries. Particularly the first strawberries of summer. They are always sweeter than the rest."

I laughed. "They are not!"

"Indeed they are. I have a palate for these sorts of things."

We kept walking, the night growing darker with each step. The stars peeped behind the clouds, blinking in the moonlight. Eventually, we got quicker at the game, trying to see which one of us couldn't keep up.

"I don't especially like Shakespeare," Peter said.

"Oh!" I added. "And I love a good book on a rainy day."

"I hate bread, except when it's toasted."

"I love little drawings on the sides of pages."

"I hate the sound of the letter 'z.'"

"I love warm blankets."

Peter stopped, took a deep breath, and sighed it out. His nose crinkled. "Do you smell that? There must be a river nearby with water mint on its shores. I love the smell of water mint."

My smile disappeared as I inhaled too, feeling the urge to gag. It should have been a pleasant aroma—it was cool and sharp and fresh—but it made my throat dry and thick. This smell that Peter loved permeated every bad memory I had of Newington.

It reminded me of Thomas.

It was in the cologne he always wore, one gifted him by his mother long before she died and Father remarried. Thomas stockpiled it, and I couldn't remember a time when he wasn't accompanied by his signature water mint scent.

My mind tumbled and tumbled, bringing up images of a black corner, memories of him yanking my arm. The helplessness I felt as my tears splattered the wooden floors.

"You look pale," Peter said, shattering the illusion.

With jerky movements, I pinched my cheeks, willing the blood back to my face. "I find I don't enjoy the smell as you do." I walked on before any more was said, and Peter followed, though our pace was much slower now. The silence thickened and a breeze blew us down the road.

I wrapped my arms around myself, scuffing the pebbles by my feet. "I hate . . ." I bit my lip at the pang in my heart, whispering, "I hate feeling like a child. Everything is so much more potent to a child—the feeling of shock, of betrayal, of . . . of not being wanted." My feet stopped of their own accord.

Peter stopped too, his expression somewhere between surprise and eagerness. His lips parted. He took a step closer, his hand finding mine. "Mary, I—" He inhaled sharply. "I suppose it's my turn then, isn't it? And perhaps I shouldn't—every part of me is telling me I shouldn't —but . . . I've wanted to tell you for some time now . . ." He finally looked up.

I swallowed, heartrate spiking.

"I've wanted to tell you that I love . . ."

Blood pounded in my ears. There were some things that should be left unsaid. I had to stop him.

"I love—"

I pulled my hand out of his grasp, and when I did, a cord snapped in Peter. He stepped back. My face burned.

He exhaled, rubbing a hand over the back of his neck, shaking his head. "I love besting you," he muttered at last. "That is what I wish to say. I love that we are friends."

"Friends!" I agreed, snatching the lifeline. I looked up at the stars, mutely thanking the heavens. "I love that we are friends as well, Peter. We will always be friends, won't we?"

Peter nodded and smiled, but it didn't touch his eyes. He looked away first, and when he did, I noticed he only had two parcels hooked under his arm.

Peter noticed it too, searching around frantically and then back down the road. "Blast," he said under his breath. "I seem to have dropped the rest of the packages. I was distracted. They'll be back that way somewhere."

Clasping my hands behind my back, I said, "You should go fetch them. I'll walk slowly and you can catch up." I needed a moment alone anyway.

Peter's foot turned away to retrace our steps. "Are you sure?" I nodded, and after a moment's hesitation, he said, "Then I'll be right back," and left, disappearing behind the trees covering the bend in the road.

Moaning softly, I let my head collapse into my hands. What was I doing? Why had I done that? And what on earth were we going to talk about when he got back? Surely the rest of the walk would be awkward now, and how I hated the feeling!

Oh, that is what you should have said, Lily! I scolded myself. *That you detest awkwardness! Why couldn't you have kept it simple and impersonal? Then Peter never would have tried to—never tried to . . . to . . .*

I rubbed my eyes with the heels of my palms, before straightening and sighing. I didn't want to puzzle out the end to that thought.

Breathing in an ocean of crisp night air, I tipped my head back and squinted at the sky. I ambled on, hugging myself, not paying the minutes any heed as twenty of them slipped quietly by.

The hair on the back of my neck rose. Then I heard it: a rustle, followed by an odd, metallic sound. I spun around, flesh crawling. There was nothing but road and trees, illuminated by pale moonlight.

"Peter?" I said in a small voice. "Is that you?" The forest was still, the world holding its breath.

Nothing.

All was silent, except for the wind in my ears and the thumping in my chest. I hesitated and looked around one last time. Letting out a careful sigh I turned and—

Oof.

A hand snaked around my waist, the other clamping my mouth, stifling my gasp. Another figure emerged from the trees, knife gleaming in his grip. I thrashed violently, whimpering. The knuckles around my mouth whitened.

"There's a good girl," the man with the knife said as he neared. "This won't take long, I promise."

I struggled. The grip around me tightened. Pain seared into my arm. My lungs collapsed. Black dots speckled my vision.

"Good," said the knifed man. "Now. Harry's going to take his hand off your mouth. And if you scream, we'll ensure your death is a slow one. Understood?"

"Not that it would do you any good," Harry's voice above my head added. "There's no one around for miles."

I froze.

Peter.

Had they already hurt him? Was he lying in the road somewhere, bruised, beaten, and . . . and dead?

My mouth ran dry. Peter *couldn't* be dead. They hadn't harmed him —he was alive and he was going to come back. He had to, or else . . .

"Understand, girl?"

My eyes flitted to the nearing man. I calmed myself before giving a slow nod.

Harry's hand around my mouth slackened, before reinforcing his hold on my arms and waist. If Peter were still alive, he would be here soon. Acting on that sliver of faith was my only hope. I had to give him as much time as possible. I had to stall.

The man with the knife was finally close enough for me to see his face. His gaze was dark, his nose slightly crooked above a muscly build, a handful of scars carving into his face. He might've been handsome in a deformed sort of way if I weren't extremely terrified of what he was about to do.

He inspected me closer. Then he bared his teeth, a different glow overtaking his face. "Well, well, well."

"The man didn't say she'd be so young," Harry rumbled behind me.

The scarred one sneered. "Or that she was so becoming." He

stopped inches from my face, his rancid breath washing over me, the cool of his knife grazing my neck. "I'm beginning to think there are a *lot* of things he didn't tell us." As his eyes raked over me again, I swallowed several times and clenched my hands.

Stall.

"Who is he?" I forced bravery into my voice. "Surely I merit an introduction."

He ignored me. "We might be inclined to let you go free, if you can top the fifty pounds he's paying us."

I listened for approaching footsteps. There were none.

"Can you?"

I whipped back to the scarred man. "Can I what?"

"Can you top fifty pounds?"

That was quite an extraordinary sum. Was it Mary they wanted? Was she actually in debt and had hired a diversion to stay at Ambleside so she could sneak away to France? Were these men debt collectors, instructed to kidnap me and drag me to court if I refused to pay?

"Fifty pounds?" I barked a laugh, thinking quickly. "Is that it? Do you not know who I am, sir? I am Mary Raynsford, a rich heiress and niece to Lady Phoebe Raynsford. What do you plan to do if I don't come willingly? Are you instructed to kill me?" I laughed again. "If so, then whoever hired you would want proof of my death. How are you to convince him of my identity, since I am not wearing my aunt's token? Do you intend to cut off my head? It doesn't seem you brought along a bag to take it with you."

The scarred man's eyes flickered with a sliver of uneasiness. "We're not here to kill you, only take you with us. Willingly or no."

"That would be such a fantastical sight, too," I went on. "Blood spurting and soaking everything—and I do think you'll have a difficult time sawing through my neck with that short blade. It might take a while. Will you commit the deed here, or do you intend to carry me off and cut me up later? I don't see your horses, so you must be staying in town. Hopefully you've allotted enough of your earnings to bribe the innkeeper not to say a word when he has to clean up the bloody sheets."

Harry's throat moved against the back of my head as he gulped.

"And what sort of guarantee did this employer of yours give you that he won't have you killed, to cover it all up? If you would just let me contact my solicitor, I can pay you a far more generous sum. Now who should I make the note out to? Mister Harry and Mister . . .?"

"Reggie," Harry said, but it wasn't toward me, "maybe we ought to listen to her. The gentleman said nothing about her being so high-born. Maybe we should forget the whole thing."

"I'm not leaving without finishing the job," Reggie growled.

"You must know you have the wrong woman." My fingernails burrowed into my palms. "Kidnapping is an atrocious crime to begin with, but to kidnap the wrong person! I cannot fathom the humiliation."

Reggie snarled. "If we did let you free, you wouldn't give us the money—you'd turn us in the moment we turned our backs."

Yes, I would. "Then at least tell me who wishes this upon me."

"We've been over this." He narrowed his eyes. "You're stalling."

I bit my lip, looking over the man's shoulder one last time.

There was nothing. No one. And I was out of time.

"If you think I'm stalling, then what are you waiting for, sir? Did this mysterious employer of yours want something more from me than my disappearance?"

Reggie's lips turned up into a leer. "No, miss." He came closer, clasping my chin in one hand, knife positioned delicately on my cheekbone. "But I do."

Oh Peter, please be nearby!

Reggie lunged for me, and I screamed, pulling and pushing and shoving and thrashing, hitting the ground at a painful angle. *"Peter!"*

The man was ripped off me and flung to the side. Peter's hand snatched my arm and pulled me up. He had enough time to shove me away and shout, "Leave!" before Harry charged, throwing several fast jabs. Peter deflected them, catching a stray blow in the arm. Harry put his weight in a single punch. Peter ducked, kneed him in the stomach, and shoved him to the dirt.

I bolted, blood pounding, every muscle and nerve strung high. I scoured the ground for the knife, sounds of the skirmish ringing out. A battle cry, the crunch of gravel under boots, a grunt, steel clattering to the ground.

A flash of metal came from Reggie's hand as he barreled forward. "Behind you!" I shrieked.

Peter turned, catching his arm. But Harry had recovered and stood, pinning Peter from behind. Reggie gave a few teasing swipes of the blade before he charged again, knife raised. At the last second Peter ripped his arms free and dove to the side, the knife lodging into Harry's stomach instead. He screamed in agony, crumpling onto the gravel.

Peter turned to Reggie. Face steady but livid, he took off his coat and threw it aside.

Reggie bellowed, throwing one punch, two. Peter dodged easily. The third punch found its mark. Peter grunted, but used the momentum to rotate and return his own blows.

One. Two. Three. Four. In the stomach, side. Along the jaw and neck. Five. Six. Seven. Reggie heaved and collapsed, blood oozing from his nose and temple. Peter took a menacing step toward him. He scurried back in the dirt, turned, and hobbled toward the forest. Harry was nowhere to be found.

Reggie crossed the road and disappeared into the trees, leaving behind the mess of the struggle. Peter's chest heaved as he watched him scamper away. The new silence rang disconcerting. Peter remained taut for a moment before he exhaled, relaxing, raking a hand through his hair. It stopped midway.

"Mary," he whispered. He spun around, looking wildly about. "*Mary!*"

I took a wobbly step forward. "I'm here."

He sighed in relief. "Don't frighten me like that." He neared, eyes still angry and frantic. "Tell me, did they hurt you? On my honor, if they did . . . Blast it! I shouldn't have left you alone. I should *never* have —Oh Mary, look at me." He cupped a hand to my face, lifting it. "Are you hurt?"

That was all it took for the tears to start pooling. I bit my lip and shook my head. He glanced back and forth between my eyes for perhaps half a minute, before he was finally convinced. But he didn't let me go yet.

"Did you know those men?" he asked gravely. "You didn't recognize either of them?"

My lower lip trembled. I shook my head again.

"Is there anyone who might have a motive for harming you?"

"No, no one."

He sighed, then pulled my face closer, gaze solemn. "I will find whoever did this. I promise you."

I nodded. He looked as if any moment now he would scoop me into an embrace, but instead he stepped back and took in the messy scene. He rubbed a hand over his face at the sight of ripped packages and dust clouds still settling.

My gaze snagged on his ripped, discolored sleeve. It took a moment to find my voice. "B-By all England, you're bleeding!"

Peter inspected his body and found the cut on his arm. "So I am." He lifted it up to see better in the moonlight, and when he did, I sucked in a breath. The deep gash ran the length of his forearm, blood running everywhere. "We can't let anyone see this." He looked back to where my attackers had disappeared, then spun and headed toward the foliage in the opposite direction. "This way."

I grabbed his crumpled coat that had been trampled in the brawl and followed Peter through the bushes and trees until we came to a river. With surprising ease, he rolled up his good sleeve and tore the lower half of the damaged one off. Bending over the stream, he shoveled water and rinsed away the blood, not making a sound when he scrubbed the dirt out of the deep cut, though it must hurt terribly.

My eyes stayed glued to where his cravat had been, now lost in the scuffle. To where the top of his collarbone glowed in the moonlight. And to his forearms, muscle and sinew flexing and working under bared skin. I hugged the coat tighter and made myself look away, peeking back again only twice.

After cleaning the wound, he bandaged it using his torn sleeve, tying it off using his teeth. He held out his hand for his coat. I gave it to him and he put it on slowly.

"There," he said, straightening it.

His cravat was still missing and I was still shamefully staring. When the silence grew awkward, I realized he was watching me, waiting. I ripped my eyes away.

"I'm sorry," I mumbled. "I didn't mean for you to get hurt."

"It wasn't your fault. I've been in significantly worse scrapes than this." He paused, gaze serious and full of an oath. "And I will find them. Come. Let us return."

We revisited the carnage to gather up the scattered parcels, dropped in haste to rescue me, and started back on our way.

We were both quiet, both sweaty, both dirty, both exhausted. We walked the last mile or two with only the moon as our guide. Twice, when Peter thought he heard something, he reached a protective hand over to stop me. Once he was satisfied it was nothing, we continued trudging.

At last, we crested the final hill and saw the dim, flickering lights of Ambleside in the valley below. Sluggishly, we plodded up to the mansion. Peter led me away from the main stairs, opting instead to enter through the servant door.

He dropped the parcels on the kitchen counter as we went. Climbing the servant's stairs to the second floor, we passed through several rooms and hallways before stopping in front of my chamber door. Laughter and music drifted up from the main level along with the faint hush of conversation. The life of tinkling crystal and silk gloves was such a drastic contrast to the last few hours—making it seem as if it never happened.

But it had. And I was doing my utmost to keep the memories at bay.

"You're weary," Peter said. "Sleep. I will convey your excuses to the party."

He turned to go, but I grabbed his good arm. "What about you? You're more exhausted than I am, and that cut can't be pleasant, either. You should retire as well."

The side of his mouth lifted, but he shook his head. "No, I must make an appearance. I am the host." He inspected himself, his dirty shirt, his wrinkly coat. "Though I think a change of clothes would suit."

"What are you going to tell them all?" I asked, realizing how it must look—arriving back with Peter so late, and then coming in secretly.

Again, he shook his head. "Tomorrow." A tentative hand reached up, grazing my cheek just once. "And you shouldn't be alone. I will send someone up to look after you." He turned and disappeared down the corridor.

Eyes and feet heavy, I entered my room, not caring if the servants gossiped or not as I disrobed and climbed into my nightgown. I collapsed on the bed without washing my face or re-pinning my hair, trying not to replay the frightening scene in my mind. Trying not to feel hands around my waist or a knife pressed to my face.

A soft knock sounded, followed by Katherine quietly entering. She brought in a ball of yarn and knitting needles, settling into a chair in the corner before quietly knitting away. *Tap. Tap. Click. Click. Click. Tap.*

Peter had been right. I needed to not be alone. And the last thought I had before sleep finally overtook me and I drifted away to a place without threats, evil men, frightening fights or dark nights, was that I was eternally grateful to him.

CHAPTER 14

I SAT UP AND GASPED, BLOOD PUMPING FAST. EYES WIDE BUT unseeing, I clutched my blankets, shadowy images passing through my mind. A few moments passed before I could blink them away by gulping down big breaths.

I was back at Ambleside. I was safe. I relaxed my fists.

Katherine had disappeared sometime during the night. Another knock sounded at the door—the first of which had awakened me. Wondering who it could be, I slipped out of bed and cracked the door open, eyes bleary, hair mussed, and nightgown slightly askew. A servant handed me a slice of paper bearing only one word: *Rooftop.*

Quickly, I braided my hair, wisps of curly brown tresses escaping the rushed bind. I threw on my overcoat and slippers and slithered out of my room, careful not to disturb the sleeping house.

The soft plod of my feet filled the silence, and then the muted moan of the library door creaking on its hinges. I crossed the room, pinching my cheeks as I went. Climbing the secret staircase, my imagination ran wild.

Did he want to talk about last night? Why up here? And why now, instead of at a decent hour?

I lifted the hatch and clambered onto the rooftop. Fog engulfed me, the outside world gray and hazy. A yellow glow rose from the east, morning dew still kissing the ground. Peter leaned on the ledge and riffled through some papers. He turned when he heard me approach, setting the papers aside.

"I was surprised to get your note." I yawned and formed a wobbly smile. "Luckily for you, I'm an early riser."

"Yes, I can see that. Lucky for me." He came closer, taking in my rumpled nightgown underneath my coat, my messy braid and frazzled hair. He chuckled. "You could have gotten dressed first."

My mouth twisted, embarrassment mounting. I nodded to the papers still sitting on the ledge. "Were you working?"

He glanced over his shoulder. "Yes, actually. I like to go over accounts and ledgers in the morning, and I like to do it up here. Helps me think."

"Rather strange habit." I followed him to the ledge, stretching then shivering. "Are you going to tell me why you asked me up here, or are you going to continue to be mystical?"

His hands grouped together and he reclined on one elbow. "I wanted to discuss last night."

"Yes, I thought as much, but why here?" I yawned again. "And why now?"

"I know it is inconvenient, but it's important we get our stories straight—and also that we discuss it alone. I managed to stave off most of everyone's questions last night, but they were all curious, and I shouldn't be surprised if we are to be quizzed at breakfast."

"You mean we're not going to tell anyone what really happened?"

He shook his head.

The tranquil dawn, filled with the chatter of jackdaws, lay shrouded in the thick fog. I hugged my coat tighter against the chill. "But . . . but you saved my life."

"So I did," he said with a lopsided grin. "But I'd rather not have to recount the tale."

"Why ever not?"

"Three reasons." He sighed theatrically. "Firstly, because I would be such a hero. 'Peter the Angelic' they would call me. 'Come,' they would say, 'marry our daughters and take our fortunes.' And how is a poor man like me supposed to refuse? They would write books about me—songs too—and heaven knows from this day I wouldn't get a moment's peace."

A bubble of laughter spurted out of me. I didn't know if my nerves were high-strung, or if I just needed to forget the frightful events of last evening, but I was grateful for the levity. I nudged him with my shoulder. "The angelic? That doesn't suit you at all."

One corner of his mouth twitched. "Secondly, Eliza and my mother would coddle me the moment they discovered this gash." His thumb stroked his forearm, and he started to chuckle. "And then I *really* wouldn't get a moment's peace."

I laughed again. "And the third reason?"

"Well." There was a sudden seriousness to his tone. "Everyone knows those men probably wouldn't have attacked had I been there. Which would mean you would've had to be alone with them, at least for the smallest moment. At night."

I stared at him blankly, waiting for him to elaborate. And it could've been the lack of light, or a trick of the mind, but if I didn't know any better, I would've thought he was blushing. Understanding struck.

"Oh."

"And that would mean," he went on, swallowing hard and struggling with the words, "at least in everyone else's eyes, that no one can know what did or did not happen. People simply love to gossip, and I wouldn't give them the material to do so if I could help it. Especially where it concerns you."

Now it was my turn to blush and look down. Here he was, more concerned with Mary's reputation than I was myself. The thought hadn't even occurred to me. "What happens when they discover we walked to the manor, alone and at night?"

"It is not so scandalous if we explain that the lace delivery was late and our carriage broke down. The hour was indecent, but what else could we have done? They will understand, and we shall simply omit the part about the highwaymen."

He had it all worked out; had obviously been thinking about it since the attack, possibly before. He was willing to lie, and hide that wound that would develop into a scar on his forearm. For me.

A rush of emotion clogged my throat. "Thank you, Peter. I forgot to thank you last night. I can never repay you—"

He shook his head. "I shouldn't have left you in the first place. It was thoughtless of me, and I'm only glad nothing worse happened." The growing sunlight painted more colors on the world. "There was another matter, one that must be reviewed while we're still alone. It's about those men." He scratched the back of his head. "Are you sure you didn't recognize them? I know it was dark, but was there nothing familiar about them? Nothing that stuck out, nothing that might give us a clue to their identity?"

I thought back. "One of the men had scars on his face." My face pinched as I tried to recall every detail. "And they said they were hired —by a gentleman."

Peter's boots scraped as he turned. "Really? . . . Do you think they were telling the truth?"

"Yes, I do."

"Then can you think of any gentlemen who would wish you harm?"

My mouth ran dry.

Of course, there was my half-brother.

But he couldn't know I was here—not again, and not so quickly. Or did he see me at the fair? Had he tracked me down from there? Even if he had, to attempt kidnapping? It seemed extreme, even for him.

And even if it wasn't, I'd have to explain my connection to Thomas Markley to Peter, and that was a conversation I could not have. Those men had been after Mary, I was sure of it. They must be connected to her somehow.

"No," I said at last. Peter's brows drew together, concerned and skeptical. I cleared my throat. "There's no one."

Peter sighed. "Then it might be difficult tracing those men back to someone. I'll relate the details to Mr. Minton. He has enough connections that he might be able to glean some additional clues."

"Can you trust Mr. Minton to be discreet?" I asked, worried about the possibility of Mary's debts.

"Of course. He's been loyal to my family for three decades and has gotten us out of many a tight spot. I'll see if he can do anything, and will keep you informed of any updates."

I exhaled in relief. "Thank you."

We stared at each other for a lengthy time, unsure of what came next. And again, something in the air palpably shifted. Maybe it was the way he rubbed his fingers together with one of his hands, or the way eyes strayed to a lock of my hair that had come undone.

I swallowed. "Well, if that is all you—"

"Yes, that was all." He looked away.

"Then good, I am glad we—"

"Yes, so am I. No, there was nothing more."

I turned and walked back across the rooftop, opened the hatch, and disappeared.

PETER HAD BEEN RIGHT. A MYRIAD OF QUESTIONS KEPT US COMPANY at breakfast—each one more grueling than the last—but we managed to get through it with relative ease. Now, most of us sat outside, sweating in the humid afternoon.

Unlike at dawn, the day was stiflingly hot, each of us clinging to the shade of various trees. Servants mingled about the small party, serving appetizers and drinks. A quiet breeze ruffled the blades of grass and brought relief to the perspiring throng. I sat at Eliza's side underneath a great oak. Quincy was there too, and Sir William Bentley—but I did my best to ignore him.

Just looking at him made me nervous.

"I was quite surprised to find you at Ambleside, Miss Raynsford," said William. He lay on his side with an elbow propped up beneath him, one hand plucking the grass. "Last I knew, you were heading to Paris for the summer. What caused your plans to change?"

Biting the inside of my cheek, I folded my hands in my lap. "It was my aunt who insisted I come. She is very good friends with the Wycliffe's."

"As am I," he countered. "Which is why I find it perplexing you would not have told me. I am your dearest friend, after all. Excepting Eugenia, of course." His eye contact held steady.

My smile grew tight. "Of course."

"And when last I talked with her, she mentioned nothing of Ambleside. Quite odd indeed—for surely you told her, as you tell her *everything*."

I wet my lips. "Of course."

"And as you know, she can never keep a secret." He blinked innocently. "You do *know* she can't keep a secret, do you not?"

I frowned at him for a long moment, gritting my teeth.

"Indeed, I even asked after you. I said, 'Dear Eugenia, where is Mary going to spend the summer?' And on my word, she replied, 'Why Paris, of course!' and that was the end of it." He relaxed onto his back, doubling his hands under his head and propping a knee up. "Strange, is it not?"

"Strange indeed!" I said, seizing the opportunity. "You must've talked to her before my plans had changed. And I think, Sir William, you judge a person harshly. For how is anyone to know if someone cannot keep a secret, excepting the owner of the secret? Though someone may divulge some things, they might keep others hidden, and you would be none the wiser."

From his reclined position William turned his head, intrigued.

"Perhaps I have thousands of secrets I have told Eugenia, and from among them she has only told you ten. And you, not knowing any better, have branded her a gossip! You should be ashamed."

His dark brows dropped, mouth parting. "I beg your pardon. I see the truth of it, and I humbly apologize." The look on his face was anything but apologetic. Still, I exhaled with a smidgeon of relief.

But really, I should've known better.

He sat up. "How disappointed you must be to have studied French for so long, only to be thwarted in visiting the country. Your French had really gotten quite good."

The air went out of my lungs. *French?*

"You flatter me sir," I stammered. "I do not consider myself skilled in the language."

"Ah, but you do know the basics! I am quite proficient myself." He laughed mockingly. "But of course, you already knew that."

My tongue felt like lead. "Yes—"

"C'est une très belle langue, n'est-ce pas?"

"Indeed," agreed Quincy, obviously versed in French.

I was really sweating now—and not just from the heat. I snatched my dormant fan from the grass before me, snapping it open and waving it rapidly.

William leaned forward. "Pourquoi ne répondez-vous pas? Êtes-vous nerveuse?"

Eliza linked her arm in mine. "How you tease her, William," she said. "Of course she is nervous—and I can see is embarrassed too."

"Yes!" I said, stealing the excuse. "I have never spoken the language in front of so many people—"

"Such modesty!" he cried. "And from one who participated in the French poetry reading last summer at Lady Iris's tea party. You did not seem so embarrassed then." His brows met, his lips pouted, his hand twirled circles in the air as his devilish innocence continued to pervade the conversation. "I can't quite wrap my mind around it—these sudden changes in you. It's almost as if . . . as if you're a completely different person." A hint of a smirk touched his lips.

My nervousness converted into annoyance and resolve. I took a big breath, touching my hand to my collarbone. "Oh, how could I forget Lady Iris's tea party! Yes, I was mortified. All those people, those faces —I could barely stumble through the verses. I was so embarrassed, in fact, that I haven't studied French since! That is why I am rather unpolished now, I'm afraid."

While Eliza and Quincy voiced their sympathies for my horrible experience, I held William's gaze. At last, he sat back—no longer aggressive, but far from defeated.

From across the lawn came a fit of laughter, the undertones of Lady Wycliffe and one of the servants, and a hand shake from some chess players. Even in the shade, the humidity continued to swarm.

"What a lovely day for croquet," Quincy leaned over to me and said. "How I love a good lawn game! Don't you?"

"Yes! Croquet!" cried Eliza, jumping up. "William, wouldn't you like to play?"

He looked to me, a smile playing upon his lips. "I should play if Mary does."

"Oh Mary, you shall play, won't you?"

The eagerness in Eliza's face stopped me from refusing. "I suppose." I stood and eyed William. "If Sir William promises to let me win."

A grin split his face. "Always."

Eliza sent one of the servants into the manor for equipment, and in a matter of minutes the game was assembled.

"Choose your color, madam." William held out four mallets. Lifting my chin, I selected the red one. He took the green mallet for himself, Eliza chose the yellow, and Quincy was left with the blue. Armed with our mallets, we lined up at the first stake and Eliza took her turn.

Quincy was just about to go when Peter and Miss Caldwell strolled up arm in arm, returning from wherever it was they'd been. A surge of disapproval washed over me at the sight of them. I twirled my mallet in my hand, refusing to focus on the contradiction they were.

"There you are, Quincy," said Miss Caldwell. Quincy straightened from his hunched position, obviously flattered with her attention. "You are from Kent, are you not?"

"Born and raised," he nodded with a bright grin.

"I am not familiar with the families in that area. We were drafting up invitations to our ball in three weeks, you see. Peter's been away in London, so he's not very familiar with them either. So I was wondering —that is, if it is not too much trouble—"

"Say no more, Miss Caldwell, I am at your disposal." Quincy bowed with a flourish.

"What a relief! I should hate anyone to think we neglected them."

My twirling stopped. Miss Caldwell had been helping draft the guest list, something reserved for the woman of the house. *We*, she had said. And in such a casual way! My eyes whipped to Peter, but he was looking off in the distance, as if this significant conversation were anything but significant.

By all appearances they were attached. If Peter wanted to continue to pretend they weren't, he should be concerned at Miss Caldwell's bold insinuations. Yet he stood there. Indifferent.

Let him start a scandal. What did it matter to me?

I fanned myself with my spare hand, the heat of the afternoon getting to me. "If Quincy leaves we shall only have three players. Perhaps we should save croquet for a milder day."

"Peter could take his place," Eliza suggested.

"Yes, Peter, you should," Miss Caldwell said. "It is only fair since I've spoiled it all."

He came out of his thoughts to offer, "Of course."

"Perfect!" Eliza brightened. "It is your turn now."

Quincy handed Peter the blue mallet then escorted Miss Caldwell across the lawn, discussing the invitations. Several family names floated back to my ears before they were too far away to hear. The couple disappeared into the mansion.

There was a prodding on my back—William nudging me with his mallet. "Your turn."

I looked back to find that Peter had already taken his. "Sorry." I approached the starting stake and positioned my ball.

Behind me, William muttered, "You need to keep your head in this game, *Mary*, if you intend to win it," his double-meaning anything but subtle.

I hit my ball with brutal force, sending it well beyond Eliza. "I shall win, sir," I said, gazing after my ball. "Not because I have your promise of surrender, but because I am fully capable." And I flounced away.

"I do love croquet," Eliza sighed when I joined her. "There is something about it that equals the playing field between the sexes." She sent a longing look behind me toward William.

"And provides ample opportunity to catch a husband?"

"Mary! That is not at all what I meant." Her cheeks colored as she subtly glanced toward William again, confirming what I already suspected.

William had apparently been a friend of the Wycliffe's for years, so likely her interest stemmed from a childhood wish. Eliza was barely fifteen. I wondered if I should warn her he was not a very generous character before she grew too attached.

Now that I thought about it, it was odd William and Peter didn't know each other better. Although William was warm around Eliza and Lady Wycliffe, he treated Peter with aloof civility—as if they were new acquaintances.

William's ball landed a few paces ahead of me. When Eliza took her turn, she passed us all again, leaving the three of us behind. Peter decided to aim for my ball.

"I shall get even if you hit my ball," I said in warning. "You know I can."

He laughed. "Yes, and the prospect is frightening." He bopped his ball, sending it rolling into mine with a *chink*. "But well worth it, I'm afraid."

I exclaimed in mock annoyance as Peter swung his mallet in victory. "Sir William was closer! Why did you not aim for him?"

"Because he is not nearly as entertaining to tease." Peter flashed me a cheeky grin, ready to swing again.

"Well, *Miss Smith*," William said. "Your prospects of winning aren't so bright now, are they?"

My lips parted.

In my peripheral, I saw Peter's smile slip and his body freeze. He raised his head. "Miss . . . Smith?"

William sauntered away, the fox content with the harm he had caused. He thought no one knew about my other name—thought I would have to devise an explanation as to why he had called me it. Well, William had done damage, but not in the way he had anticipated.

Peter's eyes flitted from the back of William's head, to me, a question in them. "Miss Smith," he said again, in a way that almost sounded wounded. He'd thought Julia was someone just the two of us shared; a joke I had conjured that was unique to him. I swallowed, wishing there was a way to explain it away.

But at the same time, why would he care so much? What concern of it was his if someone else knew my other name? A name that in actuality wasn't even mine? It's not as if I expected him to not have any secrets with Miss Caldwell. And hang what he told me. He was going to *marry* her by all appearances.

I took an awkward step towards him. "Peter, it is not what—"

"You don't have to explain." He recovered quickly with an understanding smile, but it seemed forced. "You cannot keep Julia in hiding forever."

Peter turned back to the game and hit my ball away. But when he looked up, his eyes narrowed, scrutinizing William with a new, intense interest.

I hit my ball again in frustration. It whizzed past Eliza, coming to land only a few paces from the muddy banks of the river. William happened to be near, aiming for the next wicket. I sidled up next to him with my freshly assembled wits, placing the hammer side of my mallet on the grass and leaning on it.

"What, pray tell, would compel you to address me so, sir? I hardly know anyone by the name of 'Smith.'"

Without warning, William switched his mallet to the other side of his ball and whacked it into mine. Then he also leaned on his mallet, mirroring me. "Oh? Have you forgotten all about your closest and most trusted friend, Eugenia Smith?" He tsked, sighing. "You are forgetting quite a few significant things these days, Miss Raynsford. One might wonder why . . ."

I clamped my mouth shut. William had the overwhelming advantage. He knew everything about me—or, who I was supposed to be—whereas I knew next to nothing about him. At least nothing to use as leverage.

I distorted my expression into one of regret. "Have you not heard? Before I left to come here, we had a long conversation where I quarreled with Eugenia—oh, I can scarcely bear to say her name!" Cupping my forehead and then my mouth, I pretended to be overcome with emotion. I took a moment to compose myself for extra measure, then sighed, longingly. "Though once there was never a secret between us, I daresay it's true that I hardly know who she has become."

William's eyebrow rose along with one corner of his mouth, amusement brimming. In my peripheral Eliza and Peter approached. They had taken their turns, their balls lying a mere few feet away.

"And what could cause so great a divide between you?"

I grabbed the first logical thought. "A suitor."

Too late, I realized that Peter and Eliza were within earshot now, listening. William's gaze flickered to Peter for the slightest moment. "A suitor! Who could it be? Surely you would not keep us in suspense."

"It is such a highly improper thing to speak of—"

"Come now, my dear. We are all good friends. Do you not trust us with your secrets?"

I glared at William, sending him a message that said, *I would sooner trust a wolf with a herd of sheep.*

Exactly how close was he to Mary, anyway? How much did he know about her? About her personal affairs? There was no telling.

My thoughts darted to all the possibilities. If I imagined up a fictional name, William would see through it and call me out on it. I couldn't say the name of an actual gentleman, on the likelihood of his being acquainted with William. Or Peter, for that matter.

Everywhere my mind turned, it saw a trap. I was neatly snared. He probably knew all about Mary's various suitors; those she was interested in, those she had rejected. The only person he might not know Mary's thoughts on was . . .

"Well? Who was it? Who did you quarrel over?" William smiled in thinly-veiled satisfaction, and he turned to nudge Peter. "We are all dying to know, aren't we, Wycliffe?"

Peter regarded me vacantly for several heartbeats. "By all means," he murmured. "Enlighten us."

Trapped, trapped, trapped.

I schooled my features and turned to William. "Why, it was *you.*"

The silence that followed was rife with tension and discomfort. Five whole seconds—that's how long I was able to withstand Peter's burning stare. I gave in and glanced at him, seeing his eyes sparking . . . angrily? He looked down and away, jaw working. Though I had escaped the trap, I had far from won.

William's laugh rang out. "Forgive me, I should not have pushed you had I known!" He bent down to my ear, his voice suggestive and low so the others couldn't hear. "And had I known you felt so about me, I would have treated you differently."

My face burned—even more on such a warm day. I smothered the sneeze before it had a chance to surface. William stayed near several moments more, murmuring, "Perhaps I shall, going forward . . ." before pulling away and sauntering off with his mallet. Apparently, the game was over.

"Mary, I do think you had the right idea earlier about saving croquet for a pleasanter day," Eliza said, face tight. "It is much too warm out here. I think I shall retire." She turned and left, leaving Peter and I alone in an uncomfortable silence.

Unable to bear his continued staring any longer, I picked up my mallet and ball. As I passed him I said, "I do not care to hear your disapproval, or your questions. Just know that it was all a lie."

I wasn't sure why I added on that last bit. Perhaps because the confused resentment on his face had sickened me further than I cared to admit. Because it was what I imagined his expression would be, if he ever discovered my identity. I never wanted to see it there again.

After stashing the pieces in the canvas bag, I turned to see that Peter had followed. There was usually something lurking in the glint of his eye or the corner of his lips, but he stood before me as stone-faced as a statue.

"What place is it of mine to question you? To voice my disapproval?"

The words stung. If it was anyone's place, it was his. This was his house, I was his guest; but more than that, he was my closest friend.

"What claim upon you do I have?" he added quietly, sounding like he was asking himself more than me. "I would not rebuke you for the way you would treat me. But if it was all a lie like you claim, then have a care, Mary. Have you no regard for Eliza's feelings?"

My heart skipped a beat.

Eliza. She, who was moonstruck for William, who had confided her interest in him to me only a moment ago. I had not considered the implications my lie would have on her. Surely she detested me now. The thought gutted me.

What a heartless, thoughtless, bumbling fool I was! "I will apologize. It was tactless of me, and I am sorry."

He was still exasperatingly unreadable, but he emanated disappointment—a fact that made me desire even more to make it right.

"What hold has he over you?" Peter asked, head knocking the direction William had gone. "Enough to bring out such a competitive nature—where you disregard others for yourself?"

I gripped my arm behind my back, unwilling to answer. Ashamed that Peter felt the need to reproach me.

"Tell me something. What did he whisper to you?"

I bit the inside of my cheek. Peter was too shrewd for his own good. There was no way I was going to repeat what William had uttered. "That he and I should remain friends." My voice caught slightly on the invention.

Peter took a moment to absorb the information, then cocked his head. "Really? That is not what his eyes said. Quite the opposite, in fact." He looked my face up and down, the crook of his mouth lifting sadly. "I can tell when you're lying, Mary."

I clenched my teeth, disliking this disdainfully-amused expression even more than his unaffected one. Disliking this conversation and the entire afternoon. Blast my wit—it was only digging my grave deeper, transparent to the people I tried hardest to deceive.

I can tell when you're lying.

CHAPTER 15

Eliza stood on a carved bridge overlooking the scintillating river.

As I neared, I chewed my bottom lip, feeding on my despicableness. I stopped next to her. Fish gamboled near the reeds at the bank, splashing playfully in the last hour before dusk.

". . . Eliza?" No response. "I came to tell you I am sorry."

She tossed pea-sized pebbles into the stream, staring at the ripples they created. By her blank expression, I would've thought she hadn't heard me. The song of nightjars filled the air with a gentle thrum. I leaned my forearms on the bridge, waiting to be acknowledged.

"William is a fine catch," she said at last. "You are the perfect couple—and you are so much prettier than I, it is no wonder he should prefer your company."

I shook my head.

"No, it is true. I don't blame you. I don't feel betrayed, or even hurt, really. I only don't understand. I thought you and Peter . . ." She exhaled and bent over the water.

"Oh, Eliza. I came to say how truly sorry I am, and to try to explain. You see, I lied."

She glanced at me.

"I didn't really quarrel with my friend, and I most certainly didn't quarrel over William. I only said I did because—well, because we were just playing a silly game," I finished in a small voice.

"A game?"

"Yes."

Eliza's expression brightened slowly, until it was beaming. I linked my arm through hers and led her down the bridge. The late light of day streamed through nearby trees, creating patterns on the grass.

"And," I went on, "you are decidedly prettier than I. Ask anyone and they should tell you." Eliza blushed and laughed as we strolled along the river's edge.

After a few minutes of silence, I licked my lips and jumped in again before I lost the nerve. "Speaking of William, do you not think he is a bit . . . demanding?"

Her face scrunched. "How do you mean?"

"I mean do you not find him arrogant?"

"Oh no, not in the least!" Eliza scooped up a rock and tossed it into the river. "Though I can understand why others might find him so."

I eclipsed her, determined to help her see the truth. "But it's been some time since you were close, has it not? It wouldn't be surprising if he has changed."

"William? Oh, never!" She picked up another rock and fingered it. "He has been the same since we were children."

I wondered if I should proceed, and if so, how to go about it. I didn't want to hurt her feelings again.

Eliza did a double take at my expression and stopped short. "Why? Do you have reason to believe he is not honorable?"

I took her hand in a sisterly move. "I would only warn you to be wary—for I do not wish to see you hurt. That is all."

She smiled. "There is no need. I know William in a very different way than you do." She looked around—though she needn't have bothered. We were entirely alone. "I'm not sure I should tell you this, but I am going to, if only to help you understand."

I waited, my curiosity awakened.

"Peter and William were childhood friends," she began. "Since our mothers were close, William would often come and stay the summer here, and he and Peter would go on adventures or play pranks together —often on me. When they grew to be around Matthew's age, Peter went to Eton and William went to Harrow. Gradually, they grew distant—even more so when they enrolled in different universities.

"When my father died, it was so very hard on Peter. He stayed away in London as a way to cope with his grief. My mother was also crushed. She needed consolation, reassurance—but most of all, a man to depend on. She has always been like that."

My brow furrowed. I had lost a father, and it was horrible enough. What must it feel like to lose a husband—the other half of one's soul?

"William did not attend the funeral," she went on, "but he visited a few weeks after. With my father dead, Peter gone, and my mother in an overwhelming amount of grief, things were in a ruinous state.

"Then, without having to be asked, William stepped in where Peter should have. He managed the estate and visited the tenants. He embraced my mother with tenderness and care, lending his shoulder for her to cry on." Eliza glanced up at me, tears suddenly brimming in her eyes. "He took away the burden of trying to make everyone else whole, getting me to laugh again when I never thought I would."

Speechless, I scrutinized Eliza, trying to imagine her hopeless. It must've been incredibly hard for her, too. She must've tried to do everything herself, all while comforting her mother and trying to be strong for a littler Matthew.

And Peter had abandoned them?

As if Eliza read my thoughts, she said, "You mustn't blame Peter, though. When he wrote us letters, inquiring after things, Mother forced me to say everything was fine. As far as he knew, the estate was thriving. Had he known the truth, he would've moved heaven and earth to get back to us."

"Still," I said, a little anger surfacing, "you can agree it was inexcusable for him to leave in the first place."

Eliza hesitated, and sighed. "Perhaps. But who am I to know how he felt? And what I would have done in his place? As the eldest son, the one expected to carry the title, the legacy, and all the importance that goes with it? Peter never wanted that life. And yet, it has always been the only one open to him."

Her beseeching hand found my arm. "You must understand. There is something extraordinarily special about Peter, in that when he loves someone, it is with a depth that very few of us can fathom. The loss of my father was more devastating to him than it was to anyone else— even my mother. There were times when I thought it was his soul that had broken, more than his heart, and none of us knew how to help him heal."

The thought of Peter, broken, unsettled me, niggling at me in a way I didn't care to acknowledge.

Her hand gave my arm a squeeze. "While he was coming to terms with the loss, William was here, picking up our shattered pieces. So while I know you think him conniving, there is much more to William than you know. Beneath all of that teasing, is someone who truly cares for our family. Who truly cares for *me*."

I studied Eliza in a new light, seeing for the first time how strong she was, how her family would've fallen apart without her. How, just like the rest of us, all she wanted was to be loved. I embraced her.

She was the daughter of a Peer, and I a servant out of necessity. Our dreams and hopes and futures were worlds apart—and yet, I felt permanently tied to her through the deaths of our fathers.

As soon as we broke the embrace, we left the water's edge and wandered back to the manor, our hearts feeling quite full.

Since William Bentley had arrived on the scene, the seating order for dinner had been rearranged. I was now to Peter's left at the head of the table.

I planned on apologizing to Peter as well, not sure if I'd been forgiven yet. But, either Eliza had apprised him of our reconciliation or he had completely forgotten my offense, because when we sat at the table, he was pleasant and amiable once more.

William sat across from me but one place down, and I dreaded the thought of speaking to him again. As Mary Raynsford, I had declared affection toward him. He was undoubtedly planning to give me grief about it, so I ignored him, as well as Miss Caldwell who studied me from the other side of the table.

My appetite had soured with the game of croquet earlier, and as I stared at the boiled vegetables atop my plate, I discovered it still hadn't returned.

I stabbed one of my boiled carrots and pushed it to the top of my plate. Another carrot almost identical to the first slushed its way up to its companion, forming the eyes. Corralling the peas with my spoon, I arranged them underneath the carrots, referencing Sir William as I did so. They trooped into a crooked line, their extra companions making up the eyebrows.

Now the nose. I surveyed the available vegetables on my plate, finally selecting a small radish. The rosy color would go well with his complexion, I thought. With the radish in place, my masterpiece was complete. I leaned back in my chair, studying my design with approval.

The face staring back at me resembled the satisfied look he had worn during the croquet game. In fact, the likeness was astonishing, given that it'd been fashioned from vegetables.

I snickered silently. Out of habit I looked to Peter, wanting to show him my creation, but I didn't have to. Peter's eyes were already fastened to my plate, his head tilted, mesmerized. He must've watched me as I had formed it.

He raised his gaze, a knowing smile creeping across his lips as he fluctuated between me, and William, and my plate. Smile widening, he looked down and added another hushed chuckle to tonight's collection.

Quincy, who sat to my left, happened to look over as well. He barked out a laugh.

It was unfortunate timing, as the guests were currently conversing Betty's cousin, and how she had recently fallen into poverty. Mouths dropping, the people around the table quieted.

Quincy cleared his throat. "I beg your pardon . . ."

Peter and I struggled to contain our laughter while Quincy bumbled through a handful of explanations.

And so there we were, heads forever facing our laps and shoulders shaking as if an earthquake were taking place underneath our chairs.

Then the conversation changed to one I was unprepared for.

". . . are all invited to go to Newington, tomorrow," Lady Wycliffe said at the far end of the table. "He was quite insistent, Sir Thomas Markley. How he must long for your company, Clarissa."

My napkin that I had been clutching under the table tumbled to the floor. I lifted my paling face.

"Indeed," Miss Caldwell said. "My brother-in-law is eager to meet all of you, and he is not to be dissuaded, you know. Olivia always loved that about him."

I tuned out, mind reeling. *Her brother-in-law? Thomas?*

But of course, now that I thought on it, Thomas had married a Miss Olivia Caldwell. Why hadn't I made the connection before? In a twisted way, that would make Clarissa and I sisters. But why were we all invited to go to Newington, a much smaller estate? And only a day after I had been attacked? A panicked feeling clawed its way up my throat.

It is him. He knows.

No he doesn't, Lily, my sensible half reasoned. *It is as Lady Wycliffe has said. He is related to Miss Caldwell, and that is his only reason for the invitation.* I swallowed the lump in my throat, determined to stay calm.

Peter's voice broke my contemplation. "I wonder if Sir Markley knows what a large party we are hosting. I shouldn't like to inconvenience the man."

Miss Caldwell waved her fork in the air. "Of course he does. I daresay he is quite anxious to meet you. And every time Mama writes, she begs for your company, as she hasn't had it in months! She's been ill lately, but she is sure to be there, at Newington. Oh please, Peter." Her lips turned down into a pretty pout.

"Of course," he said after a slight hesitation. "I shan't disappoint your mother. We shall all go."

The blood drained from my face. I looked about the table, hoping for someone to denounce the idea, but everyone either nodded in agreement or expressed their excitement. My eyes snagged on William, who watched me in suspicion. His eyebrow quirked.

I jerked my head away, keeping my gaze on my lap as I had done minutes before—only this time, for a completely different reason. I pinched and twisted my dress under the table

"What of Sir Markley's sisters?" asked Mr. Cunningham. "Shall they be in attendance?"

I sunk into my chair, wanting to slide out of my seat and crawl away.

Miss Caldwell scoffed, annoyed that the addled old man was so behind in hearing the rumors. "Of course not. They were disinherited years ago."

"On my word, I heard the most scandalous news the other day," said Miss Betty Hartford, dabbing a napkin on her lips, "about the little Markley girl. Though it would seem she is not so little anymore."

I stiffened. *The little Markley girl.* My head swam with an onslaught of memories, dreading what the next words spoken would be. I'd assumed that by coming here, I would escape . . . well, myself. Escape the endless lies tied to my name. It appeared no matter how far I ran, my reputation always caught up with me.

Other branches of conversation quieted, everyone more interested in this new scrap of gossip.

Eliza leaned over her plate. "The Markley girl? The elder one?"

"No, the younger," said Betty, "for the information I heard came from the lips of Mrs. Wilshire. 'But of what great importance is that?' you might ask. I tell you it is of the *greatest* importance—for Mrs. Wilshire has had the Markley girl under her employ for the past *eight* years."

Exclamations of shock resounded around the dinner table. The servants entered, burdened with platters of stuffed tomatoes and roast fowl. Dazedly, I watched as the plate bearing William's face was switched out.

"Eight years!" Lady Agatha cried out after a moment, scowling. "To shelter someone with such disgraceful character—and for such a long period of time. Why, Mrs. Wilshire must have taken leave of her senses!" Murmurs of agreement rippled through the group.

"Oh, but that is the best part," said Betty, bringing her voice down. Everyone joined Eliza in leaning over their plates. "As it turns out, she had been *unaware* of the girls' identity, and so had been treating her like a daughter!"

All gasped in astonishment.

"How could Mrs. Wilshire have loved someone so shameless?"

"Surely she had not been unaware?"

"Miss Lily was using a different name, not her real one."

"Still, I would have spotted the girl a mile away!"

This was the first rumor I'd heard about me that had an ounce of accuracy in it. But the tale reopened old wounds, ripping my heart like it was a letter containing dangerous secrets. Overcome with the desire to sob, I closed my eyes, aching more than ever for my sister.

A warm hand rested on mine under the table. I looked over and saw Peter, his touch bold and reassuring. "You dropped your napkin," he said softly, passing it to me. When had he picked it up?

"That is the least of her scandals, I'm afraid," said Miss Caldwell. "The girl can't help but cause grief to her family."

"What other scandals?" someone inquired.

"It started with her sister. She pursued some reprehensible activities, and because the sisters were so inseparable, it ruined the younger by default. Even more regrettably, it didn't stop there. The younger Miss Markley began to gain a reputation for herself, following in her elder sister's footsteps. And when the elder ran away, Miss Lily trailed her."

"What reprehensible activities?" Sir George asked.

"All sorts. Thieving and gambling to name a few. And, shall we say, others of a less . . . *delicate* nature. There was one particular incident involving her cousin."

My face burned; my chin quivered as a single, hot tear escaped down my cheek.

"Oh my!"

"Disgraceful girl!"

"Poor Sir Markley!"

"Certainly you cannot believe these rumors to be true, Miss Caldwell."

Everyone hushed. It was William who had spoken, and a quick glance told me he was in earnest. To others he might've appeared amused or indifferent by his careless posture, but there was steel behind his hazel eyes.

"Why, Sir William, of course I do. I know Thomas Markley intimately. Surely he would not lie about this." Her eyebrows dropped into a glare. "Just as surely as you now snub him for these misfortunes."

"I do not snub him." William's tone was light as he played with fork, twirling it around in one hand. "I merely question his motives for perpetuating these *unfortunate* reports. What has he to gain by it but a tarnished reputation himself?"

"Upon my word, how can you say that?" Miss Caldwell looked

about the table, soliciting support. "What other reason could he have had for disinheriting them?"

"I cannot know, but does a man need a reason to do anything?"

Eliza intervened. "That is just such the thinking of men—and why we women shall never understand the other sex."

There were a few light chuckles, but Miss Caldwell plowed on, oblivious to Eliza's attempt for peace. "A sensible man has a motive for every one of his actions—and I know Sir Markley to be such a man."

William set his fork down. "What sort of *sensible* man would turn away his own flesh and blood in a scandal? Is that not the opposite of sense?" His tone tipped into heated, and several at the table shifted in their seats. "They must have been only children at the time."

"The elder was sixteen. That is not quite a child, I should think—and quite old enough for the rumors to be true."

"Yes, but the younger would have been no more than eleven." Gone was William's amused façade, his face contorting angrily. "A little girl, likely too grief-ridden to be capable of eating, let alone malevolence. Tell me what unforgivable crime such a child could commit. One so atrocious her own brother should scorn her?"

A lengthy, awkward pause settled in the room.

I studied William, noting how he saw through Thomas's lies where no one else could. Perhaps Eliza had been right. Perhaps there was more to William than I knew.

Miss Caldwell chuckled nervously. "Good heavens, Sir William. I did not know you to be a man of such passion. Come, Peter, will you not support me in this matter?"

Silence.

Peter and Miss Caldwell held each other's gaze. But then, in the smallest moment, his eyes flicked to me. I saw him swallow.

"I daresay I agree with Bentley," he said at last. "It appears cruel and undeserved."

She took it in stride. "Well, I do not know the reasoning of my brother-in-law, but I do know he is justified. Pray, let us all call a truce!"

Her cheeks dimpled. "Let us talk of the impending visit. What fun we shall all have! I happen to know that Newington boasts of endless rows of raspberry bushes."

The conversation continued with the best recipes for raspberries, Peter arguing that the first raspberries of the season were the most delicious. I had no taste for raspberries, nor the lavish iced oranges with chocolate cream the servants brought in for dessert.

Somehow, I survived until the end of the meal, at which moment I excused myself from the joining the others in the drawing room due to a small headache. Instead of fleeing to my chambers, I strolled onto the stone terrace, feeling hot and in need of fresh air. Wrapping my arms about me, I leaned on the balustrade, heaving a weary sigh, grateful for the peaceful moment to contemplate my predicament.

What was I to do? I couldn't very well go to Newington. And what if someone had seen my reaction and suspected something? There had been that funny look from William . . . and then he had defended me so animatedly . . .

I knew the exact moment Peter stood behind me.

"Eliza told me of your apology," he said. "I wanted to thank you. It means the world to her."

I smiled, grateful for the reprieve from my weighty thoughts.

There was a pause. Then, "I take it you won't be going with us tomorrow?"

No, I wouldn't. I would simply have to fake another headache—which wouldn't be too hard since I had already planted the seed that I was unwell. Instead I asked, "What makes you say that?"

"You were less than enthusiastic about going, to put it mildly. And it is so very easy for women to pretend to be ill. They hardly have to be anywhere they do not wish to be."

Oh, dash it all. He'd been paying more attention to me than I'd thought.

". . . At dinner, for example."

"How churlish of you, Peter." I circled about to face him. "We females cannot help that we are more prone to illness."

He leaned against the frame of the double white French doors leading into the house. "Or more prone to pretending," he said with a sardonic smile. I turned back around and he joined me. "Are you going to tell me the reason you looked so shaken?"

"It was my headache, of course."

"I meant the real reason."

"Then no, I'm not."

He let the matter drop, the quiet resuming. The fresh smell of river, grass, and spices permeated the air. A symphony of chirping crickets and frogs accompanied the glorious, gilt sunset. I gazed into the hastening dusk, taking comfort in the thought that Jennie might be staring at the same spot at this very moment. I heaved a weary sigh, looking out at the world where somewhere, very far away, she was waiting for me. A deep emotion flared up from within, and suddenly I was totally exhausted of my charade.

"Do you ever tire of having to pretend?" The wistful words escaped on a sigh. I knew the question left me defenseless in so many ways, but all at once I wanted—no, *needed*—to be me for a few minutes. To be Lillian.

Peter shifted beside me. "Pretend?"

"Yes." Snapping out of my daze, I said sarcastically, "Don't tell me you've never had to pretend to like someone. Being a viscount, you must associate with dozens of people you wish you didn't have to. Me, for instance."

Peter laughed lightly. "What? I have never pretended to hide my loathing for you."

I cracked a grin.

Peter gradually sobered, then said, "I do know what you mean, though. I know all about gluing a smile to your face and pretending to be friends with someone, when you really want to be far less than that." A pause. Then Peter glanced me over and looked out in the distance, his jaw ticking once. "Or far more."

My insides did a flip. The boyishness in his face fled under the setting sun, the light casting Peter's face regal and older. Shadows lurked in his dark hair, his blue eyes morphed into a glittering gold, taking on a sharpness that had never existed before. It transformed him from that endearing boy into a powerful man, a fire unleashed in his gaze.

Unsettled, I turned away. Soon the sun would drift below the horizon and leave me in the dark with this . . . stranger. I needed to leave.

"What are you pretending, Lily?"

I froze. Sucked in a breath. "What did you call me?" Had I heard him wrong?

Peter looked at me, brows sloping together. "Mary."

What was wrong with me? I was letting my guard down, taking pointless risks, wishing like a fool that I could just once hear my name on his lips, and now I was hearing things? I needed to focus, to stop letting futile wishes get the better of me. Peter didn't appear suspicious, though, or even confused. In fact, I didn't know at all what his expression was.

"So what is it?" he asked again, softly. "What are you tired of pretending?"

I flung the absurd thoughts from my mind, concentrating instead on how to answer Peter without giving anything away. I dug deep inside, searching for the right words. "I am tired of pretending I am strong." The statement left me naked, bare—but I continued, relieved at sharing some of the cumbersome truth. "I tell myself I am, but who am I fooling? I am tired of trying to show the world that it cannot touch me. That I do not care. Because if there were ever something I know so profoundly, it's that I do."

I stared awkwardly at my hands, wondering what Peter would make of my revelation. Would he laugh at me? Tease me?

His hand shifted until it rested atop mine on the stone balustrade, warm and reassuring. "Look at me."

I did, and his breath tousled the top of my hair.

"I may not know what it is you're talking about, but if there is one thing *I* know, it's that you're the strongest person I've ever met. If you ever need someone to lean on . . . to confide in . . . I am here."

Peter's words struck a chord in my memory. *"There, there, Lily . . ."*

Peter was offering to do what my father had always done. To be a comfort, a balm for my soul. My throat suddenly thick, I managed a nod. He inhaled as if he wanted to say something more; but then he sighed and offered me part of a smile instead.

But I could see those questions, still sparking and burning—Peter dousing them just enough so that they never escaped past his lips.

"Why, Peter?" I whispered, unable to help myself. "I must seem quite a contradiction at times—and I can see your confusion. It rages behind your eyes. You struggle to keep the questions inside, so why do you never ask them?"

A thick silence ensued.

I turned my face away, wishing I hadn't been so honest and open. I had just invited him to ask me my deepest secrets. What was wrong with me?

Maybe I did want to get caught. Maybe I was so exhausted between juggling William and Peter and Mary and my developing feelings that I—subconsciously—thought it would be easier to be done with the lot of it. And maybe I thought . . . if anyone was going to expose me, I would prefer it to be Peter.

His eyebrows furrowed. "Come," he said at last, extending his arm.

I took it hesitantly. "Why do you not ask them?" I repeated, needing to know.

He pulled me toward the house. "Perhaps I am not as interested in your affairs as you are in mine."

"And are you going to tell me why you're skirting the question?"

"Because it grows cold, and you are without your wrap."

I halted. "I meant the real reason."

One corner of his mouth lifted. "Then no. I'm not."

I pursed my lips, disinclined to smile. Peter led me across the terrace and inside. When we reached the entryway, he paused and slanted his head toward the doorway of the drawing room.

"Will you be joining us?"

"Mm, I think not." I extracted my arm from his grasp. "I fear my fake headache is worsening."

"How dreadful." He clucked his tongue. "I do hope you recover by morning, or you shall have to forgo travelling to Newington with the rest of us."

"Indeed," I said, face sulking. "And I was so looking forward to it!"

CHAPTER 16

FINALLY, THE HOUSE WAS SILENT.

I'd sequestered myself away until half past noon, pleading an illness just as Peter suspected I would. Now, I put one finger up to the glass of my bedroom window, tracing the dots of carriages as they thundered away toward Newington.

"Oh, Lily," I whispered, smiling to myself. "Though it is only one half-day, you are free." I laughed and fled from the window, seizing my shawl on the way out. Lady Wycliffe emerged from the parlor, halting me in my mad dash down the stairs.

"Ah, Miss Raynsford!" she said. "I was informed you were unwell, and was on my way to visit you."

"Oh. Yes, I was just about to ask the cook for some tea."

"How strange." Her hand rested on the marble bannister. "You look quite well . . ."

"I have just this very moment felt recovered enough to come down." I descended the rest of the steps between us. "Though I don't think I could have borne the trip to Newington. I should have been exhausted by the time we arrived."

"Yes indeed." She took in the large, vacant room, her countenance sobering. "I was about to ring for tea myself. Perhaps you would like to join me? I find I don't relish solitude as some do."

I studied Lady Wycliffe closely and somehow knew she was talking of her late husband. "I'd love to." We proceeded into the parlor where Lady Wycliffe rang a dainty bell.

"So Miss Raynsford, how are you finding your stay?" she asked once we had settled in. "Is your room to your liking?"

"Very much, ma'am."

"I'm glad to hear it. You must forgive me for not being a more attentive hostess. My health is not what it used to be."

A maid entered carrying a tray topped with a light blue porcelain tea set. After setting it down, she left and then reappeared with another tray, this one filled with scones, biscuits, and jams. She closed the doors behind her. Lady Wycliffe poured the tea, asking me if I liked cream or sugar. She tapped the spoon on the ridge of her cup, filling the silence with soft *chinks*.

After several quiet minutes passed, I noticed an extra place set. Its tea sat there, steaming up in wispy shapes. Lady Wycliffe didn't seem to think anything of it.

Is she expecting someone else?

The double doors behind me opened and Lady Wycliffe sat back, smiling. "There you are, William."

I peeked over my shoulder, hoping against hope it wasn't the William I thought it was. Fate was especially cruel today, for steadily walking toward us while shrugging off his black great-coat, was Sir William Bentley.

"You are late," Lady Wycliffe said, giving him an admonishing look. He neared, then bent and kissed her on the cheek. His mud-splattered pantaloons and hessian boots left a perfume of grass and fresh air in their wake.

"So sorry, Aunt Rebecca. I ran into some unavoidable business in town and peeled myself away the moment I was able."

She smiled up at him lovingly. "I grew tired of waiting for you, so I solicited Miss Raynsford for company."

William spun around and gave me a once over. "Why Miss Raynsford," he said, coming to my side and kissing my hand, "you are as radiant as ever."

A blush crept up my neck and I extricated my hand from his. "What sort of business kept you, sir? Hopefully nothing too troubling. What a shame it would be if your pressing affairs cut your visit short." I batted my lashes.

"A shame indeed." He brushed past me and flapped his coattails back before sitting. "I shall spare you the boring details of managing my investments. But I think you would agree, Miss Raynsford, that my business here is much, *much* more important."

I wrung my unseen hands in my lap, struggling to remain confident in Sir William's presence.

"So Miss Raynsford." William inclined his head and took a sip of his tea. "How is your aunt?"

"Yes, how is dear Phoebe?" inquired Lady Wycliffe.

I cleared my throat. "In my last letter, she chastised me for my spending habits. I think she should be very proud to learn I have not spent anything since coming to Ambleside. As for her health, she is very well, ma'am."

"Oh?" William lifted his chin. "Has she taken a turn for the better recently? She was not well the last time I saw her."

". . . You've seen her? Well. Then it must've been some time ago—"

"On the contrary, it's not been two weeks." William smiled wickedly. "Surely you have not seen her more recently than that. And you've not had a letter from her. How could you know she is doing better?" His face was innocent for Lady Wycliffe's benefit, but the fox was just underneath the surface.

My civil smile stayed glued to my face with the knowledge that William was checking my correspondence. Perhaps not him personally, but he wasn't teasing when he said he had connections. I would have to be more careful.

"How do you know she has not written me? Did she tell you so, or are you bribing the postman?" There was a barb inside my tinkling laugh. "No, no of course not. That would be absurd."

Not the least bit fazed, William said, "Indeed, quite absurd. Yet, you have just admitted she has not—which begs me to ask again, how do you know she is better?"

My jaw clenched before my expression warped into a sad one. "Truthfully, I do not. But she swings between being well and ill so often, you see. I am filled with endless joy at her recovery, only to be brokenhearted when she takes a turn—and it happens dozens of times in the course of a year!"

My cup clinked as I set it on its saucer and back on the table. "No. My physician informed me that my emotions cannot continue under such a strain. I have determined to look on the bright side until the very worst happens. That is all I can do, and that is why I said that she is well." I put my hand atop William's, resting on the table. "Forgive me if I seemed uncaring. It is only that sometimes, ignorance is for the best."

William stared at our hands, before his gaze slid up. His lips twitched. "Your physician must be very attentive. And you are so young! By all appearances vibrant and healthy. I should be honored to know a man so dedicated to his profession. Pray, what is his name?"

I faltered, withdrawing my hand. "His name?"

"Yes, his name. For I know every doctor in London, and I should like to thank him for so diligently looking after my friend." To Lady Wycliffe, he sounded like a caring friend, but a jeer was all my ears heard.

I swallowed, even as I cast William a withering stare. "Why, he is the same one that attends to my aunt," I tried.

"Ah, yes." William's face crinkled. "Though I cannot recall his name. Now what was it? I shall remember when I hear it. Mister . . .?" He looked at me expectantly, knowing very well the name—but if I blundered and said the wrong one, he meant to ensnare me. And I couldn't pretend as if I'd forgotten it—for I had just declared that I knew him quite well.

"Mister . . .?" William repeated.

"Perry," finished Lady Wycliffe, and I nearly heaved a sigh in relief. "John Perry. I remember Phoebe mentioning him on several occasions. And I have heard from numerous sources that he is the best physician in England."

"Yes, John Perry," William said at last, but he watched me with half-lidded eyes, letting me know how lucky I had been.

Lady Wycliffe crunched on a biscuit then turned to me. "So Miss Raynsford, you are acquainted with Miss Julia Smith? Though I try, I cannot seem to remember who she is. Tell me, who are her relations?"

Taking a big breath, I turned to William, spotting a rare opportunity to flip the tables. "To be honest I have not met her family, but Sir William knows Miss Smith—perhaps *he* could tell you about them."

"Do you know them, William?" Lady Wycliffe asked.

He thumbed his bottom lip. "Hmm. I know of two Miss Smith's. One is Mary's dear friend Eugenia, but whether the other one is Julia remains to be seen."

Lady Wycliffe frowned. "There. That is just the sort of cryptic answer I always receive regarding her. Isn't there anything you can tell me?"

"Yes!" I said. "Tell us your opinion of her, sir."

He leaned forward in his chair tapping his fingertips together. "My opinion . . . Well, I am still forming my opinion. But this I can tell you —she is no ordinary girl."

"And what is she like?" asked Lady Wycliffe. "Has she a sweet temperament?"

He looked at me, smugly, for far too long. "In a naïve sort of way."

"I think she's a sweet girl," I piped up. "She might not be as confident as some, but she is quiet. She has a good heart. And she desires only the opportunity to go about her business undisturbed and unthreatened."

"Indeed," said William. "In a naïve sort of way."

Lady Wycliffe set down her cup and saucer with a quiet clank. "Perhaps I have never met her—though Peter insists that I have. In fact, he seems to be so preoccupied with the woman that I cannot help but worry."

William's gaze slinked over to mine. I didn't know how much he knew about Peter's engagement to Miss Caldwell, but judging by how well he knew the family, he knew enough. Did Lady Wycliffe think I was trying to sabotage the union? Did William?

She sighed. "Ah, well. Now if you'll forgive me, I suddenly find I am quite tired. Will you excuse an old woman?" She stood gracefully, and William stood with her.

"*Old*, ma'am?" He flashed her a grin. "Why, it was not so long ago I thought you and Eliza sisters!"

Lady Wycliffe laughed in her throat. "Oh William, you are too good to me." Then with one hand, she cupped his face in a gesture that couldn't be described as anything but motherly. "Never change, William. Never change." She tapped his cheek twice before leaving.

What Eliza had told me must be true—at least to some extent. Lady Wycliffe's eyes glowed at William nearly as much as they did at Peter.

We were alone now, and I was uncomfortable at the thought. I stood, ready to follow Lady Wycliffe out of the room.

William spun around. "Miss Raynsford, I wonder if I could beg for your company this afternoon."

"Me?" I wanted to hide.

"Yes. Since I know how fond you are of nature, I thought a picnic might suit."

He was mocking me. Or the real Mary. Or both. "How I'd love that. But I think my headache is resurfacing—"

"Oh, but you must." He extended his hand. "I insist."

Definitely both.

"You do realize we are alone?" I crossed my arms. "You need not pretend to be so gallant."

His lips twitched. "I haven't pretended that bit."

"Nevertheless, I can be quite candid when I say this: I do not wish to go." I glanced again at his outstretched hand, then put my hands on my hips. "And since there is no one to pretend in front of, you have no means of coercing me into saying yes."

"True," he conceded. "But you must be curious . . ." He extended his hand even more with a slight bow, smile slowly spreading. After a heavy hesitation, I took it.

As much as I hated the fact, he was right. I was curious about this side to him—the side that had defended me at dinner. And what else was I to do while everyone was away? I could read, or embroider, or explore—or perhaps I could analyze my biggest enemy, find his weakness, and determine how to exploit it.

Once William led me out of the room, I fetched my bonnet and parasol. When I came down again he was already waiting, his topper under one arm and a large basket in the other.

"Should we not have a chaperone?" I asked, suddenly quite nervous.

"Come now, Miss Raynsford. We are the oldest and dearest of friends after all."

"Mary might know you, but I know you very little, sir. Frankly, I do not trust Mary's judgement, and what I have seen so far of your character is not encouraging."

"Surely you trust Lady Wycliffe? Or Eliza? I believe they would give me impeccable reviews . . ."

Hm.

Since they both trusted him, I suppose I could for a few hours. Still, I kept a wary eye on William as I descended the stairs and we left the mansion.

Instead of calling for a carriage, William guided me in the opposite direction toward the river. The walk took a few minutes and neither of us talked. A simple dory nodded on the river, and William stopped before it.

"All aboard." He set the basket down and gestured flamboyantly to the little boat, waiting for me to get in.

I nudged the boat with the toe of my boot. "You cannot be serious."

"Why would I not be? I went to great trouble to secure this dory, Miss Smith, and I will not be put off simply because you are afraid of a little adventure."

"Eliza is the adventurer, not I." I tossed my parasol into the dinghy.

"Here." He hopped in. "I shall even assist you, if you wish."

"How gentlemanly of you," I answered wryly.

He offered his hand again, but as I bent to take it, he grasped my waist and hoisted me inside, setting me down in front of him. And then wouldn't let go.

"Sir William!" I cried, trying to remove his hands without toppling into the river. He chuckled and the boat rocked from my struggle. And then we both lost our balance: William, catching himself on the rower's seat—I, sprawling backward and landing in an inelegant way on the hull. Water sloshed in on the sides, wetting my shoes. I huffed as his laugh rang out.

"You see, Miss Smith? Already we are having such fun!"

I scrambled up into the seat opposite his, face flushed. "I have a mind to push you overboard!"

"I would only pull you down with me." He smirked. "Returning to Ambleside unraveled and wet is something you would rather avoid, yes?"

I didn't merit that comment a response. He retrieved the basket and oars, untied the anchor line from a nearby post, and shoved off.

Oh, why did I agree to this? I asked myself as he began to row upstream. *I'd almost rather be at Newington.* I snatched my dampened parasol from the bottom of the boat and opened it, determined to hold my head high. We inched past Ambleside.

"If I recall correctly, there is a quaint little pond upstream. I used to play there as a child, you know."

"Back when you and Peter were friends?"

His eyes lazily flicked to me. "What makes you think we are not friends now?"

We glided underneath the bridge Eliza and I had conversed on, blocking the sun's heat for a few moments. "Perhaps it is the way you shoot daggers at each other when you think no one else is looking," I said.

"My, aren't we observant? I did not think you noticed me that much. Oh, I like Peter well enough, and I think he feels the same way about me—it is only that we have a matter on which we disagree."

"Which is?"

He stopped rowing for just a moment and cocked his head. "Croquet."

What an odd thing to say.

William looked behind him, upstream. "Ah." He took up the oars again. "We are nearly there."

I leaned out the side, watching the water widen into a large pond. Plump cattail stems decorated the edges and several ducks swam through the glossy water. Willow trees dappled most of it, their fronds leaving trails in the water whenever the wind blew. William steered the dory beneath one of these sheltered parts of the pond.

Instead of docking, he heaved the oars in and started pulling parcels of bread, chicken pudding, potato and apple pie, and lavender cheesecake out of the basket and setting them on the hull.

"What are you doing?" I asked, snapping my parasol shut.

"Setting up our picnic."

"In the boat?"

"Of course in the boat. And how lucky you are that I invited you, Miss Smith. How many people can say they've had a picnic on a pond?"

I looked all around me, wondering if there was anyone else hearing this nonsense. William continued unloading, unconcerned with my reluctance. At last finished, he dished me up a slice of pie and handed it to me.

I glanced at my plate and then at him.

"Well, go on then." When I didn't start eating, he chuckled and added, "Where is your sense of adventure? Indeed, and I thought the pond was a rather romantic idea."

I nearly dropped my plate. "What need have we for romance, sir?"

"None, I suppose."

How William befuddled me. Peter didn't always say what was on his mind, but I never questioned his sincerity or his motives when we talked. But whenever William said something, it felt as if he really meant something else. As if he was hiding some dark part of him that he never let anyone except me glimpse.

I stabbed the pie with my fork, took a much-too-large bite, and chewed with big motions, letting William know that I was only doing it for his benefit. He laughed and portioned out some food for himself.

I swallowed and gazed out across the glistening pond, watching four adorable ducklings as they followed their mother. The one in the rear lagged behind, giving out a little quack. The family reached the bank, waddled ashore, and disappeared behind the fronds of a willow tree.

I reeled my focus in, only just noticing a niggling thought at the edge of my mind. I set my plate on the hull. "You must be very pleased with yourself, Sir William," I said, "to have managed an outing such as this. You obviously planned it—but what confounds me is, how?"

"How?" He finished his last bite and returned his empty dishes to the basket.

"Yes. It was not made known that I was feeling ill until just before eleven. You could not have managed this feast between then and now, which means you must've requested it early this morning." I leaned forward, forehead creasing. "But then you wouldn't have known that I would be staying, so how?"

William laughed. "Wouldn't you like to know? I told you I have connections."

"No one has those kinds of connections—the ability to summon a feast like this in a matter of hours. You must tell me how on earth you managed it."

He reclined back on his arms. "I managed it because I started the arrangements last night."

"Last night! You would not have known to."

"Ah, but I did. For I knew you would not go to Newington." He reached out of the boat, plucking a white waterlily from among the lily pads nearby.

"*How?*"

"Honestly, for being so clever, you can be rather slow at times." He twisted the flower around lovingly and then brought it up to his nose, still twirling it under his unbreakable stare.

What is he implying? Why is he so smug? And why won't he stop fingering that silly flower and tell me what he . . .

My eyes magnetized to the lily, and I stopped cold.

William's smirk broadened. "Yes, that's right. I know all about you, *Lillian.*" The flower fluttered in the breeze. William pinched it tighter and examined its delicate petals while he continued.

"Disinherited and ran away at ten. Your sister got a job as a scullery maid under Mr. Melbourne, but they couldn't afford to keep you, so her friend found you a job under Mrs. Wilshire. Through long years of hard work and devotion, you worked your way up to lady in waiting— only to be tossed out just like your brother had done eight years before. Somewhere in the midst of it all, you managed to cause no less than nine scandals, among which were the nasty things listed last night. And after all that, you embroiled yourself in Mary's scheme." Finally William looked at me and his voice grew quiet, sultry. "The infamous Lillian Markley. Alone with me."

I swallowed, debating whether to be more impressed or frightened.

I forced myself to laugh. "That is not so remarkable sir. Anyone could find that information if they cared to look."

"But no one ever does, do they? No one cares about the little Markley girls." He sat forward. "Though you are right. It is not extraordinary because it is only half the story. The other half I have yet to discover. The why of it."

"The why?"

"Yes. Why you agreed to play Mary in the first place. For money?" He studied me closer. "Of course it was for money, but for what? A pretty thing? Accrued debts? To get back in good graces with your brother? I have yet to decide." He backed away, regarding me from the corner of his eye. A hefty pause. Then, slowly, "You realize a deception like this could land you in prison."

I gripped the sides of the boat tightly. "I knew well the implications when I took this on."

"Yes, I knew you would—which means you're desperate." He leaned in, this time much closer, blocking my vision, murmuring, "What is it that you want?"

I held immaculately still, afraid he would see the truth if I moved. I dared not tell him about America, about Jennie. If I clung to that morsel of secret, I still held some control. Of course he already knew enough to do whatever damage he wanted, but if William knew the whole of it, there was no telling what more he could do. What he *would* do.

After a long silence, he laughed and retreated. "Still playing the game, then? Very well. I shall simply have to learn it on my own."

"You flatter me with your attention, sir," I said, desperate for a change in subject. "I was a servant for a long time, as you have discovered. I am not used to such inspection. For years, no one spared me a second glance."

"Except for Wycliffe." He picked up the oars, moving us out onto sunlit water. "He has spared you quite a few . . ."

No more was said on the subject, but the air which had been merely uncomfortable before, was now stiff and taut.

William turned away and the sun caught his dark golden hair. I studied his profile, struck again by how attractive he was. Even with his languid posture, he possessed a noble air about him—a frustrating aura that magnetized my gaze. That was something Peter had, too.

His coloring was very different than Peter's, though, the more I thought about it, the more alike they seemed to be. Both were mischievous and superbly handsome, both liked to play games, and both smiled at me a great deal too much.

The only big difference between them was in the way they executed those things. Where William knew he was handsome, Peter never used his looks to his advantage. Where William threatened, Peter only poked fun. And where William laughed at me, Peter laughed *with* me.

Still, William was a fine-looking man. Even if he knew it.

"Tell me something about yourself," William said, shattering my thoughts like a rock thrown on an ice pond. "Something you've never told anyone else."

He lolled back in the dory, drinking in the sunny haze as he waited for my answer. I stared at him, unsure whether to trust this new, earnest William, or the rascally fox I knew him to be.

While I know that you think him conniving, there is much more to William than you know.

Eliza's words rang in the back of my mind. Maybe there *was* more to him than sarcastic remarks and sideways glances.

"I like rain," I said at last, avoiding a topic too soul-searching.

His brows popped up. "Rain."

"Yes, rain."

William was obviously waiting for me to explain, so I took a big breath and plowed on.

"There's something comforting in the thought that even the heavens need to grieve. That even they are overwhelmed at times. For if that is so, it must not just be an earthly thing—grieving, longing, growing." The tension-filled space between us relaxed, William's gaze taking on a dreaming quality.

"Just think of what would happen if it didn't rain," I went on. "The grass would die, trees would shrivel up, and we would soon find ourselves living in a much uglier place. I think I find comfort in it because it is what makes us human. If we refuse to cry, or mourn, or *feel*, then before too long, our souls would dry up. They would wither away and leave in their place a wide emptiness that cannot be filled. We would become not just broken, but ugly. And then we wouldn't be able to feel anything at all."

William was quiet, barely breathing or blinking. I was surprised at myself too, at the thoughts that had tumbled out on a wistful tongue. Knees pulling together, I looked away and added, "That's why I like rain."

In my haste to avoid thought-provoking matters, I had discovered a zeal I didn't know existed, and had essentially given him a sermon in the process. I cleared my throat. "Now it's your turn." I smoothed a lock of walnut hair that kept twisting free whenever the wind picked up, tucking it behind my ear.

His eyes tracked the movement then broke away. "To tell you something?"

"Yes. Something you've never told anyone." I was unsure if I wanted to know something intimate about William—but it was an opportunity to learn something I could use to my advantage. There was a small silence.

"I find life boring," he muttered.

I blinked, unprepared for the confession.

William's hand reached out the side of the boat, tracing circles on the ponds' surface. "It lacks purpose. There is only money and connections and everlasting ladders to climb. You are introduced to someone important, which gets you higher social status, which lets you marry into money and gain a reputation. Then you're introduced to someone more important which leads to more money and more standing and it's the same thing over and over—" he slammed the water with his fist, sending up a tall splash, "—and *over* again." His face crumpled as he stared into the rippling water.

He seemed so . . . sincere. I hadn't expected him to dive headfirst into his most plaguing insecurities, and it tugged my heart in a surprising way. Maybe it was because of what Eliza had said, or maybe because of the way he had defended me at dinner.

Finally, he looked up and searched my face. "Is there nothing else to be had in this world?"

"Of course." I thought of the little happy moments that had started to seep back into life after my father died. "If you have the courage to find it."

It was something William had to discover for himself. One corner of his mouth lifted, and for the first time since being in his presence, I didn't feel threatened by him. In fact, I detected truce being called— perhaps even a friendship budding.

It was strange, how one moment he was dangling a carrot in front of me and then . . .

His face relaxed, eyes darting down the length of my face for the slightest instant. "I wonder . . ."

He leaned in, and my heartrate spiked. "I wonder," he murmured, his breath tousling that defiant lock of hair that had escaped again, "if I might have my hand back?"

My head shot down to see I was indeed holding his hand. I dropped it as if it were on fire, wondering how on earth I had come to be holding it. My face burned. I snapped my parasol open, averse to acknowledging . . . *whatever* it was that had just happened. The boat rocked as in my peripheral, William picked up the oars and steered us back the way we came.

Now what? I thought. Should I embrace this precarious friendship, one that might have happened on its own had we not both been wrapped up in Mary's scheme?

I sensed something new in William. Perhaps not a kindred spirit, but someone who was . . . lost, in his own way. And if there was one thing I had experienced, it was being lost; inside, I was still that ten year old girl, wandering about, unable to find my home.

"You remind me of my sister, you know," he said, bringing me out of my musings.

"I didn't know you have a sister."

"Had," he corrected as we left the pond behind. "She died when I was thirteen."

My eyebrows knitted together. "I'm sorry."

"She was older than I, but just too young to be coming out at the time. I remember how full of life she was." He chuckled, shook his head, and then stalled his rowing. "I remember her saying she liked the rain. Saying something very similar to what you just told me."

My lips parted. So that explained his confession. Why he had suddenly opened up.

"It is mostly your determined spirit that reminds me of her." A reluctant smile stole across his lips. "She too, refused to lose—though all odds were stacked against her."

Begrudgingly, I smiled back, embarrassed, but somehow flattered too.

Since we were going downstream on our return, it was much easier to cover the distance. William hardly had to row as we floated down the river, and when we reached our makeshift dock, he leapt out of the dory and sloshed up the bank, towing it ashore.

I stood and took a wobbly step. William grasped my hand and led me to the helm. Once there, I found his hands around my waist again, lifting me up and setting me down on the grass, lingering for just a bit too long.

"Thank you," I whispered a little breathlessly.

"I wonder," he said. He let the words hang in the air. ". . . I wonder if I've already found what I've been looking for . . ."

I glanced up at him, weighing his words. But his eyes glazed over—

a mask that kept me from deciphering him completely. He proffered his arm, which I took, and as we headed back into the mansion and toward more pretending, I rallied my courage one last time. "Does this mean you won't torment me anymore?"

"About what?"

"My name. About how I'm an imposter."

Halting midstride, he turned and laughed. "Now where would be the fun in that?"

CHAPTER 17

THE NEXT DAY I RECEIVED A NOTE.

It was an odd little thing, only a small slip of paper with a confounding riddle neatly penciled on its surface. There was no address and no signature—and I would've presumed it to be intended for someone else, had I not found it just inside my door. It read:

> *My first is a sphere through which all things behold.*
> *My second is that of which poet obsesses,*
> *And is given to champions both valiant and bold.*
> *My third is a woman of curly white tresses.*
> *And fourth is a floret, whose heart is of gold,*
> *Whose beauty in depths, no other possesses*

KATHERINE, THE HOPELESS ROMANTIC SHE WAS, DEEMED IT TO BE A love note from a secret admirer. A *handsome* secret admirer, she said, for what other kinds of secret admirers were there?

I was more skeptical. My first thought was that it was from Matthew, but after thinking on it, decided he was much too forthcoming. Rather than mysteriously leave a riddle under my door, he would simply tell it to me on one of our reading days.

My next guess was Peter. It could be him trying to get ahead in our game. But then why wouldn't he have given it to me in person? And why this morning, when we hadn't even spoken yesterday? It seemed unlikely.

My other suspicions were Eliza and William. Eliza had such a—not exactly mischievous—but playful spirit, and William was the one holding the noose around my neck. He no doubt wanted to tighten it a little.

After an hour of fruitlessly trying to unearth the riddle's meaning with Katherine, I put it away in my vanity's drawer next to my father's pocket watch, deciding it could wait for a rainier day.

"But miss!" Katherine protested. "He'll likely be waiting for a response!"

"*He*," I said, scooting into the chair opposite the mirror so she could arrange my hair, "could very well be a woman. Besides, timely responses are not the nature of riddles. I think whoever sent this wouldn't mind waiting a week or so."

"A week!" She moaned. "What agony you put him through."

"Or she," I added.

"He'll be an emotional wreck. He's probably already done his share of waiting—only now has he worked up the courage to give it to you."

I laughed. "Or *she*."

With a wide comb, Katherine started gently working through my tangled curls. "Though I'm not at all surprised at something like this. You are quite lovely, miss, if I do say so."

I swallowed the compliment as best I could. "Thank you."

"All the other maids turn green whenever I tell them how the young master dotes on you."

My head snapped up.

"He's never been so attentive to any lady before," she went on. "I am practically a lady's maid to the next mistress of the house! How jealous my friend Isabelle is!"

My blood ran cold, and I thought I was going to be sick. If people were beginning to talk, I had let mine and Peter's friendship go too far. My departure was only a fortnight away. Two weeks, and I would trade Peter for my sister. It was a sacrifice I always knew I'd have to make, but had been reluctant to acknowledge it.

Mary Raynsford might be able to marry Peter. But I couldn't.

"Do not say such things, Katherine." In a smaller voice, I added, "It will never come to that."

It was time I faced the truth. It was time I sever my ties before things got too out of hand. Before I broke his heart too severely. And mine.

I bit the inside of my cheek, chagrined. "You think Lord Wycliffe sent the note?"

She looked at me in the mirror, suddenly timid. "All I know is what his valet says—Mr. Tillman. When Master Peter comes in to change into his evening clothes. Mr. Tillman always asks the young master what he did that day. Some days he's been with his mother, or Miss Caldwell—but Mr. Tillman says he can always tell when Master Peter has spent the afternoon with you, because when he has, he can't for the life of him stop smiling."

Oh, this was bad. This was so very, very bad—worse than I feared. I had let romantic ideas—fickle, girlish dreams—sweep me away from my one and only goal: To come here, to leave, and to move on in my life with Jennie.

Though, I had never considered that I might not . . . *want* to move on . . .

No!

I would see this through. I owed my sister everything—for taking me under her wing, for giving me footprints to follow in and loving me unconditionally when no one else did. The reasons were endless.

There was nothing to decide. I would avoid Peter in the future. I would do all I could to spare his feelings. And if he confronted me about it, I would deny . . . What? Our friendship? Every good memory we've shared together? My heart?

Yes, I answered myself, dreading such an event. *I will deny it all. I must.*

But this firm resolution didn't make me feel any better. In fact, I felt nauseated. Peter didn't deserve this, any of it. I'd been so selfish, thinking mine were the only sentiments being laid on the chopping block. I shouldn't have been so careless. I should've come with a locked heart and a mismatched key.

I'm sorry, I told him, knowing he would never actually hear the words. *I'm so, so sorry.*

Katherine's compliment swam around in my mind. I studied my reflection with curled lips as she retrieved pins from the nightstand. "What a fickle thing beauty is. How much simpler things would be if we were all born beautiful."

"But, miss." Katherine's face scrunched. "If we were every one of us beautiful, then none of us would be."

"On the contrary . . ."

Thoughts of Thomas, whose silky words and becoming face could charm throngs of women but sour instantly upon seeing me, sprung to mind. And Jennie, who, according to the servants at Newington would "never be as handsome" as I, yet whose heart overflowed with charity and goodness. And me. I studied myself once more, seeing my cowardice, my cynicism, my pride, my utter disregard for people's feelings.

"That is when the real beauties would shine," I murmured. "I wonder how attractive I would be then."

"Stuff and nonsense, miss." Katherine tugged my hair up and pinned it in spotty places. "I'm sure whoever sent you that note thinks you're the most beautiful creature in the world—inside and out. And he obviously wants you to know it."

A weak smile twitched my lips. "Or she."

Avoiding Peter was proving to be harder than I'd anticipated.

It wasn't as simple as keeping company with other people—it was not looking at him when someone said something clever, or when someone said something ridiculous, or when someone said anything at all. I hadn't realized how much I looked at him.

Or him at me.

I sensed when his eyes shifted, studying, lingering. They would move away, occupied by one of the other guests, only to flick back, caressing my heating cheeks, my downcast eyes. All through dinner his gaze singed the side of my face, until I couldn't stand it any longer and I finally risked one little peek.

He was waiting for me, brows slightly furrowed, liveliness and concern fighting for dominance in his features. He offered me a smile and nodded down to his plate.

I glanced at it, and then wished I hadn't.

He had taken my little dinner-plate trick to new heights, using tonight's selection of vegetables to fashion a despondent face. Though they were only vegetables, I could tell that its face was meant to be mine. That he was teasing me.

My heart tugged when I saw how much time it must've taken him, and how he was attempting to cheer me up. And how I couldn't let it.

When I looked back up, he was aglow with expectancy. A pit cut in my stomach. I made myself turn away, vacant, and then I never looked back, too troubled by the prospect of what I might find if I did.

His staring got worse after that.

You can do this, Lily, I strengthened myself as the servants carried away the last of the nougat almond cake we had for dessert. I'd deliberated throughout dinner whether or not I should beg another headache

—but judging by how well my "headache" had gone over last time, I might as well trudge through the rest of the evening. Besides, Peter would see through it anyway, and then a confrontation about it would be unavoidable.

The men settled in to talk business and drink port while Lady Wycliffe stood, cueing the rest of us ladies to follow her to the drawing room.

I had an hour to regroup my forces before going back to battle. I breathed a sigh, falling down onto the drawing room sofa, unsure how long I could keep up the charade with how high-strung my nerves felt. This was proving to be problematic.

I chased the thoughts away, rubbing my temples in an attempt to ease some tension. The women tittered, gossiped, and played cards, scraps of their conversations drifting to my ears. I retained none of it, though, and the majority of the hour passed in a blur.

"You've been reserved all night," Eliza said, plunking down beside me. "How about a nice round of whist?"

I grimaced. "I'm in no mood for cards."

"Then why don't we play a different game? I know how fond of them you and Peter are."

The groan was out of my mouth before I could stop it. Eliza meant well, but this wasn't helping at all.

Her cheery countenance sobered. "Whatever is the matter?" There was a hefty pause. "Is it about Peter?"

"No. At least—not necessarily." Any moment now I was going to chew through my lip. Perhaps there was a way to explain my predicament without revealing too much. "Oh Eliza, I don't know what to do. I plan to travel extensively after my stay here, but I cannot bring myself to tell Peter. He obviously hopes for something I cannot give him, for I don't foresee myself returning to Ambleside anytime soon. What am I to do? Tell me what I should do."

Her eyebrows furrowed. "There's not much I can say that isn't biased. I will say this, though." Her face grew grave. "If you are not going to return, you should sever all ties. To remain friends would torture him."

As I thought. It was better this way—it had to be. I sighed again, and said in a small voice, "I do care for him."

"Has he made his feelings known to you?"

I shook my head.

But then, I thought of that moment outside my chambers right after William had arrived, or when we were walking back from town before I had been attacked. I tucked in my chin. "That is, I suppose I've never given him the chance. But that might not matter—after all, are not he and Miss Caldwell secretly attached?"

"Not technically." As soon as she said it, Eliza gasped. Her hand flew to her mouth, eyes going wide.

"Why 'not technically'?" I pressed, sensing some answers at last. "Why would he say they're not engaged, but let her act as if they are?"

This was good. If they were engaged, it would be so much easier to break away from him—it would justify my actions, give me an excuse he would believe. It would prove to my foolish heart how utterly impossible everything was.

Eliza gnawed on her bottom lip, debating something, then gave in. "You must promise not to tell any others. It is not exactly a secret, but it is what allows Peter a choice in the matter."

A choice?

Eliza took a big breath. "It was Father's deepest wish that Peter marry into the Caldwells. They were astonishingly rich, and Father had great influence over them, but they were also old friends of his. So how could the match be unsuitable?

"Peter didn't mind in the least. Clarissa was pretty and sweet and he adored her completely—and he would do anything to please my father, so it was settled. Or, so we had thought."

Eliza glanced around, ensuring we didn't have eavesdroppers, voice dipping lower. "Father grew ill suddenly and died, making Peter a viscount. The day after the funeral, the Caldwell's came to cash in

Father's promises. They wanted a wedding, and they wanted it within the month, forgoing the mourning period. But Clarissa had changed in the years since we had last seen her. She had become demanding and spiteful, and saw only the title when she looked at Peter.

"Naturally, Peter was hesitant. We were all deep in mourning, after all. But their pressuring led to bullying, and eventually threats to bring in the authorities. I couldn't stand seeing my brother in such turmoil any longer. I asked Mr. Minton for the certificate that sealed the agreement. To our surprise, a document was never signed, and without written agreement, nothing was official.

"The Caldwell's could not force the marriage. So they changed tactics, trying to win Peter over with pretty smiles, preying upon his love for my father by reminding him of how much he had wanted the match. Peter didn't know what to do. He was confused and hurting for my father. So he left. Went away to London. And he stayed away for a long time."

There was a heavy pause, and then Eliza let out an even heavier sigh. "Clarissa went after him, and I was told later that they continued their acquaintance over the course of the Season. At first, I assumed Peter had made up his mind to marry her. But I saw how things were for myself last summer. Peter was still in turmoil, but couldn't bear the thought of calling things off—because even with all their scheming, the Caldwell's had been right. Father had wanted the match. Peter was doing his best to honor that."

My mouth hung open. "But still," I said, "to let her pretend they are engaged? If she flouts it to the world, the rumors could force him into it—whether he wants it or not."

Eliza shrugged sadly. "I'm sure he knows that, but I think he feels he has no other choice. Either he lets her do it, or he must call it off and insult my father's memory—and he can't do that." Eliza paused. "Though I would be lying if I said he hasn't been thinking about it of late." A look passed between us.

I grimaced again. I had thought this would help, Eliza telling me the history between Peter and Miss Caldwell, but it wasn't. It was only making me pity his situation more, just before I was about to make it worse. Like me, he was also trapped. And unlike me, his trap was not of his own making.

The doors opened and I jumped up, watching the men file through the doorway. My heartbeat pounded in my ears. I wasn't ready yet.

But Peter didn't come near. He sauntered toward the card table in the opposite corner and leaned against the wall. He kept his distance—something that seemed calculated, if the way he stared at me was any indication.

I turned away and bumped straight into William. "Easy there," he said, his hands finding my waist and steadying me, "we wouldn't want to cause a scandal. Though I suppose you are used to those by now, aren't you?"

Conscious of Eliza who was overhearing our exchange, I removed his hands. "Yes, Aunt Phoebe has been quite the handful for our family, so I'm told. It is fortunate she was born wealthy, or society would never have forgiven her so readily." Eliza chuckled as William steered me back to the sofa and sat between us.

"How cruel toward your aunt, you are," he said. "I wonder that you are really related . . ."

Eliza nudged him and laughed again. "Oh, but they are not, according to Matthew. He claims there were discrepancies between Phoebe's description and Mary's real appearance. When Mary first arrived, he wouldn't stop talking about it—going on and on about how suspicious it all was."

"Is that so?" William's head sluggishly swiveled back to me, revealing a face that said, *Now I've got you.* I gulped.

Eliza tilted her head in thought, scanning me with a thoughtful stare. "Come to think of it, he hasn't mentioned it to me in over a month. Hm. He must've changed his mind."

"Why, I wonder?" William said, relishing my squirming. "Especially when they are all valid points? Explain to me, Mary, why these incongruities occurred."

My lips pressed into a line. "As I have told the Wycliffe's, Phoebe's memory isn't what it used to be. She thought me to be a young, green-eyed girl with blonde hair. But as you can see, that is not so."

"Interesting." His eyebrow cocked. "Though as I recall, last Season you did have green eyes."

"You must be mistaken—"

"On the contrary, I remember because Mr. Hayman wrote you those verses declaring his love for you—and two whole stanzas devoted to your sage eyes. It caused quite a stir, as I recall. What, do you not remember?"

Eliza's eyes peeped over William's shoulder, face in a question. I stood, the higher ground making me feel cleverer. "Yes, I do remember, now that you mention it."

He grinned. "How convenient."

"But my eyes have always been temperamental. They change with the season, the lighting, what I'm wearing—"

"They are decidedly blue right now."

"—so as you can see—"

"Like an early spring sky."

"—you shouldn't put much stock in what Aunt Phoebe thinks she remembers. Or Mr. Hayman's poetry. For all you know, he could be blind."

"Now of that, I can assure you, he is not." William stood, too. "Or he would not have spouted your beauty from the rooftops."

Face heating, I met his stare, unable to control the itch to say it. "He did not spout of *Miss Smith's* beauty though, did he?"

"Perhaps he would have," he murmured, leaning in so no one else could hear, "if he saw her as I do."

I felt a fire in my chest, eyes blazing away and catching on Peter on the opposite wall. He was still watching steadily.

Eliza let out a forced laugh. "You two befuddle me. I shall go find a game of cards. And Mary?" She stood and straightened her skirts, pointedly avoiding my face. "If you find you have any more questions . . . about what we were talking about earlier . . . I shall be happy to answer them." She walked away, joining Quincy who was reading in the corner.

For what felt like the hundredth time that day, I mentally kicked myself. Driving away one friend just wasn't enough for me, apparently.

"What were you talking about earlier?" William retrieved a deck of cards from a nearby table and shuffled it in his hands. Something about the move seemed deliberate. Almost threatening.

"About Miss Caldwell."

His shuffling stopped. "So you finally know the truth, do you? Engaged but not engaged. A messy situation indeed."

It didn't surprise me to learn William knew the whole of everything. He was close to the family. But even if he weren't, he seemed like someone who would've unearthed it on his own, whether by his own shrewdness, or because it amused him.

"Lady Wycliffe is set on her son marrying into their family," William went on. "To honor her late husband's wish."

"And what is your opinion, sir?"

With two fingers, William held up a card and stared at it thoughtfully. The queen of hearts. "For myself, I couldn't care less who Peter marries. But if Lady Wycliffe wishes it, I will do everything I can to see it done. Everything." He slipped the card back into the stack. "She is dearer to me than my own mother. And Eliza . . ."

He never finished, making me wonder what he'd stopped himself from revealing.

Instead I asked, "Did you mean what you said yesterday? About me reminding you of your sister?" For unfathomable reasons, I needed to know he had been sincere—that there was some part of him that was good. Because if there was, then he didn't truly intend to expose me.

He set the deck aside. "Of course," he said lightly.

I put a hand on his arm, forcing him to look into my eyes. "I mean really."

For a glimmer of a moment, a raw emotion overtook his features. "I meant everything I said yesterday. Everything." He paused. "And many things I didn't." Before I could decipher what those things were, he turned away and followed after Eliza.

Alone now, I sank onto the sofa, mulling over the interaction. I lost myself in my thoughts before involuntarily, I glanced at Peter. He was still watching.

As sure as I was sitting there, I wasn't going to initiate anything. *Just stay over there,* I told him. *Stay there, and all will be well.* I turned my attention to a clock above the mantle. 8:50. Just ten more minutes until it would be acceptable to retire. Just ten more.

Still, anything could happen in that time. It only took that long to be talked into coming here for two months, and look where that got me—

"Enjoying your evening?"

Drat. Why couldn't he have waited ten—no, nine—more minutes?

"Yes. Splendid," I said, tone bright.

Peter sat on the other end of the sofa. Too far to be touching, but much too close for my liking. A quick peek at him told me absolutely nothing. He was choosing to be unreadable again.

"Enjoy dinner?" he asked.

"Yes."

"And your day yesterday?"

I nodded. Why was it I had a whole field of vision, but he seemed to take up every inch of it?

He folded his hands in his lap. "Did you do much?"

"Not really."

"But you enjoyed yourself."

"Tremendously."

He stooped his head to the side, trying to get me to look at him. I gave in. There was a neat crease between his eyebrows, his eyes maddeningly soft. "Why have you been so distant? And why were you so peculiar during dinner?"

I licked my lips. "Scallops really aren't my favorite."

"What is your favorite? If it will put you in better spirits, I shall have cook prepare something special for you tomorrow."

There he was being thoughtful again, confound the man. My eyes brushed the clock again. Seven more minutes.

"Thank you, but no."

In my mind I pleaded with Peter to let it go now, to walk away and spare me from having to spell out hurtful lies to him.

Well. More of them.

But of course he couldn't make it that easy. He leaned forward, capturing my gaze. "Are you well, then?" The corner of his lips twitched. "Are you actually ill this time? For I can't imagine how you didn't find my plate humorous."

I bit my tongue, then pushed the words past my teeth, wrapping them in scorn. "Having my portrait made out of food is hardly flattering. And though it may come as a shock, Peter Wycliffe, you are not as charming as you think you are."

Peter's expression froze, then his eyes hardened—not in offense or anger, but solid confusion. "I have this strange feeling," he said, his voice low, "that something happened yesterday while I was gone."

"Nothing happened. I spent the day with Sir William."

The silence grew thick. Peter breathed a scoff and sat back, and I thought I heard him mutter, "Exactly," but couldn't be sure.

Five more minutes.

"Is this about the note?" he said.

I blinked. "What do you know about it?"

Now it was his turn to act surprised. "I saw him slip it under your door last night."

So it really was from William. Well, that solved that riddle. Now if only I could decipher what it said.

"Did it upset you?" he went on. "I can think of no other reason why you'd be acting like this."

"It is not about the note. Truthfully, I don't even know what it says yet." I didn't want to confront Peter about this. Not tonight. I wasn't strong enough yet. I looked back to the clock. Still four more minutes. There was no way I'd last that long. I'd have to distract him.

"What a day you all must've had at Newington, to be gone so late into the evening! I trust Miss Caldwell gave you good company."

It was cruel of me to bring Miss Caldwell into this after finally knowing the whole truth from Eliza, but I was growing more desperate by the minute.

"Yes," Peter responded slowly, not one bit fooled by my change of topic.

"Were the raspberries just as delectable as she promised?"

"Is this about her, then?"

How was I supposed to tell him that I was trying to distance us because I was an imposter, destined to ship across the sea in two weeks? He would never believe it. And even if he did, it would be so much harder to part if he detested me, rather than just be confused at my sudden detachment.

"No. I simply want to know about the raspberries."

His brows plunged. "On my word Mary, you are acting strangely. Tell me whatever it is that is bothering you. I promise not to . . ." He drifted off, eyes catching on my necklace. It was the one Eliza had bought for me at the fair, with the porcelain watercolor.

"That necklace." He studied the thing resting on my collarbone. I grew warm under his gaze. His tentative hand reached out and thumbed over its surface, his stray fingers brushing my skin. "I have not seen you wear this before now. It's . . ."

I swallowed. "A—a waterlily," I finished for him. My voice sounded high-pitched and wheezy.

He stared at it for the longest while, something pensive in his face, his body tense as if he were fighting some internal battle. His fingers curled around the necklace and lifted it up for closer inspection, leaving a trail of tingles where he made contact. He stroked it thoughtfully.

"It suits you," he said at last. Then our eyes locked, only there was something in his stare. Something veiled and intense.

The clock on the mantle tolled, announcing the hour and breaking me out of my stupor.

"Well look at that." I shot up, yanking the necklace out of Peter's grasp. "Nine o' clock. Already my bedtime. Goodnight Peter."

I spurted out of the room, making my escape.

CHAPTER 18

FOXGLOVE.

Katherine arranged the freshly-cut flowers in a vase on my night-stand, taking care to keep the snippers quiet. She adorned the bouquet with twigs of primrose and sage—a combination pungent enough to bring anyone back to life, quiet snippers or no. I blinked slowly, clearing away the cobwebs of sleep.

The night had been fitful. Three weeks had passed since William's arrival, and every day it became more and more difficult to juggle my three identities. It was the worry that kept me up most nights, wondering how on earth I was supposed to survive these last ten days. Now as I lay in bed smelling the foxglove, I wondered if perhaps this whole adventure had been a mistake.

"Ah, you're awake, miss," Katherine said when she noticed me. "I hope I wasn't too loud."

"No. I'm a light sleeper." *These days.* I slipped my feet out of the covers, sitting up on the edge of the mattress.

"Quite an unexpected morning this one has been." Katherine gathered up the plant trimmings and tucked them in her apron. "First Mr.

Minton calls, and then Miss Caldwell leaves so suddenly! Quite bizarre. Who ever heard of a visitor in the morning?"

My eyebrows drew together as I slid into the seat of my vanity. "Miss Caldwell has left? What news did Mr. Minton bring? What's happened?"

"I've only heard the gossip, mind you, but it would seem that Mr. Minton came expressly to see the Master—on some urgent business, or so he claimed. He wouldn't say another word to anybody. Although . . ."

Through the reflection of the mirror, I saw her rub her lips together, then walk up behind me. Her voice lowered. "One of the servants happened to be cleaning the hall outside of the study while Mr. Minton and Master Peter were meeting, and she overheard bits and pieces."

"You mean she was snooping?"

"No!" Katherine reared in offense. "No, no, no, never that. Not *snooping*. Of course not. What kind of servants would we be?" She picked up some pins, working through my tangled curls. "No, it was more like eavesdropping."

I breathed a laugh, shaking my head. "All right then, let's hear it."

Pins in mouth she said, "Well. There were only three words that Martha was able to pick up, and they've confounded the rest of us. *Information*, *attack*, and *gentleman*. Don't know what he'd be talking about. Do you make anything of it, miss?"

My eyes froze in the mirror. Peter had news about my attacker. I should go see him. Or would he send for me? Perhaps I shouldn't go at all—I was supposed to be estranging myself after all. But what if it was important? Or . . . revealing?

I cleared my throat. "No, I'm sorry. Quite intriguing to be sure."

It was only fifteen minutes before Katherine had finished pinning my hair and I was hastening downstairs. Opening the study door, I peered into the dark room. A single lamp burned at a desk, and in its light, Peter slumped over open books, seemingly asleep. I slipped further into the room, leaving the door open just a crack. Walking as quietly as I could, I neared.

I had imagined Peter's sleeping face would be peaceful, serene; but it was neither. His brows angled down, a frown upon his lips, his breathing ragged.

One of my feet turned back toward the door. It felt wrong to see him like this. Too intimate. And how was I supposed to wake him without startling him?

As it turned out, I didn't have to.

He inhaled sharply and sat up, blinking his eyes open. I waited for him to jump at seeing me standing in his study, without an invitation. Instead he said, "Mary." He ran a hand through his mussed hair. "Forgive me, I uh . . . I fell asleep." He flipped through the books and papers on the desk, searching for something.

I stood there like a statue, unsure what to say, or do. He hadn't been surprised. Indeed, he almost seemed to be *expecting* me. "Turbulent night?"

His searching stopped. "Uh, I um . . ." He looked away, scratching the back of his head. His eyes darted to me, then back. "Yes, you could say that."

I had never seen him this undone. "Is it because of the visit from Mr. Minton?"

"Not entirely." Then his eyes cleared, just before he rubbed them with two fingers. "Ah yes, Mr. Minton. That's right. I was going to tell you." Peter continued to shuffle through papers.

What else did he think I was there for? What else could I *possibly* be there for?

Oh, I shouldn't have come.

At last he found what he was searching for, a small slip of paper no bigger than my hand. He offered it to me, and I took it, reading through the contents. All that was scribbled on its surface was a date and a time.

"That's when the kidnappers were hired," Peter supplied. "Mr.

Minton made inquiries into every inn and tavern within a twenty mile radius, finally finding someone who recognized his description of the men. It was at a pub ten miles north of here where he found someone. The man absolutely refused to disclose any amount of information about the employer, even with substantial bribing. But at long last, he did finally say when the transaction occurred, and that's what you see there."

I studied the date again, squinting in contemplation, heart beating erratically. What if I had been wrong? What if it really was Thomas?

"That was the day of the fair," Peter went on, and my thoughts ground to a halt. "With all the extra crowds and strangers, it would've been the perfect time to hire kidnappers and then disappear. It's still unclear where they planned to put you afterwards though."

I nodded. Peter expected me to be disheartened at this news, but instead my shoulders sagged in relief. For if it happened on this day, one thing could be sure.

It wasn't Thomas. I had seen him there, in the throng, which means he couldn't have been at an inn ten miles north.

No one else was a suspect. Either those men had been mistaken, or they were after Mary. The situation was still unsettling but had turned out better than I'd feared. There were men out to get Mary, but at least they weren't out to get me.

"Ah, well," I said. "Perhaps we should just forget the whole matter."

Peter straightened up, smoothing his clothes. They were the same ones he'd been wearing last night. "How can you say that?"

"I don't wish to relive it. I would rather let it rest." Not to mention that if the men were debt collectors, Mary probably wanted to keep her financial ruin a secret; I wasn't about to draw more scandalous attention to myself if I could help it.

Peter shook his head, looking slightly impressed. "You might be able to forget, but I cannot." He stood. "I will ask Mr. Minton to continue the investigation, and if we come to a dead end, then so be it. But I will not give up hope just yet."

My smile turned sideways, taking in Peter's rumpled clothes, his cheeks still rosy from sleep. This wasn't good for me. "I understand Miss Caldwell has left. I assume you know why."

"There's been a death in the family. Her mother."

My mouth hung open. "O-Oh. Was it sudden?" Peter knew her—and Clarissa's mother had been one of the strongest advocates for their marriage. Was it plaguing him? Was that why he looked as if he hadn't slept at all? Or was it another reason? One that . . . had to do with me?

"Not too sudden, fortunately. Miss Caldwell was shaken but seemed to take it well. The services are today—immediate relatives only. I understand the family will forego the mourning period as well. It's all rather scandalous and hushed."

"But surely Miss Caldwell won't be returning."

"On the contrary, she told me she shall return tomorrow." He rubbed the back of his neck, blowing a sigh. "I don't understand it but, if that is her wish, who am I to refuse?"

"Does she not want more time to grieve?"

"I don't know what she wants." It was a simple enough answer, delivered in a way that had nothing to do with the conversation. He sighed again and moved out from behind the desk. "Forgive me. I'm out of sorts this morning." He halted. "It *is* morning, isn't it?"

I half laughed. "Yes, of course. Just after nine."

His smile turned genuine. "Good. Then I still have time to turn myself into something resembling presentable before breakfast." He worked his way to the door.

"You are well, Peter?" I called to his back.

He turned. "Of course. Or at least, in a few moments I will be."

PETER HAD BEEN TRUE TO HIS WORD. THERE WAS NO LINGERING remnant of the man in the study for the rest of the day. No one would have guessed his state from early that morning.

"Are you able to visit the country very often, Miss Raynsford?"

We were in the drawing room, entertaining ourselves with riddles, rhymes, and jokes, though Peter was nowhere to be seen. A game of cards was in motion in one corner, another occupied by a table boasting tarts, jams, and biscuits. Matthew sat at my side, paying attention to his surroundings half as much as he did his novel, and William was doing his utmost to slip me up.

I forced a laugh. "Why William, you know the answer to that."

"Indeed, but I doubt the others do. Do tell us, *dear friend* all about your recent country visits."

The twins applauded and begged for my story. It was a trap, of course. I had no clue as to whether Mary had visited the country lately or not. Was it a recent trip that sparked such hatred for the outdoors in her? Or a childhood trauma? I gulped and opted for an easy way out.

"I would not wish to bore you—"

"Oh, but Miss Raynsford, I do insist!" cried Miss Margaret.

William grinned. "Please, Mary. She *insists*."

How I tired of this caged feeling!

And that's when I realized, at the very worst, no matter what I said, it was my word against his. If William denied my story, I could simply claim he didn't recall it properly, and no one would be the wiser. I jutted my chin out and stood, bolstered.

"Very well, Miss Margaret," I said, "my story you shall get." I sauntered around the back of the sofa, facing the crowd and the half-dozen pairs of eyes now fixed on me.

"It all started around noon on April, the twenty-second, when I was invited to a dear friend's house. Her name is not pertinent to the story, but we shall call her Jennie for the sake of detail." A dry laugh sputtered out of William. I ignored it. "She had been sick for some time, so I decided to take her a basket of pastries. My friend loves pastries."

"As do we all!" declared Quincy. Everyone laughed.

"On my way, my carriage was rudely halted by a Mr. Vinney. He had the eyes of a devil that day, although his hat was rather handsome." They all laughed again, and I ambled slowly sideways, drawing in my audience like a fish on a hook. "He was on foot, and me in carriage, yet somehow he managed to catch me. Oh, how I wished I could escape the man!"

"You knew him?" Eliza asked.

"Indeed, he had long been an unfavorable suitor of mine. Anyway, he convinced me there were pretty flowers in the woods nearby, and that surely my friend Jennie would like a bouquet. Jennie liked flowers nearly as much as she liked pastries. Nearly."

Smiles spread round the group. Even Lady Agatha's frown had disappeared, and Matthew's eyes peeped over his book.

"So I left my carriage and plunged into the woods. It was not long before I spotted a meadow, full of the most richly-colored blossoms I'd ever seen. Bright yellows, and deep pinks, and blooming purples that looked like a sunset." I used my hands to describe their shapes, and now the card game in the corner had stopped as well, everyone fixated.

"I was so hypnotized in the enchanted meadow that I hardly realized the hour had grown late for visiting. With enough for a dozen bouquets—each one looking like a paradise—I raced back to my carriage, bidding the driver to make haste. To my relief, we arrived just at the stroke of four." My voice took on a suspenseful tone. "But, upon entering the house, my relief quickly vanished."

"Oh, what?" Miss Margaret bounced up and down. "Pray tell, what happened?"

I moved away slowly, the sound of my footfalls uncannily loud in the silent room. I waited just long enough for the suspense to ripen, before turning back and saying, "When I beheld Mr. Vinney."

They all collectively gasped. Except William, whose lips quirked in amusement.

"Mr. Vinney it was—and he'd delayed me only for the purpose of arriving there before me! But, that is not the worst of it." My audience looked between each other, then leaned in closer.

"'Good day, Mr. Vinney,' I said after giving dear Jennie her pastries and a bouquet. 'To what do we owe the pleasure?' And he said, 'As you know Miss Raynsford, I am quite in love with you.'"

"Scandalous!" Lady Agatha said.

"Yes, quite," I agreed. "But there is more. 'As you know Miss Raynsford I am quite in love with you, but I find I am torn. For I am also quite in love with Miss Jennie.'"

"No!" the audience gasped as one.

I nodded. "Yes. You can imagine our surprise. Needless to say, we both shouted angrily at his lack of decorum. Just then, my coachman entered with the rest of the bouquets. Mr. Vinney grabbed one of them, offering it to me, pleading with me."

Eliza clasped her hands together. "What did you say?"

"I didn't have to say anything. For, the bouquet in Mr. Vinney's hand was one I had picked specially for him. It contained a hefty amount of poison ivy in it, and he had an immediate allergic reaction."

The room cried out triumphantly.

"He ran from the room, yelling and scratching at his eyes. Mr. Vinney has not bothered me since, and I think it is safe to assume he never shall. But, dear friends, I don't believe I shall be visiting the country again anytime soon. For it is better to be safe than sorry." I gave a small curtsy. "The end."

Everyone laughed and clapped loudly.

For the next several minutes, I was smothered in smiles and remarks of 'Well told, Miss Raynsford,' until at last everyone returned to their previous activities. I walked to a tall window, watching a gardener trim the hedges that lined the paths outside.

"Lovely little story," William said as he joined me. "Though on my word, I am certain I have heard it before. Now where was it?" His expression cleared and he snapped his fingers. "Ah, yes! Little Red Riding Hood."

I folded my arms. "Any similarities between my experience and the fairytale are purely coincidental."

"Interesting coincidence."

"I wonder that you did not expose me for it."

He turned around, looking on the room, lips twisting slightly to one side. "Indeed. I wonder that myself. Perhaps it is because you wove your web so delicately, I was too charmed to care that I was caught." He blinked over to me, head turning just a fraction. "By the way, I thought you should know that I took it upon myself to review the guest list for the ball."

My eyebrows rocketed up. "Why would you do that? Are you trying to steal Miss Caldwell's attentions?"

"Heavens, no! No, I only wanted to ensure that Mary shan't be exposed."

I stood shocked for two beats before an unexpected laugh bubbled out. "Is this truly the William Bentley I know?"

He chuckled. "Think what you will of me, but I really do care for Mary. And even if that weren't the case, I seem to have changed considerably these last few weeks."

I linked my hands behind my back, setting them on the windowsill. "I like it. These changes."

"I wouldn't depend on them if I were you. I only saved your skin this time because my friend happens to be entangled in this mess."

I smiled and turned toward the sound of Miss Betty Hartford laughing triumphantly over the round of cards.

"Which is a shame," William sighed, "as I was looking forward to seeing the looks on everyone's faces when they discovered your sister is in the colonies."

Gut twisting, I swiveled my head back, mouth dropping open. William was all innocence leaning against the wall.

"And that she's working at a bakery in New York," he went on, "earning 15 shillings a month. She's been there for about five months now, has she not?" His thumb came up to stroke his chin. "And you know, the thought occurred to me: If she wrote to you the moment she landed in America, which she most assuredly would, you would've gotten the letter around . . ." He pretended to do the mental math. "Ah. Around the time you arrived on Mary's doorstep. Another interesting coincidence, is it not?"

He grinned at me, his hand reaching over to finger a lock of my hair. "It must be challenging to be so very far away from one's only family. You must be aching to go to her side." He tucked the curl behind my ear, bending and whispering, "Even desperate." As his hand fell, it grazed my neck—a neck that was reddening by the second. I could tell he enjoyed watching the blush creep up my face, because he stared at it a long while.

Finally, he murmured, "That is why you are doing this, is it not? Because of your sister?"

I blinked at him, hard and fast before looking away, at last managing a fragile nod.

"I thought as much. I got them to take Mary's acquaintances off the list, but . . . I should be very nervous if I were Lillian Markley."

My thoughts halted. Of course. If Miss Caldwell was related to Thomas, then surely he would be invited. "Do you think you could persuade them to take my brother off the list as well?"

He inhaled through his teeth. "That is a tall order."

"Please." I grasped his arm. "If I did, it would only raise suspicion —I have no reason to ask them—"

"And you think I do?"

"I think you are very persuasive."

He laughed softly. "Very good, Miss Markley. Where force fails, flattery succeeds."

"So you will do it?"

He ran his tongue over his teeth behind a closed mouth. "I will do it. But only because now you shall be in my debt."

As if that was what I needed. More favors. More entanglement. More lines that blurred together. But what other choice did I have? I was trapped into attending the ball, and Thomas *could not* see me.

"Thank you," I said at last. Then he left, finding Miss Margaret and engaging her in a game of tiles.

I tarried, brooding over the exchange. At last, I let out a slow, heavy sigh. Another fit of laughter started at the card table, followed by what sounded like someone plunking drinking glasses down.

"Look at that dreadful weather!" Lady Agatha scowled out the window, her face competing with the clouds to see which could look more ominous. "It is about to rain!"

Everyone let out little moans of despair, which quickly turned to cries of delight as their various games continued. I glanced out the window, and sure enough, churning clouds darkened the sky. My spirits perked up. A little rain and thoughts of Jennie would do me some good.

I excused myself and rushed upstairs to retrieve my bonnet. I took extra care with my overcoat and making my cap secure, excitement pulsing in my blood. I hurried out of doors in the direction of my favorite tree.

The ash.

CHAPTER 19

I WAS OUT OF BREATH BY THE TIME I REACHED IT, BUT MY SMILE broadened, memories of The Great Toppling surfacing in vividly painted pictures. I stood for a moment, relishing them in my mind and adoring the fact that they existed. A rumble of thunder echoed across the sky, tumbling through the clouds like an enthusiastic toddler. Any moment now the downpour would ensue.

"How did I *know* you were headed here?" Peter stepped out from behind the other side of the tree.

I gasped and fell back. After a moment, I put a hand over my thudding heart. "Y-You startled me."

Peter laughed, shaking his head. "*You* are getting more predictable."

"I never claimed otherwise." I swallowed and untied the ribbon of my bonnet, before taking it off.

Patting the tree to his side, Peter said, "Honestly, Mary, I had thought you learned your lesson last time. Climbing trees only results in topplings and sneezes." He rebuked me with his expression—but it was all just a mask, his eyes lit up with mischief.

"Who's to say I was actually going to climb it? Perhaps I merely came to this spot because it is my favorite tree in all of Ambleside."

"Oh, I have no doubt of that. But once you've strayed into the devilish practice of tree-climbing, there is no going back. Once a tree-climber, always a tree-climber."

Peter folded his arms and reclined against the tree, rather delighted at his cunning and his uncanny ability to best me. But, despite the smug look on his face—or perhaps because of it—he looked rather dashing. In the manor, he was elegant and refined, commanding and handsome. Out here under the ominous clouds he looked powerful and daring, wild and adventurous. The wind tousled the hair that curled at his temples, distracting me for a moment with thoughts of touching it.

Peter had very nice hair.

It was wavy and rich, stopping just under his earlobes and weaving a chaotic pattern over his head. It was so full and reckless in the slight breeze. I found myself imagining . . .

Peter's smirk catapulted me back to reality. He was watching me watch him—and for how long we had been in that state, I didn't know. He stared off in the distance, trying not to laugh. "Just can't get enough of me, eh Mary?"

Of all the conceited—!

I itched to slap that handsome face and pull that glorious hair I'd been admiring moments ago. It was one thing for me and all of England to find him attractive, but another wholly different matter for him to know it. He and William were incredibly alike in that way.

"I think I've had rather too much of you, in fact." I punctuated each word with annoyance. "And who gives a fig that I would come here to climb a silly tree? I should think you wouldn't mind in the least —for it seems to fill you with such happiness. Though you are convinced I enjoy staring at you all day, no one else has ventured after me, Peter. If we are drawing conclusions here, one might think that it is *you* who can't get enough of *me*." I nodded to myself, pleased that I was able to turn the tables so quickly.

But all that my challenging words produced was a muttered, "I never claimed otherwise."

That was the last straw.

I was tired of losing, tired of giving in to Peter and his unsurpassable wit. I tramped up to him so abruptly and stopped so closely that his laughing subsided and his eyes began to travel my face in a daze. I forced myself to look at that face and that hair and those lips, to ignore how my heartrate spurred into a gallop.

Oh, I desperately needed him to leave. "I did not come here to climb a tree. I came here to be alone, and I daresay it's time for you to go."

"Ah, but I came to be alone as well. This is, after all, my favorite tree. And in fact, I *was* here first. Perhaps it is time for you to leave."

"We both know you did not come here to be alone." My patience was cracking under that annoyingly delighted face. "And though you were here first, on my word, I loved this tree first—for reasons I will not divulge, it is sentimental to me."

"To me as well."

"Peter, it is my tree."

He laughed. "Not so. It is on my land, and I am the one who owns it. Though I suppose that it *could* be yours, too . . . someday." A mischievous smile crept across his lips.

My face pinked, and I felt the urge to sneeze clawing its way up my throat and nose. With a colossal effort I pushed the sensation down, knowing it would only delight him further.

"Though, of course, for obvious social reasons, my wife must be able to dance," he went on. "One who does not possess such a quality could never be considered."

"Perhaps I don't want to be considered."

He sighed dramatically. "Just as well. I can't begin to imagine the injury my toes would sustain, trying to teach you."

"Is that another trait your future wife must possess? Toe-avoiding skills?" Even as I hated myself for succumbing to Peter's charms, I couldn't stop the begrudging smile pulling at my mouth. I was undermining all the work I'd already done, extinguishing the bridges I'd already lit.

He smirked. "Among other things."

Too late, I realized I was watching him in a familiar way again. Swapping my look for one more sober and hesitant, I inhaled, preparing to excuse myself from his company.

He stopped me by saying, "I could teach you, if you like."

After a flash of surprise, I laughed, dubiously. "Out here? Under the tree? In this mud? I am no fool—you only want to watch me fail miserably."

"It is not so muddy over there." He knocked his head toward a drier patch a few paces away. "Besides, *Julia*, you promised to make an appearance at the ball. Would you prefer to fail miserably in front of me, or in front of a crowded ballroom?"

He was right. I didn't want to embarrass myself in front of all those people. Yet to dance with Peter would be to walk a dangerous line—to flirt with disaster.

"Why must it be you? I could likely get some other person to teach me."

"Who else would risk their toes?"

"William."

I don't know why I said it. Perhaps I was more desperate to avoid contact with Peter than I let on. Perhaps I truly believed William would help me—that I was not the friendless girl I was before. Whatever the reason, in the instant that I said it, Peter's expression shuttered closed.

"Oh?" His voice was quieter and guarded now, devoid of any feeling. "Would you prefer he teach you?"

The question lifted his eyebrows, giving the impression that he didn't care about my answer. But I saw the truth in the way his hand at his side tightened, in the way his feet planted and his jaw clenched. All subtle signs, but confirmations that Peter didn't like William—and refused to say why.

"That depends," I said carefully, "on who is the better dancer."

Peter seemed to relax a little, some of his easy manner slipping back. "I cannot vouch for William Bentley, but I was the most sought-after dancing partner in London last Season." Before I could say no, Peter untied my overcoat and took my bonnet from my hand, placing them carefully on the grass a few paces away. He came back and put his hands on my shoulders, positioning me correctly then stepping back the proper distance.

"Now, the minuet is very simple. It's mostly just a series of bows and sequences."

"Aren't *all* dances?" I asked wryly.

His eyebrow quirked. "How would you know, Oh-Un-Danceable-One?"

"I've observed. It's just as horrid and pointless as all the others."

Without warning, he stepped forward, and I fell back. "No, no. You're supposed to step towards me and we meet in the middle. See?" He demonstrated again, stepping back then forward. Slowly, he walked me through each of the steps, showing me how to mirror his movements.

He blew a frustrated sigh after several failed attempts that each ended with me stepping on his toes. "You're not very good at learning this, you know."

"Perhaps it is because I have a horrible teacher." Peter scoffed, and I threw my hands up in defeat. "I told you I'm an awful dancer! To mindlessly follow such a tedious pattern, especially without any music, is senseless and boring."

"Boring?" He put his hands on his hips. "Dancing is anything but boring, Mary. It is personal . . . Sensuous."

"Not in my experience."

"Perhaps you never had the right partner." His head cocked to the side. "I think I've been going about this all wrong. Maybe I need to approach it in a different way . . ."

In the distance, thunder cracked again, the sky darkening to charcoal. The first few, fat drops of rain fell through the tree and spattered my shoulder, foreshadowing the deluge. Peter considered me a moment. Then he approached, gently taking my hands in his, as if to begin again.

My stomach turned somersaults at his changed expression. It was no longer mischievous, or even necessarily *happy*. But whatever it was, it whispered of fervor.

"To dance is to be an artist," he said softly. "Your partner is the brush. The ballroom floor, your canvas. Together, you can paint a masterpiece."

With an exhale, he pulled me toward him and my breath caught, unable to think or do anything except follow his lead.

"Yes, the steps are predetermined, but there is a world of possibility in every glance." Our eyes locked. "In every touch."

I reminded myself to breathe, to not contemplate how close we were. Slowly, we started to go through the steps of the dance. I didn't think about my feet or the movement. All I could think was: Peter.

Peter.

"Like time, dancing is a circle." He let go of my hands and we turned as one. "We may separate, but there is still that thread that ties us together, pulling us back to the beginning. Pulling us back to each other."

Gazes fixed, we circled each other, breaking away but always coming back. The fresh rain swirled around our dance, gradually becoming heavier. With careful steps on the wet grass, we glided back and forth, moving in perfect synchronization. I had never danced like this, without thought or error—knowing the next step merely by the way my partner moved.

"It is an impossibility. You must be strong, yet soft. Grounded, yet flowing." We finished turning and started a new set, stepping close again. "Passionate, yet restrained," he murmured. The air between us crackled with energy, my heartbeat hammering to the imaginary music. A strange sheen fell over Peter's eyes, and with each step the energy built, growing and swelling with an overwhelming force. We were two separate beings—but together, we were one thought, one breath, one soul, gracefully creating that masterpiece beneath our feet.

When we were apart, I could feel his raw stare upon me, his anticipation to return. When we were close, I could feel his tender hands against mine, his warm breath on my cheek. And when we danced like this, I could feel his passion burning deep within, his restraint despite it. I tried to pull myself away, to break the hypnotic fall of our steps, but Peter's deep blue stare held me suspended, banishing all thought of turning away.

And still, we danced.

A flash of lightning split the sky, the rain pouring harder. I was soaked, but I paid it no heed—because another, far deadlier storm raged inside me. It thundered in eagerness and fear, splitting me two different ways as it destroyed all the flowers. Everything I felt was a contradiction of excitement and dread, of confusion and clarity, of "I don't want this" and "I do."

I don't know when our feet stopped moving, but suddenly Peter was above me and my back was against the tree. Still enraptured from the dance, from floating on a cloud and dreaming what it would feel like to just let go, I peered up at him through my lashes. Peter's chest rose and fell, his forearm resting against the ash just above my shoulder, his breath heavy as he wandered my face. I clung to the tree behind me, my only anchor to reality.

This wasn't happening. At any moment I was going to wake up; I was going to climb out of bed and go downstairs, where Peter would be waiting with a clever comment and a friendly smile and a look that didn't make me feel so . . . *his*.

I don't want this.

I do.

Then, some of his restraint gave way, and he leaned in an inch. One small inch that was as wide as the sea. Thought fled me. Mind in a daze, I reached a tentative hand up and touched that beautifully rich, damp hair, feeling its softness beneath my fingers.

Peter stilled.

He looked at me and held his breath.

We were motionless, perfectly balancing between familiar safety and the dangerous unknown, neither of us sure which path we were going to take. His eyes were more expressive than I had ever seen them, giving me a brief glimpse of his infinite well of emotions, of how acutely he felt things. And for a small moment—like the dance—I mirrored him, letting my own feelings show. His gaze shifted to my hand that still held his hair, and slowly returned.

"What are you going to do, Mary?" Peter breathed at last. "Kiss me?" His voice was deep and hushed and serious, his question reminiscent of that first day we met. A trickle of rain fell across the side of his forehead, running down and across my hand.

Peter's mouth was closed, but I could hear him calling to me in a thousand ways. He soundlessly begged me to do it, to throw everything into the wind and give him my heart like I had always wanted to. To close the distance between our lips. To do it, or else he might.

With his enticing gaze, his magnificent smell, and his mouth so close to mine, I believed that perhaps I could.

I do . . .

My eyelids half-closed. I leaned forward. So did he.

But Jennie!

I inhaled sharply, eyes whipping open and dropping my hand like I'd been burned. My wits returned and I looked down, intensely regretting letting him dance with me, and coming outside where he could catch me alone and send my senses running, and in a way, regretting ever coming to Ambleside at all.

Every day, another string of bliss tied its knot around my heart with finality, as if it had stolen another piece of my happiness that could only ever belong to me if I stayed. Why was everything becoming so hopelessly complicated?

I could not kiss him, I could not tell him the truth, and this time, I could not laugh it off. So I let out a shaky breath and stepped out from under him, instantly feeling cold and wretched.

That was close. *Much* too close.

Wrapping my arms around myself, I turned back, feeling more vulnerable than I'd ever felt since the day my father died. I stared at him, expecting any moment now to see his eyes sparkle and a grin split his face. I imagined his resonating chuckle as he told me he was only teasing. That he didn't really want to kiss me after all.

Instead, he looked at me, blankly. Waiting. The sky rumbled around us as the silence stretched on, becoming more and more difficult to break.

Go on Peter, I thought, *laugh at me. Say something clever so we can laugh it off like we usually do. Laugh at me!*

But he only stood there in his wet clothes, breathing heavily as his hair dripped over solemn eyes. Eyes that said, *Tell me the truth, Lily. That is all I have ever wanted.*

I shook my head, taking another step back. "I can't." Before I could see his reaction, I turned and walked back to the manor with weighty steps, the rain pounding gloomily like an undertaker at the door.

CHAPTER 20

HAIR DAMP AND NERVES WOUND TIGHT, I SAT AT THE DINNER TABLE. Before me sat a plate of barely touched food, and to my left sat the man I was pointedly trying to ignore.

Peter had changed and his hair was dried, once again the perfect, amiable host—but for the life of me I couldn't bring myself to look at him. The meal passed in a haze of forced smiles and occasional nods.

After dinner we sat in the drawing room, where all the usual things happened. The double doors leading to the terrace were opened, allowing some of the stuffiness in the room to dissipate. Miss Hartford and the twins took turns performing ballads. The weather was talked about—and the ball too.

In fact, there was nothing unusual about this night, other than the fact that I felt positively vile. I still couldn't decide if I'd done the right thing, underneath the tree.

William began a duet with Molly, something in Italian that I hadn't heard before. It had a nice tune, and their voices were pleasant. Just before they finished, the card game at the table ended, and before I knew it, Peter was at my side, offering his arm.

My eyes shot up. A repertoire of memories flooded my mind as I struggled not to flush. At last, I hesitantly took his arm, and he led me onto the terrace into the starlit twilight. The sounds outside were softer, the Italian song still gracing our ears, but faded.

"I trust you did not catch cold," Peter said.

"No. Thank you."

There was a strained moment, filled with meaning and expectation. At last, the quiet words came. "Mary, about earlier . . ."

I tensed. Peter saw, and paused.

Then slowly, he continued. "I realized during dinner that I might have left you with the wrong impression. Or at least, not the right one." He took a long, deep breath, then shifted over to block my view into the drawing room.

"First, you should know the last thing in the world that I want is to frighten you, so I have prepared these words very carefully. I've spent the last three hours mulling over the right way to say this, because I want you to understand that I—oh, I haven't been able to think of anything else, because I want you to understand . . . Dash it all, I'm already getting this all mixed up."

He sighed through his nose. He swallowed. "I want to tell you that I'm in l—"

"There you are, Wycliffe." From behind Peter's shoulder, William strolled onto the terrace. Peter turned, whatever reverie that had held us, ruined. William reached us, forming a discomfited circle. "Dominating Miss Raynsford again, I see. You wouldn't mind if I joined you, would you?"

Peter cleared his throat. "Not at all."

An uncomfortable silence hung in the air before William turned to me. "The issue we talked about earlier—it is resolved now."

"Oh." My hand found its way to my throat, surprised and relieved that the fox didn't reveal more. "Thank you. I am in your debt."

He grinned roguishly. "Indeed you are, madam, and I shall ponder how you might repay me, later."

Peter's eyebrows lifted by the smallest fraction. I laughed nervously to try and cover the awkwardness, but Peter spoke before I could change the subject. "Forgive the observation, but this conversation of yours sounds rather like one Mary and I had a while ago."

My gut twisted as I watched the banter unfold, helplessly.

"Oh really?" William asked.

"Yes." Peter smiled, but it wasn't in his eyes. "It is a comfort to know that Miss Raynsford is equal in all her attentions."

William rubbed his hands together. "So you've crossed swords with this one, have you? A formidable partner she makes, does she not?"

Peter inclined his head. "Indeed."

William laughed, stepping up and putting his hand around me. So quickly that I must've imagined it, a flicker of aggression crossed Peter's face. But then it was gone.

"You should know better than to cross my Mary, Wycliffe. She's no ordinary girl."

Peter glanced from William, to me, and then settled on William's hand at my waist. Finally, he raised his gaze—and there was something pained about the way he looked at me. "Yes. I am very aware of the fact. Please excuse me." He left without another word.

When the sound of his retreating footsteps fell silent, I pulled William's hand off and turned on him. "Why did you do that?"

"What?" William's face was childlike, but I had learned to see beyond the innocent façade. I nodded to his hand. "Oh, that." His wicked grin flashed. "I was merely marking my territory."

"*Marking your*—!"

"Shh!" He put a playful hand to my mouth, but I shoved it away.

"What on earth is wrong with you, William? Just because you feel threatened by Peter—and heaven knows why—it is no reason to act like a fool!"

His lively smile dropped, replaced by something darker. "Threatened by Peter?" His tone bordered menacing, his dusky brows furrowing into a fiery scowl. "And a fool? If there is a fool here, *Lillian*, it is not I. I, at least, know what I want."

"So what is it? I have been trying to decide since the day you arrived. To threaten me? To coerce me until there is no more happiness to be found in my world? Would that satisfy you?"

Willian picked his gloves off his fingers and crumpled them in one hand. "It has been a game, nothing more."

"Save your rubbish. Games do not upheave an entire future. They do not set stakes so high that one's life will be crushed if one loses. That, sir, is called blackmail."

"I have *never*—"

"I am tired of games, William." My voice wobbled with anger, all the frustration of the past several weeks spewing out in a torrent of passion. "I am tired of losing and losing and all the wondering in between. For once, I would like to not care what people think of me. No more hidden jabs or double meanings. I want to get off this cycle of dodging and scrambling and worrying until I can't form a clear thought! So for heaven's sake, *tell me what it is that you want!*"

"You!" William tossed his gloves aside. They fell to the stony ground, forgotten.

Both angry, both breathing hard, it took several heartbeats for the word to register. ". . . What?"

Surely he'd misspoken.

But William was the most serious I had ever seen him. "I want you, Lily," he said softly. I blinked, chest still heaving from my rant, but frozen in place.

Me? It was inexplicable. Unthinkable. Impossible.

Yet, it made perfect sense. The decision to stay. The endless flirting. The rivalry with Peter.

"I come from a very prestigious and wealthy family. It made my life very easy." His hand found its way to his hair, and he blew a sigh, walking the length of the terrace and back. "All my life I have had every need met. Everything I've ever wanted before I could ask for it. All the connections, wealth, and female attention I could ever hope for. But then I knew heartbreak and all at once my eyes were opened."

I didn't know where this was going, or what it all meant. Heartbreak?

William stopped midstride, and spun to face me. "Where balls were once entertaining and full of wonder, now they were pointless. I played all the pranks, kissed all the girls, even gambled—but it no longer brought me pleasure. Pranks became childish. Women became tiresome. There was nothing exciting—nothing new to help me achieve that elusive sense of fulfillment." He played with his hands, slowly coming back.

"I was on my way back to London, when I decided to stop by Ambleside in hopes of anything mildly stimulating. I doubted there was. And as soon as I arrived I wished I hadn't come, so dull was the company."

His warm hands wrapped around my shoulders. "So you can imagine my surprise when instead of my monotonous Mary standing before me, I saw you." A half smile lifted the corner of his lips. "A beautiful, sparkling stranger that practically radiated adventure."

I stood in stunned silence. William gathered my hands and brought them up between us.

"You are that *something*, Lily, that I have needed all this time." He kissed both my hands and tucked them against his chest.

The world tilted, and I took three breaths. I shook my head, exhaling in pity. "Oh, William."

"I love you."

A trapdoor beneath my stomach opened. "You do not love me," I whispered, wilting. "For what if I *had* been monotonous? What if I had proved to be just as senselessly dull as everyone else?"

He shook his head.

"You love that I fill you with excitement, that I have broken your dreary routine. It is the idea of me that you love, nothing more—"

"I think I would know my own heart."

"What would you have me say?" I faltered, then freed my hands from his grasp and put one on his arm, choosing my words cautiously. "Think, William. You did not say you love my smile or admire my courage—only that you like how I make you feel. Though I am honored you regard me so highly, to the point where you feel you must profess your feelings . . . I cannot, in all honesty, do the same."

He tensed under my hand and his jaw ticked. "You will not accept me?"

I hesitated again, biting my lip. "No."

"Is this because of Wycliffe?"

After a moment, my face puckered with a twinge of irritation. "What has any of this to do with him?"

William laughed as he shook my hand off, his eyes flashing dangerously. "Oh, it has everything to do with him—do not pretend it doesn't. From the moment I arrived, it was painfully evident. You never showed any interest in—never even *glanced* at—anyone else. You were besotted then, as you are now."

My hands at my sides clenched. "Besotted?"

"Do you love him?"

Even in my anger, I wavered, terribly unprepared for such a life-changing question. I became immobile, fixated from trying to discount the truth that beat in my heart.

"Do. You. Love him?" he repeated, stepping so close there was nowhere else to look but in his raging hazel eyes.

I flushed. "Whether or not I love him, it is entirely beside the point."

William shook his head and scoffed. "As I thought."

He stalked away. Then, thinking better of it, he spun on his heel and turned on me. "You think he could actually love you? Even without the problem of your sister, you believe that all could work out between you?" His booming words reverberated off the stones, as if my sense of doom had its own voice.

"Face the facts, Miss Markley. Once he finds out you are not Mary, what do you think he'll do? Pardon your past? Quiet all the gossipmongers and ask you to bear his unsullied family name?" He scoffed again, face contorting. "It isn't even unlikely—it is *inconceivable*."

"You do not know that," I muttered, feeling a prick in my eyes.

He tracked back to me. "Oh yes I do. You know how much his father meant to him. Do you think Wycliffe would knowingly tarnish that extraordinary legacy his father left behind? No. He'd do better to marry Miss Caldwell, like his mother wishes. If he knew you as you truly are, he would turn you out of his house in a heartbeat. Toss you away like all the others have. In your eyes he is perfect and wonderful, but how would you feel toward your precious Peter when he's shown his real colors? Tell me how someone like him could ever love someone like you—"

With all of my fury and hurt, I smacked William across the face.

He reared back. His thumb gingerly stroked his cheek, where a large, blotchy red spot developed. The rest of him froze in shock.

"You tell me nothing I don't already know." My voice trembled on a breathless whisper, and my whole body quivered. "I know what people think of me, what they think I've done. But if there is someone who should be ashamed at their behavior, Sir William . . . it is not I." I spun around, half-running from the scene.

I fled through the double-glass doors, ignoring the group of people mingling nearby and Eliza's jolly cry of "Mary!" I fled across the entryway and up two flights of stairs, feeding on my anger to keep the tears at bay. I fled down the hallway to my quarters, longing for the security of solitude. Once I was safely and blessedly alone, I leaned against the door, panting hard and allowing my thoughts to wander.

It was true. It was all true—and that was what hurt the most. *How could someone like him ever love someone like you?* The words echoed off the walls of my mind, searching for an answer that didn't tear my heart in two.

But that was just it. He couldn't. And I had been so pathetically foolish to hope otherwise.

Peter had never been an option. I had known it from the start, so why was it so painful to think about now? Jennie was still constant. She was the only one I had left—the only one I'd ever had, really—and I couldn't let her down.

My eyes wandered about the room, taking in the delicate furnishings, the tasteful, flowery wallpaper, the sunny atmosphere that had begun to feel like home. *Not long now until I leave it all behind.*

William had no reason now not to expose me. For all I knew, he already had.

But suddenly, I had a difficult time caring.

A FEW MINUTES LATER, I DUG THROUGH THE DRAWER OF MY VANITY, ignoring my father's watch and the letters from Jennie. Bottles of cream and perfume toppled in my haste. At last I found it and hurried out of my room, pinching my cheeks with one hand and clutching the riddle tightly in the other. It was late, and he might not be there, but after my quarrel with William, I realized just how much I needed to know what the note said.

I ascended the flight of stairs that led to the third story, then made my way through great halls with wide windows, until at last I stood in front of the library, determined to get some answers. Pushing the doors open, my eyes went immediately to the spot where I hoped to find him. To my great relief, Matthew was there, his nose halfway through a thick volume.

I marched in, trusting he wouldn't be too put out when I begged for his help. He was the only one I could think to go to, not only because he was brilliant and would no doubt solve the riddle within minutes, but because he was my only friend who knew of my disguise. And, the only one I'd risk letting see what William had written me.

Matthew had been the obvious choice. But his first words made me reconsider.

"I hope you're not here for my help," he called, "because last I looked, I'm busy."

"Perhaps I'm here to read," I said. As I walked up to his chair, I was answered by a scoff and a turn of the page. "And besides," I added, "what could you possibly help me with?"

"Oh, I don't know." He sighed, still skimming his book. "How to not blunder up your charade? How to not be so predictable? How to form a clever comeback? The list is rather extensive, so unless your plans include listening to me ramble for the better part of the night, I wouldn't recommend it." Finally his gaze lifted. "And even if they did—as I said before—I'm busy." He returned to his book.

I felt like stamping my foot. How did this boy have any friends at all? I was about to despair, when it occurred to me just how someone like Matthew Wycliffe needed to be handled. Before I lost the nerve, I grabbed his book and yanked it away.

"Hey!" He hopped up as I walked off with it, eyes violent. "Give that back!"

Instead, I lifted it higher and said, "I will once you stop treating me like a nuisance."

Matthew stared me down in silence, willing me with his eyes to instantaneously combust, before muttering, "Fine."

With fluid movements that revealed nothing of his blustery mood, Matthew collected the top book from an impressive stack atop the table. He dropped back down into his chair and repositioned himself, before opening his new book and starting anew.

"Upon my word," I murmured. "Whatever have I done to offend you?" He didn't deign to answer, and I was frozen in contemplation, until understanding dawned at last. "Ah. I have been ignoring you of late, is that it?"

He stopped his perusing, his expression hardening by a fraction.

My grin bloomed. "Is that it?"

He slammed his book shut. "By all England! Yes, if you must know."

He tossed the volume away then looked off in the distance, adding darkly, "Though I don't know why I would care."

I melted, my smile exploding into a laugh. He could pretend that prickly exterior all he wanted—he was all softness and sweetness underneath. I ruffled his hair. "Oh poor, little Matthew. I didn't know you liked me that much."

"I don't." He swatted my hand away. "And definitely not anymore."

He was still playing hurt, but I could tell he liked the attention. I handed him his book back, pleased when he didn't move to open it.

"Why are you here then?" he asked after a moment.

"As it turns out, I actually did come here for your help."

He clucked his tongue and shook his head. "It never ceases to amaze me how often I am right. It's a curse, really."

I rolled my eyes, procured the folded riddle, and handed it to him. He glanced at it. "What is this?"

"What you're going to help me with."

Matthew opened it up and took a few minutes to mull over its contents.

My first is a sphere through which all things behold.
My second is that of which poet obsesses,
And is given to champions both valiant and bold.
My third is a woman of curly white tresses.
And fourth is a floret, whose heart is of gold,
Whose beauty in depths, no other possesses

"The first one is an eye," he said at last. He procured a pencil from a hidden pocket in his tailcoat. Smoothing out the note, he scribbled the word 'Eye' to the left of the first line.

I nodded. "That makes sense."

"Champions," he mused. "That could mean any number of things. I think I'll skip that one." He flicked down to the fourth line, containing the clue to the third word. "My third is a woman of curly white tresses. Rather vague, isn't it?" He shook his head, moving his lips without making any sound. Then, "I would think the white hair refers to someone elderly, like the name of a mother or grandmother. But then, why 'curly'?"

My brow furrowed. "You're right. Vague. What woman is known for having curly white hair?"

"Unless . . . unless it doesn't refer to a person at all." He sat forward, scrutinizing the spines of the books still stacked on the table. He selected one and carefully extracted it from the pile, leafing through its pages.

"Aha!" he finally said. "A sheep. Sheep are known for having curly white tresses."

"Sheep." I gave a short, disbelieving nod. "You honestly think that is the third word?"

"No, not 'sheep.' The riddle specified a *woman*, and the correct term for a female sheep," he consulted his book, "is a 'ewe.'"

I guffawed, baffled at his logic, but he wrote it down on the paper anyway.

"Now perhaps that will give us enough of a clue to guess the second word." He returned to the second clue, pondering aloud. "Something that a poet obsesses over . . ." His face puckered. "Paper? Ink?"

I chuckled. "Perhaps it means something like 'verse'? Otherwise, why would it specify poet?"

"Or something *in* the verse. Something that poets love to write about. Moonlight? Flowers?" Matthew sat up and snapped his fingers. "Love! That is what all poets obsess over." He held the paper higher, reading it again. *"And is given to champions both valiant and bold.'* Champions—champions of love." He scrawled 'Love' next to the second and third lines.

I stiffened when I realized what Matthew had discovered, my face already turning every shade of red.

"Thus far we have 'Eye,' 'Love,' and then 'Ewe.'" He stopped. His eyes narrowed, looking over the riddle and then back over his scribbled words, as if re-checking an answer to a mathematical equation. "I . . . love . . . you . . ."

His head shot up. "Who gave this to you?" It sounded like an accusation more than a question. When I didn't immediately answer, Matthew leaned forward, eyes boring through me with an intensity that tied my tongue. His voice was quieter when he said, "It's not from Peter. Is it."

Awkward silence ensued. My head started to pound so I rubbed my forehead with one hand. What exactly had William hoped to accomplish by writing this? My mind flitted back to our quarrel. Maybe I had been wrong. Maybe he *was* sincere. Maybe he had been afraid of my reaction, and that's why he wrote me the riddle.

Maybe . . . maybe it wasn't from him?

I was so confused. I needed to consider it in the privacy of my room. "I'm sorry. Thank you for your help."

Matthew returned the slip of paper to my hand. "There's still one more word. Do you not want to know what it is?"

"You already know?"

He disappeared behind a tower of bookshelves, reemerging a moment later, scanning a new book. He found what he was looking for. "I've been pondering it since the start. 'Floret' means flower. 'Heart of gold' refers to the peduncle or center of the flower. Then when it says 'depths,' it could mean a few things, but the obvious one is the ocean—or water in general. So in the end we have a flower with a heart of gold, which possesses beauty on the water."

Matthew looked up, and there was actual gentleness in his expression—something I had never seen from him before. Something that made him look like Peter. "The only thing I can think of that fits that description is a lily. I. Love. You. Lily." He inclined his head, waiting for me to explain.

So. It really was from William. It couldn't be from anyone else because no one else knew my real name. Not even Matthew. Well, that is, until now.

There was no pretending now. I licked my lips. "Matthew, I—"

"You should try to find the real owner of the note." He slammed the book shut, tossed it on the stack, plopped back in his chair, picked up his original book, and thumbed through the pages.

My explanation died in my throat. After a while I coughed in surprise. "What?"

He found his place and resumed reading. "It's obviously not intended for you if it's for Lily. Whoever left it at your door made a mistake. You should find the real owner and give it to her. Seems important."

Not for the first time, Matthew stunned me into complete silence. There was no denying he knew my name now. Yet he was still going to pretend as if he hadn't a clue.

For me. Because we were friends.

"Thank you," I whispered. I don't remember ever crossing the distance to the library doors, but suddenly I was standing at the entrance and Matthew was calling to me from his seat.

"For the record, I don't know who this Lily is, but if you see her, tell her I like her name. And also that she should name her firstborn son after me, after all I've done for her."

I bit my lip to keep from laughing and crying at the same time. "I'm sure she'll agree that is a reasonable request."

CHAPTER 21

"A LETTER FOR YOU, MISS," SAID THE TRAY-LADEN FOOTMAN AT breakfast, a sealed paper resting on the silvery surface.

I looked up in alarm, noting the stamp of the name 'Julia Smith' on the envelope. It was addressed to Mrs. Wilshire's house. Meaning, it was from Jennie.

"Thank you." I snatched it away and stashed it in my lap.

"Post this early in the morning?" said Miss Caldwell, patting her mouth with a napkin. "Why Miss Raynsford, I believe that is your first letter since arriving."

"Indeed." I laughed nervously. "One might think I matter not to my family, if their affections are to be weighed by the volume of post I receive."

There were a few chuckles round the table, but they quieted when Miss Caldwell asked, "Is it from your aunt?"

I gripped my fork tighter, clearing my throat. "Yes, as it happens. And as I am anxious to hear any news of her health, I trust you will all excuse me." The chair scraped hollowly against the floor as I stood.

"But do stay!" William's words carried a distinct bite to them. I met his angry smile and unyielding gaze, feeling an urge to be anywhere he wasn't. "We are all aching to know how she fares. You must read it to us."

He knew it was from my sister, and he still hadn't forgiven me.

"Mm!" agreed Quincy, half-chewing his food. "Yes, splendid. I do love good news in the morning. I always say."

I fingered the edges of the letter, eager to know the contents, fixing William with a hard stare. "Yes, unless . . ." I trailed off, finishing slowly, "unless it isn't good news."

Everyone halted, forks stopping midway to hanging mouths. Someone in the group coughed.

"I think Miss Raynsford deserves some privacy," Lady Wycliffe said. "It is such a delicate matter. When you are through, dear, do tell us if your aunt is well."

I smiled at her gratefully. "Of course." After rushing out of the room, I flew to my quarters and locked the door behind me. As I sat on my bed, I mentally prepared myself for what I would read. Then I broke the seal and unfolded the paper.

My dearest Lily,

It's been so long since your last letter, I worry something's happened to you. I hope all is well.

Life here keeps me busy, or I would've written oftener myself. Did I mention I am the new bakery apprentice? My duties now include pastries and tarts, as well as my own delivery route.

America is a very different place than England. It's busier and at times, chaotic. But I suppose it would be different if I left New York. There must be rolling hills and pretty countryside somewhere in this country. When you get here, let us make it our quest to find it.

I'm sorry this letter will be so short, but my only candle is nearly spent, and I have a harrowing day tomorrow. I love you, sister, don't ever forget. Stay protected.

Yours,

    Jennie

I CLUTCHED THE PAPER IN MY HAND, STARING AT IT WITHOUT seeing. Then I read it again, slower, reading in-between the lines.

She was exhausted. Unhappy. But most of all, she missed me terribly. And all this time, I'd been living a life of luxury.

Guilt washed over me. *Oh, Jennie.* She was working so hard to be happy, to look on the bright side, but deep down she was lonely. Awfully, achingly, overwhelmingly lonely.

I couldn't let her down—she might forgive me if I did, but *I* wouldn't.

I blinked away the moisture that had gathered, folding the letter back up and grouping it with my others. Gnawing my lower lip, I fortified my resolve, building up my wits, and will, and courage.

I exited my room. By now, breakfast was over, and no one was to be found. Perhaps they went on a stroll, or went into town, but I didn't care. At the moment I preferred to be alone. I strolled to the library and dropped into one of the chairs. Matthew's spot was empty, the fabric faded where he usually sat.

I hardly possessed the patience to read. Every couple sentences, my mind drifted to Jennie's situation, and mine, and how I was going to manage these last few days. Worry aggravated me, eating me away like moths on a dress. I stuffed my doubts down dozens of times, forcing myself to concentrate on my book.

Hours passed, but they seemed like minutes. I drowned in my novel, freeing myself of thought and emotion. It wasn't until the clock announced four o'clock that I tumbled back to reality. Matthew still hadn't come.

I hadn't realized it, but I had secretly hoped to speak with him— my only ally here—and alleviate some of my anxiety. Now the after-

noon grew late, and it was my duty to reappear before anyone questioned my absence.

I found the guests congregated in the drawing room, going over
plans and feeding the excitement for the ball, and slipped into the
room nearly unnoticed.

Nearly.

"—new golden tapestries from London," Lady Wycliffe said. "And if
that expense weren't enough, Peter has also ordered seven of the best
chefs to make up a host of delicacies." I sat in an empty chair at the
card table.

"Oh my! Seven!" cried Betty Hartford. "I can hardly wait to try the
delicacies!"

"Yes," added Miss Caldwell, "and over two hundred guests have
been invited."

"Two hundred!" The twins exchanged excited looks, little squeals
escaping their lips.

"Some more welcome than others," Peter said jokingly. Everyone
laughed.

"Particularly Julia Smith," Matthew inserted from behind his book.
He'd been in here the whole time. Everyone turned to Peter to answer,
including me—but I wasn't prepared to make eye contact.

"Particularly," Peter muttered. For one infinite second we stared at
each other, until I batted my eyes away, busying myself with gathering
up the cards.

"Oh, I do hope the orchestra is lovely," Miss Caldwell sighed. "How
I love a pleasant melody." The crowd murmured their agreement. "In
fact, why have we not held a concert? We certainly have the talent
among us."

"What a splendid idea!" Quincy hopped to his feet. "I have been
longing to witness Miss Hartford's skill on the pianoforte. Her reputation precedes her."

Betty blushed, even as Miss Caldwell said, "Then let us retire to the
music room for a concert!" She gestured toward the threshold with

fanfare. Chairs scraped against the floor as everyone stood and shuffled through the door. Murmurs of anticipation passed through the group. Finished collecting the cards, I set them aside, and stood.

As I moved to get in line, Peter stepped in front of me. I met his gaze.

Oh Peter, please. Don't. I tried to move past him, but he grasped the inside of my elbow and stopped me from following the others. Power- lessly, I watched as Oliver Wentworth, the last in the line, exited the room and left me alone—with the one person I shouldn't be alone with. The click of the latch as the door shut sounded like a cannon.

"Is everything all right, Mary?" Peter said.

Now. It was now that I had to deal the blow. Sever the ties. And since I was too weak to leave him, I needed to ensure he would leave me. I inhaled, mustering the courage to do what needed to be done, bracing my heart for the beating it was about to take. *Think of the letter. Of Jennie. Of the way he would loathe you if he knew the truth.*

"Of course." I swallowed. "Why shouldn't it be?" I turned away and moved to the window. Outside, the sun beamed down on an expanse of green fields, turning everything yellow . . . happy. It was a stark contrast to the storm I felt inside. Clasping my hands behind my back, I bit the inside of my cheek, wishing I were anywhere but here, with anyone but him, doing anything but this.

Behind me, I felt Peter's inward struggle of what to say next. "I cannot understand why you've been acting so strangely. Have I done something to offend you? Is this about yesterday?"

I'm sorry, Peter. "Not at all. But now that I think on it, there was something I had hoped to discuss with you."

After a moment, he prompted, "Yes?"

I built one more wall around my heart before ducking my head, turning around, and plunging in. "I do not think we are suited to each other."

His expression never changed a fraction—it was his prolonged, deathly silence that alerted me to his true reaction. At last he managed in an incredulous tone, "That's it? After all that has happened, this is what you care to say?"

I clenched my teeth, biting down the words that rose to my defense. Casting my head down, I said, "Yes."

"Is this all the explanation I am to receive, then?" A bit of anger slipped into Peter's voice. It was so unexpected that I glanced up. His face was no longer frozen. All at once it was mad, desperate, and so, so confused.

My heart tugged. "What more do you want?"

"Blast it, Mary!" he shouted. "One moment you are laughing along with me, and the next thing I know you are distancing yourself—as if I'm some despicable disease. What has gotten into you? Why do you keep your distance? What have I done to offend you so? For the love of all that is good, will you just tell me?"

It took every ounce of my resolve to keep my expression controlled. "I am sorry if I led you to believe there was an under-standing between us. Truly, it was not my intention."

"If . . . you *led me to*—!" He turned away, running a hand through his hair.

At first I thought we were finished, but he apparently thought this discussion far from over.

He spun back, his voice barely controlled, his eyes sparking. "You did a lot more than *lead me to believe*, madam. There was a certainty behind every one of your actions—and mine—that cannot be denied. I did not invent a fantasy where we bared our hearts to one another. I did not invent that look in your eyes that speaks all the words you do not say. I did not invent—!"

Peter stopped and lowered his head. Breathing hard, he took a moment to compose himself before muttering, "I think we both know you are lying."

I can tell when you're lying, Mary.

Yes, and I'm sorry. I'm so, so sorry.

But what I said was, "All this time you have been playing the long game, and I the short. My aim has never been love or marriage or anything of the kind—but the desire to best you. And since it seems as if you were blind to this, I should think the victory is mine."

"This has always been more than a game, do not deny it."

"How can I be plainer, sir? If you cannot comprehend my feelings, how should I explain them to you so that you understand?" My voice wavered. I dug my fingernails into my palms, groping for more control.

"Oh, I comprehend your feelings." The hurt was palpable in Peter's voice now. "You try to hide them from the world—and perhaps you fool the world, but you do not fool me. There is a mask that you wear, Mary—though for the life of me, I cannot understand why."

I bit my tongue as his words barreled into me, expertly cutting through those fragile threads that held my heart together. Every one of my sensible thoughts sprang away.

Peter stalked to the left, then right, pacing the rug. "What is it? What is the great Mary Raynsford so afraid of?"

"It is not Mary who is afraid—"

"Oh, so it is Julia?" He scoffed. "For once can we put all these games aside? There is no difference between you two."

"There is an astronomical difference, Peter, for the girl before you is neither of them."

He halted.

Sudden silence—so copious and tangible I could barely breathe. The confession lay heavily in the air, unable to be taken back.

"What do you mean?" Peter's frustration dissipated, his expression altering to something patient and . . . hopeful?

The moment I had wished for, dreaded, and dreamed about was here. The admission was already half-done. Hang it all! It didn't matter what William had said about Peter loathing me. He deserved the truth all the same.

"I mean there is a third I have never told you about."

Peter took careful steps toward me until we were near enough to kiss. He lifted a hand to my chin and tilted it up until I was caught in the eddy of his eyes. "Who is she?" he whispered, gaze deadly serious. "What is her name?"

Every part of me tingled in anticipation. How would he react? What would he say when he discovered I was Lillian Markley? I steeled myself for the confession, tasting the words on my tongue.

How could someone like him ever love someone like you?

Unbidden, an image of Thomas expanded in my mind, eyes rigid and lips twisted with disgust. I watched in horror as his features distorted, his light hair darkening, his ashen eyes morphing into a bottomless blue, until I beheld a monster. A monster whose lips curled away instead of up, who had wrinkles in his forehead instead of by his eyes. Everything about it was Thomas, but its face was Peter's; and it looked at me with such abhorrence it made me falter.

The picture vanished and I came back to the present, where Peter was still beautiful, and gentle and soft . . . and waiting for me to answer.

I knew then I would never be able to tell him. I would not see him repulsed by my existence. I would not see him become Thomas. And if I could never trust Peter with my heart, I knew I wouldn't be able to trust anyone.

"She has no name," I whispered numbly. "Through the years, her identity has been chipped away at all ends, leaving in its place a cowering shadow, who can't remember the glory that was once her crown. She may have had a name once, but not anymore."

Peter remained fixated for a few seconds more, before he dropped his hand and exhaled, broken from a spell. He stepped away to face the wall at my right, bending his head, loosening his cravat, looking out the window. His jaw clenched in between shakes of his head.

"There is always a way out," he seemed to murmur to no one in particular. "Always a perfect explanation."

How I longed to defend myself! To justify my actions and explain every reason behind everything I had done.

"I have never asked you for the truth," Peter went on, quietly. "You

248

said once that you could see the questions burning inside me. And oh, how they have burned at times. But I never let myself utter them, and do you want to know why?" He turned back, his cravat hung loosely around his neck. "It's because I didn't want to have to. I know there is a secret you hide. I have always known. To discover it, I was willing to wait forever, if I had to. Yet here you are, telling me this has all been one roundabout, pointless, *blasted* game?" His voice broke on the last word.

"Don't be a fool." My tone didn't quite have the venomous effect I envisioned, but I went on, determined to see this through. "It has always been a game, and one you were happy to play."

Peter's hooded gaze stayed locked onto mine, but it grew intense and resolute. He took a step forward. Then another. He shook his head. "No more."

I fell back, maintaining the space between us. His gaze was blue fire, leaping out and consuming all my rational thought. Feeling the color drain from my face—or was it flooding to it?—I fumbled backward, speechless at this change in him.

I needed an escape—dreadfully needed him to stop getting closer —but I was running out of room. Any second, my back would meet the wall and Peter would close the distance. And I would tell him all he ever wanted to know.

"I have told you all I can," I tried. He ignored me and kept advancing until I felt the wall press into my back. Marble statues blocked all other escape routes. He planted his hands on either side of my head.

" . . . Peter . . ." I sounded throaty, weak.

My determination crumbled as his hands rested on my shoulders, pushing me into the wall. My lungs shrunk. His chest rose and fell with determined breaths.

His chest? Oh stop noticing that, Lily! I dragged my eyes away, settling instead on where his throat met his loosened cravat. I pulled them higher to his chin . . . lips . . .

Oh dash it all, Peter! Give me someplace safe to look! At last, I shut my eyes, doing my utmost to snub my skittering heart. Peter's warmth and woodsy scent emanated across the few inches between us.

"Tell me your secret." He said it on a deep sigh. "*Trust* me."

If only it were that simple.

I pushed the words past the lump in my throat. "I—I cannot."

He paused for a long time. "Am I not worthy of your trust? Have I not earned it?"

"You are worthy of it." I recalled the warped image of Thomas back to mind. "But I have none to give."

Another lengthy silence, even longer than the last. Quietly, he said, "Then what of your love? Have I not earned that?"

My eyelids fluttered open, expecting to see a twinkling stare, but his attention was steadfastly fixed upon my lips.

He leaned in closer. "Tell me your feelings plainly, and I shall walk away. Not, 'I do not think we are suited to each other.' In the simplest of terms, tell me you do not care for me. Tell me, and I shall never ask you again."

I panicked, my breaths coming now in short, soft gasps. He was giving me every opportunity to break his heart. If I could only but manage a few words, this would all be over.

"I beg of you," he whispered, looking between my eyes. "Clear this uncertainty, and put an end to my misery."

If you care for him at all, you would sever all ties. To remain friends would torture him. Jennie's face swam before me, her gentle words, her loving touch, her desperate pleas of companionship bleeding through her letters. I had to sever the ties. But with Peter before me, real, in the flesh . . . I found I hadn't the heart—not while he was looking at me as if I were his only anchor. As if I alone could keep him from drifting away to nowhere.

"You are my friend," I said softly, begging him to let it go at that.

"Is that all I am to you?"

Oh, why couldn't I say the words? I was being so weak and pathetic, and everything felt so impossible. Swallowing, I studied the floor, fearing Peter would see the truth.

I couldn't say them because they were the last tie between my heart and his. If I told him now he meant nothing to me, it would be the final swing of the axe. There was a finality in them I could never take back, never amend. I would be tossing away the only friend I'd ever had.

It was cruel of him to put me in this position—to force this out of me, when all I wanted was to leave this place, heart intact.

And as I realized this, my own temper began to rise, slow and simmering. He had no idea what I had been through, what I had sacrificed, or how deeply I cared for my sister. He had no idea the anguish I suffered because of him—how every moment in his presence cleaved my heart in two.

And if I were to spare my heart, I knew I had to hurt him.

"We are too different," I said.

"We are the same!" He pushed off my shoulders and heaved a frustrated sigh. "This. This is what you do. It is never the truth with you, Mary. Why can't you answer a simple question? Why can't you even admit that you *care* for me?"

"I have given you every truth I could." I willed my voice not to shake. "You don't have to understand—and I am sorry—but my conscience is clear."

"Clear? This is not about right and wrong, it is about restoring my faith in—at the very least—our friendship. A friendship which you continue to spurn—"

I stepped forward, fists balled. "If you had cared to notice, Peter, I have spurned nothing but my own follies." My lips curled back. "From my reckless actions, to my careless tongue, to my stupid, useless heart—!"

"And what of it?" He stepped dangerously closer and closer. "Do you even know what's inside it? You dodge questions or change the subject or simply walk away—anything to get away from actually looking at your feelings and *making* something of them! Yes, Mary, I comprehend your feelings. I have always comprehended them—perhaps better than you do yourself—!"

With every ounce of rage, I pushed him away. "You know *nothing* of my heart, Lord Wycliffe, so do *not* pretend to know its secrets!"

My face burned with anger, my eyes blazed, my whole being trembled with passion. But in the next moment, I let it all go, burying my face in my hands and tamping down the tears before they could surface. Silently, I commanded myself to smother all emotion, to hide it deep inside me where I would never find it again. To put on that mask that Peter so despised.

Another infinite moment passed, ringing with finality. The thick, wretched silence that hung between us became a sound of its own, like the last song of a dying bird, or the echo of something breaking.

"So," he murmured at last. "I guess this really is the end of our game. You have stopped calling me Peter."

I held my gaze steady even as misery spread through me like a poison. There was never a scenario that would have ended well. The moment I started to care for him, it was always going to end this way.

I felt no triumph over besting him, no wash of satisfaction at being able to wound him. A sob built up in my throat. Every part of me wanted to call out to him, to apologize, to explain. But I couldn't.

Oh what have I done?

Peter let out a soft, broken laugh. "One whole point. Well. I may have won this round, but I give you the victory." He shook his head, Adam's apple bobbing, eyes hard but sheened. "I have no wish to play anymore."

And he walked away.

CHAPTER 22

Despite my most fervent hoping, the day of the ball arrived. The whole house burst into an activity of last-minute preparations—for the decorations, the food, or one's wardrobe.

My dreading of this night had exponentially mounted over the past several days. Matthew had been kind enough to help me practice my dancing, so at least I was fairly confident on that score. Still, relations with Peter and William continued to prove strained, at best.

It had been three days since Peter and I argued. Three days of him avoiding all interaction with me. Of him never even glancing my direction—and I would know, because I had waited for him to make eye contact just once, so I might apologize with my eyes.

And every time he didn't, I realized it was probably for the best. I still couldn't tell him everything, so there could still be no reconciliation.

Instead, he disappeared, often for the entire day, not returning until evening. When Peter was home, he holed up in his study, making an appearance at mealtimes but immediately excusing himself afterwards.

Dinner had been the most excruciating—to be seated right next to him and still be clandestinely ignored. He laughed at every joke made, skewering my heart each time. I fancied he laughed too forcefully, or that his eyes didn't twinkle as brightly, but who was I fooling? It was as if we were strangers, and wasn't that what I wanted?

All the lines were beginning to blur together into one big, unruly mess.

At the moment, Katherine was dressing my hair for the ball, embellishing it with studded pearls to complement the soft pink ball gown draped over the bed. Matching muslin overlaid the base layer, with white embroidery at the hem, bodice, and sleeves. Mary had had it made especially for me, and the things it did for my complexion were breathtaking.

"Shall I do more, miss?" Katherine asked me in the mirror.

"No, that is quite enough, thank you."

Katherine stepped back and locked her hands together, admiring. "Even the handsomest gentleman shall have the hardest time not stopping to stare."

I stood and examined my reflection for a long while, stomach queasy. Katherine retrieved the dress from the bed and situated it about my shoulders. She fixed a lock or two mussed in the dressing, then spread the lightest dusting of rouge to my cheeks. Not that I needed it—I was already flushed at the thought of what tonight might bring.

Katherine fetched the pink ribbon I'd purchased, holding it out to me. I eyed it in the mirror, chest squeezing at the memories. I shook my head, and without question, she tucked it away.

A few raps sounded on the door. Eliza let herself in, along with the faint sounds of stringed instruments being tuned. "The first of the guests are arriving, so Mother said it was time for me to retire upstairs and I thought I'd—Oh my!" She stopped, gasped, and rushed over. "Mary! You are positively stunning!" She moaned. "How I wish Mother would let me go! The look on Peter's face alone is going to be priceless."

I didn't feel like answering that, so I walked to the chair where my long white gloves lay, freshly pressed. As I slipped them on, Katherine applied a perfume to my neck. It smelled like lilacs in the rain.

"There! All finished now." Katherine cupped her hands under her jawline, admiring her work.

Eliza sighed again, smile bursting as she grasped my hands. "Oh Mary! You are going to have such a lovely evening."

Inside, I grimaced. How I wish that were true.

Only the thought of my reunion with Jennie comforted me enough to return Eliza's beam. Eliza always meant well.

"Don't stay up too late fantasizing," I teased.

She laughed. "You know I will."

I took one last critical look in the mirror before giving Eliza's hands a squeeze and striding out of the room. The drone of a crowd grew louder as I neared. I paused at the top of the stairs, breaths erratic, longing to spin and flee to my chambers where I could wait out the rest of the week locked away. Squaring my shoulders and lifting my chin, I glided down, ready to face the night.

People mingled everywhere; in the entryway, in the drawing room, standing about in alcoves and hallways. All these were just the first to arrive? I had no escort, so I went to the ballroom in hopes of finding a companion.

Connected to the drawing room by the stone terrace at the back of the mansion, the ballroom was easily the largest room in the house. Brightly lit by the sparkling chandeliers above, couples danced in the center of the room to a lively quadrille. Throngs of party-goers sat by the sidelines, talking and sniggering over the music. A miasma of heady perfumes wafted through the air.

I glanced around, pretending not to know who I was searching for. Finally, I spotted a dark head of hair, a familiar figure not twenty paces away. He stood with a group of young men wearing the languid expressions and scowls of condescension only noblemen could possess.

A man with black hair and a cravat of starched linen drank from a glass, surveying the scene. Our eyes met over the rim of it. He lowered it, the corner of his mouth lifting. He said something to his companions, gesturing my direction.

As one, the group twisted their heads around, and I blushed, hard. Peter turned and saw me for the first time in three days. He froze. Stared. Looked me up and down, lips parting.

"Good evening Miss Raynsford!" Mr. Cunningham bellowed, appearing at my side. "How are you enjoying yourself?"

It was all I could do to stutter through a half-thought reply. Mr. Cunningham rambled on about his recent visit to Bath and its refreshing air and cleansing waters and . . . I stopped listening, instead chancing a peep back at Peter.

He still stared, mouth slightly agape. Then he saw me watching him, and his head whipped the other way.

Oh. How my heart ached.

". . . and that's why I shall never again go sea-bathing." Mr. Cunningham finished. "My dear? My dear Miss Raynsford?"

I turned back to him. "Sea-bathing?"

"Yes." His face took on a hurt expression. "Were you not listening?"

"Oh! Sea-bathing! Yes, of course."

He shook his head. "Dash it all, people never listen to me anymore. They think I'm just an old fool."

"I'm sure they—"

"You're just like all the others, aren't you Miss Raynsford? You think I'm an old fool like everyone else, don't you?"

"On my word, I—"

"Miss Raynsford perceives many men to be fools," a deep voice behind me said, "whether they be or not."

Mr. Cunningham turned to the new arrival with a delighted smile. "Ah, Bentley!"

William stepped forward in a deep red tailcoat and shiny latchets. "And as you know, Mr. Cunningham," his gaze settled on me and he inclined his head, "we men must all bow to Miss Raynsford's wisdom."

Seizing the fan hanging from my wrist I flicked it open. It was getting too warm in here, what with the pressing of bodies and my traitorous cheeks. And here William was trying to pick a fight, when all I had ever wanted from him was to be ignored.

"I suppose you are right," Mr. Cunningham said. "Miss Raynsford does know better than us all."

William pretended to consider this. "Indeed. One might further say she knows us better than we know ourselves." It was a jab, meant to remind me of our quarrel. *I would think I know my own heart.*

Mr. Cunningham didn't seem to catch the sarcasm in William's tone. He nodded reverently as if William had just unearthed the secret of life.

William turned to me. "I have come to solicit Miss Raynsford's hand for a dance." When I hesitated, he added, "I recall her saying she would, if one asked like a gentleman."

Finally, I managed a slow but stiff nod before he led me onto the dance floor and he held me at his side, poised to begin. What was I doing, dancing with him? There was no way it could end well.

"You're a sensation," William said out the side of his lips. "Mary Raynsford is the name on everyone's lips tonight."

"I thought you said none of her acquaintances were invited."

"They weren't. But your name has spread like wildfire. Everyone wants to know who 'that fetching young girl' is. I can't count how many people have petitioned me for an introduction."

I sighed and shook my head. "What exactly is Mary supposed to do when she re-meets all of these people as herself?"

His hand at my waist tightened. "*Now* you care about Mary? Only *now* have you thought about what you're going to do to her? What you did do to her the moment you took this on?" He blew a long, cynical laugh. "Ironic, is it not. Only after you have destroyed everyone's lives do you begin to care."

"I have always cared."

A violin introduction sounded the beginning of the song. We faced each other and bowed. His face marginally softened, and just as we stepped forward to join in the middle, we locked eyes and he murmured, "Just not enough." We each turned away to dance with a different partner.

I promenaded a full circle around him, mirroring the other dancers until we formed a line of couples, waltzing forward, then back. "Why did you send me that riddle?" I asked once I returned to his side.

"Riddle?"

"Yes. Why did you go to the trouble if you were going to profess your feelings so soon anyway?"

We separated again, and it was half a minute before he returned with an answer. And what he said couldn't have surprised me more.

"I did not send you any riddle."

I stopped short, then spurted forward, remembering I still had to dance.

It wasn't from William? But of course it was. It had to be.

The couples on the dance floor laughed gaily while the stringed instruments played a melancholy tune—the light summery dresses of the women contrasted against the dark tailcoats of the gentlemen. It all slowed, whizzing by with muffled, distorted sounds. My feet moved mindlessly, eyes zipping back and forth as I tried to fathom it all.

If not from William, then . . . who?

Who knew my real name?

"What did the riddle say?" William asked, breaking through the ringing in my ears. I beheld him dully, for a moment not understanding.

I shut my eyes and shook my head. "You must know, surely it was from you." My voice rose. "It could not have been from anyone else!" The dancers nearest us glanced over.

William and I separated again, a cello now soloing. The dance was about to end. I turned with an older gentleman, once, twice, then finally returned.

"On my honor, I sent you no riddle," he said. He stared at me with a deep sadness. The last note from the cello held, decrescendo-ing into silence. Couples bowed to each other and clapped.

We stared at each other, the mystery of the riddle suddenly the last thing on my mind. In this moment, all I could think of was how sorry I was. Sorry about Mary. Sorry about coming here. Sorry about the ruined look in his eye. The other dancers drifted away, like leaves from a tree on a warm autumn day.

"William," I said softly.

His brow furrowed.

"We are friends, are we not?"

He watched me for the longest time. We were nearly the only ones left on the dance floor now, and soon we'd be joined by others, ready to begin the next set. But I didn't care. I needed to know.

He sighed like it cost him everything to do it. "Yes."

"Truce?"

He looked at me, then down, then back, an inward struggle raging. "Yes."

I offered him a part of a smile. "Good." I stayed a moment more before turning to go.

"Lillian—" His hand reached out and didn't quite find my arm, instead grasping the fabric of my dress.

"Yes?"

He licked his lips. His head, arm, and expression fell. "Nothing. Never mind."

I hesitated for half a moment, before returning to the edge of the room, wishing Jennie was here. For if she was, I would laugh at her shyness and inability to make friends, effectively covering up my own insecurities on the matter. The applause and gleaming teeth bombarded me, repeating the same phrase over and over: *You don't belong.*

"Miss Raynsford," Lady Wycliffe greeted as she strolled up. "Why are you not dancing? I trust you are enjoying yourself."

I forced my smile to break through. "Immensely, my lady."

"Let us see if we cannot find you a partner."

"Oh really, that is not necess—"

"Lord Ruthford!" We were soon joined by the man. I bit my lip, face heating. He had pleasant features, though I was as tall as he was—if not taller.

"Lady Wycliffe," he said bowing and kissing her hand, "how youthful you appear this evening."

She waved her closed fan in the air. "Oh, do go on! Lord Ruthford, this is Miss Mary Raynsford."

He bowed to me. "Enchanted."

"Don't the dancers look lovely this evening?" she said once he straightened.

"Ah, they do indeed."

"Miss Raynsford was just remarking to me how she loves to dance."

He turned to me. "Do you? I admit, my dancing days are almost over, but I would be remiss if I didn't stand up with such a charming young lady."

I laughed awkwardly. "Thank you, sir, I would be delighted."

We swung around the dance floor to a cotillion and came back bright eyed and out of breath. Lord Ruthford was all smiles. "I underestimated my partner," he said to Lady Wycliffe. "If that is the last dance I ever have, I shall die a happy man indeed."

Lady Wycliffe inclined her head amicably, then gestured to a figure at her side. "Lord Ruthford, you know my son, Peter."

I stilled. Peter stood just beyond Lady Wycliffe, and I hadn't noticed. He twisted around, stepped forward, and bowed his head in welcome.

I didn't know if I should stay or flee. I wanted to do both. The atmosphere erupted with a strain that had nothing to do with the music—though neither Peter, Lady Wycliffe, nor Lord Ruthford seemed to notice.

"Pleasure to see you again, Wycliffe," Lord Ruthford said, pumping Peter's hand. "Feels like it's been longer than a couple months."

Lady Wycliffe gestured to me. "Peter, I don't believe you've greeted Miss Raynsford tonight."

A cough rose in my throat. Peter glanced at his mother sharply, a look passing between them. A muscle in his jaw jumped.

At last, the civil words came, bereft of a smile. "Good evening, Miss Raynsford. I trust you've been well." He was looking at me now, but I could tell he was trying not to. His face was a blank sheet of paper, his gaze its only spot of ink.

"Well enough," I murmured.

He lingered for one heartbeat. Two.

"I should attend to the other guests," he said. "Delighted to see you again, Ruthford."

Now Peter would leave and avoid me for the rest of the night. For the rest of my stay. For the rest of my life. The whole conversation felt like an utter defeat. So I was shocked when he grasped my hand, bent, and kissed it slowly, thumbing over the kiss once it was finished.

"I hope you have a pleasant evening," he said quietly, eyes not quite locating mine. He departed with a short bow.

I stared after him, wide-eyed, blood pounding, hand shivering. I gripped the dry, crisp piece of paper he had left in my palm. I didn't have a chance to read it though, as Lady Wycliffe and I were approached by a woman wanting an introduction.

One woman turned into three, then five, and soon I realized it was because I was still by Lady Wycliffe, whom everyone wanted to converse with. Clutching the paper tighter in my fist, the note grew warm, crumpled, and slightly damp. I feared it would be soggy and illegible by the time I was able to read it.

The night wore on, the festivities building to a crescendo. Glasses tinkled, skirts swished, and a harpsichord plunked joyously for the dancers. The air grew stuffy and hot with the scent of sweat and old perfume. Every time I plotted to make a dash for an open window, another stranger materialized, paying their respects to Lady Wycliffe and introducing themselves. My head pounded from trying to remember all the new names and faces, and my face muscles hurt from holding a smile for over an hour.

Finally, I couldn't take it any longer—I needed to breathe. In between another introduction, I managed a mumbled excuse, rushing away and dodging the individuals in my path.

I burst into a long, deserted hall just off the ballroom, where the noise of the party was muffled and distant. It was much cooler and surprisingly dark. Light spilled from the doorway, revealing grim faces in the hanging paintings. Their stares were watchful, wary as I passed them. I folded my arms and came to a halt, unnerved.

As soon as my eyes had adjusted to the lack of light, I opened my hand. Reverently unfolding the paper, I squinted to read the scrawled words.

The favor you owe me. Rooftop. Midnight.

The favor . . . the one in return for him going to the fair. He had promised me it would not be anything improper, yet being alone with him at such an indecent hour most certainly was. My exhale was cut short by my mind screaming the question that had plagued me all night.

What was I doing?

Why had I come here, really? Was it to see my sister again, or was it possibly because what I craved most of all was a sense of belonging? I was a servant—a servant gallivanting about as an heiress. I had reveled in my belonging, stringing hearts along, but in the process butchering the one I had tried to protect most.

My own.

Letting the paper tumble to the ground, I cast my fan away. And I didn't stop there. I tore off my silken gloves, pulled the studded pearls out of my hair, and unfastened the watercolor necklace Eliza had bought for me, tossing them onto the pile. None of it belonged to me. Not really. This life wasn't mine.

It could never be mine.

The items lay in a heap, gloomy and useless. I gritted my teeth against my watering eyes as I stared at it, mentally throwing them away along with all the lovely memories I'd created here. The paintings watched on, and I sensed their approval. They knew I didn't belong with their master. They knew I was not an heiress—just a servant, pretending to be one.

I exhaled sharply, glad to be rid of the heady perfume of the ballroom. But as I took a deep breath in, my chest tightened on an astringent, new scent. Fresh and clean, it burned my throat. Mint. The soft plod of boots came to a stop behind me. I turned.

There, in front of me, was the man that had caused me so much pain, Father's gold ring on his finger, the aroma of water mint oil stronger than burning wood.

I froze. "Thomas?"

"Hello, little sister." His gray eyes bored into me, cutting me down like sharp knives.

"When—how did you find me?" My voice quivered, my hands started to shake.

He laughed and loomed over me, a tower of intimidation, a curly brown lock sweeping onto his forehead. "Not so clever now, are you *little Lily*? It took me nearly eight years to find you last time, but only two months this time around. Either I'm getting better, or you're getting sloppier."

I hated the way my confidence shriveled up. I was suddenly ten years old again, small, cowardly, and helpless, recalling the voices of the servants whispering, "*Wherever will she and Miss Jennie live?*"

"How did you find me?" I repeated, satisfied when my voice didn't waver.

"I saw you at the fair—it was only a glimpse, really, but that was all I needed. Those men were utter failures. I should've done the job myself."

My blood ran cold.

In my mind's eye, I relived that night; the hands around my waist, the knife on my cheek, the foul breath on my neck, and I shuddered with hatred. "That was you? You hired them?"

Thomas snorted. "Who else? Everything would be so much simpler if you were gone, but those fools blundered it all."

Thomas despised me, I knew, but to attempt *kidnapping*? How could he? I reeled with shock and fury, anger and terror. My limbs stiffened at the dark scenes flashing through my memory.

"It took some digging to find out you were staying here," he went on. "Even more digging to find out why—and I nearly couldn't believe the truth of it. What a charade you have been leading! You, pretending to be a lady for money—all for an asinine sister who is a continent away. What a joke!"

I blinked, and my lips parted in surprise. Quietly, I said, "How do you know that?"

Thomas chuckled. The sound of it fed my courage.

"Where did you hear that? I was the only one Jennie ever told about going to America. I've never told another soul—not about her, not about Mary, not about that blasted nine pounds! There is no one else who knew the truth, so *how could you possibly*—!"

My eyes caught on a lone figure, standing in the distance beyond Thomas's shoulder. His head held high, his jaw clenched, his hazel eyes fixed on me with an apologetic stare.

William.

The force of his betrayal knocked into me. I faltered back a step. My heart wrenched in my chest, wringing out the fragmented bits of trust that had shattered, impaling it like shards of glass. William approached, face set.

Thomas noted the direction of my gaze. "Yes, your friend was quite useful in that regard. He sent me a note not three days ago, saying he had information that would be worth my while." Three days. Right after we'd quarreled.

Why? . . . Oh William, why? He reached us, suddenly able to look anywhere but at me.

"How could you?" I whispered, finding my voice.

"You're late," he said to Thomas.

Thomas frowned. "Yes. Thanks to you, I had a difficult time obtaining an invitation."

William swallowed, hard. "No matter what you may think, I am not doing this for you. You're despicable and you don't deserve her. Not then, not now—"

"Yet here we are."

"*William.*"

At last he managed to look at me, his stare protective and concerned but far from sorry.

"How could you?" I repeated, unable to fathom him. Any of him.

So minutely I almost didn't notice, he shook his head, voice low and hoarse. "It is best this way. For Lady Wycliffe. For Eliza. Even for Peter, though he chooses not to see it. I gave you a way out of all this, but you threw it away. I had no choice."

I will do everything I can to see it done. Everything.

"How can you say that? How *dare* you say that? You had every choice—but you cannot see beyond the scope of your own desires!" All the confusion and pain of disloyalty made my hand itch with the desire to slap him again. "I trusted you!"

His head lowered, nostrils flaring. "You shouldn't have."

My vision flickered, and I wanted desperately to go back. To take it all back and erase this nightmare.

He turned to Thomas, a challenge in his gaze. "You promised you would not hurt her. You will keep that promise."

"Of course."

William tarried, ensuring that his message was clear. Then he took a step back, faltered, and eventually retreated down the hall, leaving me alone with Thomas once more.

"It's a good thing I had the help of your friend. I never would have figured it out otherwise."

I turned on my half-brother, attacking the tears, pushing them back down. "Why do you care so much? Yes, I've been pretending, but why should it trouble you so? In less than a week, I shall have enough money to leave and disappear forever. You'll never have to see me again, so why do you care?"

Thomas grabbed my chin with one hand and laughed, amused. "I always knew there was some fire in you. Just like your poor excuse of a mother." He thrust my chin away. "If you want to embroil yourself in scandal, then by all means do so. I care not what happens to you."

I flinched. Even after his constant abandonment and displays of cruelty, some small, childish part of me had still hoped for a bit of kindness, or acceptance. Forgiveness. This just showed how soft I had become; how willing I was to hope and to trust and to love. I had forgotten that people do not care. People do not change.

"My only concern is for Clarissa," he went on. "She is my wife's sister after all."

I blinked fast. He was able to care about her, a girl only tied to him through marriage—and whom he had only known for a few years—more than his own family? It felt so wrong and unfair. He had never given us a chance. Had never given *me* a chance.

Thomas sniffed. "It was the old viscount's deepest wish for Wycliffe to marry her, but he died before the proper negotiations could be documented. Through the years there has always been an unspoken understanding between the two families. When Clarissa came of age, they would wed. Until recently, that was our under-standing."

His eyes darkened. "It became known to us that Wycliffe was . . . wavering. He no longer showed an interest in Clarissa. And though I had seen you that day at the fair, it never occurred to me you were the object of his pursuit."

I folded my arms. "Yes, Peter pursued me. But I would not abandon Jennie for him. Go ask him yourself, he will tell you I do not love him. I chose Jennie. I would choose her every time—only a heart-less monster abandons their family."

He leaned in close, snarling, "I did not abandon you. I would have sheltered you had you not run off with that worthless sister of yours."

Liar. You turned us away. You turned me away.

"She is not only *my* sister. From the moment father married my mother, she became *family*. And family does not throw each other to the gutter!"

Thomas's chin jutted and he stepped forward, backing me into a corner. But there was no stopping the words now.

"You hated me long before father died. If I had stayed, my life would have been miserable. Admit it—you were glad to be rid of me. You were glad you no longer carried responsibility of me. But no, you could not stop there! You had to drag my name in the mud just as you did our sister's, to ensure I could never, *never* be happy!"

Thomas grabbed hold of my arms.

"If that was your aim, then you have got your wish." Tears pushed to the surface—of regret and anger and might-have-been's. "I am sorry, Thomas. I am sorry for how I acted thoughtlessly all those years ago—I truly am. But I will not apologize for being born. I will not apologize for being loved better by Father. That was not my folly, it was his."

His hands pinned my arms in a death-grip. They squeezed impos-sibly tighter, before releasing me completely. He backed away, lips curling back. "Neither will I apologize. Thanks to you, I came to know who my true enemies are. Now as enjoyable as this is, I am not here to reminisce with you. I have come to offer you a deal."

I looked at the floor, gently rubbing the blood back into one arm.

"Clarissa is a rich heiress with powerful connections. All you are is a pretty, little distraction—someone Wycliffe occupies himself with when he is bored, but would never seriously consider. I have no doubt he would see the light of his unfortunate choice without my interference, but Clarissa's family grows impatient. They will not risk you influencing him until the end of the week. In fact, they will not wait another day."

Without raising my head, I glanced at him in suspicion.

"I will give you this money you're so desperate for. You can pack your bags and head to the colonies—go gallivanting off with that sister of yours. I'll even grant you a sum to help you get on your feet once you're over there, if," he grew gravely serious, inching closer, "and *only* if, you'll sever all connections with Lord Wycliffe and leave tomorrow."

I stopped breathing. Tomorrow? That was so soon. I'd have to say goodbye to Matthew, and William—no, not William—but to Eliza, and Lady Wycliffe, and Peter.

Oh, Peter.

I licked my lips. *What's wrong with you, Lily?* my sensible half screamed. *Isn't this what you have always wanted? Why you came here in the first place? Here is the freedom you've worked for years to obtain. It is hanging in front of you, only an arm's length away, yet you falter!*

"I realize you have little reason to trust me, so trust this: I want you gone." He scowled. "You know firsthand I will do whatever it takes to make that happen. Naturally, you cannot breathe a word of my interference to anyone. There's no telling how the Wycliffe's would take it—they are, after all, a sentimental lot. You will say you left of your own volition."

"But what excuse do you expect me to give them?" I asked with a tad of desperation.

Thomas waved his hand dismissively. "Say you grew tired of your stay or missed your *fictional* aunt. Lie. That shouldn't be too difficult for you."

No. It shouldn't. I had always been good at lying.

But that didn't make it easy.

Seeing my hesitation, Thomas jabbed a finger down the hall and muttered darkly, "And if you refuse to go, I shall drag you into that ballroom and expose you for the fraud you are. You will never see your sister again if you are in prison. The choice is yours."

I wavered, trying to swallow my dread. The choice was obvious, but that made it no easier to accept. I steeled myself to say the words, mentally going over all the possible explanations I could give Peter for leaving, knowing he would believe none of them.

You don't belong.

"All right," I whispered numbly. "I will leave tomorrow."

"Excellent. I knew you'd see things my way. I shall send my carriage to pick you up at six 'o'clock sharp. Do not wake the house."

He turned on his heel, leaving me to stare impassively out the hall window, wishing the night would take pity and swallow me whole. I knew what he meant; he wanted me to say my farewells tonight and leave unceremoniously in the morning, before someone could convince me to stay.

Tomorrow. So soon.

A clock on the wall chimed, announcing the hour. Startled out of my daze, I glanced at it. Was it already midnight? Sighing, I headed toward my chambers. I needed to get to bed if I was to get an early—

Midnight.

I halted, remembering the small slip of paper Peter had snuck to me. *The favor you owe me. Rooftop. Midnight.*

I glanced back out the window into the blackness, deep and encompassing. I wasn't prepared to say goodbye, but this might be my last chance. It took me several minutes to gather the courage Thomas had scattered. My feet were leaden, but at last I took a step, then another, and made the long pilgrimage up to the library.

The shadows that prowled on the edges of my vision bled inside and crept up, circling me in their midst. Somehow, that thought wasn't nearly as disturbing as the thought of what I would find on that rooftop.

Opening the secret door, I made my way up the circular staircase, fumbling in the dark. When I reached the top, I lifted the hatch, and stepped carefully onto the moonlit roof. The light from the heavens was pale, just like my bravery. My eyes switched from the sky to the dark figure on the other side of the rooftop, slowly making his way toward me.

CHAPTER 23

"I WAS BEGINNING TO THINK YOU WOULD NOT COME." PETER FACED away from the moon, rendering his features indistinguishable in the shadows.

"Of course I came. A promise is a promise. And Mary Raynsford is a woman of her word." *But not Lily*, I added silently. *Not me.*

"I'm glad you are here." He inhaled slowly, his words as heavy as the world. "I wanted to apologize—for the other day. Regardless of my feelings or the circumstances, I behaved inexcusably."

I folded my arms. "It is I who should apologize. I should not have gotten so angry. And it's a silly thing really, but I didn't intend to lose my conditional point by calling you what I did."

He was silent. Then, "I think you did intend it. I think you were looking for a way out. As you always do."

"What else was I to do in the face of such unrelenting aggression? I panicked. What else could I have—" I halted and crammed my frustration down. It wasn't Peter I was angry at, but myself. "Why did you ask me here, Peter? What do you want?"

"A dance." There was no hesitation in his reply. "One dance, Mary. Then I shall let you go."

No, I wanted to tell him. It was the surest way to unravel my resolve—and he *knew* it. *No, no, no.* But as I stared at the man I had lied to and taken advantage of countless times, it seemed like the smallest of settlements.

"There is no music," I answered lamely.

As if on cue, there came a faint melody on the air. There must be open doors and windows downstairs, where the tune could escape into the night. It was a melancholy song—haunting, striking a chord within me.

A soft, "*Oh*," escaped between my lips.

Peter didn't give me any more opportunity to refuse. He walked toward me solemnly, one hand propping mine up, the other coming around my waist.

"I do not know how to waltz," I whispered, frightened.

Peter drank me in in the moonlight, his clothes brushing my skin, his smell and his breath washing over me. Leather, soap, danger. "Then I shall teach you."

With no warning, he stepped forward and I followed. Back, side step, turn. Back, side step, turn. The 1-2-3 pattern of the dance came easily enough with Peter leading me. His hair shone as black as the night. Stark shadows split his face. The song rose in volume, Peter never breaking his stare. And with each twirl, he pulled me just a fraction closer.

We were alone in the world, the strains of the sad song enveloping us. Closer and closer we moved; deeper and deeper his eyes became; farther and farther I fell into them, tumbling and dropping and drowning without any hope of ever coming up for air.

The music ended on a minor chord, never resolving and clinging to my heart like a child at her mother's skirts. The dance was over.

I broke away, putting the back of my hand to my mouth. Peter watched my back mutely as I breathed in defeat. When I turned back, there was no mischief left on Peter's face, no sparkle, no twinkle, no glow. I had taken it from him.

And now I would say goodbye, preventing him from ever claiming it back.

Squeezing my eyes shut, I whispered, "I cannot do this," and moved away.

"The strangest thing happened the other day," he said so quietly I nearly didn't hear him, "when we were at Newington."

I halted in my steps. Gooseflesh prickled over my skin.

"While on a grand tour of the house, I noticed there was one room we had passed over." His gaze burned into the side of my face, taunting me to look at him. "Curious, I stayed behind, and, when no one would notice, slipped inside. It was the late Sir Markley's study—for it was dusty and hadn't seemed to be touched in the eight years since he died."

My feet trembled with the desire to flee. "That does not sound so strange to me. His son must have wanted to keep his memory. You shouldn't have intruded." I added a bite to the last sentence, uncomfortable with where this was going. A warning bounded through me that I should stop Peter—that this road didn't lead to anywhere safe.

But he persisted, seeming to know that I would halt him if he didn't. "Perhaps. But what was strangest was the large portrait that hung above the desk, depicting two little girls." His tone sounded deliberate, like he'd imagined this conversation dozens of times, and had it memorized. "At first I did not think anything of it. Though, upon closer inspection, I realized one of the little girls looked very . . . *very* familiar."

Heat rose to my face, breaths becoming faster and more desperate. His intense gaze did not let up when he said, "'Lillian,' I believe her name was."

I spun to my right, gripping the ledge with whitening knuckles. "What a lovely name. Though I don't know why she would look familiar. I do not think you would associate with someone possessing such shameful character." After drinking in the darkness, succumbing to the night, I turned back and met his eyes.

His gaze was fathomless and strong, pinning me in place. Rendering me exposed and helpless.

He knows.

It glowed so unmistakably that I wondered how he had ever managed to hide it. My throat tightened, limbs growing shaky as my deepest fear was realized.

It was *Peter* who had written the riddle. *Peter* who had been trying to get me to confide in him. *Peter* who had been trying to tell me this whole time that he knew the truth. He knew it all—and here I was, stripped bare and defenseless before him.

Slowly, he came forward. "Maybe her character is not so shameful."

There had always been the wall of my lies between us, a barrier that kept us both safe. Now that he had scaled it, there was nothing I could do to prevent the tears from forming. Mutely, I begged Peter to stop.

"Perhaps all the rumors are lies," he went on. "Perhaps she had changed her name because no one would associate with her if they knew who she truly was. And *perhaps* . . ." He stopped just inches from my face. ". . . perhaps the person who she became was Julia Smith."

"Please," I begged, finding my voice. "Stop." All of my resolve dissipated. My lips trembled as I struggled to bottle my feelings back up.

He ignored me. "Then Julia Smith became Mary Raynsford, who came to Ambleside. She came, and she stole my heart."

"Stop it, Peter!" I cried, his words piercing me so starkly that I felt as if I couldn't breathe. He tilted my chin up, forcing me to look into his star-lit eyes. His thumb grazed over my lips, once.

"I win."

No longer able to control the quiet tears, they dripped onto his hand. "Please, Peter. I don't want to hear the rest."

Again, he ignored me. He lifted both of his hands up to my face, cradling it. "I love you, Lily."

His eyes closed just as gradually as his head descended. Before I knew what he was doing, his lips covered mine.

They were soft, caressing kisses, equally pleading and desperate and hopeful. He pulled me closer, one hand finding its way to my hair, the other wrapping around me and preventing the escape I should try to obtain.

His kiss grew more insistent, and I melted into it, kissing him like I had always wanted to. I could taste the salt of my tears on his soft lips, bittersweet as he pulled my head still closer, needing me more than he did air. And in that moment, I needed him back.

He pulled away, still close enough that I could feel the warmth of his breath on my skin. "Marry me," he breathed, searching my face. "Marry me, Lily or Mary or Julia, whoever you are. It does not matter to me as long as you're mine. As long as I have you to laugh and play all those stupid games with."

I formed a sad, pathetic smile and started to shake my head, but he stopped it with his hands, unabated. "Yes, and we can dance on rooftops and fall out of trees and sneeze all about it together. What a pair we shall be!" He breathed a laugh. "And I promise to let you win, sometimes. I shall even let you gloat to your heart's content. Just, please . . ." Peter sighed and his breath hitched. "Please. I need you. *Marry* me."

There it was. Peter's heart laid bare: tender, willing, and trusting. And I had to break it.

Why did he have to be so wonderful? If he had been like all the other nobles—arrogant and callous—none of this would have happened. I would have come here and borne it. I would have endured everything until my two months were up.

But no. He had to smell like freedom and taste like heaven and be everything I never knew I wanted.

"I cannot," I finally whispered, a deep defeat welling up inside, building and swelling. "Do you not see? Why do you make me suffer so, when the answer will forever remain the same?" I pushed him away, the hot tears coming fast. "Confound it Peter, why will you not see it? Thomas will send more men. Jennie will be alone. I will ruin the

Wycliffe name—and Eliza's chance to find love! I cannot stay here. I cannot marry you. I cannot love you as I do!"

Burying my face in my hands, I exhaled, utterly spent and ruined. My broken pieces splintered a million times over, smaller and smaller until they were grains of sand, counting down the minutes in the hour-glass until I had to leave. I was powerless to stop it.

". . . I cannot love you as I do . . ." There was no fight left in my voice. Only resignation.

"You can, Mary." He took one of my cold, shaking hands in his. "Julia." He smoothed a stray lock of my hair, then tipped my chin up again. "Lily."

I backed away from his touch. "You sent me the riddle, yet you acted as if you didn't."

"Yes, I deceived you. I had thought you returned my affections, but then Bentley came on the scene, and I . . . I suddenly wasn't sure. But then that day in the rain, I could see the truth of it in your eyes. I did not doubt your feelings then."

"Then why did you not say anything?"

He sighed, raking a hand through his hair. "I wanted to. So many times, I almost did. That day at the fair—you dropped your reticule and the contents spilled into the street. I happened to glimpse the letters. I thought it strange that some were actually addressed to Julia Smith, when she was fictional—and there was another paper that contained signatures from both Julia Smith and Mary Raynsford. You couldn't be both. That was the day I first suspected something. So I had Mr. Minton do some research for me."

A faint bubble of laughter from below escaped into the night, reminding me that I needed to leave.

"At first, I didn't believe it was possible," Peter went on. "But over the course of the following weeks, the pieces fell into place, and it all made sense. That day at Newington, I only slipped into the study because I had to know the truth. Once and for all."

The moonlight rendered his eyes cloudy and silver. "And as for why

I didn't say anything, I have already told you. What hurt me the most was not your deceit, and it was not your avoidance. It was that, despite my best efforts, you could not bear to give me a little of your trust—the one thing I wanted most of all."

"Yes," I admitted, backing away. "I couldn't. And I shall tell you why—it is because trust breaks. I trusted William to keep my secret, and just now he has betrayed me. I trusted Thomas to take care of me, and he sent me away. I trusted my father not to die. I trusted my sister to stay beside me—not leave me behind, scared, scarred, and alone! Trust *breaks*. And I could not bear to see you shatter it once I had given it to you."

Peter shook his head, face firm. "That is not trust you speak of—that is life. That is *love*. And is it not better to have the happiness with the sorrow, than to guard your heart with such vigilance that you never feel anything at all?"

His words resembled the ones I had said to William about the rain, and the hypocrisy in it was deafening. I chose to ignore it. "I will not marry you, Peter. I am leaving."

As if Mother Nature had heard me, the breeze ceased, leaving the rooftop dissonantly still. Peter looked as if all life had gone out of him.

"You will see once I am gone that it is for the best. I will embrace my sister, never to be parted from her again, and you will marry Miss Caldwell, as your father always wanted. Everything shall be as it was meant to."

"No, it shall not," Peter said, chin setting. "I will never marry Clarissa. I had already decided in my heart, long ago. That is why I called things off while we were at Newington."

I blinked. "What?"

"Once I knew everything, I did not doubt what I wanted. So I spoke to her parents and to her. They didn't take it well, but we came to an understanding." He lowered his head. "It was wrong of me to keep her guessing for such a long time. I treated her terribly in that respect."

Thomas's words echoed through my mind, about how Clarissa's family couldn't wait another day. Regardless of Peter's feelings, they were still set on her marrying him, and hadn't given him up.

Peter did not know Thomas as I knew him. If I didn't leave and if Peter didn't marry Clarissa, Thomas would ruin Peter too, dragging his whole family's name through the mud as he had mine. If Clarissa could not have Peter, no one would.

He inhaled sharply, bringing me back to the present. "And though you might find contentment with your sister in America, I know what will happen to me. I would look for you in another girl, look for a soul that fills me with the same happiness, and I know I shall never find you again."

"So that is your solution?" I asked, sadly. "For me to never see my sister again? To tie yourself to a woman rumored to have—" I stopped, unable to say the words.

"You did not do those things—"

"How can you be so sure? Can you say that through the years you would never doubt it, or wonder if you were wrong?"

"Yes, I can." He glanced between my eyes, stepping forward and putting his hands around my arms. "For I *know* you. And even if it is not reciprocated, I trust you completely."

My heart twisted. "While I have never done the things I've been accused of, it would be unwise to trust me with your heart, Peter, for it will break every time. Can you not see? I am a chaos. I am not worth the trouble, the whispers, the stares."

"You are to me. There has to be a way." His touch trailed down my arms to grip my hands, face beseeching . . . begging. "There must be."

I pulled away. "I will not do it to you—or Eliza or Matthew, for that matter—and there is nothing you can say to change my mind." A hefty silence reigned, before I looked down and added in a small voice, "And I love my sister."

Peter breathed deeply through his nose, looking as helpless as I felt. The inevitability of it all was beginning to dawn on him fully. I was going to leave, and he could not stop me. We stared for the longest while, drinking each other in for undoubtedly the last time.

And there we were, alone with our hurt on a moonlit rooftop, unwilling to break the moment, for fear we would break altogether.

"Goodbye, Peter," I said at last, turning away.

When I reached the hatch, he called, "Will you be happy?"

I halted.

"In America? With your sister? . . . Happier than you would be with me?"

My eyes welled up with more silent tears. I had told myself that I would be, that my sister meant more to me than he did. But it was one thing to lie to myself, and another to lie to the man I loved. Time and again I had fed him the untruth. Not this time. I would give him this one last piece of myself—a truth I could never utter again.

I took two deep breaths, then whispered, "No."

I fled through the hatch, unable to look back, because my heart was already breaking with each step. I don't know how I made it to my quarters, but I did. Closing the door, I leaned against it and slowly sank to the floor.

There is something extraordinarily special about Peter, in that when he loves someone, it is with a depth that very few of us can fathom.

I'm sorry, Peter. I'm so, so sorry.

Because one thought kept recurring so vividly: that he and I were the same after all. I remembered the tree that I fell from, and landing on top of him. I remembered the card games, the dancing, and pretending to be Julia Smith. I could hear his laugh, see his smile, feel his hands on my face as he told me he loved me. Memories of the last two months flashed through my thoughts until I couldn't bear it any longer.

My world shattered, just as it had when my father died, and I broke down into heaving sobs. I pulled out my father's pocket watch, stroking the golden clasp and telling myself I only had thirty more seconds.

"There, there, Lily," I said. "You should not encumber yourself so, for your mother would have been p-proud . . . Look here . . . You have thirty more seconds to cry b-before you have to be . . . happy again . . . before you *have* to be happy . . ."

Each time I recited it, it would end in a wrenching turn of my heart and a pain that burrowed deeper. I gasped aloud, the tears coming faster than I could swipe them away.

I could not stop.

Over and over I tried to time myself again, saying that I had to stop when the seconds were up. But I couldn't.

Just as I couldn't when my father died.

The seconds turned into minutes . . . and the minutes, into hours. Hours that passed in agonizing slowness until the pink-grey light of morning drifted through the window.

CHAPTER 24

THE CARRIAGE RUMBLED FORWARD, HEADING TOWARD LONDON harbor at a grueling pace.

I had gotten what I set out to do, and I was going to see my sister. I should have been feeling at least hopeful, if not happy. Yet, no matter how I tried, I couldn't shake the sense of gloom that had nestled inside, protecting me from any warm moods.

More than once Mrs. Bumbridge, the elderly chaperone that Thomas had sent with his carriage, had to repeat her questions. After the first few hours of her echoing herself, she finally realized I preferred the quiet.

We shuffled in and out of the carriage, to stretch or settle into an inn for the night. The pattern could've lasted for one day or a hundred —I wouldn't have known the difference. Each night before Mrs. Bumbridge retired, she would put a palm to my forehead, and ask if I needed anything. My soft reply was always the same. "No. Nothing."

At last, the smoky plumes of London came into view. Long before we entered the jungle of buildings, I could smell the putrid stench of smoke, fish, and poverty. Factories whistled and gulls cried while grimy children zigzagged through the streets. Carriages rattled on the cobblestones.

Mrs. Bumbridge pulled out a pocket watch attached to a chain. My eyes sidled over to it, dull, and frozen.

"We are early," she announced. "The boat doesn't leave for another two hours, at least. Hmph. I suppose it is better than being late." She tucked the watch away, grabbed her cane, and rapped the top of the carriage to get the driver's attention. We slowed. "Take us to the nearest coffee shop."

After stopping in front of a row of shops, the footman swung the door open. Mrs. Bumbridge gathered her skirts and stepped out. I did the same, not possessing enough presence of mind to do anything but follow suit.

The shop was loud, and smelly, much like the rest of the city. Mrs. Bumbridge shooed away two men from their table, then motioned a man over and ordered two cups of coffee. I sank into my chair, oblivious to the noise and crush of bodies.

"Well," Mrs. Bumbridge said as she sat, "you are not the most pleasant young woman I've conversed with."

I glanced up, really seeing my chaperone for the first time. Her hair was graying, face round and worn. And there was something familiar about her soft expression.

"Forgive me," I said. "I do not mean to be rude."

"Something is troubling you."

I hesitated, the din around me swelling. "You could say that."

A man appeared with our coffee, setting the steaming cups on the table and then disappearing through the crowd.

"Highly irregular, you running from your fears instead of facing them."

"Yes, but there is no victory for me. Not in this." I reached for my cup, hand freezing just as it reached the handle. *You*, she had said. As if she knew me.

"You do not remember me, do you?" she said at last. I shook my head dumbly. "I thought not—though I remember you quite well. What a spirited little girl you were. So full of life! I've often wondered what became of you, but I'd never have thought you'd become such a shell."

My eyes narrowed. "Who are you?"

After taking a sip from her cup, she leaned back. "I watched you, you know. Sometimes from a distance, sometimes as you cried yourself to sleep in my lap, longing for your father. It is natural you would not remember me. In your mind I was a simple servant."

"You were employed by my father?" A fragmented memory surfaced. Warm hands stroking my hair, lips touching my forehead. But that was all.

She nodded. "And then your brother." She tsked. "It is shameful, what he did to you and your sister. None of the staff have ever forgotten it. But your brother has treated me fairly and I have no room to complain." Waving her hand, she added, "You are the one I wish to discuss."

I looked away, at the bodies milling about the tables and doorways. "It is too lengthy a story."

"We have time yet."

For the first time since leaving Ambleside, my heart stirred. I held fast, unwilling to let it wake again. Tears gathered in my eyes as holding on became just as painful as letting go.

A compassionate gaze overtook Mrs. Bumbridge's features, and she grasped my hand resting on the table. "You are not required to bear your burdens alone," she said softly.

I wilted. And I told her everything.

I started with leaving Newington, and Jennie, then moved on to becoming Mary Raynsford and coming to Ambleside. I told her of Peter, and William, and America, and Thomas's threat if I didn't leave. The words that I had bottled up so tightly for so long spilled out. Mrs. Bumbridge didn't interrupt, only nodded every so often.

We sat in quiet once I had finished. A lot of time had passed, but I didn't know how much. Fewer people occupied the shop now. I wanted Mrs. Bumbridge to say something, instead of staring meditatively at her empty cup.

Done mulling it over, her eyebrows shot up. "My. What a tale. And what a predicament you find yourself in." There was another stretched moment. She set her cup down, pulled out her watch again, and stood. "If we do not leave soon, we shall miss the boat."

My head lowered, disappointed somehow. What had I expected? What had I wanted her to tell me? That I was doing the right thing? . . . That I wasn't?

We left the shop for the carriage, once again heading toward my future, toward Jennie. So why did I feel so . . . disconcerted? When next we stepped from the carriage, it was on the docks where I could taste the salt in the air.

Those on sea shouted to those on land as they loaded barrels and crates onto various sailing vessels. Throngs crowded the docks. Mrs. Bumbridge grasped my hand and pull me in the right direction. By the time we arrived at *The Endeavor*, my trunk was already being hauled up the cargo plank.

"Here is where I leave you," she said, handing me my ticket.

I took it and gawped at the giant ship, suppressing a gulp. I was ready now. I could do this. I wanted this.

Before I could stop myself, I walked up the gangplank, pausing at the top. Waving goodbye to Mrs. Bumbridge, I passed rigging to the port bow. Staring out to sea, I sucked in the sour air, tucking all of my memories of the last two months back where they belonged now—permanently locked away.

A hand touched my shoulder, making me jump. My heart thumped faster. Harder. I turned.

It was only Mrs. Bumbridge.

He hadn't come.

And I was angry. Not at him—at myself. How could I—how *dare* I —hope, after the way we had parted, after the path I had chosen? I was putting him behind me, once and for all. And I would not regret it. I would not.

"I admire you, you know," Mrs. Bumbridge said, joining me at the rail, "for making such a difficult decision. I do not know if I could, if faced with it. But I thought it interesting that, as you told your tale, you kept restating that you needed to go to America for your sister. Which made me wonder, do you even wish to?"

I drew back. "Of course I do. I want to see her and—"

"I do not mean for your sister. I mean for you. Besides her, is there any other reason you have for leaving?"

Stopping short, I searched for the answer. America had been my dream, *our* dream, a hope we had clung to through the years. But now as I stood on this ship, Mrs. Bumbridge's question hanging in the air, I found that it wasn't so anymore. My dream had changed.

There were other reasons why I couldn't stay. Eliza, Matthew, Mary, Thomas, William, and the half of England that would gossip if I showed my face again. But if, suddenly, Jennie didn't exist, all of those reasons would melt away. The one reason I had to stay would dwarf them, no matter how I looked at it.

"I think you have your answer," she said, turning away.

"Wait." I snagged her arm. "It still does not matter. My sister *is* in America, and I promised I would come to her. Nothing can change that." Even as I said the words, I foolishly hoped she would counter me again. Give me the answer I longed to hear. "If I stayed, it would tarnish the Wycliffe name. Who knows what Thomas would do to them—or to you for that matter?"

"Oh, pish posh. Have no worry for me, girl. This is not about them. This is about you. What *you* want." With a perceptive smile, she patted my arm. "I know it is a difficult choice, and one you had already made. You can still stick to your decision, or you can change your mind—but the choice must be yours alone." She cupped her other hand up to my cheek. "My only advice is this: Lead your heart to where it already knows it belongs."

She left, and I sputtered and glanced around in a panic.

"All aboard!" The shout came from the captain, and suddenly the deck was suffocating and crowded. A whistle blew and I looked back to shore, undecided. Everywhere, there were people, and crates, and net, and sound. The wind in my ears, the shrill cries of the seagulls, the drone of the people chattering all around.

The noise grew, and grew, increasing into a cacophony of jarring sounds. I squeezed my eyes shut against it, but it was too loud. It built, harsh and thunderous and disturbing.

Then a face came into my mind.

The noise faded. Time ground to a halt. All I could hear then was the slowness of my breath. In. Out. In.

"Home," I whispered. And I knew exactly who that was.

CHAPTER 25

Suitcase in tow, I ran down the docks, my pocket loaded with Thomas' money. I needed to find a carriage that would take me back, but I hadn't a clue where to find one, or if—

I pushed through the congested throng, making my way to one of the side streets that was less jammed. The cobblestones were still slick from an earlier shower. Picking my way across, I hopped over puddles and bumped into a man I hadn't seen. My luggage spilled out of my hands as the man steadied me. The case was wet now, and likely my dresses too, but I found I didn't mind.

"I beg your pardon," I said. "Please forgive me, sir."

A long crooked nose and rosy cheeks graced the elderly man's face. "Not at all, miss." He retrieved my luggage and I took it from him with thanks.

I dusted the suitcase off then spun on my heels to run down the street to find a carriage and—

Oof.

In my haste, I had not noticed the man's companion, and we crashed to the ground together in a splendid heap, water splashing away as we did. My trunk landed beside me in the puddle, my skin going cold from muddy water.

My cheeks turned beet-red. I had run into a complete stranger and tumbled into him in front of a crowd of onlookers. My dress was milky with dirt now, and my other dresses were ruined, and I was on top of a man in a most scandalous way. Could this possibly get any worse?

Yes, it could.

I groaned and blinked my eyes open. We gawped at each other, immobile save for our eyes that widened. After a long moment filled with whispers around the gathering crowd, one corner of his lips turned up.

"So *you're* my wife," he said.

I sneezed.

We both blinked in surprise.

I scrambled up, trying to rub off the mud on my dress, but smearing it instead. He got up too, wiping his face. "You really ought to stop doing that."

"I'm so—you see, I was going—oh, I am sorry. Are you hurt? Oh, your clothes are all dirty now—"

"Why are you not on the boat?" Peter asked simply.

I halted, folding my arms across my chest. "I was, but then I . . . then I got off."

"Why?"

The throng began to disperse, apparently accustomed to scandalous situations. Now no one stopped to stare at our mucky pair. I crossed my arms, fingers fiddling with my dirty shirtsleeves. What if it was too late? What if this was some terrible coincidence and he did not want me back?

"What about you?" I said instead, disbelieving his existence. "Why are you here? *How* are you here?"

One finger tugged on his cravat. "Oh, that. Well, erm. I came because . . . you left this." He held out his hand, the porcelain watercolor dangling from his fingers. I took it, stroking it with my thumb.

"There was another reason," Peter went on. "Mr. Minton, why don't you explain?"

Mr. Minton turned to me, and I noticed it was he who I'd bumped into first. I had been in such a rush, I hadn't recognized him.

He cleared his throat. "I have spent the last several weeks gathering information on your brother. The same day you left was the day I upturned some crucial evidence. I caught one of the men who attacked you, and he's willing to testify—though of course, there are still a few things we need to obtain. Documents, substantial evidence, more testimonies if possible. Though your brother is of good standing, there is a very good chance he would go to prison for his crimes. Or at the very least, a lawsuit would restore your good name."

"So you see," Peter cut in, "I am here, because . . ." He hung his head, face devoid of hope. "I know it is unfair of me, but I am here to ask you . . . to *beg* you to reconsider."

Hope fluttered to life in my chest. All of my tensed muscles relaxed. Vaguely, I registered Mr. Minton excusing himself to give us some privacy.

"As for your sister, this is all I could think to do to remedy her situation." Peter extricated a paper from his tailcoat, fingering the edges. "I wrote it a dozen times over, unsure if you would be pleased with the idea or not, but. It is a letter to your sister, inviting her to come live at Ambleside.

"I know it is not really my place, but I could think of no other solution. I don't have to send this letter if you do not wish me to. I only thought you shouldn't have to choose between us. And if, even after all this you still choose her, I understand."

My mouth hung slightly open, eyes misting over. "You would do this for me?"

"I would do much more." But he must've misread my reaction, because he started grimacing. "And now I've made a complete fool of myself." The horn from the boat blew, and we both glanced toward the harbor. It blew a second time. "If you do not hurry, it is going to leave without you."

"I got off in the first place because I wanted to tell you that I love you." Pressing my eyes shut, I savored the words on my tongue, and opened them again. "I love you," I repeated, softer. "And as I boarded that boat, what has been so indistinguishable to me for so long, suddenly shone out in clarity. The thing I most wanted, the thing I most needed—when I searched, I found the answer. And that answer . . . was you."

Peter froze in shock, before sagging back.

"I know I am not the most trusting person," I went on, "and I have decided to change that, so, here I am. Trusting you'll take good care of my heart."

Peter shook his head and looked up to the sky, laughing softly as he stepped forward. The twinkle returned to his eye as he wrapped his arms around me. "Oh, darling," he said. "I always have."

Interlocking my fingers around his neck, I thought on all the mistakes I had made, all the things I should have done differently. "I am sorry for all the lies, and all of my stupidity." He pulled me closer. "Oh, Peter," I muttered, drinking in his face. "Can you ever forgive me?"

He grinned, a smile that was all warm and dazzling and glorious. "Only if you promise to never sneeze on me again. That bit is getting rather tiresome, madam."

I laughed through my tears, pulling his lips down to mine.

And then I knew he had won. All along, we had not been playing trivial social challenges, we had been playing a game of love. I had gambled my heart, and he had won it. Peter had known it from the start. He had entered the game, *knowing* I would be the prize—and, as always, he had come out the victor.

And so there we were, kissing in the muddy streets of London, perfectly, wonderfully, and indescribably happy.

As it turned out, I wasn't very clever after all. For though I was able to puzzle out hidden meanings and ensnare others in their own words, I did not always see what was right in front of me. Or what was most important.

Time is meant to be filled with memories. And though I had always timed myself when I was depressed or crying, I had never counted the seconds when I was happy or truly living—and that time added together far outweighed the others.

I hadn't realized it until this moment, but I had a whole lifetime ahead of me that was made up of thirty second increments, just waiting to be filled with sneezes, and stories, and games. And it didn't matter what they were going to be; because whether they were filled with sadness, or joy, crying, or laughter, pain, or love . . . they were going to be filled with Peter.

EPILOGUE

Dear Miss Julia Smith,

I cannot thank you enough for your disguise at Ambleside this last summer (though you did leave a little early . .). I received a note from my Aunt Phoebe the moment I returned from France. She didn't suspect a thing—and how proud she was that I had done as she wished and was making an effort to change my ways! How can I ever repay you?

I was quite distressed to hear how much trouble Bentley gave you—and he almost ruined the whole thing! Rest assured knowing I gave him the scolding of his life. He seemed duly repentant, and though I do not condone his actions, you should know that he's a good sort of fellow at heart.

As for the rumors running rampant about London—I have lied to anyone who has asked, testifying that I was indeed staying in Hampshire. I understand Lord Wycliffe has been backing my reports (though one might wonder why?).

The only thing I cannot understand is how a name like Lillian Markley got mixed into this mess. I heard about her recent engagement to Lord Wycliffe, but where did she come from? Surely she was not present? (And wasn't it truly awful the accounts her brother has spread about her, all these years? I am glad he is now behind bars for slandering a woman's reputation like that.)

*At any rate, I am forever indebted to you. If you will send me your address,
I shall forward you the £9 as promised.*

Yours etc.
   Mary Raynsford

PETER STOLE THE LETTER FROM MY HANDS, HOLDING IT UP TO THE
waning light of the sun drifting below the horizon. "Now what is this?"
he asked, squinting at it. "Ah, Hampstead House? And who lives at this
house, hmm? A close friend?" He smiled cheekily. "An *admirer?*"

The wooden planks of the boardwalk squeaked as I hopped up and
snatched it back. "*Mary Raynsford* happens to live at Hampstead
House."

"Mm, but how can that be, when she lives at Ambleside?"

"Not yet, she doesn't." We were, of course, referring to me, not the
real Miss Raynsford. Even now, several months after the truth had
been revealed, Peter still insisted on calling me Mary. Now, he was
looking at me in that way of his that made my face turn every shade of
red. "And she never shall, if you keep staring at her like that."

His grin widened. "Does it bother you?"

"You know it does. And that is why you do it."

On the crowded dock, everyone awaited the arrival of the boat
from America. We gazed out onto the sparkling ocean as a bulky trans-
port ship glided ever closer.

"Are you nervous?" Peter asked.

I sucked in a breath of briny air. "More than I care to admit. It has
been so long."

He put his arm around me and squeezed. "It shall make your
reunion all the more wonderful."

"I'm glad you could be here with me," I said.

"I wouldn't miss it." His face screwed in contemplation. "But you

know, the thought did occur to me—it would be enormously embarrassing to have to turn your sister out of the house, if we ever got
divorced."

My mouth dropped open. "You would not turn her out! And how
can you joke about such an event? Are you planning to fall out of love
with me anytime soon?"

"Of course not!" He looked back out on the ocean, the sunrise
glinting off his face. "No. No, unfortunately it has already happened."

I shoved him away as his laughter rang out.

"I cannot help it, Miss Raynsford! Another woman has caught my
eye, and I simply must have her."

"And who is this other woman?"

His face turned thoughtful and he held up a finger. "You know, I
believe you are acquainted. Indeed, practically inseparable, if I recall.
Miss Julia Smith."

"Mm, and what happens when you fall out of love with *her*? What
then?"

"Fortunately, if she falls through, I have one more replacement in
mind."

The ship sailed closer, the British stripes flapping in the wind. I
felt, more than saw the distance between us shrinking. The people on
the ship shouted to those on the mainland, now at a recognizable
distance. A woman aboard the deck linked arms with a gentleman. She
scanned the dock, her brown eyes frenzied and hopeful. My arm shot
up, waving frantically. "It is her!" Peter followed my gaze and he raised
his hand too.

Then our eyes locked. Her lips turned up and I saw her laugh, but
the sound was lost in all the commotion of bustling bodies and sailors
dropping the anchor and the ocean lapping at the wooden beach.
Jennie waved back, leaning so far over the rail, I feared she'd fall into
the harbor. I saw her calling my name, shuffling along in the line to
disembark.

"What if you do not like her?" I asked Peter, smile bursting off my face.

"I know I shall—especially if she is anything like you."

I turned back to him, shooting him a teasing look. "So you *do* love me then?"

His eyes sparkled. "Of course, my dear. I love all three of you."

THE END

Enjoyed the book? Leave a review on Amazon, Goodreads, or Book-bub, to help other readers discover it too!

Want a free ebook about the real Mary Raynsford? Sign up for Jessica's newsletter at jessicascarlett.com and stay up to date on all her new releases!

AUTHOR'S NOTE

While "German whist" exists, as well as a variation of whist called the "elimination version," I took a lot of liberties in twisting them together for the purposes of this story. The coinciding fairytale that Peter tells Lily in the library about the king and queen of hearts is completely fictional.

ACKNOWLEDGMENTS

Once upon a time, I woke up and decided I wanted to write a novel. *It will be fun*, I said. *It can't be all that hard*, I said. *And I definitely won't lose my mind or hundreds of hours of sleep slaving away for people who don't actually exist.*

Turns out all those things I told myself were lies. Writing a book is *hard*. And I know I'm not supposed to admit this, but half the time, I didn't even know what I was doing. There were so many murky puddles to wade through—and an uncommonly high number of Pringle cans—but I finally turned Lily and Peter's story into something I was proud of.

Each of these people helped in their own way:

God comes first. This Podunk story doesn't matter in the grand scheme of things, but He inspired me whenever I came to a place where I was stuck, giving me peace that I was going to finish. All glory to Him.

Thank you to all those beta readers who read this story in its early stages. I especially want to give a shout out to Kimberlee Turley and Chrissy Cornwell. You guys gave such great suggestions and encouragement, this book wouldn't have been half as good without you.

Thank you to my mom, who inspired a love of language in me. Well, more like beat it into me, but hey. It did the job.

Thank you Alayna, who became my overnight fan—and who also watched my daughter for hours on end while I was busy editing. *In Nacho Libre voice* Yewer the behst.

I guess I should mention my friends here, seeing how this book is dedicated to them. Allie, 'Laine, and Kj: You gave me suggestions, courage to face my fear of writing, and confidence that I was good enough. But more than that, you gave me unfailing support. (Well, except for those couple times when you failed to suggest something not utterly, eye-rollingly stupid. I forgive you.) I love you guys. Thanks for needing to know how it ended. *Finger guns*

Last of all, I want to thank my husband, Daniel. You . . . little punk. How dare you refuse to read my book until it was published. (And I know as you're reading this you're thinking, *Um, YOU refused to LET me read it until it was published.* To that I say: Whatever, sir.)

Basically, you were my muse for Peter in all but appearance. Our experiences together were the fuel behind Peter and Lily's love story—and without you, I wouldn't have my own. Thank you for that. Thank you, *thank you* for encouraging me in my pursuits of happiness. All of them.

ABOUT THE AUTHOR

Jessica Scarlett grew up in rural Utah, where lots of wide-open space served as a blank canvas for her rampant imagination. Along with being an author, she is a songwriter and a huge Broadway fan, so don't be surprised if she hears the people sing or defies gravity on a regular basis.

Being mother to two crazy-eyed kiddos, she has been forced to develop a deep appreciation for humor—which is probably why she laughs so much at her own jokes. Though Jessica currently writes regency romance, she loves dashing heroes from all eras in history, and hopes to one day branch out.

Connect with Jessica on social media!

Made in the USA
Monee, IL
05 September 2020